Off the Grid

OTHER BOOKS BY MARK YOUNG:

Off the Grid
A Gerrit O'Rourke Novel

by Mark Young

Off the Grid
All rights reserved
Copyright © 2011 by Mark Young

This is a work of fiction. Names, characters, places, and incidents are either the product of the author's imagination or are used fictitiously. Any resemblance to actual persons, living or dead, events, or locales are purely coincidental unless specifically acknowledged.

Mass market © 2013
ISBN-13: 978-0-9832663-3-4
ISBN-10: 0-9832663-3-6

Library of Congress Cataloging-in-Publication Number: 2013918342

Joseph Costello

A man who peered into the future

And understood the good and the bad

Acknowledgements

Publishing a novel is not a solo endeavor. I want to recognize some of those who have made this novel a reality. First and foremost, my wife Katie, always my inspiration and encourager in this writing journey—proofreading, editing, and formatting print books, just to name a few of the hats she wears. I would be remiss if I did not mention some of my friends and acquaintances who pitched in to make this dream a reality.

My fabulous editor, Julee Schwartzburg, finally succumbed to my pleas for help and took this project under her wing. Thanks, Julee, for helping me to reach that next level. I hope we can partner on many other projects. I want to express a deep appreciation to eBook formatters, Rob and Amy Siders of http://www.52novels.com/ who continue to provide outstanding professional assistance and support in getting my novels to the readers. They make an awesome team. And, thanks to Peter Ratcliffe at http://peterratcliffe.com for coming up with an eye-catching cover design. Great work!

A special thanks to my lovely daughters Ingrid, Julia and Jacqueline, for their love and encouragement from the very beginning. All those hours of emails, phone calls, and conversations ad nauseam about the writing life—thanks for hanging in there.

To my friends who faithfully read my stuff and care enough to correct: Carol Young, Carole Neal, Denise Fehlman, David and Melody Jones and all those who'd rather not be mentioned—thanks for your time and patience. A special thanks to Kevin Pickron, for patiently guiding me through the confusing world of computer technology.

Lastly, I would like to give recognition to authors Grant R. Jeffrey and Bill Salus, whose writings help me create a long-term concept of what the future might hold. First, Dr. Jeffrey's book, *Shadow Government: How the Secret Global Elite Is Using Surveillance Against You* (Waterbrook Press, © 2009) helped shape some of the ideas already floating around in my head. His book has became a great resource regarding the advances of technology, documenting a growing concern over the erosion of our right to privacy. Secondly, I'd like to recognize author Bill Salus' book, *Isralestine: The Ancient Blueprints of the Future Middle East* (High Way, © 2008) as he shares a look at current events in the Middle East as they might relate to our future. He put such world events as The Arab Spring and the suspected proliferation of nuclear weapons by Iran into perspective as our world edges toward future confrontations.

Prologue

Fallujah, Al Anbar Province, Iraq, December 2004

They were on their own.

Diesel growls from M1A1 Abrams tanks beckoned from a distance. Tanks circled the city like lumbering metal horses of war, though their mighty firepower could do him and his men no good here. Narrow city streets permitted only pedestrians and small vehicular traffic to squeeze through. No room for armored cavalry to maneuver, only small arms and hand-to-hand combat worked in these tight places.

Gerrit O'Rourke eased himself to the dusty floor, quietly resting his rifle against the wall. Gazing upward, a black cavernous hole in the ceiling, carved out some time ago by an explosive fist from an artillery shell, offered him a glimpse of a blue heaven. Next to him, a stairwell led to where his men stood watch on the second floor after they ate. His turn for a break after a long tense watch.

A puppy—caked with dust the color of sandstone—clambered over rubble. Gerrit eyed the dog as he heated his MRE, Meals Ready to Eat, featuring chicken with salsa. He studied the four-legged creature as it cautiously drew closer. A tiny rib cage, poking through matted fur, announced just how hungry the animal might be. Dark, mournful eyes stared at Gerrit's meal.

He lowered a green plastic pouch and squeezed out a few morsels of meat onto a flat stone. "Hey, dog, wanna try a little spice in your life?"

The puppy snapped them up like a hungry bird, then sat on its haunches whimpering for more.

He squeezed out another hunk of meat just as an enemy sniper opened up.

Gerrit scrambled for his M16 assault rifle and sprinted up the stairwell to the second floor. As he low-crawled toward an open window, he glanced at the rest of his team, sprawled out below several other windows, to make sure everyone was present and accounted for.

"You see where it came from?" Gerrit whispered, pressing against the wall and slowly peering around the window frame.

"Yeah, Lieutenant. Somewhere at twelve o'clock. Don't think he spotted us." The Marine—a gangly young man from Georgia nicknamed *Peaches*—lay on his side, glancing at Gerrit. Peaches carried one of the radios for the team. "I think he was shooting away from us, sir. In that direction." He pointed in the direction where the sniper lay hidden, toward the west, where the late-afternoon sun slowly sank toward the horizon.

Nodding, Gerrit edged his head higher, scanning the rooftops beyond. No movement. They had been sitting here since before daybreak, easing into position during the chilly predawn darkness.

Something nudged his leg. Looking down, he saw the puppy sniffing his pockets. Somehow, those short legs made it up the stairs.

Peaches grinned. "Hey, Lieutenant, who's your friend?"

Gerrit reached down and patted the puppy's head. The dog peered up, tail wagging, too young to be afraid. "This little guy is hungry."

He surveyed the street—scarcely more than an alley—as it cut a canyon between low, squatty buildings, a dusty corridor draped in shadows and protected from the onslaught of the afternoon sun. Movement on the street made him tighten his grip on the M16. He spied several figures moving in single file fifty yards away, sneaking toward his position.

"We've got company," he whispered, pointing toward the gunmen. "At least five, heavily armed. No, wait. There are more. Plenty more, coming our way."

He motioned toward his radioman, carrying one of the unit's AN/PRC-148 radios. Peaches handed over the external handset. Gerrit grabbed it and, in a few moments forwarded their coordinates and the direction and travel of the enemy.

Yesterday, he and his men from the 1st Reconnaissance Battalion had been ordered to sit tight and report without contact—if possible. Eyes and ears only. Intelligence believed they would be greatly outnumbered in this part of the city, with other Marines too far away to help. After a month-long push of door-to-door combat, a small lull had crept across the war-torn city as Operation Phantom Fury bore down on this ancient city. Some old-timers were comparing this battle to the U.S. Marine operation in Hue City during the Vietnam War because of the nature of the operation and the high number of casualties.

This brief winter lull in Fallujah might be coming to an end. But not today.

Gerrit crawled over to his men. "Get ready to rock and roll. We have units moving into place. They want us to hunker down. Just be ready to fly if need be."

The others nodded and spread across the room as quietly as possible.

The puppy nudged Gerrit's pocket, whimpering.

He stroked the animal's matted fur, hoping this would keep the puppy quiet. More movement caught his attention. An Iraqi resistance fighter, dressed in loose-fitting clothing and carrying several bandoliers of ammunition, loomed into view, an AK-47 held at the ready. He stealthily moved out of Gerrit's line of sight in the direction of the other fighters.

Just as a second fighter crept by, the puppy yelped. The gunman jerked his head up toward the window.

Tensing, Gerrit waited. He did not think the man could see him from the street, but just in case he gripped his rifle and withdrew into the shadows of the room.

Motionless, Gerrit watched the fighter scan the building, rifle pointed toward their position. His mouth felt dry as he waited to see if the man might spot them.

Finally, the gunman lowered his gaze and moved out of sight as another combatant followed close behind on his heels. And another. And another. A minute slipped by. Silence filled the dry, warm air as the waning sun still baked the clay walls. He could hear footsteps below and saw more men moving in single file.

Soon, the street appeared empty. The enemy had moved farther down the street. He estimated about twenty men had slipped past their position. Maybe more.

Booom! The crunching sound of a mortar round hit about a hundred yards away. Other rounds quickly followed until it seemed one explosion blended into the next with a continuous blast.

Peaches rolled over and tapped Gerrit. "Sir, how'd you give out those coordinates without looking at a map? I've seen ya do this before, but I forgot to ask."

Gerrit glanced toward the explosions. "I memorized them when we set up here. Just recalculated where the Ali Babas would intersect with our units."

"Man, that's so cool."

Gerrit shrugged. "Let's get ready to move. As soon as it gets dark enough, we're pulling out."

Peaches jutted out his chin. "Lieutenant, you got a new recruit."

Looking down, Gerrit saw the puppy huddling next to his leg, explosions making the tiny animal shake. The louder the sounds, the more the dog shoved against Gerrit's leg trying to find a place to hide. He scooped up the dog and held it against him. The puppy wiggled deeper, burying its dirty head into the crook of Gerrit's arm.

"I think it loves ya, Lieutenant. Whatcha going to call him...Devil Dog?"

Gerrit laughed. "Nah. How 'bout Bones? Look at those ribs sticking out."

The younger man smiled. "That dog is one heap o' bones."

Explosions from incoming mortars suddenly ceased. An eerie silence followed until he heard the sound of men running down below. He signaled a warning to the others. Suddenly, a man's head popped up on the rooftop directly across the street. A turbaned gunman, rifle in hand, peered toward where the mortars had struck earlier. If the fighter turned toward them, he could see right through the window where Gerrit and the others lay.

Gerrit lowered the puppy and raised his rifle just as the man glanced down. Squeezing off several rounds, Gerrit saw the man jerk back and drop out of sight.

Gerrit sat up. "Let's get out of here. We've been spotted. There must be others."

Another head emerged. One of Gerrit's teammates fired back. The team scooped up their gear and scrambled toward the stairs. Gerrit realized he'd snatched up the puppy without thinking. For a moment, he thought of flinging it away to leave his arms free. Instead, he yanked open a thigh pocket on his pants and shoved the puppy inside as he ran.

Just as he reached the stairs, several rounds slammed into the wall next to him as he hustled through the doorway. One team member fired back as the others dashed to safety. Looking over his shoulder, he saw the last team member make it safely through the doorway as they single-filed down the stairs to ground level.

"Do not engage unless there is no other option," he yelled. More fighters were moving into the area. A sweep would be coming their way, and he didn't want his men caught in the cross fire. "Let's move out.

They began moving away from the sound of enemy gunfire. The building opened up on a parallel street, a large hole punched by an artillery shell. One of his men poked his head through the hole, glancing both ways down the street before crossing. Another Marine moved in to cover, as the first team member charged across the street and kicked in the front door to another dwelling.

The team cleared the next building and leapfrogged their way from building to building. They worked their way about another hundred yards before they felt comfortable the enemy had given up pursuit.

In the last building they came to, Gerrit found an interior courtyard built around a small fountain, cobblestones creating a small pool. The water, barely running, seemed fresh. Oddly, in this war-torn city, this courtyard seemed to offer a moment of tranquility.

Gerrit motioned the others to gather round. "Okay. Let's sit tight until dark. Then we'll make our way back home." He directed several of the team members to clear the building above them to make sure they were alone and directed two guys to stand watch on the top floor. The others spread throughout the building to stand guard.

Bones squirmed as he tried to thrust his nose through the pocket flap. Gerrit smiled as he reached in to withdraw the puppy and carefully set it next to the water. The puppy thirstily lapped it up, stopping for a moment to glance back at Gerrit.

He shook his head. "What am I going to do with you, Bones?" The puppy seemed to have enough water and sniffed around Gerrit's boots. The dog lifted a leg and peed on his boot. "That's how you show me gratitude, you fur ball?"

Peaches, sprawled a few feet away, tried to stifle a laugh. "Hey, Bones. Y'all got to learn a little respect."

Wearily, the Recon unit slipped into headquarters just before dawn. They'd crept through the city as quietly as ghosts, using night-vision goggles to navigate their way until they hooked up with a transport unit back to this compound.

The men plodded to their cots, anxious to catch some shut-eye before starting out again. Gerrit handed Bones off to the radioman. "Since you think the dog's so funny, you babysit this mutt till I report in. The com center says the old man wants to see me."

"Yes sir." Peaches held the dog as far away as possible. "Man, this here dog stinks to high heaven. What kinda dawg is he?"

"Looks like a cross between a mud-colored lab and a who-knows-what breed. He's a mutt."

Peaches seemed to be reading his mind. "Please, Lieutenant. Don't make me do it."

Smiling, Gerrit shook his head. "Just keep an eye on him. I'll clean this freeloader up when I get back."

Peaches opened up an empty locker—left behind by another Marine who just shipped out—and gingerly lowered the animal inside.

"Okay, dog. You can pee all you want until the lieutenant gets back — just don't poop."

Peaches always made him smile. The team slapped that nickname on him over beers after he drunkenly boasted that Georgia girls thought he was "sweeter than peaches and cream." No matter how hard he tried, Peaches couldn't shake that handle. It stuck to him like Super Glue.

Gerrit made his way to the CO's hooch, raised in the middle of the compound the Marines had taken over for the duration of Operation Phantom Fury. Enclosed in concertina wire and earthen bunkers, the battalions' nerve center consisted of green-canvassed tents enclosed by waist-high sandbag walls. Headquarters seemed to be drowning in waves of dust raised by passing trucks, Humvees, and other motorized vehicles.

Gerrit rapped on the door to the major's quarters, a plywood entryway that led to commander's tent. "Permission to enter, sir."

A growled response from within led him to believe permission had been granted. Inside, Major Jack Thompson sat at a folding table, maps spread out in front of him.

"Sir, received your message. My unit just returned."

"Take a load off, Lieutenant." Major Thompson pointed his chin toward a folding chair next to his desk. He peeled off his reading glasses and rubbed the bridge of his nose. Close-cropped dark hair dusted with gray and a wrinkled weather-tanned face gave no hint as to Thompson's age. "G2 updated me on your run-in yesterday. Good job calling it in, sitting tight, and keeping your troops out of harm's way."

"Thanks, sir. Good men. Good Marines."

Thompson frowned. "They are, but that's not why I called you here, Gerrit."

Hearing the major call him by his first name made Gerrit tense. He waited for the man to continue.

"I'm afraid I've got some bad news." Thompson turned, facing him. "There's no easy way to say this, so I'll just spit it out. I've just been advised your folks were killed in a car bomb two weeks ago. Somewhere in the Seattle area. And your uncle … he turned up missing."

A chill grabbed Gerrit's chest, icy fingers refusing to let go. His world seemed to slow down and sound became distorted. Numbly, he stared at Thompson, finding words hard to form. "Why? Do...do they know who did this?"

Thompson shook his head. "I made a few calls and learned that Seattle PD's running point on the case. The feds are assisting. So far, they don't have squat." The major leaned forward. "I've cut orders to send you back home." He paused, looking down at his hands for a moment. "I'm sorry to add to this to your load...but they couldn't wait on the funeral. Those idiots couldn't seem to find you. A closed-casket affair. A few of your dad's friends got together from MIT and buried them near your home in Boston."

Thompson's face seemed to soften. "Son, I want you to go home. Make your peace."

Gerrit felt the chill disappear. "Sir, my men...the operation."

The major waved his hand. "Our operation here in Fallujah is winding down, and orders will be coming down to rotate some of you guys in 1st Recon Battalion stateside anyway. In your case, rotation just came a bit early." **He stood.** "Go home, Gerrit. Take care of your family."

Gerrit eased to his feet. "Sir, I have no more family. Everyone's dead or missing."

Thompson placed a hand on Gerrit's shoulder. "You got your father's Irish look and his ruddy brown hair, but you have your mother's smile. They were good folks."

Gerrit shot him a quizzical look. He never knew the major knew his folks.

"I met them years ago at one of those highfalutin D.C. parties. We kept in touch over the years. Once your dad learned I was your CO, he'd drop me a line once in a while to see how you were holding up."

Something seemed to make the older man draw back. After a moment, Thompson continued. "Go home and take care of the dead, son. Your mission here's finished."

"But—"

"That's an order, Marine."

Gerrit stiffened and saluted, before turning to leave.

"And may God have your back."

Gerrit closed the door behind him without responding.

The sun was just rising, casting a golden hue as it chased the shadows of night toward the west. Black, acrid smoke rose in the distance. He heard a helicopter whirl past. An overpowering smell of diesel fuel hung in the air, a part of the stench of war wherever men and machines clashed in battle.

Unclenching his fist, he reached into his pocket and withdrew a pocket watch his father gave him the day he received his doctorate degree from MIT. He flicked the watch open and gritted his teeth as he studied the photo of his mother and father attached to the lid, protected by glass. They were smiling back, proud of their son, enjoying a moment of academic achievement as the last remaining member of the O'Rourke clan earned the right to be called *doctor*. They could call each other that now—but they never did. Status did not mean much inside their family circle.

And then—with a grimace—he remembered the last time he saw his dad. The day before he shipped to Iraqi for this last tour of duty. Angrily, his father implored him to remain at the university, to help him with a research project clouded in secrecy. "I have connections, I can get you assigned to work here with me."

When Gerrit pressed for details, his father refused to divulge the nature of the research without Gerrit's promise to help. Instead, Gerrit refused to allow his father to intercede. He knew he was needed here—in Iraq—serving with his men. It would be the last time he and his father spoke to each other in this life.

Whatever path Gerrit traveled, death and war seemed to hover. Now this dismal road led to Seattle. Car bomb? Why? How?

He trudged toward the tent where his men were most likely fast asleep. Tiredness and sadness unbearably weighed him down. The major's news had just shaken Gerrit's world off its axis, and in that final jolt, he felt all alone. He was the one who should have been in harm's way. Not his folks. Not in America.

As he reached his tent, Gerrit paused and looked at the rising sun before reaching for the door. He must start packing for the trip home, even though only the dead waited for him there.

Chapter 1

Seattle, Washington, December, Present Day

A sense of trouble seemed to bear down on him as hard as the chilly blast of wind off the water. Gerrit O'Rourke pulled his navy-blue pea coat tighter, fending off a face-numbing gust straight off the Puget Sound. Leaning over the railing, he appeared to be watching the ferry's bow plowing through swelling waves. Instead, he stole a look along the deck, studying other red-faced strangers in the crowd, small groups of commuters and tourists.

No informant yet. No killers trailing behind.

A comforting bulge beneath his coat — a holstered semi-auto .40 Smith & Wesson — gave him confidence as he thought of Nico Petrosky and the man's trigger-happy goons. The Russian crime boss planted eyes and ears everywhere — even in law enforcement.

The informant's voice had sounded tense over the phone. Gerrit agreed to this meeting because he sensed trouble. On the flipside, it would not be the first time this guy, plastered on drugs or alcohol, feigned danger while demanding more money.

Nico Petrosky was an animal. A wealthy animal. The man had been in Gerrit's sights ever since he joined the police department. Even before he was hired, though, he never revealed this fact to the background investigators.

The name emerged again a few years back when Gerrit, alerted by a tip from the LAPD's vice squad, found a shipping container stored on the docks in Seattle, waiting for transport to San Francisco. Inside, they found twenty Russian girls—ages ten to fifteen—cowering inside, half starved. The girls were bound for the sexual slave market on both the East and West coasts.

He found the body of one girl—barely ten years old—curled up in a ball. The coroner would later determine that the girl died from pneumonia and starvation. The sight still haunted him. He swore that day to hunt down those responsible for this atrocity. The girl's death and leads from the container led to Nico Petrosky. He knew this dirt bag benefited from these crimes, but so far, Gerrit's unit had not been able to prove it.

A chrome-glazed December sky hovered as if warning of pending trouble, darkness only a few hours away. He cast a glance toward sheltered passengers, comfortably ensconced behind thick-plated windows, customers bellying up to the bar for another round to ward off the cold. No one looked familiar. Beyond, Seattle's skyline twinkled with illumination across the waves, beacons of light spewing from high-rises, growing brighter by the moment across a darkening sky.

The city's silhouette brought a knot to his stomach, a reminder of the past that drew him to this seaport. Painful memories muscled in on him like the jostling crowd he was watching right now. Wrenching his attention back to the present, Gerrit suppressed those memories, pushing them deep inside. He glanced around once more for the informant.

"Maybe a no-show?" he whispered into a mike hidden near his shirt collar.

Looking toward the upper deck, he spotted Mark Taylor, another Seattle PD detective, shaking his head. Taylor's rich, dark skin stood out among the crowd of pale white commuters standing around him, the only African American assigned to the squad when Gerrit joined the unit.

It has been seven years since Gerrit left the military and surprised everyone when he applied as an officer with Seattle. He'd worked his way into special assignments, always focusing on positioning himself within the department to investigate his parent's bombing. And now he was working intelligence. The first day they teamed up together, Taylor took one look at him and shook his head.

"This ain't gonna work, bro. A military guy with a college degree and a *brotha* from Chicago's Southside just smacks of trouble." They worked out their differences over time, Gerrit finally managing to overcome Taylor's suspicions.

Gerrit keyed his mike. "Did you know that 70 percent of the people who died in boating accidents in 2009, 84 percent did not wear life jackets?"

Taylor's voice came through a transmitter lodged in Gerrit's right ear. "What are the stats on how many cops shot their partners while traveling on a ferry boat? Do you realize how cold it is up here?"

"Chill out. Until today, zero cops have fired on their partners while riding on any watercraft."

"If we don't end this soon, I may change those stats. How 'bout we call it quits? This guy's in the wind."

Gerrit turned away, resting his arms on the wooden railing. "Might as well stay with it until we hit the dock." They were about fifteen minutes out of Seattle's Pier 50 terminal, heading to Bainbridge Island.

He glanced over the crowd one more time and saw a familiar face sliding through the throng. "Got 'em, Mark. Coming my way at three o'clock. Where did this guy come from? Hiding in the john?"

Two clicks signaled Taylor understood. Gerrit pushed off the railing, one hand ready to reach under his coat for his S&W.

The informant—a gaunt, birdlike creature with raven-black hair and even darker eyes—sidled alongside a moment later. Clothes hung on the man like a straw-filled scarecrow in the middle of a cornfield. A tanned fleece jacket with blotches of dark grease flapped in the gusty wind like a seagull trying to take off.

As Birdman leaned closer, Gerrit caught a whiff of skid-row perfume—wine and urine, overpowered by fear-drenching sweat. Birdman, real name *Gregori* in the snitch file, seemed to be coming unglued.

Cautiously, Gerrit eyed the informant, watching the guy's eyes and hands for any sign of danger. "What happened to you? You're a mess."

The man next to him did not even resemble the lab rat Gerrit had rolled as an informant. He studied Gregori's lifestyle, his appetites, and found the man's Achilles heel: money and a promise of a new life. The man standing before him seemed to have lost his nerve after stealing from Nico. Gerrit had not heard from him in weeks. Now he knew where Gregori must have been hiding. In a bottle somewhere deep in a skid-row sewer.

"I th-think someone's on to m-me. I run," the informant stuttered, his lips cracked and dry. "I think dis whole thing mistake." His Russian accent and wine-influenced English dropped and smashed words together like a giant blender.

"Gregori, stay cool. You're the one who called me. Said you made copies of what Nico stole." Sometimes he needed to speak to the informant as if he were communicating with a child. "If you're not blowing smoke, then we're almost to the finish line. And you're off to Witness Protection and a new life. Don't blow it now."

Birdman straightened. "You…You drop me in danger. They like-shasrks.They smellmy blood, They…oh, man, I wish we never met. They know! I feel it."

"How can they, unless you let it slip?" Gerrit glanced beyond him, eyeing the throng once more. Something really spooked this guy. He looked for a face that might raise a warning flag. Normal crowd. Normal commuters. Bainbridge only ten minutes away. "Tell me why this was worth my time."

The man reached into his grimy jacket and withdrew a thumb drive. "Download all dis stuff. All right here."

Gerrit started to reach for it, but the man jerked back, clenching it in his fist. "First, you, how you say, immunize me. And protection. I dead man if this gets out." He waved the clenched fist holding the computer drive.

A clicking noise chirped in Gerrit's earpiece alerting him that Taylor was about to transmit. "We got a boat tailing us forty yards off starboard. They've been following us for several minutes."

A sport-fishing vessel with jet engines ran parallel to the ferry. Two men on board. Their engine throttled down to keep abreast of the bigger, lumbering vessel. "I see 'em." Gerrit leaned away from the informant to speak. "Keep your eyes on them until I finish up here."

Gregori's eyes flickered, fear widening his pupils. "What happening?"

"Nothing." He flicked his hand as if it was nothing. "And, my friend, it's called *immunity* unless you've caught some disease I don't know about. Let's get down to business."

"The boat's dropping back. Looks like they might be trailing us to the dock, matching our speed. Maybe picking up a friend?"

Glancing up at Taylor, Gerrit nodded. He did not want to spook the informant.

Gregori followed his gaze. "That one of you guys?"

Gerrit deadpanned, "Like I said, don't worry about it. We've got this covered."

"No way, man. Something wrong—" Birdman glanced over Gerrit's shoulder in horror.

Gerrit reached for his weapon. He whipped around, seeing a man a few yards away armed with a gun. He shoved Gregori to the deck with one hand just as the gunman fired off two compressed shots. The first shot splintered the deck, and the second seemed to go wild when a bystander fell into him.

A silencer. The shots sounded like compressed air hissing angry spit wads.

The gunman seemed to be trying to follow Gregori's path to the ground with his weapon. A few bystanders bolted when they saw the guns. A woman screamed, starting more of a panic. The attacker seemed to realize his chance to kill Gregori just vanished as each shot caused more chaos.

Gerrit positioned himself to protect Gregori, but he could not take a shot due to the number of innocent people. Grimacing, the shooter—a lithe man in blue denim trousers and a dark, bulky sweatshirt—turned and roughly shoved his way through the crowd, forcing at least one woman to lose her balance. The gunman dashed toward the stern.

"Hey," Gerrit yelled, trying to draw the shooter's attention. The informant hovered on the ground, chest still heaving. Gerrit activated his radio. "Taylor. We're Code 4 on this end. Shooter heading aft through the crowd. See him?"

"Gotcha. On my way."

Quickly, Gerrit knelt. "You okay?"

Gregori nodded.

Gerrit grabbed the thumb drive from the man's grasp and slipped it into his pocket. "I'll take this for safekeeping. Stay down and don't move."

Gregori mutely nodded again.

People crowded around, eyeing the man on the ground like this was some television show. One woman edged closer and saw Gerrit holding a gun. He yanked out his badge just as the woman screamed. He flashed it at the crowd.

"Police! Everyone take cover. Man with a gun." He jabbed a finger toward the stern. A young girl stared at his right hand, still holding the S&W. "Another man with a gun," he said, looking away, searching for the gunman.

People began clearing a path as he pushed through the lingering crowd. Some still crouched in place. Others ran for the enclosed bar and lunchroom inside.

Taylor's voice blared across the radio. "The shooter's on the railing. He…he jumped overboard." Frustration was evident in his voice. "I can't get to him, Gerrit. Caught in this crowd topside."

Gerrit neared the railing and spotted the attacker bobbing between waves. The fishing boat Taylor spotted earlier drew alongside. One of the crew members hurled a life preserver, attached to a nylon rope, into the water, waiting until the gunman grasped it. Once set, the crewman yanked on the rope like he was hauling in a large fish. Fist over fist until the man in the water reached the edge of the craft. The shooter clambered up a metal ladder as the vessel pulled away.

The bow rose as the boat picked up speed, heading toward the Seattle shoreline. The fishing vessel would soon be lost on the far shore. Air support was too far out, and ground units could never respond in time.

He reholstered the weapon and pounded the railing with a clenched fist.

Chapter 2

Bainbridge Island, Washington

"**Here it comes,**" Gerrit muttered to his partner. "The inquisition has begun."

Gerrit started toward the officer until the man held up a hand, cell phone planted in one ear. The man straightened and glanced toward Gerrit while shaking his head, jaw tightening as he ended the call.

"My boss told me to stand down." The officer glared at Gerrit. "Said some feds are on their way to talk to you guys."

Gerrit nodded. "I'm going to step outside for some fresh air." He gestured at his partner heading toward an exit door and followed Taylor outside.

Earlier, officers from the Washington state police tried to keep the two of them apart until investigators arrived, but in the confusion over supervision and the number of eyewitnesses milling around, Gerrit and Taylor met up and stayed together. Now, the state troopers probably thought they had already worked out their stories, so what's the point in keeping them sequestered.

He found Taylor standing in the dark a few feet from the doorway. Light from his cigarette illuminated his face as he took a deep drag.

Gerrit stood up wind from the smoke. "Task force heading our way. Probably want to do damage control before WSP gets too far into this investigation. I figure Marilynn just threw around her federal weight at the locals." Marilynn Summers spearheaded the investigation for the federal prosecutor's office.

Taylor shook his head, the cigarette bobbing in the dark. "I'll bet Summers wants to handle this herself. One of our informants almost gets wasted by a hitter right in front of us, then the shooter vanishes off a boat." He winced, his dark skin and clipped Chicago accent seeming out of place here in Washington. "I hope this doesn't come out of our paycheck. Brothers always seem to wind up in more trouble than you white guys." Taylor grinned at him before taking another hit on the cigarette.

Gerrit laughed. "White or black, we're both in trouble, partner. Don't play that race card with me. It won't fly."

Taylor chuckled. It was a politically incorrect game they played with each other, since they had become tighter than brothers. Taylor knew Gerrit would always have his back. And Taylor always backed his play even when they got into serious jams. "Where's the snitch?"

"I gave him a few bills and sent him on his way. No use letting him sit around here and give the shooter a second chance. Right now, he has a better chance running on his own than sticking around for police protection."

Blades from an incoming helicopter beat the air behind them. Gerrit turned just as the craft emerged, rotors whirling through the night like a giant wind machine. The aircraft hovered, slowly settling to roost somewhere behind the terminal building.

"Here they come. Get ready for them to turn up the heat." Taylor dropped the cigarette butt on the ground, grinding it with his heel. "Well, Einstein, did you tell the state troopers about the *evidence* you snatched?"

Gerrit shook his head, leaning against a concrete pole, hands thrust in his trouser pockets. Taylor's self-appointed nickname irked Gerrit. His right hand circled around the thumb drive. "No need to complicate their investigation."

Taylor snorted, reaching for another cigarette.

A door opened, thrusting shafts of white iridescence from inside the building across the black asphalt. It was the same WSP investigator who had been ordered to wait before interviewing them. He leaned through the doorway, one hand resting on the knob. "They want to see you inside." He thrust a chin in Gerrit's direction.

Pushing off the pole, Gerrit glanced at his partner. Taylor returned the look. "Good luck, my man."

"As far as I'm concerned, no harm, no foul. No one's dead. No one got hurt."

"Yeah, but shots were fired and you scared the crap out of everyone on that boat. I'm sure the whole thing will wind up on YouTube before we get interviewed."

Gerrit shrugged before entering the building behind the trooper. Once inside, he paused for a moment to allow his eyes to adjust. A man and a woman stood at the top of a flight of stairs to his right. The man wore a dark-blue suit and red tie, obviously FBI. The woman—Marilynn Summers—turned and glanced down at him.

"Detective, why don't you join me up here where we can talk... privately." She gestured toward a door a few yards away from where she stood. As he climbed the stairs, Marilynn turned toward the FBI agent. "Why don't you contact the other detective and have him debrief you on the incident. We'll compare notes after I'm through with Gerrit."

He tried to mask his irritation while Marilynn and the agent continued chatting. She glanced at him, still conversing with the other man. Her soft blond hair, cut shoulder length, added a certain softness to her navy-blue skirt and black waist-length leather jacket. Any softness coming from this woman was merely a means to an end.

As he reached the top landing, she gave him one more look. "Okay, Detective. Follow me and let's get this over with."

"Yes, sir."

Marilynn seemed oblivious to his comment as she opened the office door and gestured him inside. Gerrit strode into the room and leaned against the only desk, a gray metallic bruiser positioned dead center in a large, vacuous office.

She closed and locked the door from inside. A slow smile emerged as she advanced toward him. "Well, honey. I wish we could make good use of this *private office*. Door's locked and the window shades are drawn." She pulled off her jacket and flung it across the desk, pushing herself against him. Her arms encircled his waist as she moved in close. "Can't wait to get you home."

Gerrit raised himself up, grasping her shoulders. "Get a grip, Marilynn. I almost lost an informant out there, and I know my boss will be planting his boot up my butt over this. We need to get our stories straight."

"*Our* stories? Don't draw me into this. You and your partner wanna play cowboy and meet an informant without backup knowing Nico's lurking out there…well, that's your problem. Not mine."

He eased away, putting distance between them. Since when did she start playing it safe? Her willingness to take chances, to walk a fine line between the law and the lawless, to get the job done had been the magnet that drew them together. Gerrit never stomached unnecessary rules. Even worse, he hated rule makers sitting behind a desk and coming up with reasons why the job couldn't get done. Impatience always drove Gerrit to scale these obstacles any way he could.

He thought he'd found a kindred spirit in Marilynn, whose job as a federal prosecutor gave her many more rules to bend or break. Sometimes, she seemed willing to go a lot further than Gerrit. Lately, he began to have second thoughts.

And now, she wanted to distance herself from this incident. Why?

"Come on, Marilynn. We haven't much time before the suits show up to figure out who gets to tear into me first." He eyed her for a moment before continuing. "Just because your old man is a senator, doesn't protect the rest of us when things go sideways. I've got to be careful. Can't afford any more mistakes."

"Okay. Have it your way." She brushed a strand of blond hair from her brown eyes giving him an irritated look. "Did you salvage anything from this screw up with our informant?"

He circled the desk, trying to gain control. This woman seemed to know how to set him off. Spending time with Marilynn was like throwing a lighted match into a pool of gasoline. Someone always got scorched. He should have stopped this relationship a long time ago. Tonight was not the right time.

"*Our* informant?" he said. "I'm the one who recruited him months ago while working undercover. Remember? A bottle of vodka, a sympathetic ear, and a promise of a better life earned me fresh eyes and ears into Petrosky's organization. Mark and I—with Gregori's help—turned up leads to Nico's criminal enterprise. Smuggling. Narcotics. Call girls. Even stolen gasoline sold on the black market tax free."

And one bombing in Seattle. But he would never reveal that to anyone. They might question why he focused on the Russian in the first place.

"Old news," Marilynn said, her face turning red.

"I'm reminding you of this because the guy who made this case almost got killed. Because I pushed, Gregori discovered Nico stepped up to the big time. Selling technology on the black market. More money. Less exposure. The guy taking all the chances," Gerrit said, "has a name. Gregori Vasiliyevich Pyotor."

"Now, there's a mouthful." She smirked. "In any event, he survived."

Gerrit paused, clenching his teeth. "I almost got him killed because I missed something. And now the suits will want to crucify me for all this bad publicity. Wild shots on a ferryboat full of passengers. Almost getting my informant wasted. Letting the gunman slip away. Violating protocol—although whoever made up these rules never worked out in the field."

"That's why you always wind up in trouble. Making it an 'us against them' thing. That just sets people off, Gerrit—including me." She folded her arms, giving him her prosecutorial stare as if cross-examining a hostile witness. "*Your* informant has been exposed because you screwed up. Because you did not follow the rules." She let that hang for a moment. "Let's just hope you can salvage something out of this mess that'll make my boss happy. Otherwise..."

He withdrew the thumb drive from his pocket. "This ought to make him jump for joy. Gregori pulled this off Nico's own computer before my guy got cold feet and started running. Nico must have gotten suspicious and had his people watching us to see if Gregori showed up. Taylor and I didn't see the tail until it was too late."

A smile softened the hard lines around Marilynn's eyes as she reached for the drive. "Well, this gadget changes everything, sweetheart. This just might buy you a ticket out of the doghouse."

Gerrit tightened his jaw. Gregori's sacrifice seemed lost on her. "Yeah. My ticket almost cost another man his life." He saw a sudden coldness enter her eyes, a look he couldn't define. It flickered for a second, and then it was gone as quick as if she batted an eyelash.

Marilynn edged closer. "Did I ever tell you how much you turn me on when—"

A fist beat on the door. "Gerrit, you in there? Open up. Now."

He pushed Marilynn away, working his way toward the door. He recognized that voice. Trouble just seemed to follow him today. He unlocked the door and grasped the handle.

Lieutenant Stan Cromwell launched himself into the room, first glancing at Gerrit, then eyeing Marilynn's jacket still draped across the desk. "What the...?" He wheeled around to face Gerrit. "Taylor tells me you guys are being questioned by...these *feds*?" Each word doused with a heavy dose of contempt.

"Now, see here, Lieutenant. Gerrit's assigned—"

"I'm not speaking to you right now, Summers. You'll get your chance to flap your gums in a minute. Right now I wanna hear from my detective." Thirty-five years on the street weathered Cromwell's face like a desert sun beating down on parched land. He seemed to carry the weight of the department on his shoulder, broad muscular limbs matching his thick neck, fists the size of footballs strong enough to send an all-pro linebacker crashing to the turf but gentle enough to comfort a frightened child. Right know, the lieutenant did not look comforting. His neck swelled over his tight collar, veins pulsating a warning sign to anyone close enough to see.

Marilynn paused, thin lips pressing back a retort.

Gerrit faced his boss and filled him in.

"Where was your backup?"

Gerrit rested against the desk, his momentary silence making Cromwell's face turn even more threatening. "We wanted to low-key this. It was just supposed to be a simple meet and talk."

"A simple meet? Your informant almost gets blasted, the would-be killer and a couple other bad guys disappear, shots fired into a crowd… and you call this simple?"

"How were we to—?"

"You're expected to think these operations through, O'Rourke. No more of your lone cowboy stuff. That's what keeps getting you in trouble. It's why I warned them about letting you…" He stopped, as if suddenly realizing they were not alone.

Putting on her jacket, Marilynn faced Cromwell. "We picked Gerrit because of his…special abilities."

Cromwell watched as she buttoned up the jacket. "He's special, all right. A special pain in the ass."

Marilynn crossed her arms. "You know what I'm talking about, Lieutenant. His language skills, his MIT background. That's why we went to your chief to ask he be assigned to us. And besides, he and his partner were already working on Nico."

Gerrit shifted his feet. "Hey, I'm standing right here."

The lieutenant peeled his attention away from Marilynn. "I know you have a lot to offer, O'Rourke. That's why I let them talk me into creating this specialized unit. But if I feel things are starting to come unglued, I'm pulling the plug. I don't care how many high-value targets you guys take down. I won't jeopardize the department, even for you."

Almost imperceptibly, Cromwell's craggy face softened. All the officers knew Cromwell's rise in rank came at the direction of the chief, each rise up the ladder had been forced on this man. Cromwell just wanted to work cases, to work the street. Respect from the rank and file allowed him to lash out at his officers when they screwed up, where other supervisors might have wound up in the hospital with a broken nose. It was why Gerrit kept his mouth shut right now.

Cromwell seemed to relax for the first time since entering the room. "You're the best we have, O'Rourke. I know that. But I can't have you going off the reservation and taking matters into your own hands. That's how you'll wind up dead, and maybe take your partner down with you. Understand?"

Gerrit nodded.

"You're like a son to me."

Gerrit smiled.

A look of irritation flashed across Cromwell's face. "What's so funny?"

"You're fifty-four. You're only ten years older than I am—if that."

"That's not how I feel at the moment." His features relaxed until he glanced at Marilynn. He turned as if to ignore her, his voice lowering. "I know why you do what you do. That's why I have my eye on you."

Marilynn glanced at Cromwell with a puzzled look.

"I understand, Lieutenant. I never thought we'd have to call out the cavalry on this."

"Let's just get you through this mess. I hope something good can come out of it. Were you able to get anything from the snitch?"

Gerrit told him about the computer drive.

"Well, start using that brain of yours and get this Russian crook behind bars." Cromwell turned to face Marilynn. "Get this guy cleared as soon as possible. I'll handle the details on my end. And bring this case to a close before I'm forced to pull the plug on our participation. Understand?"

Marilynn nodded, giving him a look that said he just made an enemy. "I understand perfectly. So, if you will excuse us, Gerrit and I need to finish our conversation."

Cromwell glared at her, then glanced over at Gerrit. Without saying another word, the lieutenant wheeled around and marched out of the room.

Chapter 3

La Jolla, California

Darkness drenched the Pacific Ocean beyond the shoreline, the moon allowing just enough light from the shore to highlight specks of sea foam churned by pounding waves. Gerrit caught a glimpse of the water before the van door closed.

Taylor eased into the seat next to him. "Okay, SWAT's in place and Marilynn just came through with warrants. Agents en route from San Diego's federal building with the paper. They should be here in twenty."

"Marilynn's not bringing the warrants?"

"Nope. Cromwell called and said she jumped on a red-eye back to D.C. as soon as a federal judge put his John Henry on the paper."

"Cromwell? I thought he was still up in Seattle."

Taylor shrugged.

Gerrit glanced up as the monitor tapped into the target's security system. The last two months since the ferry shooting had passed with a blur of activity, almost as blurry as his relationship with Marilynn. They'd been together a couple times since that last tense meeting with Cromwell. And those few times they were together—beyond the physical—they lived like strangers going through the motions.

"Okay, I've accessed the primary suspect's computer." Gerrit typed a command on the keyboard in front of him. "Once I get into his system, I'll be able to see what he's looking at. Thanks to Gregori, we've got all of Nico's codes."

Taylor watched him hit the final strokes as the screen opened up. "Man, you always freak me out with this stuff. Learned all this when you went to that fancy school back east? How to hack into other people's business?"

"MIT. Massachusetts Institute of Technology. One of the best schools to learn how to hack and track whomever you choose. By the way, I canceled your dinner date for next week."

"How'd you know...?" Taylor glared at him.

Gerrit smirked.

"Yeah, yeah. I know. Pulling my leg again. With all your computer savvy, I never know whether you're on the up-and-up." Taylor shifted in his seat. "I can't figure you out, bro. You walk away with a doctorate in some kind of technology I can't even pronounce—to become a cop? They should've bounced you on the psychological. Must have bribed somebody in the department to pass that test. A real mental case."

Taylor leaned over and poked him with a finger. "If I was you, I'd be making a killing in the private sector—all that nano mumbo jumbo everyone's talking about. Instead, you're hanging around in a van with the likes of me. Personally, I think you've got a screw loose."

Gerrit glanced up at a monitor, and a man with a rifle slung over his shoulder loomed on the screen. "Okay, we're in business." He clicked through a number of camera locations inside the suspect's dwelling. "I count five men walking security. I think Nico's in his office or bedroom, but his security system doesn't monitor either location. I saw him walk in that direction a moment ago."

Taylor nodded. "How'd you get access to his computer, Einstein?"

"If I told you, I'd have to shoot you." He leaned closer, studying the monitor. "Same technology you can buy off the market to monitor your kids or employees—but a lot more sophisticated. Rigged up so the suspect doesn't know we climbed into his system."

Another monitor in the van caught his attention. A red dot blinked on and off. "There, he's in the master bedroom…wait a minute. We have another marker going off." Headlights flashed on yet another screen. A car pulled into Nico's gated driveway. "Uh-oh. We got trouble."

"I hate it when you say that." Taylor pulled closer.

"See that second dot? That's one of Nico's cars."

"If Nico is in the bedroom, who's using his wheels?"

"His family—wife and daughter. I thought they were supposed to be away for the weekend. Up at their place in Tahoe."

"Must be a change in plans."

Gerrit leaned back in the swivel chair. "This complicates everything. SWAT's going to hit that place in just a few minutes. And now we have two innocents in the way. One of them a five-year-old girl." He snatched up the portable. "Team leader to Alpha One."

"Go, Team Leader." Special Agent Peter Finch, SWAT leader, continued. "We just moved into place. Ready to move out?"

"Stand down until further notice. I'll eighty-seven you in two."

Finch keyed the mike twice in acknowledgment.

Taylor leaned over. "Where you going, Gerrit? The entry team's all set. Just waiting for the warrants to get here."

"I'm going in with them. Need to protect that child. This jerk might use his own child as leverage."

"Oh, man, Gerrit. Can't you just let someone else handle this?"

"Stats just changed, Mark. Before, our safety margin was high—90 percent chance of our people staying safe with shock and awe. Now, that just changed. With innocent people on board, our chances dropped 50 percent because our guys might have to hold back their firepower. I've got an idea to change that threat ratio."

Gerrit snatched up his Heckler & Koch MP5 submachine gun and several extra magazines, slipping out the door before his partner started in again. The salty night breeze swept up the hillside, off the ocean, like a cool sweep of a hand. He inserted an extension wire to his portable, plugging an earpiece in place before clipping the radio to his belt.

He scrambled toward the SWAT van a block ahead. He tapped twice on the rear door and climbed in. The target residence stood another fifty yards away, hidden by a dense cluster of trees.

Inside, Peter Finch, greased up for war, edged in Gerrit's direction. "For crying out loud, Gerrit, we're ready to go in right now."

Gerrit pulled out a portable monitor, showing GPS markers blinking in the darkened command van. "The target's family just showed up. We have to adjust our entry and takedown."

Muted red illumination inside the vehicle did little to conceal tenseness in Finch's face. "We can't change our plans. My men will separate the family from Nico when we hit the place."

"Not good enough. I have to know that the woman and child are safe. I'm going in with you, Finch."

The FBI agent bristled. "No way. You haven't—"

"Served with the U.S. Marines in three wars—Gulf War, Afghanistan, and Second Gulf War. Member of Seattle PD's SWAT team. I think I can handle a simple entry. Besides, it's my decision—not yours."

Finch surrendered. "Stay behind the entry team until we cross the threshold. Right on my butt. We'll snatch the wife and child together."

It was Gerrit's turn to relent. Nodding, he glanced at the mobile monitor patched in from the other van. A red dot emanated from the car inside the garage. "Family may already be inside. Give me updated readings from our heat sensors showing where everyone's located. I don't have Nico locked down. Taylor just advised the paper is in hand."

Finch whispered into his mike, waited a few seconds, then nodded. "You're right. A woman and child just went upstairs where Nico might be. There are five other bad guys; one at the top of the stairs and four downstairs. It's time to move out...now!"

Gerrit nodded.

Finch broadcasted his orders. As Gerrit followed him out the van, his cell phone vibrated. He pulled it out. *Marilynn*. "Hold up. AUSA calling in."

Finch let out a groan at the assistant U.S. attorney's timing.

Gerrit raised the phone to his ear. "What's up, Marilynn? We're on the move."

"I need you here in D.C. immediately. Something's come up."

"Unless it's about this operation, I don't have time to chat."

Marilynn's voice cut in before he could kill the connection. "Have Taylor connect with the FBI. They can run the show without you. I need you on a plane tonight."

"Forget it. I'm going in with the entry team. Everything's in play."

"This is much more important, Gerrit. Hand it off. That's an order."

"Marilynn, you don't call the shots on these operations." He killed the connection and jammed the phone into his pocket. Something about her voice sounded odd. Not Marilynn's normal confidence coming through. She seemed worried.

Gerrit grasped his MP5 and signaled Finch it was a go. Time to take care of business.

Chapter 4

The SWAT team huddled together, waiting for the command to strike. As he watched them line up, Gerrit tried to focus on the operation at hand, but Marilynn's call kept troubling him. Something was off. This case represented her pride and joy, an operation she'd been orchestrating since day one. For her to jump on a plane and head to the nation's capital and then to call him like that was beyond bizarre. He tried to shake it off as SWAT neared the front door.

A moment later, the SWAT leader whispered, "Now." All sources of light on the property vanished. Gerrit flicked on his night-vision scope as they scurried across the driveway, approaching the front door.

"Go," Finch hissed into his radio.

Breaking glass carried across the night air, followed by simultaneous explosions. The entry team slammed the door with a metal ram like Nordic raiders breaking into a fortified castle. "Go, go, go!"

The team rushed across the threshold and into the darkness, one man peeling to the right, the next one to the left, each trying to cross the kill zone as quickly as possible before armed inhabitants began firing.

Gerrit followed Finch inside. He saw movement to the right and a high-caliber assault rifle flashed. Several SWAT members returned fire, short bursts from their own H&Ks leveled at the gunman. Nico's man screamed, followed by silence. One down.

More quick bursts came from the rear of the house. In the lobby, Gerrit moved toward the stairs that spiraled upward. Using the wall as cover, he started to climb the first stair until he saw movement. A shooter emerged and sprayed the lobby with a Mac 10.

Gerrit found himself caught in the open. He rolled away and dived through a doorway at the foot of the stairs. Scrambling to his feet, he risked a quick peek around the corner.

Another burst of gunfire sprayed the lobby. A child screamed. The sound seemed to come from the back of the house behind the gunman.

The shooter fired blindly. The bad guy could only see what his muzzle flash showed after each explosion.

Gerrit prayed the child and mother made it to the back bedroom. He waited until the gunman went silent, then fired two short bursts across the top of the stairway where the shooter crouched. He leaped backward out of the gunman's field of fire.

Silence.

He slowly peered around the corner, allowing his night-vision scope to refocus. The gunman lay draped across the stairway, his weapon lying on one of the stairs several feet away.

Gerrit hurried up the stairway just as he heard someone behind him. He whirled and raised his H&K before realizing it was Finch. Lowering his weapon, he held up three fingers, then pointed toward the back of the house on the second floor.

Finch nodded, gesturing for Gerrit to lead.

He began climbing the stairs, staying to the far right of the stairway and brushing the wall with his body. Every few steps, Gerrit paused and listened.

Nothing.

At the top, Gerrit cautiously peered around the corner, looking over his gun sight as each part of the second floor hallway became visible. No one in the hallway. Nico and his family must be holed up in the master bedroom.

They lost the element of surprise. Nico knew they would be coming.

Gerrit ran through the sketch of the house in his mind. Before the operation, he'd studied the house's blueprints at the city's planning department. He committed these plans to memory as an office clerk watched.

"You want me to make copies?" the young man asked.

Gerrit shook his head. "No thanks, I'll remember."

And he did remember. It was a gift he possessed since childhood that his parents never questioned. They just knew his eidetic memory was a gift, and it was why Taylor kept dubbing him Einstein. Whatever Gerrit read or saw, with minimal effort he memorized.

The top of the stairs opened up to a hallway that ran the full length of the house. At the far end stood the door leading to the master bedroom with only two other doors in between. He recalled that one door, on his right, led to a large storage room. That room was his goal. All Nico needed to do was fling open the bedroom doors and fire. Anyone standing in the hallway would be killed. He would have to move fast.

Turning, he motioned Finch closer and whispered, "Cover me. I know another way into Nico's bedroom."

"What? You gonna fly?"

Gerrit ignored the barb. "When I give you a signal, call out for Nico to give up. Distract him."

Finch looked puzzled but nodded.

Gerrit handed over his assault rifle. "I can only take my S&W. I'll signal when I'm in position."

"What the—?"

Gerrit moved away before Finch finished, eyeing the master bedroom as he crept along the wall. Reaching the storage room, he eased open the door and slipped inside. Just as he started to close it, the master bedroom door flung open. He left the storage door partly open as he watched through the slit.

A girl slowly emerged from the bedroom. Nico followed on her heels, gripping her by the throat and jammed a .9mm Glock to her scalp with his other hand. "Back your men away or she dies."

Angrily, Gerrit watched Nico using the girl as a shield, a look of terror on her face. The gangster didn't seem to notice the half-opened door where Gerrit stood hiding. Instead, Nico focused down the hall as the child fought back tears.

"Don't involve the girl, Nico." Finch's voice carried down the hallway. "Calm down. We can figure this out."

"Don't tell me to calm down, you idiot. I'm calling the shots. You guys back off or someone gets hurt."

Finch relented. "Okay, okay. We're pulling back. Just take it easy."

Nico peered around the girl, his gaze darting down the hallway. A second later, Nico turn toward him. The gunman seemed to have just noticed the door cracked open.

Gerrit pulled back into the darkness, hoping—for the girl's sake and his—that Nico didn't see him.

Suddenly, Nico yanked his gun toward Gerrit and fired several shots into the storage room.

Gerrit had no place to run. He sank deeper into the shadows, expecting to be hit at any moment. The door slammed closed as the bullets passed through, leaving the room in darkness except where bullets riddled the wood.

"Hey, what's going on down there? I said we'd pull back." Finch's yell carried down the hallway.

Nico must have slammed the bedroom door closed without answering.

Gerrit fought the urge to feel his chest for bullet holes. The door looked like a slice of Swiss cheese, holes riddling the wood, allowing fingers of light to cut through darkness. He was alive and standing. He hoped the rest of his plan went smoother than this. Nico would be on the alert for anything. Next time, his luck might not hold out.

Chapter 5

"Alpha-One. You Code 4?" Finch's voice cracked in Gerrit's ear. "We can't see anything from our position." The FBI agent sounded stressed.

Gerrit whispered into his mike, "Alpha-One is Code 4. Stand down. Will advise."

The last thing he wanted was SWAT to rush in and kill Nico—or the girl. The Russian crook may be able to give Gerrit evidence about his parents' deaths. He must keep the man alive. A detonation trigger found at the scene of his parents' murders raised suspicions that a Russian crime group might have been involved. Nico was the number one crook.

He relaxed when he heard two clicks on the radio. Finch got his message.

Gerrit fumbled for a small LED flashlight. He flicked it and scanned the ceiling. *There it is!* A square panel, white plaster finish blending with the ceiling, recessed about four inches.

He pushed the panel to one side, then clenched the flashlight in his teeth. Grasping the panel's frame, he pulled himself upward, holding his breath and trying to move quickly and silently. His holster caught on the edge, making a loud clunking noise.

He froze, caught halfway through the opening. Seconds ticked away as he listened. His arms started to shake. Unable to wait any longer, he pulled himself up into the darkness.

Gerrit stood on a support beam, flashlight still clenched in his mouth. He inched forward as he balanced, wincing when wood creaked under his weight. He finally reached a second access panel above a walk-in closet adjacent to the master bath.

He pulled out a knife and flicked the blade open, working it down between the panel and the wood-framed opening. He began to force the panel up so he could grasp its edge with the tip of his fingers. Gerrit almost dropped his knife when his radio squelched to life.

"Alpha One. Status check." Finch was getting jumpy.

Gerrit carefully kept the knife blade in place so the panel wouldn't slip. He reached up with a free hand and keyed the mike twice, hoping Finch might back off for a moment. He was thankful Finch's voice became muffled in Gerrit's earpiece. He didn't think Nico and the others below could hear.

"Roger that," Finch said. Gerrit just bought a few more minutes.

He turned off his flashlight. Holding his breath, Gerrit worked the panel up until he saw a hint of light emerge. Gently lifting the panel to one side, he saw the walk-in closet below, large enough to sleep a small family.

Biting his lip, he started the hardest part of this operation, lowering himself through the opening without making a sound. He braced himself and began his descent.

Just as he reached shoulder height, he heard feet running below. Someone dashing across a hard surface. Must be in the bathroom area. The building plans showed this walk-in closet as an extension of the bathroom. Someone was moving toward his location, shoes clinking on what sounded like tiles.

Gerrit froze, sweat starting to drip down his forehead, arms beginning to shake from holding up his weight in an awkward position. He tried to stay in place for fear of making a sound if he dropped to the floor below. He was too far committed to pull himself back up into the attic, but he would not be able to hold this position much longer.

No one came to the closet door.

"Hurry up in there." Nico's voice. Angry.

Gerrit heard someone vomiting. A moment later a woman's voice called out just a few feet away from the closet door. "Give me a minute."

Her voice seemed strained, frightened. More retching. What was her name? Yeah, Cassandra.

Muscles began to burn from the strain. He could no longer hold on. He must risk it. He eased himself lower, muscles burning, until his head cleared the opening, feet finally resting on plush carpet. He allowed his weight to rest on his feet a little at a time, waiting for the boards underfoot to give him away. This close and one squeaking board might catch Nico's attention. He knew the man was waiting for any noise that might alert him to trouble.

Where was the girl?

He heard Cassandra moving around in the bathroom. Nico's voice came from farther away, somewhere deep in the master bedroom. The girl must be near the Russian gangster. But where?

He reached down and unholstered his .40 caliber S&W, slowly withdrawing it. His right thumb flicked off the safety and his index finger slid across the trigger. The closet door was only a few steps away.

Cassandra's shoes clicked on the floor as he neared the door. She seemed to be moving away. Back into the bedroom?

He paused, keyed his mike, and whispered, "Finch. When I key the mike twice, I want you to create a disturbance in the hallway just loud enough to grab the suspect's attention. Copy?"

"10-4," Finch's voice crackled over the radio, full of tension.

Gerrit lowered his free hand and reached down to grasp the door handle, slowly turning counterclockwise. He felt the knob stop and knew the door would open when he was ready. He pushed forward, opening it a fraction at a time. Bright light began to filter in as the door widened. He stopped, peered through the opening.

No one.

The door blocked his view from the rest of the bathroom but gave him a straight shot into the bedroom. He needed to get past this door so he could clear the bathroom behind him and move toward where Nico stood guard over his wife and child.

Now was the time to make his move.

Gerrit pushed the door further and stepped into the room. He started to level his weapon toward the bedroom door when he heard a sharp gasp behind him.

Whirling, he pivoted to see Cassandra's startled face. He clamped a hand across her mouth, her eyes wide with fear. She didn't resist. How had he missed her? He looked down and saw she was barefoot. She must have kicked her shoes off after getting sick.

Cassandra looked at him as if waiting for instructions.

Pointing for her to move back into the water closet, Gerrit edged around the closet door, closing it behind him while still trying to keep a visual on the doorway to the bedroom. He couldn't see anyone from this position.

Cassandra's hand squeezed his arm. She motioned toward the bedroom, gesturing that her husband and child were to the right, just out of sight. Nodding, he crossed the bathroom until he was standing to the right of the bedroom threshold. Carefully leaning to his left, Gerrit peered around the corner. The girl lay rigidly on the bed, fists clenched, staring up at Nico. Nico paced back and forth a few feet away like a caged animal.

Gerrit drew back out of sight. Maybe he wouldn't need to alert SWAT. He could end this right now.

He brought up his weapon, looking over the front sight as he edged to the left until he had a bead on Nico's head. Had to be a head shot. A shot to center mass would give Nico time to twitch and fire a weapon before dying. Now it was about the child, not his parents' death. Nico must die quick.

A shot ran out somewhere in the house.

Nico lunged toward the girl, grabbing her hair in a clenched fist. The girl screamed, crying.

Gerrit backed out of sight as Nico dragged the child toward the doorway leading into the hallway. He lost his chance to take Nico out.

Cassandra pushed against him. "Stop him, please," she whispered. He tried to restrain her.

"I told you to back off," Nico screamed through the locked door. "You want me to kill the girl."

Maria. That was the girl's name. Gerrit clenched his teeth. Why did it matter at this point? Sometimes his brain came up with information at the oddest times. Maria might be dead in the next few seconds.

Cassandra stirred behind him, eyes bulging with fear. Gerrit glared at her and jerked his head toward the bathroom. Cassandra shook her head, tears welling up.

He held a finger to his lips, trying to get her to remain quiet, as he turned his attention toward the bedroom.

Finch's voice bellowed down the hallway. "Accidental discharge. We're staying back…just like you said."

Gerrit peered into the room and saw Nico release the girl once again. He was facing the door. "Maria, get on the bed and lie down. Don't make a sound." The girl started to comply until she looked up and saw Gerrit.

She screamed.

Nico swung around just as Gerrit got him in his sights.

"Freeze."

Nico continued to take aim.

Gerrit fired.

Maria and Cassandra screamed in unison.

He fired repeatedly until Nico's body lurched back, the Russian's gun firing into the ceiling. Nico's weapon slipped from his grasp as he collapsed on the carpet.

Rushing over to where the man lay, Gerrit pointed his gun at Nico's face, ready to fire if the man so much as twitched.

Nico's eyes turned toward him, and he gave one gasp. His sightless eyes stared back.

Scratch one gangster.

The girl sobbed, and her mother rushed past him to comfort her.

Gerrit hit the transmission button. "Suspect down. 10-55. Units cleared to come in."

And another lead to his parents' death just killed.

Chapter 6

"Man, that's one sick animal. Holding a gun to his own kid's head." Taylor moved over to make room for Gerrit in the van.

"Not his kid." Gerrit eyed one of the shooting team investigators across the street before closing the door behind him. They were still holding down the scene three hours after all the shooting. It was going to be a long night. "Nico married Cassandra when Maria was a year old. Rumor has it Nico had her dad wasted just to clear the way to Cassandra. He hates the kid."

Taylor shook his head. "How'd you know about the access panel in the storage room?"

Smiling, Gerrit shrugged. "Just remembered."

"You're weird, dude. Freakin' weird. Who remembers—?"

Pounding on the van door reverberated through the vehicle. "Gerrit, you in there?" Lieutenant Cromwell's bellow was easy to identify. "Get your ass out here. Now."

Gerrit smirked. "He's such a sensitive soul. Worried about my traumatic experience." Seeing Cromwell peering through the tinted window, Gerrit edged over and unlocked the door. "Coming out, Lieutenant."

Cromwell stepped back as Gerrit swung open the door. "We need to talk. Privately." He whirled around and crossed the street to his rental car. "Get in, O'Rourke." It was a command, not a request.

Gerrit slid into the passenger side as Cromwell heaved himself behind the steering wheel. "What are you doing here, sir? I thought you'd be standing by in Seattle for details."

"Plans change. I'm driving you to the airport." Cromwell fired up the engine. "Taylor can bring your things later."

"Boss, you came all the way down here to drive me to the airport?" Gerrit looked at him incredulously. "Besides, we've got a ton of evidence and property to seize back there. And the shooting team—"

"Leave it to me to coordinate. That's why I am down here." He yanked on the wheel and hit the car horn. "This comes from the top. I mean, straight from the top in Justice. Our chief got the word several hours ago. Ordered me to hop on a plane and personally drag your sorry carcass onto the next flight to D.C. They want you there yesterday."

Marilynn's earlier phone call flashed in Gerrit's mind. "What's up, Lieutenant? Why the urgency?"

"Sometimes, we're just not given a reason. You've been in the military. When they say 'jump,' we just ask 'how high.' This is one of those times."

"The shooting team took my weapons. I've got nothing on me."

"Won't need it where you're going, although you never know about these Washington bureaucrats. Might want to consider wearing a bulletproof vest so they don't stab you in the back."

"Came here to fill me with confidence?"

"Don't give a flying leap about your confidence. Just want to make sure you get on that plane." Cromwell gave him a hard stare. "Son, be careful. Don't know what's going on, but these people are serious. Deadly serious. I've been around the block a few times, and my gut tells me you'd better watch out. Trust no one."

Gerrit watched the road ahead. They pulled onto southbound I-5. Ten minutes later, Cromwell took the exit to San Diego International Airport, runways cutting between the USMC's recruiting depot and the Navy's fleet anti-sub warfare school along the edge of the San Diego Bay. A well-protected stretch of real estate.

As they neared the airport, Cromwell glanced over at him. "Oh, they have a passport waiting when you get to D.C. I guess you won't be staying there long."

"What? My passport is locked up in a safe in Seattle."

The lieutenant shrugged. "My guess, they'll be giving you undercover creds. Passport included. You're on your way out of the country."

"Where are they sending me? And who is 'they'?"

Cromwell turned his attention back to the road. "They will tell you who 'they' is when they want to. Why they're sending you, only God knows, son. Him and those calling the shots. Watch your back."

Chapter 7

Washington, D.C.

Gerrit landed in D.C. as a steel dawn cracked the eastern horizon. A man dressed in the black and white uniform of a chauffeur stood at the boarding gate peering at each passenger as they emerged from the plane. The man glanced toward him with a look of recognition, then moved in for contact. "This way, Detective. I have a car waiting."

How did this guy get past security? The driver entered a code to access a secured door, then led him down a flight of stairs to the tarmac. A stretch limo was parked near the doorway.

The driver opened the car door to reveal a predawn greeting party for him—Marilynn; her father, Senator John Summers; and a third man Gerrit didn't recognize. The senator leaned forward. "Climb on in, Detective. Get out of the cold."

He stooped through the doorway and slid onto a black leather seat opposite Marilynn and her father. Senator Summer's gravelly voice—as if hewed from granite rocks—spilled on about law enforcement, serving one's country, and fighting the good fight. It was as if the man was trying to win Gerrit over as a voter.

After the political rhetoric, the senator leaned forward with a conspiratorial look, introduced the third man as someone from State without giving a name, then lowered his voice. "As you know, Gerrit, I sit on the Senate Select Committee on Intelligence. I also have a pipeline to the White House on intelligence matters. You know, the right hand keeping the left hand in the know."

Gerrit stared back. Where was this conversation going? Marilynn avoided his glances, as if he wasn't even here. The State guy—probably a spook—sat tight lipped, watching.

"We've got friends in a lot of key places—particularly in the business community. People willing to help us protect this country and make it a safe place to live. Know what I mean?" The senator shot him a wink.

Gerrit looked on without responding. The word *snakeskin* came to mind as he studied the senator.

"My daughter tells me good things about you and your work on this here task force she runs."

She finally gave him a glance.

"We have a *situation*, a matter of national security you might be able to help us with."

"Like what, Senator?" So far, Gerrit didn't have a clue as to why he was sitting in this plush ride.

Senator Summers sat up, back rigid, his look of friendship vanishing. Instead, a mask seemed to slip over the man's face. His eyes narrowed. "I know about your service to our country while in the armed forces. Special Ops in the Mideast, several tours of duty. Impressive record, son." The man's impassive face seemed to conflict with his impassioned words. As he spoke, the senator seemed to be sizing Gerrit up as if trying to decide whether he could be trusted.

Gerrit pursed his lips, waiting for the senator to get to the point.

"We could use your special skills in an investigation, the details of which I am not at liberty to discuss right now. I want you to meet a friend of mine: Richard Kane. He's expecting you in England later today."

Gerrit glanced at his watch. It was 2:00 a.m. in Seattle, making it mid-morning in London. He did a quick estimate. "There's no way I can get to London until nine or ten this evening. And I still don't have a clue as to why we're meeting here, Senator?"

"Your chief has been briefed and gave approval to have you work with us," the senator said. "Everything will become clear once you meet with Kane. Until then, we must maintain a certain level of discretion on our end. You understand."

"Actually, I don't, Senator. You're shooting me a wink and nod, as if we are the best of friends, and giving me a line of bull. I'm not stupid. So far, you haven't given me anything that would warrant my cooperation. Be specific."

Senator Summers's face flushed a bright red, and Marilynn shot Gerrit a shocked look. She leaned forward. "You can't talk to my father that way—"

"Sure he can, hon," the senator shot back, holding on to her arm as he apparently fought to restrain his own emotions. "We're asking Detective Gerrit to trust me, and he doesn't know me from Adam. After all, I'm a politician." He laughed and leaned closer. "Look around you, son. We're sitting out here in an unsecured location. I just can't spell out national-security information in this environment. You can understand that, can't you?"

Gerrit couldn't help himself from nodding.

"I thought you'd understand. All I ask is that you meet with Kane and hear what he has to say. He will fill you in on all the details. He has high-level clearance and will be running the operations from his place in England. Then you decide from there. Fair enough?"

"Operation?" Gerrit already felt uneasy about the situation. He recognized the importance of maintaining security, but so far he had not been given anything to work on. And now, the senator was hinting about some operation on foreign soil?

Senator Summers leaned back. "You'll land in Heathrow and Kane's people will pick you up. They'll let you get some shut-eye before heading up north where Kane's group is headquartered."

The State Department man—wearing a black fedora, a black rain coat, white shirt, and black shoes, dressed as if he wanted to try out for a bit part in *Casablanca*—finally seemed to come alive. He reached into a chrome Halliburton briefcase, withdrew a yellow package, one end already opened, and handed it to Gerrit.

Gerrit reached inside and withdrew a passport, airline tickets, British pound notes bundled together, several credit cards, and a California driver's license. He flipped open the passport and saw his photo plastered on the second page of the document, but another man's name appeared below the photograph.

John Gerrity.

Someone had switched Gerrit's first and middle name and added a letter to his first name. He glanced at the embossed name on the credit cards and CDL. Same bogus name printed on these documents.

Gerrit glanced at the guy from State, then turned toward the senator. "John Gerrity?"

The senator shrugged. "Name seemed to work. Easy for you to remember." He leaned forward and placed his hand on Gerrit's arm. "We need to be careful. No one will search you getting on or off the plane. We must keep this meeting with Kane quiet. Remove all your current identification papers and store them in your luggage. No one will look, I promise."

After placing everything back into the envelope, Gerrit set it on his lap. "You have to be kidding, right? You want me to prance through the airport with these bogus documents and board a plane for the UK without knowing what I'm getting into. I'm not an idiot, Senator."

Senator Summers seemed flustered. "Let me assure you these documents will never be questioned, nor will you. This is just to protect the secrecy of the operation."

"Yeah, yeah. I know—national security."

Anger flashed on the senator's face. "This is a matter of life and death. For many people, Gerrit. Don't be so flip with me."

"Then don't expect me to waltz into that airport without some assurance that this has been cleared with my bosses."

Nodding, the senator flipped open his phone and dialed. "Your man seems reluctant to cooperate. Talk to him." The senator thrust the phone toward Gerrit.

Gerrit pressed the phone to his ear. "Who's this?"

"This is the man who tells you what to do." Lieutenant Cromwell's angry voice boomed over the phone line. "Let me make this simple. Do what they say. That's an order...straight from the chief." The phone went dead.

Gerrit shrugged and passed the phone back to the senator. Anybody but Cromwell, he'd have asked to speak to the chief.

"Now that we have that matter cleared up," Summers slipped the phone into his pocket, "there's a commercial flight scheduled to take off in less than an hour. You are going to be on it as John Gerrity. Understood?"

Gerrit nodded and stole a quick look at Marilynn. Stoically, she sat and stared at her hands.

Summers tapped on the glass separating them from the driver. The limo began to roll toward the terminal. They left the tarmac, rolled through a guarded gate, and pulled onto a city street. Gerrit glanced out the side window and saw they were pulling up to the curb in front of British Airways east of the main terminal.

"Cheerio, Gerrit. Have a good trip." Summers extended his hand. Marilynn shot him a quick smile, the first since he climbed into the limo.

Gerrit edged toward the door, grasping the envelope.

The driver came around and opened the door. Gerrit started to step out when the senator called out, "Let's not have any further contact, shall we? Just get word to Marilynn if you need to talk. Otherwise, take your lead from Kane.

"And Gerrit," the senator added. "You've been reassigned to the State Department. Those documents you're holding provide diplomatic immunity. Cromwell has been filled in on what he needs to know. Don't expect to be hearing from him any time soon."

Gerrit crouched and stepped outside. He turned to face the senator. "Is there anything else about my future I should know about?"

Summers smiled. "If there is, you'll be told, soldier."

The driver closed the door, already holding Gerrit's overnight bag in his hand. "Here you go, sir. Have a good trip." The man tipped his hat and walked around to the driver's side.

"I'm a U.S. Marine, you pompous ass," Gerrit muttered, watching the limo pull away. Entering the terminal, he sought out a bathroom stall where he could privately trade his true ID and related documents with the falsified ones. What would the penalty be if he was caught?

In the last twelve hours, he seemed to have relinquished his own life—and identity—for something as ill defined as national security. That euphemism called *national security* covered a lot of ground, and he heard it got a lot of people in trouble on Capitol Hill. He thought of another good Marine—Colonel Oliver North—who faced a political hurricane while trying to serve his country under the name of national security. He hoped Senator Summers and the others knew what they were doing. It was Gerrit's neck sticking out here.

A few minutes later, he left the bathroom stall and made his way to a security checkpoint. A woman in a blue TSA uniform took his airline ticket, boarding slip, and passport.

"So, Mr. Gerrity. Traveling to London?"

He nodded, getting used to his new name.

She handed him back the documents. "Have a nice trip." As he walked away, a reflection in the glass allowed him to see that the woman was still following his movement. She looked until he could no longer see her in the glass. Glancing back, he saw her questioning another passenger, then turn toward the next person waiting to be cleared.

His lips felt dry and his chest tight.

As he watched airport security screen each passenger, he wondered why he felt so guilty if he was acting in the country's best interest. Maybe it was the fact he didn't have a clue what this was all about. A pawn in a game in which he did not understand the rules or the objective.

Hopefully this guy Richard Kane could enlighten him. He would just have to wait and see.

She watched as *John Gerrity* disappeared past the last checkpoint, gathered his belongings, and strode in the direction of his departure gate. She pulled out her cell phone and hit a preset number, watching the target disappear from sight. A moment later, a man's voice answered. She glanced toward the departure gate one last time.

"He just cleared security, sir. Should be boarding in just a few."

"Did he seem suspicious?"

"No. But he seemed…wary. Kept watching me as he walked away."

The man's emotionless tone sounded like an automated answering machine, but his words invoked fear in her. "You'd better not have raised his suspicions. Otherwise…"

The line went dead. With shaky hands, she lowered the phone.

Chapter 8

London, England

A blond flight attendant, her white-capped teeth dazzling against deeply tanned skin, leaned over and spoke softly. "We'll be landing in just a few minutes, sir. Pilot tells us he expects we'll go directly to the terminal upon arrival. Please buckle up."

Gerrit gave her a smile and reached for his lap restraint, clicking it into place. Only moments before, he'd watched the plane slice through a bank of clouds, leaving a pale moon behind in their wake. Darkness enveloped them. Once through the gloom, lights far below seemed to beckon.

Flashing runway lights hurled beneath them in a blur, and he leaned back to prepare for a jolt as wheels touched down. Fifteen minutes later, Gerrit shouldered a flight bag as he made his way into the terminal, still reeling from the last eight hours of sleepless travel.

As he cleared Customs, a man came alongside him. "Mr. Kane extends his greetings and wanted me to give you a lift, sir. This way." The man spoke with a southern drawl, extending a left paw the size of a grizzly as he grabbed Gerrit's bag. *Lefty* had a pancake nose and eyes of a boxer, shifting and calculating, an unspoken warning for those around him to be wary.

Gerrit followed Lefty through the terminal to a gray Rolls-Royce already parked along the curb, engine running. Another man sat behind the wheel. Lefty flung Gerrit's bag into the trunk before opening the rear door. His head jerked toward the open door.

The car peeled away from the curb the moment Gerrit's rear end touched leather. He eased back and watched the air terminal fade away, looking out on a dark, rain-swollen sky. Once on the ground, he saw the clouds close in to suffocate London with sleet and ice.

Maybe he could talk Lefty into loaning him an umbrella. Everyone in this part of the world must have one—just like Seattle. As the car weaved through traffic, Gerrit laid his head back and closed his eyes. His mind, though tired, refused to relax. Questions kept popping up like sparks from a fire. What was so important that he was yanked from a case five thousand miles away to a meeting in this foreign country? And who was Richard Kane? He had to be powerful to make a U.S. senator dance to his tune. To authorize Spyman from CIA, State, or whatever to hand deliver falsified top-quality documents. It was clear Kane wielded clout.

But to what end?

Another red flag rose back in D.C. when he saw Marilynn willing to stand in her father's shadow, to melt into the background during their brief encounter at Dulles. She never took a backseat to anyone—including her father. Totally out of character for this woman he'd come to know, publically and intimately.

Gerrit's mind must have wandered off in deep thought during the ride because the next thing he knew, the car pulled over and Lefty stood outside, opening the car door. Easing out of the car, Gerrit's lower back felt stiff from all the sitting he'd done during the night.

A recent dusting of snow coated the ground and chilled the early morning air, giving him just enough briskness to shake lingering sleep from his tired brain. Lefty, bag in hand, led him toward a light stone dwelling on the corner of what appeared to be two residential streets.

Shielded from the snow above by a pillared portico, Lefty lumbered up the expansive marble stairway to an elevated landing and rapped twice on a heavy wooden door. A gray-haired butler, face impassive to the point of disinterest, opened the door as if he had all the time in the world. Lefty impatiently brushed past without further conversation and handed Gerrit's bag to the butler as if to a meaningless servant.

Gerrit followed his guide up a curved stairway to the second floor, a tiled corridor softened by a carpeted maroon runner. They paused before an ornately carved oak door with brass doorknobs. Lefty rapped twice before barging in to the room. "Mr. Kane, your guest has arrived."

Motioning Gerrit forward, Lefty slowly backed out of the room and closed the door behind him. At first, Gerrit saw no one in the room. Then, a figure emerged from an interior doorway to the left and walked toward him. The man appeared to be in his sixties, with long ivory-white hair swept back to his shoulders and a sharply chiseled face that must have caught the eye of more than one woman.

As the man drew closer, his eyes—darkly dangerous—seemed to peer at Gerrit as if searching for information. Those eyes reminded Gerrit of a predator—cold, expressionless, and calculating.

The man extended a hand. "Welcome to London, Mr. O'Rourke. My name's Richard Kane." A Texas drawl seemed to fit the man's air of independence, a laid-back drawl that invited others to let down their guards. The man's voice reminded Gerrit of watching old television clips of President Lyndon Johnson speaking to the American people during the Vietnam conflict. Words of familiarity no one trusted.

Gerrit shook his hand, expecting to feel the ice-cold touch of a reptile. Instead, Kane's grasp seemed warm and strong.

He motioned Gerrit toward a chair near the only desk in the room, an expansive, simple desk carved from cherry wood, its reddish gleam polished to a shine. Not one piece of paper cluttered the desktop. Kane rounded it and sat down, learning forward with both elbows planted on the wooden surface, hands clasped together.

He studied Gerrit for a moment. "How was your flight…Mr. Gerrity?" It was the first smile Kane cracked.

"Long and tiring. Senator Summers sends his regards."

Kane's smile widened. "Make sure you still have your valuables after that man shakes your hand. Sneaky as all get-out."

"I wouldn't know, Mr. Kane. It was the first time I met him."

"And what did the good senator tell you about all this?"

"Matter of national security and you'd explain everything."

Kane shook his head, strands of white hair falling into his face, only to be pushed back into place. "Senator Summers always wants to play it safe. The ol' boy gives himself plausible deniability in case something goes wrong. Are you one of those guys who wants to play it safe?"

Gerrit met his stare without blinking. "I don't know what we're talking about. Anyone who knows me can tell you I like to get the job done. Whatever it takes."

"That's what I've heard. But I like to size up a man face-to-face. Helps me to determine if he's got true grit. Ya know what I mean?"

Shifting in his chair, Gerrit leaned forward. "No offense, Mr. Kane, but I'm really tired. Tired of all this down-home, *ya'll come by* bull. I got a senator who won't give me spit. A spook who hands me falsified credentials with my mug plastered on them—a felony, I might add. And I fly over two continents to meet with a man who wants to know if I've got true grit?"

Gerrit felt himself heat up. "How's this for grit?" he said, trying to calm down. "Based upon that nebulous meeting in D.C., I'm *ordered* to use those fake documents to pass through security on a trip that *might* have something to do with national security. Nobody tells me squat about who sanctioned this operation. Now, I'm not an attorney, but I'm smart enough to know that if this operation is illegal—my goose is cooked. I could face ten years in federal prison and fined $250,000 just for what I did back there at Dulles. And that's just for starters. Not to mention, my career in law enforcement would be toast. Is that enough *grit*?"

"Good enough. Look, why don't you get a little shut-eye. I know you have a lot of questions and I intend answering every one of them. In good time. First thing in the morning, we'll catch a chopper and head up the coast to a place where we operate. It is safe to talk there."

The door opened behind Gerrit. He turned and saw Lefty holding the door.

"Show Mr. O'Rourke to his room. Give him whatever he needs." Kane turned toward Gerrit. "Have a good sleep, partner. Tomorrow, I promise... all your questions will be answered."

Gerrit walked toward the door as Lefty led the way. Somehow, he didn't believe Kane. He sensed the man never revealed everything. Just enough to get his way.

Tomorrow, Gerrit had better get some answers or he was history.

Chapter 9

Harrogate, North Yorkshire, England

A black Agusta A-109 helicopter lifted off the heliport a few miles from the outskirts of Harrogate after dropping off its passengers. Gerrit gripped his bag, watching the sleek chopper climb higher against a sheet-metal gray sky. Storm clouds threatened in the west.

Richard Kane, flanked by Lefty and another man, waited at the edge of the landing site. Once Kane saw Gerrit walking toward them, he wheeled around, making long strides toward what appeared to be a small yet pretentious stone castle—Kane's headquarters.

A white gravel path wound between closely shorn lawns, neatly clipped grass looking like huge putting greens one after another, and beds of bushes and what promised to be flowering plants by next spring. Now, a harsh winter severed most of the leaves, leaving dead stems and freshly turned soil. Their destination, a gray limestone mansion replete with stone turrets at each of the four corners of the building.

Great location for snipers. Gerrit looked for signs of increased security. As he drew closer, a dark pod under one of the eaves caught his attention. A surveillance camera. Once he spotted that one, others were easier to pick out. Based on their locations on this side of the building, he surmised there was no way to approach this building without discovery.

Near a grove of trees to his far right, Gerrit saw a dark rectangular box—an unattended ground sensor—its blackened antenna sticking up like a slender finger near the trunk of one tree. He hadn't seen these since his days overseas, only those in the military had been cruder. They used them around their home base to warn of intruders approaching the camp. He imagined there might be a dozen of these sensors strategically peppered across the estate. They were walking into a well-monitored fortress.

He had yet to see weapons, but he suspected there might be at least one pointed at him this very second from one of those four turrets. Or from one of the many darkened windows overlooking the grounds.

They neared a U-shaped building, wrapped around a courtyard replete with bare rose bushes and low-kept hedges struggling to keep their green. Lefty dashed ahead and opened a ponderous wooden door. Kane and the others passed through before the ex-boxer slammed it closed.

The quiet serenity of the estate outside changed once they entered the building. A sense of urgency seemed to fill the air as they walked across the main floor. Many of the rooms had been turned into small business centers, desks sat back-to-back, manned by men and women in conservative business attire. Hardly anyone looked up as Kane and his entourage swept upstairs.

Gerrit and the others came to an office that overlooked the same grounds they covered from the helicopter. Large, paned-glass windows allowed dreary illumination from outside to creep into this massive room. Floor-to-ceiling shelves, each bearing rows of leather-bound books, crafted into the walls on all fours sides, except where doorways and a fireplace demanded their space. A desk stood in the center of the room, surrounded by several club chairs and a sofa. A fire crackled in the hearth—built from Blu **Venato d'Italia** marble—and warmth from the flames fought the cold trying to creep in from outside.

After settling himself at the desk, Kane waved the others away and motioned Gerrit to take one of the chairs.

"Now, let's get down to business. Not to be melodramatic, but I sincerely believe our country's future security is at stake. I—and the people I represent—intend to meet that challenge head-on. We could use your help."

"I'm a local cop. What can I offer?"

For a moment, Kane seemed to be pondering Gerrit's question. "I've read your file, Gerrit . You're much more than a cop. A lot more."

"I've got a few science degrees and I served in the military. Is that what you're getting at?"

"Precisely. You've got a scientist's brain, and you've got behind-the-lines military experience. I need a man just like you."

"Those skills might be useful in war, but I'm no longer in the military. And I'm behind the ball with regard to what I studied at MIT. What do you want from me—exactly?"

"Before I tell you, let me explain what I do."

"Senator Summers said you're a businessman."

"Actually, that's only one of the hats I wear. I only use my business interests as a means to an end."

"An end to what?"

"I'll share all that later. For now, all you need to know is that I am a… facilitator, a consultant, to our government and other interested parties."

"Interested parties?"

Kane leaned his hands on the desktop and pushed back in his chair. "My main objective is not important. Not for the mission at hand."

Gerrit felt uneasy about Kane's vagueness. "Does this mission have anything to do with ECHELON's major facilities only a few miles away at RAF Menwith Hill?"

Kane started to smirk, but then seemed to catch himself. "Ah yes. Everyone's heard of ECHELON, that so-called ultra secret network whereby our five allied governments spy on the world by listening in and monitoring all electronic communications worldwide. That ECHELON?"

Gerrit nodded.

"We are so far beyond that, my boy. I received permission to share certain classified information with you." He stood, gesturing to Gerrit. "Come with me. Let's mosey downstairs."

Frustrated, Gerrit stood, watching Kane head toward the door. He felt this man would never get to the point. They walked out into the hallway and down the far end of the corridor, stopping in front of what looked like a service elevator. Gerrit realized this lift—like everything about this place—was more than it appeared.

Kane peered into an iris scan and then placed his index finger on a print scanner. Once cleared, the door opened and he received authorization to navigate the elevator. Upon reaching a deep subterranean level, the door rolled open and Gerrit saw another whole floor—absent any windows—spreading out before him, much like a police squad room. Offices bordered an open bull pen that contained a number of workstations, each cubicle walled by three panels about five feet high. The offices must have been for those supervising the workforce, those minions stationed in cubicles under the watchful eyes of their bosses.

"This is where our real work takes place," Kane said. "That stuff upstairs—just window dressing."

Gerrit followed Kane along one wall of cubicles until they reached a corner office with Kane's name stenciled on an opaque glass-paned door. Kane thrust open the door and beckoned him inside. "Okay, now we can talk. There is nothing—at least in today's technology—that can intercept our conversation here." He approached the far side of a desk.

Gerrit sat across from Kane, the older man easing into the chair before speaking. "I need a man who can blend into the scientific community, into a specific field of which you are quite familiar."

"Nanotechnology," Gerrit said. "I've been out of that field for more than a decade—a lifetime in my field of study."

"You've been gone, but you can still speak the language. I need a man who can talk the talk while sifting through the unimportant and extract the important."

"Extract the important? What do you mean?"

Kane leaned forward, cupping his hands together under his chin. "I need you to get your hands on specific research material, pull out the important information, and then sabotage their efforts."

"Who are we talking about?"

A rap on the door interrupted them. Kane leaned over, whispering, "We'll talk about this later." Then, in a louder voice, he said, "Come on in, George."

A ruddy-faced man nearing seventy entered, followed by a younger and slimmer gentleman. "George Lawton, kind of you to join us."

The older man extended a hand to Kane, glancing at Gerrit with interest. "Brought the other chap with me that we spoke about." George turned to the man next to him. "Henry, say hello to a friend of mine from across the pond. Richard Kane and—"

"Gerrit O'Rourke," Kane said, without looking at Gerrit. He seemed to be studying the new man Lawton brought with him. "Gerrit, I'd like to introduce Henry—"

"Clarke," the young man said. "*Doctor* Henry Clarke, actually." Clarke shook Gerrit's hand as the two men eyed each other. "Looks like you're working for me, Dr. O'Rourke. You take orders well?" The man chuckled, but his eyes held no humor.

Gerrit rose, slightly confused. "Glad to meet you, Doctor." He turned to Kane for clarification. "I think Mr. Kane was just starting to explain my role in all this."

A sly smile emerged on Lawton's face. "Keeping everyone in the dark as usual, eh, Richard?"

Kane motioned for the others to have a seat, before looking at Gerrit. "I never got a chance to tell you. Y'all will be traveling to Vienna with Henry here in about a week. Sort of a security detail."

"Security? For whom?"

Henry pompously waved a hand. "Afraid it's for me, old chap. They think some terrorist may have it in for me." The younger man crossed his legs and folded his hands, sitting back in the chair as if he were a king holding court.

Gerrit glanced at Kane. "I'm not sure what—"

"I'll go over the details later, Gerrit. I told them about you. And they thought you were an excellent choice for the job."

The others nodded. Gerrit settled back onto his chair. Did they also know he was in this country under an assumed name? Since Kane introduced him by his real name, he assumed they knew nothing of his alias.

More secrets. And it had been a long time since he heard *Doctor* attached to his name. A long time.

Kane edged forward. "Dr. Clarke is the foremost authority in quantum computer technology and cyber-security issues."

"You flatter me, Mr. Kane. I am one of a hundred scientists puttering around in the dark in this particular field."

The man's thinly disguised arrogance—cloaked in false modesty—rankled Gerrit. There were only a handful of scientists in Clarke's field that could do what this man does. On the other hand, Gerrit could see why this man might be a high-value target for the enemy—if his own side didn't shoot him first.

Kane continued. "Henry, you're the one they chose to sit on a prestigious international panel for cyber-security technologies. And Dr. O'Rourke will fit very nicely in your entourage to Vienna."

Clarke pompously patted Gerrit's arm. "I'd be honored to have Dr. O'Rourke aboard. My secretary will send you my travel schedule to look over. She'll make whatever reservations you require."

Lawton sat quietly, watching the others interact until he gave Kane a nod. "My office will run interference."

"Your office?" Gerrit asked. "Which office might that be?"

"Let's just say Her Majesty's security office is interested in Dr. Clarke's well-being. Wouldn't do to have him popped off on my watch, good fellow."

MI6.

Gerrit looked over at Kane, whose face seemed masked at the moment. "No, that would not be good, Mr. Lawton. Let me know what you need from me."

"My friend, Mr. Kane, will give you the details. I won't be seeing you in Vienna, but I will be…available if matters turn sour. I guess we'd better be off, shall we, Dr. Clarke?"

The scientist shrugged, stood, and was about to leave when Lawton tapped him on the shoulder. "Why don't you go on ahead, Henry. There's one small matter I need to discuss with Mr. Kane and Dr. O'Rourke."

Clarke looked back curiously and then left the room. Lawton closed the door behind him. "What an arse that man is. Sorry to stick him with you, Dr. O'Rourke. But we needed that clown to give you cover."

"Cover?" Gerrit looked from Lawton to Kane.

Lawton nodded his chin at Kane. "Richard, why don't you give our boy here the details."

Chapter 10

Gerrit saw the two men exchange glances before Kane leaned forward, eyeing Gerrit for a moment before turning to Lawton. "First, I wanna make sure you know all about our boy here, George."

Lawton shook his head. "I'll take your word that this is our man. That's all I need to know."

Kane leaned forward. "No, no, George. I want you to know why I've picked this good ol' boy for the job."

Gerrit shifted in his seat, feeling like this was some kind of job interview for a job he never signed up for—nor wanted. And if Kane called him *boy* once more, Gerrit was going to grab that long-haired creep's silver locks and give him a Mohawk.

Kane reached into a drawer and pulled out a bulging file folder. "Just so I don't forget anything, I've jotted down a few notes about our boy here. Quite a history." He glanced up and gave Gerrit a wink.

Kane's index finger trailed down a page before turning to the next. "Bachelor of Science degree in 1991 before joining the U.S Marine Corp, where you entered as an enlisted man. Qualified to serve with Force Recon just before the Persian Gulf War, field-elevated to officer status based on combat service and education."

Kane shot him a look before continuing. "Let's see, you left the military in 1996 and returned to MIT to earn a doctorate in electrical engineering and computer science. Says here you specialized in nanotechnology—something to do with nano electronics."

"Mr. Kane, I don't see how this trip down memory lane tells me why I'm sitting here today. Can we fast-forward to the present?"

"Patience. My friend George needs to know he's getting the best. Like we say back home, 'Don't call him a cowboy, till you've seen him ride.' My friend here has to know this is not your first time to the rodeo, boy. And I want to refresh my memory about your background while you're here to correct me—if the record's wrong."

Gerrit leaned back, watching as Kane continued through the file.

"Now, in 2001 you started a research fellowship at MIT focused on harnessing nanotechnology by creating a…what do you call this—?"

"A nanofluidic device—"

"Right, a device capable of detecting biological warfare agents the size of a pinhead." Kane glanced up. "My, my, boy. That's got to be tinier than a little ol' ant." He returned his gaze to the file. "You just started on that project when they hit the WTC and Pentagon on 9/11. Three months later, you're called back into military service." Kane looked at him.

"I volunteered."

"Now why would you go and do something like that?" Kane seemed to be toying with him.

Gerrit crossed his arms, leaning back. "They needed everyone on board for the Afghan invasion. A couple years later, they sent me to Iraq. So, where are you going with this?"

Kane lowered the file and clasped his hands together. "That leads us to 2004. Your parents and uncle."

Those words sent a knife twisting in Gerrit's gut. The police files from Seattle PD's archives at his home came to mind. And on his wall, photos of the blackened car and what was left of his mother and father pinned up for him to face every day. Charred remains, barely enough left to bury after a closed-casket ceremony—a ceremony he missed because he was off fighting a war in the Middle East. Deep ops that lasted long after they lowered his parents into the ground.

Gerrit stood and leaned on the desk. "You had better have a good reason for dredging all this up or I am on the next plane back to the U.S."

"Calm down, my boy. Don't get your feathers ruffled—"

"And if you call me *boy* one more time, I'll take that file and shove it where the sun don't shine. Are we clear?"

Kane slowly rose. "I like a man who's not afraid to speak his mind. I'm bringing this all up for a good reason. I need—your country needs—your help. These records," he motioned toward the open file, "tell me you are a man who sacrificed for his country." He leaned on the desk facing off with Gerrit. "Why did you give up your work at MIT to become a Seattle cop? Do you still think you'll find out who killed 'em?" He seemed to forget that Lawson was still in the room.

"You read my file. You tell me."

Kane nodded. "A background investigator in Seattle asked the same question when you left the Marine Corp and turned your back on MIT to become a cop."

"So you know the answer."

"You told them it was none of their damn business."

"And I'm telling you the same thing."

"I'm surprised they took you on after that answer."

"I guess what I had to offer outweighed what the investigator thought was an impertinent answer."

Kane smirked. "I see things have not changed."

"What do you mean?"

"Still trying to be a loner. Disobeying orders. Getting into situations without any backup. In short, you're still impertinent."

"Is that a problem for you?

"Not at all, my b—" Kane caught himself. "Not at all, Gerrit. In fact, you're just the kind of man I want. Willing to think on his feet and take chances."

Kane began pacing the room. "Clarke thinks you'll be watching his back while in Vienna. That dummy thinks his backside's worth protecting.

Personally, I could care less if a terrorist caps him. But babysitting this jerk will give you a legitimate reason to be in Vienna. We have another mission for you. Another *opportunity*."

"Opportunity?"

Kane returned to his desk. "Exactly. I want you to steal something for us without getting caught."

Lawton rose. "I think I'll be off, gentlemen. Don't think you need me to discuss these details." He shook Gerrit's hand before turning toward Kane. "Richard, I know you've picked the right man. Let me know when you've knicked this thing. If you run into any trouble, I will be around in Vienna. Let's just try to keep this operation between friends, shall we?" He nodded before leaving.

Gerrit's stomach tightened as he watched the British agent leave. Whatever they wanted him to do, Lawton wanted to be able to say he was not part of this conversation. That he was never present when Gerrit got his marching orders.

Plausible deniability.

Chapter 11

Gerrit turned toward Kane as soon as Lawton left. "You brought me all the way over here to be a thief?"

"Cool down," Kane said, as he returned to his seat, leaning back before continuing. "Let me preface all this by saying national security really is at the heart of the matter. There are some documents we need to get our hands on that an American scientist is concealing. If we go snooping around his office back in the States, we might ruffle some feathers over at DOJ."

"You mean spying on American citizens on U.S. soil?"

"Exactly. Even under the Patriot Act, we'd be hard-pressed to explain why we're snooping around this guy's research facility."

"But on foreign soil, the rules somehow change?"

"Not exactly, but at least it's not on U.S. soil. And we're using foreign operatives that can get us the kind of access and information we need to pull this off while building layers between us and—"

"Foreign operatives? Do I look like a foreign operative? And what do you mean by *access*? Are you talking about—?"

"This guy is not willing to level with us. He believes he has a mandate from God to share his findings with the world. That, my friend, would not be in our country's best interests."

"What exactly does he want to unleash on the world?"

"A way to make the Internet virtually unprotected. No secrets. No privacy. No way of shielding governments from the prying eyes of their enemies."

"You mean computer technology and data open to the world? Like Internet banking?"

"Exactly. This moron—like those whackos from WikiLeaks—believe that all communication and data storage should be available to the world community. Everything open to gawk at. They want to curtail commerce to on-site transactions, for example."

"How do they expect to achieve this?"

"They've almost achieved it. By combining recent research in quantum computers, finding the flaw in the latest bio-inspired cyber security, and by linking recent developments with nanotechnology—we believe they may have reached their goal."

Gerrit shook his head. "There is no way one scientist was able to accomplish all that. He'd have to—"

"Conspire with a core group of scientists with the same goals. That's exactly what this idiot did. Joined forces with other do-gooders in interrelated fields to break down our security."

"What's their objective? Destroy the country?"

"Naively, they think by exposing all governments to world scrutiny, this will somehow bring about world peace."

"I can see some merit to that. But total exposure?"

"Exactly. This is why I detest weak-minded academia. No offense, Gerrit. Unlike you, they never lived in the real world." Kane stood. "It would be absurd to be that open in the kind of world we live in. Look at the dangers we face in the intelligence community alone."

Gerrit nodded. "Has our government sanctioned this operation?"

Kane raised his hands palms up. "Let's just say the government would like to see us succeed."

"What makes this guy so important? Can't you put pressure on him to back off? The feds ought to be good at that."

"It gets worse, Gerrit. This guy hacked into a closely guarded server the government maintains that stores every know operation—military and intelligence—throughout the world. Names, dates, times, resources, covert scientific projects, and a list of operatives and scientists in each of these operations."

Whew! "And he intends to publish this?"

Kane nodded. "That's why we need to stop him cold. To discredit his work, and take what he's already stolen."

"And if I get caught?"

Kane shrugged. "We'll try to intervene, but…"

Gerrit heard this music before. They'd intervene on his behalf about as solidly as he could tap dance on a sheet of thin ice with steel-toed combat boots. "These foreign operatives…how will they achieve what you want. Coercion?"

Kane grimaced. "Coercion is such a strong word. Let's just say they will be able to reason with him more forcibly than we could under U.S. law."

CIA interrogation efforts overseas? Gerrit heard about some of these operations, however he'd never witnessed any. He found himself divided over this issue, having seen firsthand what these terrorists were capable of. But U.S. citizens? "I won't be a part of any operation that calls for torture—whether U.S. citizen or foreign nationals."

"And you won't. All we need for you to do is grab this guy's files and extract anything that might harm our national security. He won't even be around to bother you."

Uneasy, Gerrit sat back down. This operation seemed to have been cleared through his chief, and the Department of Justice's sanction would make it appear that Kane and his people would be on their best behavior. His own boss ordered him to cooperate. "Okay, tell me more about this guy and what you want me to do."

"The target is a scientist by the name of Ron Adleman." Kane began sharing details of the operation.

As Gerrit listened, he didn't hear anything that would be outside the realm of sanctioned covert operations. It was more Kane himself that made Gerrit wonder if he was doing the right thing. Instinct urged him to walk away from this.

Instead, he sat and listened. He could not walk away from a threat to his country's security. However, the absence of a clear chain of command, a clearly identified sanction from the government meant that he would be swimming in murky waters.

And he would be on his own. No backup. No safety net.

He'd better not fall. "Okay, I'm in."

Kane smiled broadly and rose, walking toward the door. "Good. Be ready to move in about a week. We will be in touch with details. Now, return home and relax. Have a good trip."

A long trip for a short conversation.

Kane wasn't telling him everything. Lawton's chiding words about this man's lack of forthrightness seem to jive with Gerrit's gut instinct. And Cromwell's warning about watching his back with these guys troubled him. Everyone around him—Cromwell, Marilynn, the senator—all seemed to know more about what was happening than he did.

He felt like he was working in the dark without a flashlight, and he'd have a lot to lose if things went wrong.

Chapter 12

Seattle, Washington

Gerrit drew closer, sighting down the barrel of his semi-auto Smith & Wesson M&P. Squinty eyes, fat jowls, and a heavyset man slouched in the armchair, sleeping. Gerrit eased the safety off and pressed the .40 cal barrel into the fat man's forehead.

"Wake up and die," Gerrit hissed, watching the man's eyes suddenly open.

Fear and stale beer mingled with sweat on the killer's face. "Don't hurt me! I'll give you whatever you want."

Gerrit clutched the man's throat and squeezed. "Can you bring back my mother and father?"

A look of recognition and terror flickered in the man's eyes. "Are you...?"

Squeezing tighter, Gerrit drew closer. "I'm your worst nightmare. Your first mistake was killing my parents. Your second mistake—leaving me alive."

The man gasped for breath.

Gerrit felt like ripping the man's throat out. "Just one question. Who hired you to kill them?"

His eyes widened. "I can't," he gasped. "If they find out I snitched, they'll hunt me down."

"Wrong answer," Gerrit said, his voice dropping to almost a whisper. He slowly squeezed the trigger until—

Gerrit jerked awake. Light flickered across the darkened room as the black-and-white video played on the screen. A cold, wet nose nudged his hand.

Bones.

The dog placed his head on Gerrit's lap and whined.

Stroking the animal's head, Gerrit tried to clear his mind. Waves lapped against the pier as his houseboat creaked from Lake Washington's current, lights from Seattle seen in the distance through a bay window. Bones always sensed when Gerrit had troubled dreams. The dog had been with him—with a few absences—since that day in Fallujah. No longer skin and bones, the dog never missed a meal. And it showed. No fat, just muscle.

The dog had been Gerrit's jogging partner since they returned from the Middle East. Bones could run Gerrit into the ground and loved to dive off the houseboat for long swims in the lake. This desert dog loved water. At the moment, Bones was concerned about his master.

With a dry mouth, Gerrit turned and began to watch the tape he'd seen a million times as the camera operator panned the blast area. The lens zoomed downward to focus on a blackened hand, severed at the wrist, lying amid ashes and debris on the dirty-gray concrete.

One of the few parts left of his father.

As the film rolled on, investigators slowly identified other body parts, marking each one with a number for later mapping and tagging. These images still left him numb, as if he just learned of the explosion. Even after viewing this gruesome tape over and over since the blast seven years ago, his chest still tightened, his heart still ached.

As he viewed each film clip—putting his emotions aside—he'd carefully study the documented evidence trying to figure out what everyone else missed. Who triggered this ghastly killing? *Give me just one lousy lead.* A Russian-made detonator had been recovered. Nico Petrosky's group? Gerrit thought so. But as always, he came up empty. And Nico was dead.

Strewn on the floor of his small office, documents and photographs lay in small piles, all duplications from the original files. Lab reports, crime-scene sketches, and reams of reports carefully recording all the efforts of every investigator assigned to the case.

In all these hundreds of investigative man-hours and all the trained eyes focused on this case—SPD, ATF, FBI, DOJ, ICE—not one substantive suspect surfaced. Not one tangible lead emerged that might give him a clue as to who might have triggered the explosion. Not one hint as to who ordered this hit or who built this bomb that destroyed the ones he loved.

He was the only one left to mourn. The only one left to carry on this investigation. Everything changed for him the moment their lives ended. Turning his back on the military and his potential future in science, Gerrit became a police officer here in Seattle. All for one purpose—to find his parents' killers and bring them to justice. To take revenge against those responsible.

Many a night he woke up fantasizing, peering down the barrel of his gun, pointing it at the faces of his parents' murderers. There was never any hesitation in his dreams. He always pulled that trigger.

A life for a life.

Actually three lives. The only family he'd ever known had been destroyed in one night—his parents killed and his uncle disappeared.

Three tours in the Middle East had started him down this solitary road. Once his military duty ended, he planned to start a normal life. A wife. A family. The all-American dream. When tragedy struck, however, he knew his world had changed forever. His future would never be *normal*.

He picked up the file on Dr. Henry Clarke that Kane had provided in England and began to review the man's history so his cover story in Vienna would hold up. He used the flickering light from the television screen to read, too tired to get up and turn on a light.

According to the documents, Clarke supervised the UK's Communication-Electronic Security Group, CESG, an arm of GCHQ, Government Communications Headquarters. His group made sure British communications and electronic data remained intact with no security breaches. Clarke rode shotgun on any projects aimed at improving these capabilities while keeping a watchful eye out for those who might seek to breach security.

CESG worked arm and arm with Lawton's MI6, Secret Intelligence Service, and the MI5, the UK's Security Service branch. Sooner or later, all intelligence and counterintelligence communications filtered through Clarke's office.

Gerrit could see why terrorists and foreign governments might like to get inside Clarke's arrogant head.

Two quick raps on the door followed by a key in the lock made him jump and reach for his gun. Bones never growled.

"Gerrit, you home?" Marilynn Summers. He forgot she still had his houseboat key.

He put the gun back on the end table, quickly buried Clarke's file, and reached for the remote, killing the video and bathing the room in darkness. He heard her footsteps heading toward his office.

"Gerrit?" Lights came on, dispelling darkness. "Why are you sitting here in the dark? Watching that video again?" she said brusquely as she entered. Bones stood, and Marilynn gave the animal a look that said it all—she and Bones were not on friendly terms. "Why you choose to live in this damp houseboat I'll never know. You can afford better."

"It suits me, Marilynn. What are you doing here?"

"I was concerned. Never heard from you when you got back. Everything went all right in England?"

"Just fine." He took a deep breath and exhaled. "Thanks for asking."

Her intrusion ticked him off and he struggled to be cordial. Everything changed over the last few weeks, particularly after their conversation while he was in San Diego. The Nico Petrosky investigation seemed less important to her, and whatever they had going on between them had cooled. She seemed willing to move on to more important matters since their meeting in D.C. It surprised him she even showed up tonight; her actions made him suspicious. Marilynn always had an agenda.

He never kidded himself about their relationship. He knew from the first day that this wasn't going to be a forever thing with them. Marilynn wanted to climb, to achieve, and she hungered for power, a lust she learned from her father. Their relationship had become a matter of convenience. To be brutally honest, he preferred it this way. His agenda didn't include others—including Marilynn. Finding his parents' killer was his primary goal in life.

Everything else no longer mattered.

She walked across the room, tossing her coat on the couch. "Colder than Alaska in here. Mind if I turn up the heat?" Without waiting for a response, she cranked the dial to high. "There, now we can get comfortable."

"You should have called. I just got back and I'm about to hit the sack."

"Want some company?" She smiled, running her fingers through his hair. "We can really warm up this place fast."

He stiffened, causing her face to tighten. "Not tonight. I'm beat and I've got a lot to do before…"

She eyed him curiously. "Before you what, leave again?"

"I'm surprised your father didn't tell you."

Anger replaced her curiosity. "My father always keeps me in the dark. He only tells me if he needs something…*for him.*"

"I'm shipping out next week. Not sure when I'll be back. Kane seems to have cleared it with my boss and the task force."

"I'm heading the task force, or have you forgotten? I wasn't told anything." Now, her anger seemed directed at him.

He shrugged. "What can I say?"

She reached down and began to unbuckle his belt. "Are you sure I can't get you to tell me what you're up to?"

Trapping her hand on his belt, he tried to push her away. "Not tonight."

Marilynn moved closer. "You sure?" She straddled his lap, pressing against him. Her lips traveled across his cheek, ending at his earlobe.

Gerrit felt himself weaken. This was not love, not even lust for him anymore. It lay somewhere between the two—when nightmares and memories seem overpowering and two bodies coming together managed to push back the pain for a moment. He used to feel guilty, as if he might be using her for his own personal gratification. But as time passed, he realized they were using each other. He just didn't understand her purpose. Nor did he care.

She must have felt his body give in, responding to her embrace. "See. I told you—I always win." She smiled, slowly and seductively climbed off his lap, then led him by the hand to the bedroom.

Whispers awoke him hours later. He raised his head from the pillow and glanced toward the red glare of the digital clock. 3:00 a.m.

He rose and stumbled over a shoe as he padded his way toward the bedroom door. He heard Marilynn's voice, hushed, coming from the other room. The door stood ajar. He peered through the opening.

She huddled in the kitchen, farthest away from the bedroom. She must have snatched up one of his T-shirts. The green glow from the oven light fell across her body, bathing her in muted light. She covered her mouth, a cell phone pressed against her ear. She glanced toward the bedroom and he drew back. "You might wake him up."

Marilynn listened for a moment, as the man continued talking. She finally responded. "No. He is not telling me anything. I tried...believe me, I tried."

Gerrit thought back to earlier, after their passion subsided. Marilynn casually tried to elicit information about where he went in England and why he was leaving again. He chalked it up to her insatiable curiosity. Kane had ordered a lid on all this information, so Gerrit revealed nothing to Marilynn. This seemed to irritate her.

As Gerrit opened the door all the way, Marilynn jerked her head up and seemed to stiffen. "I've got to go. I'll...I'll call you from the office."

"Who was that?" Gerrit walked toward her.

"Hey, I'm sorry I woke you. Got this call and heard it vibrate. Thought I could return it in here without disturbing you."

He waited for further clarification.

"Just work." She dropped the phone on the counter, crossing her arms. "We have a surveillance going on in another case, and the guys were just checking in."

Gerrit watched her face, trying to figure out why she was lying.

She walked past him into the bedroom and began gathering her clothes. "I need to get back to the office. Need to return this call on a more secure line." She disappeared into the bathroom. "Be out in a jiffy. Why don't you go back to bed?"

He waited until he heard the shower turn on and then reached for her phone. Flicking on the menu, he thumbed to the last call received, hit the Select button, and a menu emerged. The words *Private Caller* flashed on the readout. He tapped to the last incoming call and saw the number of the caller Marilynn spoke to. He glanced at the number, recognizing the numerals immediately.

Richard Kane.

Why was Kane calling her in the middle of the night—here?

Footsteps sounded across the bedroom. Marilynn appeared at the doorway, toweling herself off. "I forget my…"—she glanced at what he was holding—"my phone."

He held it up. "Just getting it for you. Saw it here on the counter."

The darkness prevented him from seeing her expression, but her voice seemed tight. "Just drop it in my purse. I'm almost ready."

He complied, turning on a table lamp near the couch. Her purse had been left on the floor. He stooped down and slipped the phone inside. A few minutes later she emerged, fully clothed. He handed her the purse. "The cell's inside. Wouldn't want you to miss any more calls."

Her eyes, questioning, shifted from the purse to his face. She brushed his cheek with her lips. "Call me later. Maybe we can do dinner?"

He nodded, watching her leave. He heard her car start up, tires slipping on gravel. Quietness settled around him.

He slipped on some jeans and a T-shirt before walking to the glass door. He slid it open and stepped out onto a small porch that sat only inches above the lake. He looked over the water toward downtown Seattle. Cold night air made him shiver. He watched as the running lights from a small craft cut through the night, the city's silhouette beyond.

The dark water below him ebbed and flowed as small waves slightly raised and lowered the houseboat. Water carried a certain amount of force, of power, that moved like an unseen hand beneath him. Like his life, this current pushed and pulled without permission. Life seemed to forge ahead, inextricably dragging him along in its wake.

A warning blast from a horn carried across the water, bringing him back to the present. This feeling of emptiness—starting when his CO broke the news about his folks years ago—hounded him whether he was awake or asleep. There would be no peace until he learned what happened. Until then, he would just exist, even in moments when he and Marilynn lay on the bed in a passionate embrace. That phone call she fielded reminded him once again about how much his world had changed.

And who he could trust.

Chapter 13

Vienna, Austria

The trip to meet Kane and the reason for using an alias still nagged at him. Clearly, Kane or Senator Summers didn't want Gerrit's earlier travel to the United Kingdom to be flagged for some reason. Why?

Passport in hand, Gerrit approached the front counter of the Radisson Blu Palais Hotel. At least he was traveling under his right name on this trip. No hocus-pocus.

"Dr. O'Rourke." A young woman extended her hand as he approached the counter, her heavy Germanic accent seemed to add more allure to this historic site. "May I assist in your check-in? I am working with Dr. Clarke to make sure his entourage is taken care of."

"*Vielen Dank, Fräulein…?*"

"Helene." She bobbed her head self-consciously. "*Sie sind herzlich eingeladen.* You are welcome, sir."

Gerrit finished checking in as Helene stood by. When he was through, he turned to her. "I understand this hotel was originally built as two palaces in 1872."

Helene nodded. "Yes, sir. And I am pleased to point out that we are overlooking Vienna's famous Stadtpark. You will be able to see a number of monuments here, including one devoted to Johann Strauss." She pointed proudly.

As Gerrit started to reach for his luggage, Helene shook her head. "I will have someone take your bags up. Dr. Clarke is waiting in the Palaise Café." She gestured in the direction he ought to go.

He slipped money to the bellhop already grabbing his belongings. Waiting until Helene and the man walked away, Gerrit found his way to the café.

Henry Clarke waved from across the dining area as Gerrit entered. "Ah, Dr. O'Rourke. Good to see you've arrived safely. Mr. Lawton's associates have been keeping me company." Clarke motioned with his chin toward two men seated a couple tables away, a pink linen-covered table pulled out to allow both men to sit with their backs to the far wall. Teacups in hand, they looked like two NFL football players attending a women's tea party. "I feel well protected, now that you're here," Clarke said, each word liberally doused with sarcasm.

Gerrit nodded to the two men. They eyed him without returning the greeting.

"The chap on the right is heading up our party here. I will introduce you after our tea."

A waiter set a cup and saucer in front of Gerrit. Clarke leaned closer. "I hope you don't mind, I went ahead and ordered for you."

Gerrit thanked the waiter, taking a sip out of courtesy. He hated the taste, like weak coffee squeezed through a filter a dozen times before getting to his cup. Dishwater had more kick. He tried not to wince.

Clarke sipped his tea. The scientist carefully set down his cup before speaking. "Dr. O'Rourke, may I speak bluntly since we are finally alone?"

"Certainly, Doctor."

"Let's drop all this doctor stuff, shall we? You've been out of the business so long I hesitate using your title. From what I gather, you've been off gallivanting with bobbies since your parents died. Have you used *any* of your academic training since that time?"

"That is none of your concern…*Henry*."

The scientist's jaw tightened. "While you remain in my service, O'Rourke, you're just a glorified errand boy. My own private muscle, if you will. Don't embarrass me in front of my colleagues."

"Don't worry, Henry. I'm sure you can manage *that* all on your own." He instantly regretted his retort to Clarke. Focus on the primary mission, even if it meant putting up with this guy's ego. "Look, neither of us asked for me to be here. My government—and apparently yours—believe there's some risk to you. I intend to work with your folks," he nodded to the two agents across the room, "to make sure you return home safely. We can part ways at that time. Until then, let's try to work together. And I will try not to…embarrass you while I'm here. Fair enough?"

Clarke stared back sullenly. "Just stay out of my way."

Gerrit lowered his eyes to make it appear he relented. The man's belligerent attitude seemed out of place, unlike their meeting in Harrogate. Maybe Kane and George Lawton sitting in the same room forced Clarke to mask his true feelings back there. Not anymore.

Clarke leaned back for a moment, letting his breath out slowly. "I have—we have—certain pressures on the CESG right now, and maybe—"

"Forget it. Let's just get you home safely, shall we?"

Looking resigned, Clarke nodded.

One of the two NFL guys sauntered up, the man Clarke singled out as heading up security. "Everything okay, Dr. Clarke?" The man kept his eyes focused on Gerrit as he spoke.

"Just fine, James. Have you met Dr. O'Rourke? As you know, he's joining our entourage for a few days. Doctor, this is James Stafford."

The man's grip tried to crush Gerrit's hand. "We need to talk, Dr. O'Rourke. Make sure our efforts are adequately coordinated."

Gerrit gingerly extracted his hand. "Anytime you're ready."

"Meet you upstairs when Dr. Clarke is finished here?" James provided a room number. "In about twenty minutes?" The man turned and rejoined his partner without waiting for Gerrit's reply.

Flexing his hand, trying to get feeling back, Gerrit watched Stafford whisper to his partner across the room. Between Clarke and Stafford, Gerrit felt about as welcome as a vegetarian at a barbeque rib cook-off. If he didn't watch himself, they just might throw him on their grill and roast him alive.

Chapter 14

35,000 Feet above the Atlantic Ocean

Turbulence jostled Richard Kane as he reached for the phone. All the money he spent on this jet—with all its luxury and comfort—could not buy him a smooth flight. The Global 8000 business jet dipped suddenly as if a giant hand let go and allowed the aircraft to free fall. A few moments later, the pilot raised the nose, slowly regaining altitude.

Cradling the receiver in one hand, Kane dialed a memorized number and let it ring. A sultry woman's voice came on the line. "Richard, I'd know your tone anywhere."

Kane breathed heavily, remembering his time with her only a few months ago when he was recruiting. The only language she spoke was the dollar bill—or euro. She was worth every cent.

"Collette, my dear. How's Vienna?"

"Very productive. And on your end?"

Kane dispensed with the niceties. "Time's short, Collette. I have to know whether Gerrit will be a team player. Everything is set to be launched in just a few weeks. Maybe sooner. I need him on board when we launch—or terminated if he chooses to walk away. Understand?"

"I understand, Richard."

"Good. Gerrit just reached the hotel. He's in play. Are your people ready?"

"We will be when I hang up. *Au revoir*, Richard."

Kane killed the connection.

Gerrit reached James Stafford's room, trying to knock twice in quick succession. Stafford yanked the door open before Gerrit could strike a second time.

"Grab a chair." James quickly closed the door behind Gerrit.

The room was sparse, compared to Clarke's, but even so it gleamed with elegance. After Gerrit sat down, James dragged a chair across the room and turned it around so he could straddle it. "Let's get down to brass tacks, as you Yanks are apt to say. We don't need an American telling us how to protect Clarke. So...why are you here?"

"You know why I'm here."

"Hang it, man. I know when George Lawton is behind something; it's never what it seems. I don't want to get shot—or fail in my duties to protect Clarke—because you and your CIA spooks are up to no-good, keeping us in the dark. Tell me what you're up to or I'll bounce you off this detail."

"I thought the British were more tactful. And what makes you think I work for the CIA?"

Stafford glared at him without answering.

"By the way, don't you work for Lawton?"

"I work for a lot of people," he said, ignoring any further reference to the CIA, as if it was already understood.

"What did Lawton tell you?" Gerrit knew he was buying time. He tried to figure how to handle this without making another enemy. Clarke was enough to deal with right now.

"Never mind about him. I want to hear it from you."

"Just stay focused on Clarke and you'll be in the clear. That's all I can tell you."

Stafford shoved himself off the chair. "I knew it. Lawton's got his hands into something else and using this as cover."

"I'd let it alone. Better if you just do what your told...just like me."

"Playing the good soldier, eh? Could get you killed in this business."

"So could riding in a car. But we do it anyway."

"A car only gets you and other passengers dead. This business can kill a lot more people. Particularly when you don't know what you're up against."

"You have to trust the ones you're working with."

Stafford sneered. "What kind of world are you living in? In my business, I trust no one. That's how I stay alive."

Gerrit eased himself from the chair. Trust was a word he rarely used. It had been a long time since he thought of trusting anyone. The older he got, the less trust he had in people. James hit it on the head. Trust no one.

Particularly men like Richard Kane.

"I'm not an idiot," Gerrit said. "I imagine we've both worked on the dark side, taking chances and doing things for God and country that others never hear about. I know the cost of doing business. We've both paid that price. So, let's get about our business and trust that everything turns out all right."

Stafford grimaced. "This is not some fairy tale, O'Rourke. People get hurt. People die. That's just the way things are."

Gerrit strode to the door. "At times good people die and bad people survive. It's our job to try to even the score. Just do your job and stay out of my way. See you downstairs."

He slammed the door behind him, knowing that he was on his own. The story of his life in a nutshell.

Chapter 15

Vienna, Austria

Scientists could make a gunfight sound as dry as Death Valley. Gerrit couldn't take much more of this dribble.

It was the third day of the conference. Bored, Gerrit returned to his hotel room to find a brown leather briefcase on his bed. The afternoon sun streamed through the windows, brightening an otherwise drab day. He'd left Henry Clarke minutes ago as the scientist continued to drone on as a member of the panel, boring everyone in the room about cyber security.

Kane had reached Gerrit by phone yesterday, telling him to expect this briefcase and provided a combination to open it. The lock sprung open as he entered the last digit of the combination and pressed the release. He found a laptop and a zippered leather pouch inside. Opening the pouch, he found a key, an address to an apartment he was to visit, a small wad of latex gloves, and a cell phone.

Everything a burglar might need to commit a felony.

He pulled out the computer to examine it more closely. Kane had advised that this laptop was registered under the same alias Gerrit used to travel to Harrogate. He was to switch out his current ID with the John Gerrity documents.

Let the games begin.

The cell phone vibrated from an incoming call. Pressing the Send button, he placed the phone to his ear. Kane was on the line.

"You get everything we sent you?"

"Yeah. Just a minute ago. You watching me?"

"I like to think of it as protection. Yes, we're watching *over* you." Kane hesitated. "Remember, use a cab to get around. Have them drop you off several blocks away. Pay cash. Are we clear?"

"I got it. This is not my first time to the dance."

"The next call you get will be the signal. Stay put until then and be ready to move." Kane hung up.

Gerrit settled back to wait for the call. He closed his eyes, trying to fall asleep. With everything on his mind, he knew rest would not be an option.

Evening shadows now danced outside as Gerrit opened his eyes. He felt the cell phone inside his front pocket vibrate with an incoming call.

"Dr. O'Rourke?" A woman's voice.

"Yes?"

Someone knocked on his door. Gerrit, phone at his ear, moved to the door.

The woman's voice came on the line again. "Your friend from England wanted me to tell you it is time to leave."

Before responding, he flung open the door.

A woman stood in the hallway, phone in hand. She flipped it closed and walked in without an invitation. "Dr. O'Rourke, I presume. Are you ready?"

She entered and closed the door behind her. She moved about the room, prowling like a cat ready to spring, long black hair pulled back into a silky ponytail and a body that would make most men sit up and take notice.

And she knew it.

She looked back, almost defiantly, knowing she could make most men succumb. He had no doubt she used this to her advantage. Her dark, inviting eyes watched him like a feline eyeing a mouse.

"I know Kane said you'd get a call—and I did call because I always do what Kane wants." She offered a smile. "But I could not help myself. I wanted to see who my boss had picked. I have heard so much about you, Gerrit."

"And I've heard so little about you, Miss…"

"Collette. That's all you need to know about me."

"Well, Collette, now that we've met, maybe you can tell me what you do for Kane?"

She shot him a sultry look. "Now, Doctor, Kane and I must keep our secrets. You understand." She looked at him with amusement.

He walked over to the door and opened it. "Well, Collette, it's time I get to work. Will I see you again when this is over?"

She moved toward the door. "Oh, we will meet again. You can count on it." Collette seemed to float down the hallway. He watched her walk all the way to the elevator. She turned and smiled back before closing the elevator door.

He gathered the briefcase and his coat and slipped on a black ivy hat he'd picked up in London. The hat—like that worn by comic strip antihero Andy Capp—might break up his profile, make witnesses later think long and hard about what Gerrit really looked like.

As he walked through the lobby, he glanced around to see if Collette lingered nearby, but she seemed to have vanished. He piled into a taxi and directed the driver to deliver him to the Rathaus, Vienna's historic city hall, located several blocks from his destination.

"American?" The driver eyed him from the rearview mirror.

Gerrit nodded, turning his attention elsewhere. He did not want to engage the driver in small talk. Better to fade from the driver's mind as quickly as possible. In case witnesses were sought later.

Jeez, I'm thinking like some kind of spook…or crook.

Twenty minutes later, Gerrit rolled out of the cab after leaving a modest tip with the driver. Clutching the briefcase, he stared up at the Rathausmann, a statuesque knight standing guard on top of the tallest tower above Vienna's city hall. He read somewhere this figure in Renaissance-style armor had become a symbol representing the centuries-old conflict between Vienna and the Crown.

He related to the lone figure above, standing guard between local and federal forces, protecting the citizenry. He studied the building's architecture—a blending of neo-Gothic, baroque, and other period influences—before weaving his way through the Rathauspark and square, strolling toward his destination while searching for signs of counter surveillance.

No one seemed out of place or interested in his travel.

Once clear of the park, he began making his way along a sidewalk, eyeing street signs and numbers on the buildings to get his bearing. He saw the street he sought and followed the numbered dwellings until he spotted his destination about fifty yards farther down the block.

An older couple, maybe in their seventies, walked arm in arm ahead of him. He slowed his pace so he wouldn't pass them. In what seemed like an eternity, he approached the target location, a modern four-story apartment building with a white stone facade for the first two floors and pale-yellow stucco walls rising to the third and fourth floors. At the building's peak, a studio—Adleman's apartment—seemed to have been created in what once was the attic, creating a fifth floor.

Inside, a high, narrow door—solid oak with dome headers—led to a black-and-white tiled hallway and a lift. He entered, pressed the button, and the engine whirled as the elevator slowly climbed. It jerked to a stop and the door rolled open.

After pulling on a pair of latex gloves, he knocked on Adleman's apartment door, fingering the key he'd been given as he waited. He wasn't sure what he'd say if anyone came to the door. The place was supposed to be empty. The scientist reportedly used this place to meet with other cyber sleuths when they were in Europe.

He gave it a minute, then used the key to gain entry. He called out to announce his presence. No one answered. Three large bay windows allowed the occupants a bird's-eye view of the Rathaus towers with their neo-Gothic fingers clawing at the sky.

He turned from the view and saw an opened briefcase on a desktop near the far wall. He walked over to it. Inside were a bundle of business cards with *Ron Adleman* embossed in gold lettering. Right guy. Right brief-case. So where was the scientist?

Gerrit made a cursory search of the place. A door leading to the back bedroom sat ajar. He scanned the bedroom and bath. Empty. He exited the bedroom and searched the kitchen area and a sitting room before returning to the desk in the living room.

Satisfied he was alone, Gerrit went through Adleman's briefcase. It took him several minutes before he saw the file he was looking for. It was the last of about fifteen files, each one bulging with information—none of it relevant to what he'd been sent to find.

Until the last file.

Upon opening it, he smiled and reached for a thumb drive wedged in a slot inside the briefcase cover. He glanced at the hard copy and saw Adleman's abbreviated name, *Ron12Aldlemn*, and two letters: PW.

Password?

Next to those letters were a sequence of letters and numbers written in pencil.

He reached inside his own briefcase and withdrew the laptop he'd been given. Inserting the portable thumb drive, he flicked on the computer and activated the removable disk drive. After typing Adleman's user name and password, a list of files emerged on the screen, some of them matching the hard copy in the scientist's briefcase. He scrolled down the list until he came to a file titled *Quantum Leap*, a name that conjured up an old televi-sion series back in the eighties. He clicked on the file name, and his laptop strained to load the document.

He heard the elevator activate in the hallway. Someone was coming up from a lower floor. Tapping his fingers on the desktop, he waited until his screen opened up to the file menu. The file creator had categorized these documents on a number of headings, including *Correspondence* and *Latest Findings*.

He settled back in the plush chair as he read the first e-mail from Adle-man. The writer outlined a project that had nothing to do with exposing government secrets. Kane was wrong. Instead, Adleman and his colleagues seemed to be concerned about an organization aimed at bending the knee of sovereign nations to serve a greater good, a global effort to consolidate and control political power. They didn't identify the organization but indicated that the safety of Adleman and others might be at risk due to this unnamed group, which seemed bent on influencing or controlling a number of scientists from several nations.

One e-mail titled *Use of Force and Violence* immediately caught his attention. Adleman's group listed a series of incidents in chronological order—car accidents, shootings, alleged suicides, and bombings—going back more than a decade. He quickly scanned through the document until he came to 2004. There, among other incidents, a reference had been made of two people killed in a Seattle car bombing.

The report gave details of his parents' murders.

Gerrit felt like someone had just sucked the air out of the room, felt his insides tighten.

Another thought came to mind and he clicked on the document's history. It had been e-mailed to others. After opening the message, he clicked on the Send To list. One name made the hair on his neck stand up.

Joseph O'Rourke. His uncle.

Something wasn't right. Nothing that Kane mentioned could be found in these files. Instead, he found information that suggested certain scientists—and their loved ones—appeared to have been targeted.

Glancing up, he looked around the room again. He rose and began going from room to room, searching for something—anything—that would shed light on why he was sent to this apartment. He came up empty. Finally reaching the bathroom, he looked around and noticed the shower curtain drawn across the tub. He had missed that on his first sweep of the place. He flung the curtain back and saw a man lying in the tub.

Dead.

Ron Adleman.

The high and low wail of a police siren pierced the silence. He bolted to the bay window and saw an emergency vehicle more than five blocks away heading in his direction. Shutting down his laptop, Gerrit yanked out the thumb drive and tossed both inside his briefcase, slamming the lid closed.

He glanced around the place to see if he'd left anything behind, then grabbed his briefcase and dashed through the doorway into the hallway. Pulling off the gloves as he ran, he made it downstairs and out the lobby as the siren grew more intense.

He was a half a block away before the first car—its blue lights flashing—screamed past. Almost in a blur, the vehicle's gray, blue, and red markings streaked by, the word *Polizei* in white letters on the side of the car.

The officer shot a look at Gerrit as he drove past, seeming to study him. Gerrit walked until he reached the corner. Turning, he saw officers running toward the front door of the apartment next to where he'd emerged. More police cars were coming.

They're going to the wrong place.

As he rounded the corner, another thought began to nag at him. *They were sent to the wrong address. Someone was watching him?* He had no time to think this through. Time to run.

Gerrit clutched the briefcase as he looked for a cab. There was one stop he must make before returning to his hotel. Then he was getting out of town as fast as possible. This operation just took a turn for the worst, and he must figure out what just happened.

He knew one thing. If he stuck around, sooner or later he might end up behind bars.

I just became a person of interest.

Chapter 16

Gerrit turned the key in the lock to his hotel room and slipped inside a darkened room. No one lurked outside to talk to him. Good sign. He took two steps toward the bedroom before he sensed someone in the room. He turned to face the intruder, mentally searching for something close to use as a weapon.

A lamp flicked on, illuminating Richard Kane's features. "I see you managed to escape unscathed, Gerrit. You bring anything back with you?"

The two men eyed each other. Gerrit looked away, searching for anyone else standing in the shadows. They seemed to be alone.

"The briefcase and everything with it is lying at the bottom of the Danube."

"What a waste. That computer was a gift to you."

"Was Adleman's body another one of your gifts?"

"That was a surprise to us, too."

Gerrit couldn't tell whether the man was lying. "Once they discover the body, the cops may well come looking for me as a person of interest if they start canvassing the neighborhood. Someone might have seen me."

"Don't worry. We will protect you. Just leave Vienna as soon as possible."

"Protect me from what? From whom?"

"Have a seat, Gerrit. We need to talk."

Gerrit remained standing. What the heck was Kane up to?

"Suit yourself." Kane paused. "I have had my eye on you for some time. You're a man with many talents and I want you to come to work for me…for us. You'll be well compensated, and you will be doing work that is really meaningful. To you. To our country. To the entire global community."

"I already have a job. And I have unfinished business back at home."

"I know why you're really in Seattle. It's about your folks and uncle, right?" Kane hunched forward. "I can help you with that unfinished business, Gerrit. Whatever it takes. I…we…want you to find out what happened to them. I promise you unlimited resources will be at your disposal. And you can use whatever contacts we have to open those doors. You need to put this business behind you in order to focus on the future. Our future."

"And who is *we*?"

"I was hoping you'd ask that question. *We* are all those who believe we are entering a new era, a new world order that recognizes the potential and danger of new technology."

Gerrit shifted the weight on his feet.

Kane clasped his hand together as if to pray, resting the tips of his fingers under his chin. "Technology is about to lead us into a world beyond comprehension of the average citizen. I know you are aware of these developments as a scientist and recognize the potential."

Gerrit found himself nodding, even though he disliked the man sitting across the room. "This is not new. Governments have been gearing up for years."

Kane shot him a look of irritation. "Governments do not have a clue what the future holds. They are too busy looking over their shoulders, making sure their backsides are covered, that they don't see what is right in front of them."

The man rose and began pacing the room. "Molecular manufacturing—nanotechnology some call it—is about to make significant breakthroughs that will make the industrial revolution look like a hiccup in man's history. On the military side, biological, nuclear, and chemical weapons capable of mass destruction will be made cheaply and numerously while hidden in quantities too small for us to detect. Rogue nations will be able to join the arms race—nations we have been able to prevent from getting their hands on this technology and resources so far. The rules are about to change, and these countries will soon become viable threats to our national security."

Gerrit watched the man, still pacing, seem to lose himself in his own one-sided conversation. He'd just let Kane ramble.

"Not to speak of the economic tsunami that will roll over us when molecular manufacturing becomes feasible on the open market. Inexpensive manufacturing costs coupled with replication of designs will cause economic upheaval and environmental devastation on a global scale never before seen."

He stopped pacing and turned toward Gerrit. "We have to contain and control this before it gets out of hand."

"Who is *we*," Gerrit asked again, trying to prod the man into divulging those Kane represented. "The United States has been on top of this for more than a decade. Isn't that what the National Nanotechnology Initiative and the White House Office of Science and Technology policy is all about? Coordinating efforts so our country can control and contain this information?"

"Ever known a politically motivated body to do what is in the country's best interests?" Kane scoffed. "They are too busy protecting their own budgets and keeping their own power base to spend time on the greater good."

"So people like you—and whoever you work for—have the country's best interests at heart?"

Kane shook his head. "Not just our country's—the world's. The whole world must share in these breakthroughs with some controls and power resting with a few reasonable leaders."

"And who decides this?"

"The group I represent will decide this. We will keep politics and self-interest out of the equation."

Gerrit couldn't believe what he was hearing. "Listen to yourself. Whomever you represent, they are setting themselves up as the ultimate power brokers. The ruling elite. How does democracy and representation by the people factor into all this?"

"People have elected representatives to protect the country's interest. These representatives—like Senator Summers—can see the national security issues voters might not recognize. We in the U.S. work to ensure these interests are protected. In turn, I work with other like-minded individuals around the world who are working with world leaders, representing countries with similar agendas. Together, we can help shape international policy to allow these responsible countries to retain control collectively in this new era."

"You mean a one-world order?"

"I mean a one-world collective looking out for the interests of all people. An organization of leaders powerful enough to cut through regional politics to shape human history, to effectively protect our world from those who wish to destroy us."

"As if the United Nations has done a bang-up job getting people to work together. And how do you decide who's the enemy?" Gerrit asked.

"The world community of leaders, supported by their constituents, will delegate those decisions to those in the best position to protect our global community."

"You mean someone like yourself?"

Kane shrugged one shoulder. "Whoever is called upon to serve."

"And what are you willing to do?"

"Whatever it takes." Kane's reply came back like a rifle shot. He slowly lowered himself into his chair. "My question to you, boy—are you willing to do whatever it takes? The lines are drawn and the war has begun. I need to know which side you're on."

"What happens if the interests of the United States conflicts with your global community's interests? Which side will you take?"

Leaning forward, Kane peered at him with hardened eyes. "I choose the survival of mankind."

"Even if it means bringing the U.S. to its knees in submission to other countries?"

The man leaned back. "Which side do you choose?"

"Time for me to head home, Kane. I consider myself a patriot. We will never see eye to eye on this issue."

"I'm sorry to hear that, Gerrit. I had such high hopes for you. Maybe after you have time to chew on this, you'll change your mind."

Gerrit threw his suitcase on the bed and began packing. "Don't hold your breath. We're finished here."

Kane just held his hands out as if in surrender. "Whatever happens will fall on your head. I gave you a chance."

"You're asking me to betray my country. That'll never happen in my lifetime."

"Be careful, Gerrit. Without me, you'll be on your own with no connections. A very dangerous place to be."

"*On my own* has been the story of my life. I'm used to it."

Kane just shook his head before walking out the door.

Chapter 17

San Francisco, California

Touching down on U.S. soil, Gerrit began to breathe easier. Maybe Kane never alerted Interpol and the Austrian police about his presence at the crime scene. At least not yet.

He glanced at his watch as he strode through San Francisco's International Terminal, weaving through a crowd of passengers as he worked his way toward Terminal 3. He slowed down when a departure monitor flashed information that he had more than an hour before boarding his connection to Seattle.

Great. More time wasted.

Sixteen hours in flight, not counting a short layover in London, left him feeling sore and tired. He needed a shot of caffeine and spotted a Starbucks a short distance ahead. He had plenty of time to grab a cup and relax before boarding. His checked luggage would probably beat him to Sea-Tac.

The adrenaline rush of passing through security in Vienna—looking over his shoulder for Kane's people—had ebbed a long time ago. Making the switch in London had been this side of boring. Vienna police apparently hadn't singled him out in their investigation, so he surmised Kane hadn't burned him—yet. Gerrit became more relaxed the farther he traveled from Europe.

He guessed that walking away from Kane was not an everyday occurrence. There would be repercussions at some point, but when the man might drop that hammer could be anybody's guess. Gerrit agonized through every security checkpoint and the stress tired him out. He needed a java fix.

As he approached the counter, a woman laid her hand on his arm. "Detective O'Rourke. May I have a moment of your time?"

Startled, he drew back for a moment. The woman was tall and gracefully lanky, a few inches shorter than his six-foot frame. Her hair, dark and straight, cascaded over her shoulders, and he estimated her age just shy of forty. Wearing hardly any makeup and with eyes the color of his coffee, she possessed a quiet beauty that might easily be overlooked in a crowd. Unless a man took a closer look. Right now, she caught his full attention.

As if reading his thoughts, she smiled. "I am sorry to alarm you like this, but it is very important that we…how do you say, speak alone." Russian accent, but not native. Her chocolate-brown eyes glanced away as she seemed to be searching the crowd. She motioned toward a table farthest down the corridor. "Shall we sit?"

Now it registered. Jewish and Russian? Odd combination. He gathered his coffee and followed her to the table. "How do you know my name? Have we met?" He sipped the coffee and studied her, knowing he'd never crossed her path.

She settled into the chair next to him, making sure she faced the crowd as they conversed. *Just like a cop.* "We know about your meeting with Richard Kane in Vienna. And we know you've been followed ever since—a team of three, two men and one woman."

Gerrit glanced around. No one seemed particularly interested in them, although several men glanced their way in passing. "So, where are they?"

She briefly smiled. Her furrowed brow seemed to relax for a moment, and her eyes carried a gentleness he never once saw in Marilynn's. And yet, there seemed to be an edginess about her, an attitude shared by those who must always be on their guard. "The men are in the bathroom trying to rid themselves of the last of their lunch. They can barely walk."

"And the woman?"

"She got off the plane and *tried* to connect with your flight to Seattle."

Gerrit raised a brow. "Tried?"

"A canine unit hit her."

"Hit her?"

"They found a small package of C4 in her coat. The dog almost ripped her clothes apart trying to reach the explosive. She's currently being interrogated by security." Again, the smile.

He briefly eyed the cameras.

"For the next forty-five minutes, those cameras are looped back to show the crowd that passed here about an hour ago. We will be long gone by the time the surveillance cameras return to normal viewing."

"You did all this, Miss...?"

Once more, she placed her hand on his, not in a flirtatious move, but more like how a friend might touch another. "Gerrit, we have been watching over you for more than seven years. Waiting for this time."

He tensed. *Watching over or spying on me?* "Waiting for what?"

"For someone like Kane to approach." She leaned closer, lowering her voice. "We know you turned him down in Vienna. That was a very dangerous thing to do. He is a *khutspe*, a very arrogant man. He does not like to lose. Be on your guard. If you need to contact us"—she withdrew a cell phone from her purse—"use this. Once you use it, destroy it. We'll provide another."

"Who are you and what's your connection to Kane?"

She shook her head. "We do not have the time. Just be careful. If we feel you are in imminent danger, we will move in. Keep that phone near you at all times."

Standing, she looked down. "Have a good flight."

He rose. "What's your name?"

After a moment's hesitation, she said, "My name's Alena." She touched his cheek with her hand before turning away, disappearing into the crowd.

He started to reach for his own cell phone, then changed his mind. Alena's information made him suspicious of everything. It took him a few minutes to find a pay phone. He slipped in the coins and dialed.

"Hey, partner. Gerrit here."

"Hey, bro. Where in the Sam Hill are you?" Mark Taylor's voice sounded incredulous. "First, you disappear on me and when I ask the boss, he tells me it's none of my damn business. What's going on?"

"I've been out of the country—"

"I'll say. Your last message came to me from a hotel in Vienna two days ago. I checked. Thanks for leaving me with all that paper in San Diego, by the way. Now you're calling me from a 415 area code. San Francisco? Bay area? What kind of gig you running?"

"Look, I don't have much time. I'll fill you in face to face. Did you get my overnight package?"

"Yeah. Stashed it in that place where we kept our informant for a few days." Taylor had picked up on Gerrit's implied vagueness. "I hid it under the floorboards."

"Great. You look inside?"

"Nope. None of my business. Figured you'd tell me if I needed to know."

Gerrit breathed easier. "Believe me, partner, the less you know, the better. I'll be in touch." He hung up and studied those standing nearby. No one seemed to give him a second glance. He made his way toward the boarding gate.

Alena's information put him on edge. He always thought he could pick up a tail. If she was right, there had been three people traipsing after him and he never spotted them. Either he was too preoccupied or they were really good.

As he stood in line to board, he scrutinized every passenger on his flight. No one seemed too suspicious. He took one last look before entering the plane.

Everything seemed to be normal, but he no longer trusted himself to sniff out danger. After all, he'd just learned that others watched him for seven years without his knowledge. What else might he be missing? All he saw looking back were the faces of strangers.

Chapter 18

Seattle, Washington

His tired mind swirling with thoughts of Kane and the dead man, Gerrit almost missed a clue that something was amiss at home. Lights streamed through the windows of his boathouse as he drove up, lights he knew had been turned off when he left the house a week ago.

Exhausted and wary, he gathered his bag and let Bones out. After locking the car, he made his way onto the floating dock. The place had been closed up tight and dark when he left on this trip. He was glad he rearmed himself after leaving the airport. He started to reach for a weapon when he saw Marilynn's black Mercedes coupe parked a few stalls down from his car.

Bones gave a low growl as they approached the house. Moments earlier, Gerrit picked up his dog from a neighbor down the road, a woman he sometimes went jogging with and who always seemed glad to dogsit when he was away.

Bones, on the other hand, was not pleased. Gerrit swore the dog gave him an attitude when they reunited, but now—all seemed forgiven. At times, his four-legged friend seemed more trouble than a girlfriend.

He shouldered his bag and tried the door. Unlocked. He entered without announcing and smelled the aroma of pasta sauce emanating from the kitchen. *Marilynn?* She must have heard him close the door, because a moment later she emerged from the kitchen, watching him drop his bag.

"Welcome home, stranger." She moved closer and wrapped her arms around his waist. "I want to hear all about it. But first—dinner. I imagine you're starving?"

"How did you know I'd be home?"

Her eyes shifted away for a second. "Dad called. Said he'd talked to Kane and mentioned that you were on your way. So…here you are. Come on, let's sit down to eat. And you can tell me every intimate detail."

She eyed him momentarily, ignoring Bones. "Oh, there is a package that came for you. I left it on the bed."

He placed his sidearm on the coffee table as she clasped his hand and led him into the kitchen. "Open up the wine, and I'll get the bread from the oven. Everything else is ready."

He uncorked the bottle and poured for each of them. As they sat down, he watched her settle in. "You never struck me as a domestic diva, Marilynn. I'm impressed."

She smiled and waved her hand. "Just another Martha Stewart without all the billions of dollars. Don't get used to this. Now, tell me all."

He took a bite and sipped from his glass before responding. "Not much to tell. Met Kane in London, as you know. Came back here, then left for Vienna. Now I'm home."

"I know your travel plans," she said, her words laced with annoyance. "I want to know what you did…not where you went."

He took another sip. "That part I can't share. Kane's orders."

She pursed her lips. "I know you left Kane on bad terms in Vienna, Gerrit. Dad called me yelling and screaming. Not a smart move. I urge you to reconsider. Kane is a man who has our best interests at heart."

Gerrit stared back, not believing what he was hearing. "Do you know anything about this man? Do you have any idea how he conducts business?"

She met his gaze. "I know he plays for keeps. That he is a man you just don't want to cross. Tell him you are on board. Tell him you've reconsidered and agree with his point of view. Before—"

"Before he kills me? Is that what you're trying to say?" For the first time, he saw fear in her eyes.

"Gerrit, I'm begging you. Don't dig in your heels on this. This will be good for both of us if you work with him. There will be no limit where you can go."

"Good for both of us? And if I don't?"

Marilynn lowered her eyes, fingering her wine glass. "Time is running out, Gerrit. Make the right choice."

He crossed his arms. "My mind's made up. I can't work for a man who'd jeopardize our country's interests for his own agenda. I would think you'd feel the same way."

Slowly, she folded her napkin and placed it on the table before rising. "I've already made my choice. If you are not smart enough to see what must be done…" She left the meaning for him to figure it out. "I need to get back to the office. Call me if you change your mind."

A moment later her car door slammed shut and the engine roared to life. Her tires slipped on loose gravel as she rapidly drove away. He began collecting the dishes, carrying them to the kitchen. Once he finished the dishes, he remembered the package Marilynn mentioned. He found it on his bed. He carried it into the office and sat at his desk as he tore it open. Inside, he found a DVD and a note.

Just a reminder of what might happen if you don't cooperate. Give me a call.

No name. Just a telephone number.

He slipped the DVD into his computer's disc drive. Surveillance footage from Adleman's apartment building leaped onto the screen, with dates and times stamped in the lower-right corner of each camera shot, four fixed locations that showed the exterior and interior entryways, elevator, and the hallway leading to Aldleman's apartment.

He saw himself emerge on the first screen as he approached the building, and the cameras documented his path through the building to the scientist's apartment. A time lapse cut in, and the cameras followed him as he rushed from the building after finding the body.

Angrily, Gerrit reached for the phone and dialed the number given. Kane answered. "Got my present?"

"You set me up."

"You have a decision to make. Do you want to help us help the world, or are you going to start running. Because if you are not on our team, Gerrit, the police will start looking for you as a person of interest. We will leave just enough clues to make sure your world turns upside down."

"Forget it, Kane. There is nothing you can do to change my mind. This was a setup, and I will prove it."

"Good luck," Kane said, before the line went dead.

He slammed down the phone and began pacing the room, considering all his options. Call his supervisor and spill everything about his contact with Kane? Sit tight and see what happens? Running was not an option. He must face whatever Kane threw at him and try to prove his innocence. Work it like any other case, only Gerrit was the one who might be facing charges.

Agitated, he walked to the kitchen to make some coffee. It would be a long night, and he had to try to figure out a game plan. As he crossed the dining room, he heard his sliding glass door open. He glanced up and saw two dark-clad figures emerge.

He started to move to his gun on a table about five yards away but stopped when he realized he'd never reach it. Not enough time. He glanced back at the intruders and braced himself, preparing to go hand-to-hand with them. Both wore black wet suits, dripping on his rug. The first person through the doorway ripped off a black neoprene hood.

Alena.

The next person was much bigger, a giant of a man carrying another person over his right shoulder like a sack of flour. Motionless flour.

Alena held up her hand as if to silence him. She placed her index finger across her lips. The giant carried his burden into the bedroom and threw it on the bed. Gerrit moved closer and saw the person sprawled on the bed was chalky white.

They just dumped a dead man on his bed.

Gerrit edged toward the coffee table to arm himself.

Alena silently motioned for him to remain quiet. She snatched up a pad of paper and began writing. Once finished, she held it up for him to read. *Kane ordered you killed. They are listening. This house is set to blow at any moment. Follow us into the water—now.*

She motioned for her partner to leave through the glass door before turning back to him. Waving her hand, she beckoned him to follow her. He balked as he saw them exit. A moment later, Alena stuck her head through the doorway and mouthed the word *please*, urgently signaling him to leave.

Reluctantly, he followed. Worst-case scenario, his house would be blown to bits. Best-case scenario, Alena was wrong and he would get really wet. The only thing he risked by going with them was he might wind up with a cold. If he stayed…

He scooped up Bones and dashed toward the door. Slinging the dog out into the lake, he dived in and began paddling. Bones paddled alongside him—not heading back to shore. Good. He followed Alena and her partner through the water, spotting the silhouette of a blacked-out motorboat about one-hundred yards away.

He got about twenty yards offshore when night turned to day in a flash. Gerrit glanced back and saw a huge, fiery ball where his home once stood. The concussion hit as the blast swept over him. He felt a secondary heat wave microseconds later, debris raining down on him.

He saw parts of his house falling from the sky. Then blackness.

Chapter 19

A roar of an engine woke him up and he started shaking. He found himself struggling to breathe. Alena held him in her arms, her warmth warding off the chilly night. He tried to get his bearings.

She glanced at two others on the boat. "He's awake. Get us out of here."

He tried to sit up but felt woozy, pain knifing through his brain.

She pushed him down. "Stay still. You got knocked out and almost drowned. Just rest for now."

Bones edged over and licked his face. The dog was a survivor.

The motor craft's bow rose in the air when the motor roared to life. They must have dragged him to the boat. "What happened?"

Alena looked back toward where his house had been. "They rigged your place to blow up on command. A chunk of your house must have struck you in the head. We have to get you out of the area before others come."

He lay back for a moment, her arm cradling his head. "Who are you people?"

She looked over her shoulder again. "Be patient and we'll tell you everything. Right now, you need to disappear while there's still time."

He tried to raise himself again, but the exertion almost caused him to pass out. "I've got to get something I shipped from Vienna. I need to get to it tonight."

Alena shook her head. "We've got to get out of the state. Immediately."

Once again he tried to sit up. He almost threw up. "I'm not going anywhere until I get my hands on that package. It must not fall into Kane's hands."

She let out a breath, obviously annoyed. "Okay, then we get you to safety. Agreed?"

He nodded and lay back down.

As they drew closer to the far shore, the vessel's engine cut back and the boat feathered alongside a low-lying pier, a black Suburban parked on the wood dock. Alena reached inside her wet suit and withdrew a set of car keys. The vehicle lights came on briefly and the doors popped open when she pressed a button.

Alena's hefty partner lowered himself next to her, and they lifted Gerrit to his feet. She put one of his arms around her shoulders. "Move slowly."

He felt dizzy, light-headed. He was in no condition to argue. They eased him onto the wooden pier and into the backseat of the Chevy. Another man operating the boat pushed the vessel away from the pier before disappearing into the blackness with a roar.

As they pulled away in the vehicle, Alena—sitting in the front passenger's seat—turned toward him. "Tell us where to go."

He gave directions as they left the lakeside and headed for the outskirts of Seattle.

The man cringed as Kane's voice screamed over the phone line. "I told you idiots not to move until I gave the order."

He glanced at his partner next to him in disbelief. "We did not set the charge off. I am sitting right here with the transmitter turned off. I never got a chance to use it."

"Well, it did not blow up by itself, you imbecile. Did you guys screw up setting the charge?"

"Sir, it just blew up. I can't tell you anything more."

"Any witnesses?"

"Not that we can tell. Saw a boat out on the lake, but as soon as everything blew up, the boat hightailed it out there."

"Who was in the house."

"Just O'Rourke. The woman left a few minutes before everything went up in smoke."

"You still have someone on her?"

"Yeah. They're bumper-locking her as we speak."

"So she failed?"

"Uh-huh. She said the guy would not change his mind." The phone line remained silent for a few seconds. "Sir, what do you want us to do?"

Kane's voice came back, low and terse. "Clean up the mess. You know what you have to do. And take care of the other matter as soon as you leave the area."

"His partner?"

"Do I have to spell it out for you. Clean up loose ends and get out of the state. Now!"

The man heard the line click and the connection die. He pocketed the phone and turned to his partner. "Let Bravo-Two know to move in and take care of business. We've been ordered to clear out and head to our second objective. The boss has a team coming in to shadow the investigation." He pointed with his chin at the smoking heap of wood and twisted metal below.

Sirens began to wail in the distance. "Here comes the cavalry. Better late than never." He chuckled as he dumped everything back into a black drop bag. "And we're out of here."

Chapter 20

Gerrit's body felt like he'd gone fifteen rounds with a heavyweight champion. Head pounding, he eased himself from the backseat of the Suburban and tried to stand. The other two quickly shed their wet suits. They emerged from both sides of the vehicle wearing blue denim trousers and dark shirts. His legs felt weak, and his head throbbed like a madman beating on a set of drums.

"Let me help you," Alena said, rushing over. She put his arm over her shoulder and supported him as they walked toward the house. He heard the dog's nails clicking on the concrete.

Tall, scraggly weeds and dry grass in the front yard advertised what this building represented—a dwelling abandoned by foreclosure. An under-the-table agreement between the police department and certain rental agencies allowed detectives to use selected residential housing to put up protected witnesses or give informants a place to crash during short-term sting operations. This was one of those places he and Taylor stashed Gregori before the ferry shooting.

"Reach under the second rock, near the front steps." He pointed to the right of the concrete steps. "There should be a key."

Alena's heavyset partner stooped down, flicked over the rock. "Here it is." The man sounded like he'd grown up in New York, a heavy Brooklyn accent, a strange contrast to Alena's Eastern European inflections. The man stood, leaped up the front steps, and popped the door open. He turned back toward them. "Now where?"

Gerrit made his way up the steps with Alena's help. Once inside, he extricated himself from her grasp and tottered toward a rear bedroom. He dropped to his knees and leaned under a queen-size bed. "Help me move this."

Once they dragged the bed to one side, he found where loose boards had been pried up. Mark's handiwork. Yanking up the boards, he saw it— the briefcase he had been given in Vienna. Opening up the case, he sighed with relief when he saw the laptop and thumb drive inside. He closed the case, then glanced up.

"Got it. Now let's get out of here."

Alena momentarily eyed the briefcase. "How do you say it here in America. Let's scram?"

Gerrit smiled. "That's what we say." He rose to his feet and then his world turned black again.

Marilynn Summers climbed out of her coupe, closed and locked the door, before activating the alarm. She walked from her assigned parking space in the federal building toward the stairway leading to the lobby.

She began to relax, knowing that once inside she would have complete protection. She knew security cameras recorded her movement right now. Any hint of trouble and security would be running to her aid.

The only unease she felt at the moment had to do with a man a thousand miles away. Richard Kane. He had sent her to change Gerrit's mind. That was her mission and she failed. Kane did not tolerate failure.

What was he going to do? Shoot her? Daughter of Senator Summers? *I think not, Mr. Kane.*

The more she thought about it, the more secure she felt. Being John Summers's only child brought some perks. Nobody but the senator could mess with her—and survive politically.

Footsteps echoed behind her.

She turned her head to see a man a few yards away. Funny, she had not seen another car enter the garage.

"Ms. Summers?"

She turned toward the voice as the man drew closer and her chest suddenly tightened. Just for an instant she saw a metallic reflection from something in the man's right hand.

A gun.

Her brain registered an explosive flash. Then pain. Then nothing.

Chapter 21

Clearwater River, Idaho

Daylight streamed through a dusty cabin window when Gerrit finally managed to open his eyes. He tried to remember the details of the ride from Seattle during the night. He must have slipped in and out of consciousness several times. He barely remembered climbing into bed.

Noise from a television drew his attention, his eyes slowly focusing on the screen. A news reporter, mike in hand, stood near where Gerrit's boathouse once stood.

"A joint local, state, and federal task force investigation continues as authorities sift through what is left of Seattle Police Detective Gerrit O'Rourke's home. A source close to the investigation revealed that there appears to have been a body inside the residence at the time of the explosion, possibly that of the missing officer. However, investigators refuse to confirm the identity as bomb experts continue to search for clues. A spokesman for SPD did confirm the explosion was intentionally set."

Gerrit closed his eyes, a headache nagging at the backside of his brain. He reopened them to see that the television screen moved to another crime scene at the Henry M. Jackson Federal Building in Seattle. The garage entrance was taped off, and two uniformed officers stood guard, prohibiting a number of reporters and television camera crews from entering. The same announcer's voice continued.

"In a related investigation, task-force representatives are looking into the shooting death of federal prosecutor Marilynn Summers, whose father sits as chairman of the Senate Select Committee on Intelligence. Police say Ms. Summers was shot and killed after she parked her car and began walking toward the U.S. Attorney's office. And in a third killing— Wait, we just have this in. Seattle Police Department has an announcement to make. We switch you live to Seattle PD headquarters."

Gerrit raised himself onto one elbow, peering at the television screen, gritting his teeth. A knot developed in his stomach. *A third killing? Oh, God, no.* He seemed to know what was about to be disclosed.

Lieutenant Stan Cromwell, his craggy face tired and angry looking, loomed on the screen. It seemed the lieutenant had aged ten years since Gerrit last saw him. His boss approached a sea of bristling microphones, his broad shoulders rounded and hunched.

Cromwell glared into the camera. "I'm going to make a short statement and I will not answer any questions. Our patrol units were called to a warehouse near the waterfront shortly before nine o'clock this morning. They found the body of Seattle Detective Mark Taylor who has been missing for eight hours. He'd been shot at close range, and there is evidence he had been subjected to torture." Cromwell's voice cracked.

Gerrit pounded the bed in anger. *No. No. No.* Mark had nothing to do with anything. Kane reached out and killed his partner just to send a message. *No one ever turns his back on Kane.* Raised voices on the television drew him back to the screen. He watched with clenched fists, a wave of fury pounding his head with pain.

A flurry of voices followed.

The lieutenant waited until everyone quieted down. "Let me finish my statement."

Silence followed.

Cromwell brushed the corner of his right eye before continuing. "There has been a body recovered from the explosion at SPD Detective Gerrit O'Rourke's residence. There is no identification on the body, however, it is believed that the remains may be that of our officer. Lastly, we are continuing to investigate—along with the FBI and other state and federal agencies—the shooting death of the federal prosecutor, AUSA Marilynn Summers."

Cromwell paused and took a swig from his water bottle. All eyes focused on him.

"We're pursuing all possible leads. The only connection we have at this time in all three deaths is that these victims were connected to a strike force case involving Russian organized crime groups. The primary suspect in that OC case was killed by Detective O'Rourke during the execution of search and arrest warrants in a San Diego, California, residence a few weeks ago. We're continuing to investigate. There will be no further comments at this time."

Cromwell turned and walked away. No one seemed brave enough to follow.

Gerrit dropped back on the bed. He felt weak, and the news seemed to wrench away any strength he had left. So the cops thought that Russian organized crime might be responsible.

Richard Kane covered his tracks well.

He thought of Senator Summers. Could he be involved in his own daughter's death? This seemed highly unlikely. The senator might be the person to start with to get some straight answers. Maybe Marilynn's father finally had enough of Kane and might be willing to talk.

He heard several sets of footsteps on the porch outside. The door swung open and Alena and two men entered. She smiled as he turned toward her. "We are so pleased you are alive. I worried." She came to his bedside, stroking his forehead. "How do you feel?"

He glanced at the television before speaking. "Two of my friends are dead, and the world thinks I was blown up. Other than that and a bad headache, I'm doing just great," he said, anger building up with each word. "How do you think I feel?"

Her eyes softened. "I'm sorry, Gerrit. You heard."

He looked away and focused on the other two men.

"I want to introduce you to a very special man, my good friend Joe Costello." She pointed to the older of the two men, who had been intensively watching them as Gerrit and Alena conversed. The man stepped forward, extending his hand. His freckled face and curly reddish-brown hair—lightened by the onslaught of gray—complemented his hazel eyes. The man looked to be pushing seventy.

"Glad to meet you, Dr. O'Rourke. I've been wanting to talk with you for a long time."

Something about the man's voice sounded very familiar, as did the man's eyes. Very familiar. "Have we met before?"

Joe smiled. "A long, long time ago, Gerrit. Before we get into all that, I want you to meet a very good friend of mine: Travis Mays. This is his cabin. He's a professor at Washington State University in Pullman."

Travis stepped forward and shook Gerrit's hand. "I am glad to see you awake and breathing, Detective. You gave us all a scare."

Gerrit felt something cold and wet press against his arm. A dog's nose. He glanced down, thinking it was Bones. It wasn't.

Travis laughed. "Let me introduce you to another member of this household. Sam...Sam Spade." A yellow lab nudged his arm almost on command.

"Glad to meet you, Sam." Gerrit smiled as he stroked the dog's head. Bones emerged behind Sam, tail wagging. Gerrit looked up at Travis. "Thanks for putting me up here."

"Hey, glad to help. And Sam's thrilled to have a new friend."

"I'll try to be out of here real soon."

Joe took a step closer. "That's what we need to talk about. A lot has happened while you were out." Joe drew up a chair and nodded at the others. Alena and Travis headed toward the door, with Sam padding behind. Alena turned for a moment. "We'll take a walk and give you two a chance to talk."

Bones seemed undecided. Alena coaxed the dog outside and closed the door.

Joe watched them leave and then turned and smiled at Gerrit . Those eyes seemed so familiar to Gerrit, just like his... No, it can't be.

The man seemed to fathom what Gerrit was thinking. "So you are starting to understand."

Gerrit stared back. "It's impossible. My dad and mom…" He couldn't bring himself to utter the words.

The man leaned closer and took Gerrit's hand. "Your mother and father were killed because of what your father tried to do. To make the world safer for everyone. They died as true heroes."

"Some lowlife blew them up and got away scot-free. Wrong place. Wrong time. How do you figure they're heroes?"

"Because they were willing to put their lives on the line for something they believed in. Just like you did in Iraq and Afghanistan. A family of heroes…and one coward."

"One coward?" Gerrit stared at the other man.

"I should have died that day with your folks. Instead…"

An eye-piercing pain shot through his forehead as Gerrit tried to focus, tried to understand. "Are you telling me—?"

"Joe Costello's not my real name, Gerrit. I'm Joseph O'Rourke, your uncle." Joe faced Gerrit. "Reconstructive surgery can really change one's features."

"I thought you were dead."

"I should have been," Joe said, a look of sadness in his eyes. "I should have died that day with your folks."

"What happened?"

"Before I tell you, I just want you to know that I—along with Alena and others—have watched over you ever since we believed Kane might be targeting you. It has taken seven years, but Richard Kane finally made his move. Finally tried to kill what he thought was the only surviving member of the O'Rourke family."

"Why is Kane trying to do this?"

"That's what I am here to tell you. About Kane, and about a war going on inside our own country. It is about whether we will survive as one nation under God." Joe leaned back in his chair. "I'd better start from the beginning."

Chapter 22

Before his uncle could begin, Gerrit heard a car braking outside and looked through a cabin window. A patrol vehicle with Nez Perce Tribal Police markings pulled off the highway on the far side of the river. A man in plain clothes and a woman emerged. Police officers?

He glanced at his uncle. "Should we get out of here?"

Joe shook his head. "They're on our side. His name is Frank White Eagle, chief of the Nez Perce tribal police, and his daughter, Jessie. Both are close friends of Travis Mays."

"And how does Mays figure into this?"

"He helped me disappear after they killed your parents. We met through the university many years ago when I was a panelist on a cyber-security symposium in Seattle. Travis was an ex-cop teaching criminology. He introduced himself and posed some interesting questions that made me pay attention to this guy. We struck up a friendship, and when—"

"You were there when Mom and Dad died?"

"Nearby. I was in Seattle at the time. Found out that night I might be the next target. At the time, I knew very few people in law enforcement I could trust. Travis was one of them. He put me in touch with an FBI agent. Together, they and another person helped me disappear." Joe looked around the cabin. "That's when it all started. The day I became Joseph Costello."

"And your face? I see you still have my father's eyes. And I remember your voice. But everything else…"

"Yeah. I had them reconstruct my face and Malloy—FBI Special Agent Beck Malloy—contacted a source in the U.S. Marshals office. Between the four of us—and my knowledge of computer systems—we created who I am today."

Gerrit steeled himself. "Tell me why you called yourself a—"

"Coward?" Joe finished the sentence, a look of regret darkening his face. "First, you need a little background. Your dad, through his work at MIT, became aware of certain outside influences on some of his fellow researchers in the area of nanotechnology, quantum computers, and biotechnology. Governmental and private interests working together to gather and control any research developed in these fields—particularly in the U.S."

"That would be impossible to control," Gerrit said. "There are too many studies and too many researchers to allow any one group to control their efforts and findings."

Joe nodded. "True. However, what your dad learned was that this group—whoever they are—was able to control government financing for any projects of interest. This was a big hammer to wave in front of those researchers scrambling for money. And what this group could not control, they began to monitor and sabotage."

"You mean like blow up and destroy?"

"In a way. Key scientists yanked from their projects through any number of dirty tricks—trumped-up criminal charges, accidents, medical issues, fabricated claims about their characters. The list just keeps growing."

"And my folks?"

"This is why your dad was upset when you redeployed to Iraq. He wanted you to return to MIT, where the two of you could start digging into this. He didn't know who to trust."

Gerrit lowered his eyes, thinking back just before his last tour of duty overseas. He had gotten a weekend pass to fly to Boston and meet with his folks before shipping out. His father could barely hold in his anger after Gerrit refused to allow him to intercede to get him removed from full duty.

His father wanted to use his military and political contacts to have Gerrit return to MIT.

"I have something really important I need your help with, son. Others can serve their country over there. You already sacrificed. And they don't have your special skills—those gifts you can bring to the table to help me in a special research project. It is important."

But Gerrit dug in his heels.

Vainly, his father persisted "It's a matter of life and death, Gerrit. I need your help."

"Tell me what it is. I have people depending on me to keep them alive over there. What can be so important on that campus that I should turn my back on them and help you?"

His father's angry eyes bore down on him, jaws clenched. "I can't tell you—unless you are cleared to work with me."

Gerrit's stomach tightened as he thought of that last day. "I can't, Dad. I've given my word. My men need me."

"I need you, son."

Gerrit slowly shook his head. He watched as a look of abject failure crept into his father's eyes.

"Then we have nothing further to discuss." His father stormed away. They never spoke to each other again.

Voices outside the cabin caught Gerrit's attention. He heard Alena speaking to another woman. The group walked back toward the river, leaving Joe and Gerrit to continue their conversation.

"Your dad came to me after I joined Argonne National Laboratory outside Chicago just before his death. He knew we both were going to be in Seattle for a conference, and he wanted to introduce me to some of his contacts in an investigation he had quietly launched. He didn't tell me any details but mentioned that they kept hearing about a project called Operation Megiddo. He didn't know what it represented or who was be-hind it, but he learned the project had to do with significant breakthroughs in computer technology. A part of it dealt with my field—cyber-security technologies."

"Megiddo?" Gerrit sounded it out. "Among other references, Megiddo is a place in Israel, a historical location. And you know what it means translated into the Hebrew?"

Joe nodded. "Mountain of Megiddo. Better known as Armageddon. Biblical references tell us that in the end times, Christ will return to defeat the anti-Christ in the battle of Armageddon, although I believe the actual battle will take place near Jerusalem. Satan's forces will gather at Megiddo before that final confrontation."

"Interesting choice of the word—Megiddo." Gerrit grappled with this implication. He didn't want to get into a theological discussion about eschatology. They had enough to worry about in the here and now. "Did you find out more about Operation Megiddo?"

Joe held up his hand. "Let's take this one step at a time. It gets very complicated." His uncle stood and walked toward the window, peering outside for a moment. Finally, he turned to face Gerrit. "Tom—your dad—warned me they had learned that several scientists died under questionable circumstances. But he could not get anyone to tell him the specifics of their deaths or the investigations into these matters. It was like some powerful hand clamped down on these cases. Once each death investigation was closed, the findings became classified as accidental death or death by natural causes. Your dad even mentioned he and your mom received threats. That they were warned to keep their noses out of other people's business. He felt they might be under surveillance and wanted me to come on board to help."

"Did you?"

His uncle's head lowered, an expression of regret painted across the man's face. "At first, I said I would. Then one day, as I was leaving Argonne, two men in an unmarked vehicle pulled me over. They yanked me out of the car, dragged me into the back of their vehicle, and drove to a commercial high-rise under construction. They took me to the top floor, an unfinished level without walls or railings. We must have been twenty stories high. They grabbed me by the ankles and flipped me over the edge, dangling me in the air while I screamed for help."

His uncle clearly was reliving that moment. "What happened, Uncle Joe?"

The older man looked up, a look of fear lancing in his eyes. "They let me scream until my voice turned hoarse. I thought they were going to kill me, looking at the ground and knowing I was about to fall to my death. They eventually raised me up to safety, pulled me inside, and threw me on the ground. I can still remember their laughter, like it was some big joke."

His eyes glistened, and Joe covered his face to hide his shame. Gerrit remained quiet, allowing his uncle to gather himself.

"They said this was just an example of what they'd do next if I helped your folks. Next time—if I didn't play ball—they'd let me suffer a long time before killing me. Slowly and painfully." He looked up at Gerrit. "I believed them."

He came and sat next to Gerrit. "I met your dad in Seattle and told him I wanted nothing to do with his investigation. That I thought he was a fool to continue to poke his nose where it did not belong."

"And what happened?"

"Your folks and I met in that garage—where they were killed. After we argued, I jumped out of the car and made it to the stairs when the bomb went off. It threw me to the ground. The ringing in my ears was so bad, I couldn't hear anything for a few minutes. I finally ran back to find… " He choked back the words and wiped a tear from his eye. "It could have been me that day."

Flashes of the video came back to Gerrit, remnants of what was left of his parents. His voice grew hoarse. "What did you do?"

"I realized that they intended to kill all of us. I started running. In a way, I've been running ever since."

"So, you never found out who was behind this bombing?"

Joe gave him a rueful smile. "I found out one name."

Gerrit slowly raised himself from the bed, his whole body suddenly rigid. "Who? Who did this?" His mouth felt dry as he waited for Joe to answer.

"I could never prove it, but I know who was behind it—Richard Kane."

Chapter 23

Harrogate, England

A rap on the door drew Richard Kane's attention from a file on his desk. "Come in."

George Lawton barged in, his face flushed and rigid. "What the bloody hell's going on, Richard? First, that incident in Vienna. Now, three murders in Seattle? What have you gotten us into?"

Richard pushed away from the desk and ran his fingers through his long hair. "What do you mean?"

Lawton leaned on Richard's desk, fingers knuckled to support his weight. "You send Gerrit into Adleman's place—using a cover we set up for you guys—and the next thing I know, Gerrit's on the run and Adleman's dead."

Richard studied the British intelligence officer for a moment. "Things don't always go as planned."

"As planned? Nothing's gone as planned. Gerrit was supposed to go in there and fish around Adleman's apartment to see what he might turn up. Low-key and quiet. Now, Gerrit may have been blown up in Seattle. Not only that, but the prosecutor he's shacking with is gunned down and his partner is tortured and killed. Not going as planned? This is not acceptable. What did you unleash?"

Richard bristled. "Don't know what you're talking about, George. The thing in Vienna…mishap of the trade. Adleman died. Who knows why?"

Lawton leaned closer. "Who are you trying to kid?"

"Prove otherwise."

"I don't have to prove anything. I just have to pass along my suspicions. Those up the chain will have you jerked tomorrow."

"Don't think you want to do that, George. After all, they acted on your recommendation. You set up the Vienna cover. Now you have cold feet? How's that going to look…up your chain?"

Lawton glared back. "And what about Seattle?"

"What about it?" Richard stood and faced his visitor. "Looks like the handiwork of the Russian mob. Bombs, torture, killing a federal prosecutor in her own backyard. You do know that all three were working a case against Russian organized crime. In fact, Gerrit shot and killed one of their leaders. Maybe they were just trying to get even, retaliate for one of their own getting wasted."

"You think Senator Summers is going to swallow that?"

"As far as I am concerned, this all seems plausible. And, by the way, Adleman's death has been classified as a heart attack—a ruptured aorta, I believe, is the way they described it."

"You never cease to amaze me, Kane. The degree by which you manipulate events. So where does that leave you"

"Leave me" Richard's eyebrows rose. "Are you part of the team or not, George?"

Lawton's head lowered. He gave a heavy sigh and lowered himself into the chair. "I guess I'm still in. It just feels like we have too many loose ends. What if everything begins to unravel?"

"Who's going to poke his head into this mess? Gerrit's probably dead and Senator Summers knows he has to play ball or his backside will be exposed."

"But his daughter—"

"His daughter is dead. The senator is a practical man. He has nothing to gain now by fighting us. Nothing to gain, and everything to lose."

"And if Gerrit is alive?"

Richard relaxed. "Then he is still out there chasing ghosts. Thinks the Russians had something to do with his parents' murders."

"And why would he believe that?"

"Because I tainted the evidence from the bomb site and made sure a Russian detonator was seized as evidence. And I made sure the crumbs of evidence led Gerrit right to Nico."

Lawton shook his head. "Unbelievable. All this time, O'Rourke believed the Russians were behind the bombing? That's why he was so fixated on that criminal organization?"

Richard nodded and just smiled. At least until Gerrit found out he'd been set up in Vienna. It was a good thing the man died in his houseboat, or the detective could have given them real trouble.

Richard would have to make certain Gerrit had died in the explosion.

After Lawton left, Richard sat back down and dialed a number on a secure line to the United States. "How y'all doing out there? Any complications?"

"Sir, we got people on the ground, covering the houseboat and the federal building. So far, all fingers are pointing toward the Russians. They're still sifting through evidence."

"And Gerrit. Have they identified his body?"

"Not much to identify. Talked to one of the bomb guys. Said there might not be enough left to run DNA. The fire burned hotter than even our people expected."

"What are you saying? Someone added to the blast?"

"We don't know, sir. Talked to the guy who was set to activate things. He said the blast went off before he had a chance to trigger it."

"You mean the blast went off all by itself?"

"No...um, well, maybe. That's just it. Our guy said someone could have piggybacked his signal and set it off on their own. But he's not sure how they did it...if they did it."

"I want your people to go through everything. Make sure Gerrit is dead and there aren't others out there involved in this thing that we don't know about. Understand? Gerrit knows too much to be left out there alive. If he did survive, he might be able to start putting pieces together."

"I don't see how he could have survived it. And the investigators are pretty sure there was a body that burned up in that blast."

"I don't want any guessing. I want to know for sure. Are we clear?"

"Yes, sir. We'll keep on it."

Richard slammed down the phone. There was too much at stake. He had to get everything under control. If those who empowered him started to question his abilities, it would only be a matter of time before they retired him. Permanently.

That wasn't going to happen. He was a survivor, willing to do whatever it took to stay on top. To do that, he had to be aware of all the options. He needed to know who he could trust and who he needed to purge.

There was one person who might be able to help. No one but Richard knew about this person. Contact between them must be kept to a minimum. He couldn't risk exposing this person. At least until now. He needed to know right now! Whatever the cost.

Kane sent off a message and hoped it slipped through undetected.

Chapter 24

Clearwater River, Idaho

Kane was involved with his parents' death. And here Gerrit was, stuck in bed as weak as a lamb. Irritated, he eased himself to the side of the bed, his head still woozy. Planting both feet on the rough-timbered floor, he slowly raised himself, grasping the headboard for support.

His uncle looked concerned. "Take it slow. Doc said you had a serious concussion and to keep a close eye on you."

"A doctor makes house calls out here? I remember a guy coming during the night. Can't recall much else."

Joe nodded. "Travis knew a local doctor he trusted. Had him come check you out. The guy said you belonged in a hospital, at least until your head cleared and you could get on your feet. We couldn't run that risk, unfortunately. You need to stay still for a day or so—doctor's orders." Joe smiled, patted a pile of folded clothes, and glanced at Gerrit's bare legs. "Travis left these for you. Might want to slip into these unless you're set on giving the women a real thrill."

Gerrit stood and reached for the pants. A gentle knock on the door made him lunge. He had one leg started when Alena came through the doorway. She took one look and tried to stifle a grin. "Joe, you guys have a chance to talk?"

He nodded. "We got to the point where Richard Kane's name popped up."

Gerrit finished putting on his pants, zipped up, and slipped on a black T-shirt with white lettering. Again, Alena smiled, glancing at the inscription. "Looks like Travis must have gotten that from a homicide school. *My day starts when your day ends.* Travis has a sense of humor."

Gerrit glanced down at his chest. "My day would have ended if you and your friend hadn't bailed me out. Never did thank you."

Her face turned serious. "You are welcome."

Joe pointed to a large sofa near the fireplace. "Alena, this is a good time for you to join the conversation." He glanced at Gerrit. "Let's get comfortable while we try to bring you up to speed."

"If it's all the same to you, I'd like to stand a bit longer, try to get my sea legs back. Why don't you guys have a seat and tell me what I've been missing for the last seven years."

They sat down and Joe started in. "First, let me fill you in on some background. While I tried to sort out what happened in Seattle, Travis reached out to an FBI contact he worked with a few years ago here in Idaho, a guy named Beck Malloy. This agent is like a ghost—pops here, there, everywhere, and then disappears again. Back then I wondered if he really was with the FBI."

"Is he?" Gerrit asked. "I really need to know about the people I'll be depending on to stay alive. You've got this guy Travis, plus an Indian tribal police chief and his daughter. Man, it's like some kind of family get-together around here. I don't know any of these people. I'm supposed to be dead. I wanna keep it that way until I can fit these pieces together."

"Funny you should use the term *family*, because that is exactly what we've become. One extended family. I trust Travis and his friends with my life. They've proven they're trustworthy. You're the last member of my physical family, Gerrit. I would never endanger you again."

Gerrit frowned. "Again?"

Joe nodded, looking over at Alena for a moment. "After Malloy hooked me up with the U.S. Marshal's office, I quickly realized that my life—as I knew it back then—was over. I needed to recreate myself if I was going stay alive—just like you will."

"So you became Joseph Costello. Wanted to keep that Irish thing going?"

That drew a smile. "Not many people would know Costello is an Irish name. Once Irish, always Irish. No better calling, me 'boy."

They heard Travis and the others coming up the pathway. Alena pushed herself off the sofa and went outside. He heard her talking to the others. They began to walk away as Alena rejoined Joe and Gerrit. "They're going down to the river for a while. Give you more time to catch up."

Gerrit turned toward Joe. "So how did you endanger me?"

"Not intentional. You were off in Iraq. Ironically, I learned that you might have been safer over there. Then you came to Seattle and became a cop. That changed everything."

"I came to Seattle to find my parents' killer. And all the time you knew who that was? Too afraid to share it with me? Let me go for seven years without knowing why they lost their lives?" The anger in Gerrit's voice made Joe flinch.

Alena walked over and placed her hand on Gerrit's arm. "That is not really fair. Your uncle did not know the details for several years. He is trying to explain. Give him a chance."

Her softly spoken words cooled his anger. "Sorry, Uncle Joe. Just tell me what happened."

The older man took a deep breath. "Malloy and I started from the beginning—the incident in Chicago. While I was off getting my features altered, he used his resources to start to put together what happened on that day I left Argonne National Laboratory. He collected surveillance footage—before and after I left—and captured information on both vehicles seen in the vicinity on several occasions. They must have been tracking my movements. He hunted down vehicle registration, credit-card use, and traffic-cam footage. He even returned to the scene where I was threatened and collected more evidence. From that, we started putting names and companies together to piecemeal the events in Chicago and Seattle."

"Kane's name popped up?" Gerrit asked, impatiently.

"Not at first. Once Malloy knew what to look for at your parents' crime scene, he latched on to the evidence—particularly the videotape and crime-scene log of everyone who arrived on the scene. Several names didn't match up. He even used facial-recognition software I helped to develop to build these leads."

Gerrit began to feel irritated again. It seemed like his uncle was drawing out this information way beyond necessary. "So where did it lead?"

"I'm getting there," Joe said with a twinge of frustration. "You always were impatient." He shifted on the sofa. "Malloy ran this information through the Department of Homeland Security's new US-VISIT program and a yet-unreleased program the CIA is using for tracking and identifying terrorists."

"Got a hit?"

"In a way," Joe said. "He locked on to a couple of guys who used to work for the CIA and began to run this down when he got a cease-and-desist order from the attorney general's office."

"Since when does the AG's office tell the FBI what to do?"

"Malloy did some checking and learned that a power broker—a consultant with the government and a former spook himself—put pressure on his contact to shut down Malloy's investigation."

"Richard Kane."

"Bingo." Joe rose and walked to a window near the front door. He peered outside, seeming to gather his thoughts for a moment. "Richard Kane became our focus—scratch that. Became my focus. Malloy, for the time being, had to back away from investigating this case. He has been giving us back-channel help ever since."

"So when do I meet this Beck Malloy?"

"If you are lucky—never. I think there's a target on Malloy's back. Anyone who goes near him will be identified and tracked. We need to stay as far away from Malloy as we can get unless it's an extreme emergency. If he needs to communicate, he'll find a way."

Gerrit was done waiting. "For the last time, how did you endanger me?"

"I thought if I remained out of the picture and kept you in the dark, Kane and his people would think you were not a danger to them. But you joined the police department and started kicking over rocks about your folk's deaths. That triggered Kane's interest. He started to build a surveillance net around you—Marilynn Summers and others—to keep tabs on where you went with this case."

Gerrit's throat tightened. "So Marilynn was a plant." Thinking back on everything, this made sense, but it still hurt. "Why did they kill her... Marilynn?"

Joe clasped his hands together. "Because she must have failed in her mission. She was the bait Kane dangled out there to get you to help them. He does not tolerate failure."

"How long have you been keeping tabs on me?"

Alena edged closer. "Like I told you in San Francisco, we've been watching you for years. Ever since you moved to Seattle."

Joe looked away from the window. "Son, I've been watching over you from the very moment I started looking into this mess. One way or another, you have never been out of my sight."

Gerrit gazed at Alena. "That just leaves you. How did you and my uncle connect?"

Alena and Joe exchanged a glance before Joe spoke up. "We'll get into all that later. Right now, we need to figure out our next move."

Gerrit sensed the two were hesitant to bring up the past. He'd leave that alone for now. But sometime soon he'd push for answers. "So, what's the game plan? How do we take Kane down?"

A look of relief showed on their faces. Joe tipped his head toward the window. "Let's go outside while I give it some thought. I think Travis and Jessie have dinner plans for all of us."

Chapter 25

Bone's wet nose nudged Gerrit's hand, the dog's tail waving in the chilly mountain air. Seated at the outside table, Gerrit cut off a piece of steak from his plate and held it out on his open palm. The dog snapped it up in one gulp. Sam wedged between Bones and Gerrit, looking up expectantly.

Gerrit cut another piece for Sam.

A cold, freezing wind started to reach into the canyon as it swept off the mountain above them. Hot coals from the nearby barbeque staved off some of the chill.

Travis peered down at his dog. "Don't turn him into a beggar, O'Rourke. Sam knows better than to beg at the table." The others, seated round a pinewood table on the front porch, laughed as the dog tried to beg once again.

"Sorry about that, Travis, but those eyes just made me give in. And Bones…he's always been a beggar—that's how we met."

Gerrit was about to take a bite when a tribal police car pulled up. Frank White Eagle had excused himself a few minutes before, riding the aerial lift across the river where the other vehicles were parked. The police chief talked to the officer in the car, then shook the driver's hand before the officer sped off. Frank waited until the officer was out of sight before returning to their side of the river.

His uncle followed Frank's movement, a look of concern on Joe's face. They both waited for the chief to return. Frank's features, wrinkled and cracked like weathered leather, were serious as he drew nearer. The wooden steps creaked as Frank climbed the stairs to the front porch.

Frank looked over at Joe. "I arranged for low-key security for your flight out of here at the Lewiston airport tomorrow morning. No questions asked."

Joe nodded. "Thanks, Frank. Anything else?"

The chief sat before answering. "Maybe…maybe not. My office received an all-points bulletin in connection with the killings in Seattle." He glanced at Gerrit, then back to Joe. "The FBI and DHS want to know if a person matching your name and date of birth surfaces anywhere in the Pacific Northwest. They want to interview this man as a person of interest in the killings."

Gerrit's stomach tightened. "They want to talk to me?"

Frank shook his head. "Not you, Gerrit. They want your uncle."

Joe's eyes hardened. "They want to talk to Joe Costello or Joe O'Rourke?"

"Neither. They want to talk to a Joe O'Reilly." Frank began to fill his plate with a second helping of steak. "The photo that came with the BOLO looked just like you before you changed your looks."

Joe seemed to relax and then began to chuckle.

Frank raised an eyebrow. "What's this all about, Joe?"

Joe just shook his head. "That is not the FBI or DHS—this is Kane's handiwork."

"Why are they trying to locate you now?" Gerrit patted Sam's head.

"Kane never gave up looking for me. He must have known I never died, although I don't know how he found out I survived. He's using this investigation into your death to try to flush me out."

"How come they have the wrong information about you?"

"Well, I took that information and reversed everything about my history, right down to my date of birth. Kane never saw me face-to-face and used his data searches for identification purposes. A system I corrupted. I went into every system known to man and changed my photo. I recreated

Joseph O'Rourke and became Joseph Costello. I used a face that was close, but not the same. Even my own colleagues might be confused if investigators flashed that photo in their faces."

"Where did the name Joe O'Reilly come from?"

"Another good Irish name. Just one of my many aliases."

"What about those clowns who dangled you off the roof in Chicago? Won't they recognize you?"

Joe grimaced. "Malloy tracked them down before he was called off the case. Learned they were later found floating in Lake Michigan."

"But they didn't fail with you. They persuaded you not to cooperate with Dad."

"Actually, Kane never knew that. All he knew was that I might have not been with your folks when they died. I disappeared. I guess those two thugs must have disappointed Kane. Or maybe he learned I had a change of heart. Again, how did he know?" His uncle just shrugged.

"Where are we going tomorrow?"

Joe glanced at Alena before answering. "Let's just finish our meal. We can talk later—after I finish washing the dishes."

Travis and Jessie, seated across the table, looked at each other and smiled. Travis responded. "Jessie already volunteered since she loves the domestic thing."

She dug an elbow into Travis's ribs. "Don't believe him, Joe. This clown knows I don't cook or clean another man's kitchen. He knew that from the first day I showed up here."

Gerrit watched the two smiling at each other and felt an emptiness inside as he thought of his last night with Marilynn. Flashes of her emerging from the kitchen upon his return from Vienna, wearing an apron, a smudge of red sauce on her upper lip. Everything he and Marilynn had together had been a lie. She was a plant to keep an eye on him. To spy on his movements. To recruit him. The betrayal dug deeper into his chest. The way Travis and Jessie looked at each other, the love they seemed to share, only made his own life seem shallower.

He thought of what others shared. Love. Marriage. Family. Things he had always put off for another day. First, his academic pursuits took every bit of his attention. And then his military service never allowed him to even think of settling down with someone who wanted to build a life with him. His time with Marilynn had been more of a relationship of convenience—for both of them. Not once did they speak of a long-term relationship. Always living in the here and now. And now—with what Joe told him—he understood more clearly. It has been a relationship built on a lie.

He felt emptiness closing in. When his parents died, it was like that door of normalcy closed forever. He had one mission in life. Find his parents' killer. And now…maybe…he knew who that killer might be—Richard Kane. At least he knew who probably ordered the hit. Maybe bringing Kane down would give him a chance to enjoy a normal life some day.

That thought drew his attention to Alena seated next to him. She was watching Jessie and Travis joking together. He thought he saw a look of wistfulness in her eyes. What was her story? She was very attractive. A woman like that must have a man waiting for her to return.

Then he thought about their first encounter in San Francisco. She admitted to watching him for several years. That didn't sound like a *normal* life. A normal woman didn't don a wet suit, sneak into a houseboat at night, and force him to leave moments before the place blows up, leaving a dead man inside. That's far from normal.

Maybe he and Alena shared the same difficulties—unable to live like the rest of mankind. Might that draw them together? Then Marilynn's face flashed through his mind. *Get a hold of yourself, Gerrit.* One woman—a traitor—lay dead. And now he was thinking about another woman, this *Mission Impossible* gal who seems to have no history.

This concussion might have jarred his brains loose. *Better focus on your own problems, pal.* His track record with women seemed bound for failure. *Better focus on staying alive.*

Like his uncle, he might be running and hiding for the rest of his life. Kane was just the tip of the iceberg. Other people—wielding even more power—must lurk out there in the grayness of politics, government, and business. Powerful individuals who determined he was a liability. For the moment, Kane and the others thought he'd been eliminated. How long would that last?

Joe rose from the table and began gathering dishes. "Why don't you folks relax and I'll have these done in a jiffy." As he gathered the last dish and entered the cabin, Jessie leaned over the table and took Alena's hand. "It was so nice getting to know you this afternoon. I'm sorry you have to leave so soon. We women need to stick together in this group."

Travis laughed. "Hell-raisers more like it." He winked at Gerrit. "We have something in common, my man."

Gerrit leaned back. "What's that?"

"Women and water." Travis grinned. "The first time I met Jessie, she tried to drown me."

Jessie slapped Travis on the shoulder. "You drowned yourself, honey. I stood by to make sure you didn't kill yourself."

Travis continued. "I hired her as a river guide to get me through the white water upriver from here. Instead, she watched as I almost killed myself in one of those rapids. And when I bounced back from death's doorstep, she was laughing her head off."

Jessie gave him a hug. "You survived, so I did my job."

Travis shook his head. "Back to my point—women and water. So Alena drags you outside moments before your place is bombed to smithereens."

Gerrit gave a quick look at Alena. She lowered her eyes, blushing.

Travis continued, unrelenting. "You know what they say about the debt you owe someone who saves your life, buddy. You're tied to them forever. So, I guess it is foreordained that you two—"

"Stop it, Travis." Jessie gave a threatening look. "You're embarrassing them. I think it's sweet that Alena risked her life to save Gerrit. Let's just leave it at that."

Suddenly, Gerrit felt uncomfortable. "You know, I've been cooped up in bed and need to stretch my legs. I think I'll take Bones and Sam and head down to the river, if you guys don't mind."

Travis smiled. "It would do Sam good to run some of this dinner off. Go for it."

Relieved, Gerrit patted his leg, looking at the dogs. "Come on, guys. I snagged a couple pieces of Travis's steak with your names on it." He held them up for the dogs to see as he made his way to the stairs. They came bounding after him, tails wagging, eyeing the meat with hungry eagerness.

He climbed down the steps and walked a few yards down the gravel pathway when he heard footsteps behind him. Turning, he saw Alena following.

"Mind if I tag along? Needed to get away from Travis."

Gerrit nodded. "I know what you mean."

"He is a great guy. Helped us in the past when we needed assistance. But sometimes, he gets on my nerves."

Gerrit bent down and let each dog have one of the chunks of meat. "Welcome the company. By the way, do you know where we're going tomorrow?"

"Where we first met—San Francisco."

"Why there?" He wiped his hands off and began walking down the path.

"That is where I live when I am not running around chasing you." She smiled for a moment. "Seriously, we thought it best to relocate you there until things cool down. I am all set up and can provide a good cover for you while we start to fill in your backside."

"Backside?"

"You know, the story about your fake past."

"Oh. You mean *backstory*?"

"Whatever you Americans call it. Anyway, Joe and Willy—you haven't met him yet—will recreate your past with a new name, ID, the whole thing. Make you a new person."

"What name should I use?"

Alena stopped for moment, looking into his eyes. "I like the name David. David from the Bible."

"Why him?"

She came alongside as they neared the river. "He was a warrior, a leader of men. And he was very brave—like you, Gerrit."

"I'm not a brave man, Alena."

She took his arm for moment. "You forget. I have been watching you for more than seven years. I know just about everything there is to know about you. I say you are a David."

Suddenly her closeness made him feel uncomfortable. He never let anyone get close before. His first inclination was to back away. Build a wall. "You know everything about me? Like what?"

Alena just smiled. "Come on, I think the dogs want to go for a swim."

"What is your last name?"

"Shapiro. Alena Shapiro."

"That a Russian name?"

She nodded. "A Russian *Jewish* name."

"How did a Russian Jewish woman wind up in San Francisco working with my uncle?"

Her eyes darkened as if she suddenly pulled down a curtain. "A long story, Gerrit."

"Give me the *Reader's Digest* version."

"*Reader's Digest*? What is this?"

"I mean, just give me a brief story about how you met."

She took a deep breath. "It is not a happy one. When I was about nineteen years old, my parents finally obtained a visa to Israel for all three of us. A lifetime dream of theirs and they wanted to get me out of Russia. We resettled in that country and I had an opportunity to go to school. When I was twenty-two years old and serving in the Israeli army, my parents took a trip to visit my father's brother in Buenos Aires, Argentina in 1994. My relatives were showing my family around the city, including the AMIA building."

Gerrit looked at her sharply. "*Asociación Mutual Israelita Argentina?* I remember the incident."

She nodded, eyes downcast. "I'm impressed. You even have the pronunciation right."

He shrugged. "What can I say? It's a gift…or a curse. My memory."

Sadness washed over her. She closed her eyes, and words seemed to catch in her throat. "Eighty-five people killed, including my folks. The handiwork of Hezbollah and the Iranian government."

"I'm sorry, Alena. I shouldn't pry."

She angrily wiped away a tear. "Sometimes it feels like it happened years ago. And I have been at war ever since. Other times, like right now, I close my eyes and I feel like it just—"

He saw she could not continue. He knew not to dig any further. "Loved ones can leave a hole in your soul that can never be filled," he said, quietly.

She nodded. "Time and God may heal the soul, but scars will always be there—never letting you forget."

They walked in silence to the river's edge, the swollen Clearwater River running swiftly past their feet as evening shadows fell. An arctic chill swept down the canyon as winter let them know another snowstorm might be coming their way. Spring was a long way off.

As dusk settled, a momentary sense of peace descended, as if the land and the river promised shelter from the pending storm. The forest around them seemed quiet and content, ignoring winter's threat.

Both dogs stood with their paws planted in the water, listening to something Gerrit could not hear. There was an inquisitive look in Bones's eyes as he turned and stared at Gerrit for a moment. Then the dog turned and dashed upstream against the ice-cold current, Sam running to keep up.

Chapter 26

Lewiston-Nez Perce County Airport, Idaho

A Cessna Citation XLS taxied off the runway toward their waiting cars at the edge of the tarmac. Frank leaned against the driver's door, arms crossed, watching the pearl-white business jet draw near. "Holy cow, Joe. You guys know how to travel."

His uncle extended a hand to Frank.

"Thanks again. Tell Jessie and Travis to stop fooling around and get hitched. You need to have some grandchildren running around before you get too much older."

Frank grinned, eyed Gerrit and Alena gathering their things. "You know how it is, Joe. Can't tell these kids anything nowadays."

Gerrit walked over and shook the man's hand. "Thank Travis again for taking care of Bones. I don't know where I'm going to end up. I hope to come get the dog when I'm settled somewhere."

Frank nodded as they watched the plane draw near. They both knew that time might never come.

The jet's engines powered down, and a door cracked open to allow passengers to enter. Joe followed Gerrit and Alena up the stairway, waving back at Frank before he disappeared inside. "Okay, let's get this thing off the ground."

Gerrit waited for Joe into to get into the cabin. "Very ritzy! Who owns this plane?"

"Don't ask and I won't have to tell you no lies. Let's just say I have friends in high places."

Joe walked forward to the cockpit as Gerrit found a seat near a starboard window and settled in. As he eased back to get comfortable, a giant of a man squeezed from the cockpit and lumbered into the passenger quarters toward him. A teardrop tattoo under the man's left eye and a neck embroidered with prison tattoos of black and blue ink made Gerrit wonder if he stumbled onto a *Con Air* movie set. The man's biceps bulged from a short-sleeve T-shirt, and when he stooped to whisper something to Alena, his neck muscles rippled as if they wanted to climb out of his skin.

Alena kissed his cheek, then turned to Gerrit. "Let me introduce our pilot, Hank 'Redneck' Schneider." She turned toward the giant. "And Redneck, you already met Gerrit at his house the other night."

Redneck gave him a studied nod. "How's the ol' noggin, copper? Knock any sense into you yet?"

"You're the guy who dumped—"

"The dead guy on your bed. That's me, jarhead."

Gerrit heard a flush and glanced up to see a lavatory door open. Redneck muttered, "Here's my gutless copilot, Willy Williams. Wesley Snipes he ain't." A young man about the size of one of Redneck's thighs emerged, his ebony skin looking ashen.

"Lost your lunch again I see." The white giant smirked. "Get belted up, Willy, we're about to take off. Joe will help me this time."

Willy sank into the nearest chair and nodded a greeting to Gerrit. "Can you believe Joe would trust this plane to the likes of him?" Willy and Redneck exchanged glances, as Alena leaned forward.

"Okay, boys. Play nice. We have company."

Redneck was about to respond when Joe yelled back, "Come on back here. Let's get this thing fired up." Redneck turned and squeezed back inside the cockpit. Gerrit wondered how the man fit in that small space. A moment later, the engines came to life.

Willy smiled. "Don't let that giant pea brain get to you, Mr. G. It's just his way. You ought to see him when he gets down and dirty."

"Mr. G?" Gerrit frowned.

"Oh, that's how I'm going to keep you and Joe apart. You know, Mr. G for Gerrit O'Rourke and Mr. J for…well, you can figure it out, right?" Willy looked out the window and saw they were taxing to the runway. "Oh, boy, here we go again. I'm glad Mr. J has the controls again. Redneck thought he would play a trick on me on our way down here. Rolled the plane over a couple times because he knows I hate flying. I felt like capping his—Sorry, Alena. I try to talk polite when you're around." Willy appeared nervous. "I can't wait to get my feet back on the ground."

Alena stifled a laugh. "You know, Willy, air travel is safer than car travel. And Mr. J will have us back to the city in no time. Why don't you try to take a nap."

"Take a nap with Redneck at the controls? You gotta be kidding." He reached over and grabbed a laptop from the seat next to him.

"Got to wait until we are in the air, Willy." Alena smiled again. "Mr. J is at the controls now. He'll keep our gentle giant from any more tricks. Trust me."

Willy raised one eyebrow. "I do trust you, Alena. I just hope Mr. J can control that jerk." He plugged in an iPod, inserted the earplugs, and leaned back, closing his eyes.

She turned to Gerrit. "As you can see, we are one big family. Well, what do you think of the team?"

"The team?" Gerrit leaned closer. "These are the guys you depend on?"

Her eyes softened. "With my life. Do not let looks deceive you. They would die for each other at a moment's notice—you just cannot tell it by the way they interact."

"So are you…kind of like their mother?"

She looked at Willy, his head back, eyes closed, keeping time to whatever beat he was listening to. "More like their older sister."

"And Joe?"

"He's the glue that keeps us together."

The aircraft cleared the runway and banked toward the rising sun.

"You know, statistically you're wrong about air travel."

She looked at him. "What do you mean?"

He glanced out the window and saw where the Clearwater and Snake rivers joined together far below, the Snake creating a blue-green line between the cities of Lewiston and Clarkston.

"Airline companies always spout that traveling by air is three times safer than railroads and five times safer than cars, but their statistics are highly skewed. Did you know that 70 percent of the crashes take place on takeoff and landing, which is only 4 percent of the average trip."

"That still sounds like it might be safer to travel by car," she said. "Would it not?"

He looked at her, shaking his head. "A more realistic figure is to compare fatalities in these accidents by the number of journeys made. If you factor deaths per 100 million passenger trips, it's a much different picture—2.7 death by railroad, 4.5 by vehicles, and 55.0 by aircraft."

"Really?" She squinted at him. "Are you making this up?"

"Nope. By my stats, you're twelve times more likely to crash in the air compared to riding in a car; twenty times more likely to die on a plane than taking a train. Makes you think twice, doesn't it?"

"Well, don't tell Willy any of this," she said, studying him. "He'll never fly again."

"Speaking of your siblings, tell me about Redneck and Willy. I just can't see those two working together."

"They fight like brothers, and no one ever wins." She leaned back on the headrest and turned her face toward him. "I came across Willy in San Francisco, a place called Hunters Point."

"I'm familiar with the city. A lot of gang activity when I saw it last."

"Those living in the Point have always been promised a lot by the politicians over the years, but the promises always turn up empty. Willy was born and raised on those streets, never knowing his father and his mother barely keeping the family together. He was a smart kid, though, and attracted the attention of gang leaders. He was wearing colors and banging when I first saw him."

"How did that happen?"

"I was mentoring kids through our church, tutoring them on subjects they were struggling with in school. Caught Willy trying to steal one of our computers."

"You had him arrested?"

Her eyes twinkled. "It took me about two seconds to realize this guy has a razor-sharp mind. I made a deal with him. I'd let him use our computers if he'd help the other kids with their homework and continue with his education. He picked up math and science like a sponge. It was amazing to watch. Got him enrolled in a community college class to learn about information technology—programming languages, computer software and hardware, cyber security. I already knew Joe, and the two of them were a natural fit. He taught Willy IT programs and security systems the college never dreamed of. Willy soaked it up and now runs their company."

"Runs whose company?" Gerrit glanced over at Willy and saw he was listening to their conversation.

"Ain't it a trip, Mr. G? I get paid to go into rich folk's homes, rummage through their hardware, and install security systems so guys like me don't break in. And they pay me good money to boot."

"Where do you 'rummage through their hardware,' Willy?"

"Oh, Mr. J moved me back to Virginia, just outside D.C., where we operate the company. Gives us a cover to do what we really are about—going after guys like Kane." He started to put the headphones back on. "Can you image a guy like me living in the same hood as all those white crackers?"

"Hey, Willy. Mr. J taught you better than that. And so did I." Alena's face took on a stern look.

"Sorry. I know—turn the other cheek. WWJD. I've got a ways to go." He shot her a smile before inserting the earplugs and wrapping himself up in his music.

"WWJD?"

She turned to Gerrit again. "You know…What Would Jesus Do."

He looked away. "So, you're a—"

"Follower of Jesus. I confess I am. Does that bother you?"

He shrugged. "I think whatever gets you through the night is okay with me, Alena. Just not my cup of tea."

"You don't believe in God?"

"I didn't say that. I come from a scientific background—my folks raised me that way, and my experience and education is based upon hard, irrefutable facts. God is not a quantified entity I can prove. And if He exists, I don't think He and I would ever see eye to eye."

"Why don't you think you could relate to God?" She seemed genuinely interested in his answer.

"Because the world's not geared up for turning the other cheek or loving your neighbor. It's about getting ahead, protecting your own interests, and getting what you can now—because there is no tomorrow."

"What if God showed you otherwise?"

"If He comes down off His mountain and shows me a better way—I might listen. So far that hasn't happened, and all I've seen in this world is pain and death."

"You mean like your parents?"

"Yeah, like my folks, your folks, and hundreds of others I've seen killed, tortured, or victimized. So short answer: God goes His way; I go mine." Gerrit paused for a moment. "Now, tell me about Redneck. How does he connect to this…family?"

It seemed to take Alena a moment to focus on his question, seemingly troubled by what he just said. She glanced toward the cockpit where Joe and Redneck sat. "Our gentle giant is not what he appears to be."

"You mean a white racist with a low IQ? I saw the prison tats."

Alena frowned. "Looks can be deceiving. Yes, he used to be caught up in all that. But he has changed, and let me tell you—this guy is a walking calculator. He can figure out complicated flight plans in his head or take a look at a set of books and quickly pinpoint any errors. And you never want to have to go up against him—his street-fighting skills would make Muhammed Ali quiver."

"How did he connect with you and Joe?"

"It was Joe. Back when Joe still lived in Chicago, he came across Redneck in an alley, facing off against three other attackers. Joe grabbed a two-by-four and waded in to protect him. After it was all over, they became friends. First a beer here and a lunch there. Then more they hung around each other, the more he grew on Joe.

"Redneck was trying to go straight at the time. I will let him tell you about that part of his life if he chooses. Anyway, Joe saw potential in this guy, made a few phone calls, and got him hooked up with an accounting firm."

"An accounting firm? You gotta be kidding."

"I told you he has a mind for numbers. After a few years, Redneck started his own accounting service with Joe's help, and they stayed in touch ever since. After Joe…had to leave Chicago, he reached out to let Redneck know he was okay. Redneck wanted to help pay back what Joe did for him. So here we are—a muscle-bound accountant who can fly planes and toss people around with hardly any effort at all."

Gerrit looked over at Willy, then at Joe and Redneck in the cockpit. "This is certainly a strange group. Which just leaves you. So, what's your story, Alena? You a race-car driver? A belly dancer?"

Alena laid her head back and closed her eyes. "Maybe I will tell you sometime. Right now, I need to rest. We are going to be quite busy very soon."

He looked at the ceiling for a moment and then out the double-paned window. The Pacific Ocean glistened off to his right. The sky was an ocean of blue, allowing him to see far into the distance. Glancing across the aisle, he saw Mt. Hood, capped with snow, off to his left.

He started to ask Alena one more question, but she was already asleep. He watched her breathing for a moment, slow and rhythmic. Her brow furrowed.

What are you hiding, mystery lady? And why were you watching over me all these years?

Gerrit settled back to rest until the end of the flight, determined to find out all he could about this mystery woman. In a few minutes, he felt himself slip into another world, darker and more sinister.

A wicked, twisty path led him down the face of a cliff, rocky shale making each step treacherous. Above, bare trees stood dark against a star-pocked sky, like angels of death pronouncing sentence upon his soul. Their gnarled limbs twisted out in agony as they struggled to pull him back into their grasp for final judgment.

Down below, only darkness and a bottomless pit. A familiar voice seemed to be drawing him down into the bowels of the earth, where more voices called out. He had no choice. Angels of death loomed above. A dark abyss lay below.

As he slipped and slid down the rocky slope, something inside compelled him to continue, as if promising answers to all his questions if he would just submit. Give in. Suddenly, his feet gave way, and he began to fall into the deep cavern, screaming.

"Gerrit, wake up."

He shot his eyes open to see Alena leaning over, shaking his arm.

"You seemed to be having a bad dream."

Sheepishly, he sat up and stretched his arms. It was the same reoccurring dream. And it always ended with him falling, pulling him toward what he feared most—that unknown beyond death. This dream began after he visited his parents' grave sites and continued ever since.

Sleep always came at a cost.

Chapter 27

Harrogate, England

Richard clutched the phone. "Give me some good news, boy. I've got Senator Summers waiting in the lobby." One of Richard's contacts just called in about the Seattle murder investigations.

"We got the piece of evidence you wanted hidden at the bomb site before the first units arrived. Just a matter of time before they link the trigger to the Russians. We did everything but stamp *Russia* on it. I don't know if the feds will release that information or withhold it to verify a suspect's confession."

"What about the body?"

"Still unable to identify it, sir. I knew where the explosives were set, but additional charges had been placed around that bed. The body almost vaporized. They'll be lucky to gather any of the remains. And even if they do, it's so charred they may not be able to pick up any usable samples for identification—even DNA. It's like we had two separate explosions that went off simultaneously."

"Let me know the second they learn anything about the remains. I want assurances that Gerrit was in that house." Richard lowered his head, frustrated. "And that incident in San Francisco. Have them check all the security cameras, boarding information, everything. I want to know what happened to our people on the ground. I mean, C4 in her purse? Two guys wind up in the head because someone slipped them poison? I want to know who did this. I want them interrogated and disposed of—permanently. Am I clear?"

The man on the line paused before responding. "Sir, we've already been over that—the security cameras, travel records, everything. I don't know whether we will be able to come up with anything."

"Don't you dare tell me you can't find any information on one or more people operating in a highly protected international air terminal. We've got all kinds of electronics in those buildings. If need be, use our satellite surveillance feeds to isolate this crew. I want to know who they are."

"I'll get right on it, sir."

"There has to be a connection between Gerrit and what we're trying to do. I know his uncle is still out there somewhere hiding. Did they connect? It's imperative to know whether Gerrit is dead. Alive…he is serious trouble."

He slammed the phone down and yelled to his assistant through the closed door. He jerked his head toward the ceiling when his assistant poked his head in. "Senator Summers is upstairs in the lobby. Escort him directly to my office. Don't let him take any detours."

The assistant nodded and slipped out of the room.

Richard leaned back in his chair, trying to calm down. So much at stake here, and too many unresolved issues. No matter how hard he exerted control over this operation, people seemed incapable of giving him any resolution to these matters. How hard would it be to determine whether that body was Gerrit's?

What if his suspicions became a reality? What if Gerrit is still alive?

He jumped up and closed the door to his office, then returned to his desk and snatched up the phone. He redialed the same number he'd called minutes earlier. The same voice came on the line.

"Look, let's assume that Gerrit is alive."

"But he—"

"Shut up and listen. If he's still alive, then he had help. Go back to the first bombing where his uncle disappeared in Seattle. Take that man's life apart. Check every contact, every move he made, leading up to Gerrit's parents' deaths. I want to know everybody and anybody Joe O'Rourke may have contacted when he started running. I want to know where he landed in his efforts to hide, who helped him."

"That's going to take—"

"I don't care about anything but tracking these guys down. We need to eliminate any exposure to our project. Get on this right now."

A sharp rap on the door made him turn toward the sound. "Got to go. Let me know what you find." He hung up the phone. "Come in."

A haggard-looking John Summers entered the room as Richard came around the desk, extending his hand. "Senator, I am so sorry about Marilynn. Please accept my condolences."

Summers's jaw tightened, broadcasting the man's state of mind. "I don't need your condolences. I want answers. I want to know how this happened."

Richard pulled over a chair. "Sit down, John. I'll tell you what I've learned."

The senator balked. "Tell me you had nothing to do with this. Everywhere I turn, I'm getting stonewalled. Just the way you like to operate."

A look of shock crossed Richard's features, an expression he'd cultivated over the years. "I can't believe you'd think—"

"Save the innocence for someone who might swallow that bull, Kane. I flew all the way to this godforsaken place to meet you face-to-face. I wanted to look into your eyes when I asked this question. Did you have anything to do with Marilynn's death?"

"John, I swear to you, I had nothing to do with her death. I will do everything in my power to find out who did."

The senator's whole body seemed to wilt as he sank into the chair. "Since her mother and I split up years ago, Marilynn was the only family I had left. We've had our differences, but I did love her. I had great hopes for her future. And now…this."

Richard lowered himself in his chair, letting the man talk.

"I can't get any answers. You'd think the chairman of the Senate Select Committee on Intelligence could get information on his own daughter's murder. DOJ, FBI, Seattle PD, ATF—they're all giving me the runaround.

I want to know who did this." He seemed to have run out of energy as he studied Richard across the desktop.

Gritting his teeth for control, Richard leaned on the desk, clasping both hands together. "We are looking into this because her death is a great blow to our efforts. I, too, had great hopes for your daughter. She was bright, articulate, and filled with drive that would have taken her anywhere."

"So what happened?" The senator's voice softened, his tone almost pleading.

This was not the senator Richard remembered only a week ago. He was like a beaten man. He would have to monitor Summers more closely. If this man fell apart, all of them would have serious exposure. He might jeopardize everything.

"John, here is what I just learned from some of my people on the ground. As I suspected, I believe the three deaths—Marilynn's, Gerrit's, and the other cop's, Mark Taylor—are all related."

"Who killed my daughter?" The man's voice sounded hoarse.

"You remember the last case Marilynn worked on? The Russian mob?" The senator nodded.

"They have found a part of the trigger that set off the explosion in Gerrit's house. Russian made. And we started picking up other chatter about the dead gang leader's members. It seems this was clearly retaliation for that gang leader getting killed in San Diego. The shooting Gerrit was involved with just before you met him at the airport in D.C. Marilynn and the others are all tied to this one case."

John Summers drew himself up, pointing a finger at Richard. "Find those responsible and take them out. I do not want them to wiggle out of it in court someday. Find them. Kill them."

Richard stared back. "If that is what you want, John. Consider it done."

Standing up, Summers seemed to gather himself, gaining back composure that eluded him earlier. "Tell me when it is finished. I want to know every detail."

Richard nodded and watched the senator turn and exit as if the matter was settled. As his assistant stumbled after the senator toward the elevator, Richard thought back over the whole investigation since

Gerrit returned from Vienna. *And what do I tell the good senator if Gerrit rises from the dead?*

An encrypted message appeared on his computer. He glanced at the code and sucked in his breath. The message he had been waiting for since the explosion.

Gerrit is alive. Everything under control. No one is suspicious. Soon, I can hand the whole team over to you. Make sure that money gets to my account.

Richard stared at the message and saw the coded name that signed off. A slow smile crossed his face. *Got you, Gerrit! You and your uncle will soon join the rest of your family beyond the grave.* He could not risk having this Lazarus talking to the world. Only death would keep Richard's secret safe.

He reached for a phone and dialed a number in Seattle. When a man's voice came on the line, Richard almost whispered his message. "Make my boy out to be dirty. Then have him killed."

"But I thought—"

"You're not paid to think. Just obey. Gerrit is alive." Richard killed the connection.

Chapter 28

San Francisco, California

Gerrit watched the jet taxi into a private hangar like a hawk returning to its nest. Once the engines whined down, Redneck climbed out of the cockpit, lowered the stairs to the ground, and clambered out, marching toward the hangar doors. The giant hit a power switch on the far wall, forcing the door to slowly close.

As Joe emerged from the cockpit, Gerrit and Alena made their way to the stairway. Willy was already down the stairs before they got to the opening. Gerrit cocked his head. "Where do we go from here?"

Joe rubbed his jaw. "Willy and I are flying out tonight. We'll drop Redneck in Chicago on our way home. You," he looked at Alena before turning back to Gerrit, "stay with Alena while she gets you set up. San Francisco, for now, is your new home."

Gerrit caught Joe and Alena sharing a look. "I've always liked this city. Never thought I'd settle here, though."

"Don't get used to it," his uncle said. "In our business, we learn to leave everything at a moment's notice and start new somewhere else. That's how we stay alive."

"I survive by attacking the enemy. Not hiding somewhere until the war's over."

"If you live long enough, you'll have plenty of time to fight. Right now, we need to make sure you can survive in this war. That's what Alena can give you."

Gerrit looked at both of them and shrugged. "Fair enough. But I need to be able move soon, Joe. I'm going after Kane."

Joe rested a hand on his shoulder. "I know. And we'll help you. But we must work together like a team. Otherwise, they divide and conquer."

Alena and Joe left the aircraft. Gerrit followed them toward an exit door leading to a small parking lot. Outside, they climbed into a red Toyota Sienna, the van easily accommodating everyone except Redneck. The giant squeezed into the front passenger seat, pushing it all the way back. The man looked uncomfortable. Gerrit slid the van door open, climbed in, and took the backseat, allowing Joe and Alena the middle section. Willy drove, weaving across acres of asphalt before finally leaving the airport and reaching the on-ramp to westbound 380.

As Gerrit looked back toward the bay, the sky painted a golden haze as he tried to make out the East Bay Hills. Ahead, the highway abruptly ended, forcing drivers to go either north or south. Willy merged onto northbound 280 until they reached 19th Avenue's stop-and-go traffic.

Gerrit leaned forward, watching them approach Golden Gate Park. "What part of the city are we headed for?"

Alena smiled back at him. "Remember the Haight-Ashbury?"

He nodded, watching Willy cut off a car as he punched the accelerator, swerving across two lanes of traffic to get to the right-hand turn lane.

"I have a place near The Panhandle. I commute to…where I do my job."

"And what is that?"

"I repair old books and documents."

Joe leaned back. "She is also very good at creating documents—like driver's licenses, passports, whatever we need. She's an artist."

Gerrit raised an eyebrow. "And where did you develop these skills?"

Alena looked away. "In a past life."

Midway down The Panhandle, Willy pulled over and parked in front of a fire hydrant. "You guys bail out here and I'll go find a parking space. Hope I can find one between here and the Golden Gate Bridge.

"Always whining," Redneck said, peeling himself out of the car. He stood and stretched. "Try not to get lost, *Buckwheat*."

Willy stuck his head out the window. "Don't call me that, Hillbilly. This is my town. I know every inch of this city. Only hicks like you get lost."

Alena stepped forward. "Hey, settle down you two. This is my neighborhood. Try to keep it to a dull roar."

Gerrit watched the exchange between Willy and Redneck, with Alena intervening like some kind of mother hen. Joe looked on in bemusement. As Willy drove off, Gerrit wondered how this oddly matched group ever got anything done. They would be matching wits with people like Richard Kane, Senator Summers, and those working in the shadows. How could Joe have any confidence in this crew?

Gerrit shook his head as he followed them toward a white Victorian, metal bars across the first-level windows. Alena looked at him. "This is home, Gerrit. At least for now."

"And where do you work?"

"Down near the water. I've got a place along the Embarcadero. Take you there in the morning."

She climbed broad steps leading to the front door, wooden stairs painted the color of naval ships. The building, however, was brightly painted in an off-white, with windows, cornices, and trim delicately etched in muted reds, sea green, and dark blues, like a painting where the artist fills in shadows and darkness to bring forward the lighter sections. At the top of the stairway, under a deeply recessed overhang, three doors led to individual entryways for each level of the building.

Alena opened the door on the left, leading to the ground floor, and gestured them inside. Speaking to Gerrit, she said, "I have this floor, and the landlord leases the other two floors to others—very quiet, very considerate neighbors." She eyed Redneck for emphasis. "Very quiet."

Redneck shrugged and lumbered inside. All three gathered in a sitting room off to the right, which overlooked the park.

"Make yourselves comfortable," she said, heading for the kitchen. "I'll start some tea for anyone who might want some."

Redneck grimaced. "You know I never touch the stuff, Al. Got a beer?"

Gerrit looked at Alena, silently mouthing the name *Al.* He raised his eyebrows.

"Redneck and Willy shorten everyone's name. Willy started it, and now Redneck has picked it up. They call me *Al.*" She gave the giant a look that made Redneck grin. "And he affectionately calls Willy *Pea brain*—although, come to think of it, that really does not shorten anything."

The big man eased himself into a wicker chair, his weight causing the furniture to threaten to collapse. "Pea brain just seems to fit. And besides, he hates it."

Alena looked at Gerrit. "Willy already started calling you Mr. G, so I guess that will be your handle."

Redneck shifted and one of the strands of the chair snapped in two. He bent over to see the damage. "I think I'll call this guy *Einstein.* We know his history and his partner…" The man stopped speaking and grimaced. "Sorry, man. We picked that up when we were tailing you."

"Mark was a good man," Gerrit said, feeling tension suddenly fill the room. "Maybe with your help I can find who did this to him—and Marilynn. Just get me the names and I can take it from there. I'm no longer a cop. I left that behind when they killed my friends and destroyed my home."

Joe watched them as he stood near the window. "This is not about vengeance, Gerrit. Whatever we find, we turn over to the proper authorities—those we can trust. We're not a group of vigilantes."

They heard footsteps outside as someone bounded up the stairs. Redneck gingerly pulled himself out of the chair. "That must be Pea brain. I'll let him in." They heard the two men bantering as Redneck unlocked the door.

Willy came over and sat near Gerrit. "Al, I almost drove down to your place on the Embarcadero before I found a parking spot. How do you manage around here?"

"Easy. Take a taxi, a bus, or walk."

Joe walked toward them, drawing a chair with him. "Let's get started. Willie, Redneck, and I need to get back to the airport in a few hours. The faster we cover what has to be done, the faster we can be on our way."

Joe started to sit down, then reached into his coat pocket and pulled out a cell phone. Gerrit watched his uncle use his thumb to navigate the phone, apparently searching for a text message that just came in. As he read the message, a worried expression crossed his face.

"Another problem. Someone started checking into my background—again."

Redneck leaned forward. "You mean the stuff back in Chicago?"

Joe shook his head. "I mean everything. They're searching phone records, police records, the whole nine yards. Gerrit, they're looking at the records around the time your parents were killed and comparing them to the attempt on your life this week."

Gerrit found his throat tightened. "What are they looking for?"

Joe raised his eyes and looked directly at him. "I think they're looking for you. Someone must think you're still alive. And they are hunting for both of us."

Placing the phone back into his pocket, Joe looked at each worried face in the room. "We have got to move fast. We have to make Gerrit disappear."

Chapter 29

Joe hunched forward, looking from one to the other. "This is primarily for Gerrit's benefit, but the rest of you…jump in with any questions or comments." They nodded, letting the older man speak.

He turned to Gerrit. "These people never give up, son. They'll keep coming until they track down all of us — unless we can thwart their search. So far, Willy and I have been able to hurl digital chaff into the mix, sending their search engines off following dead ends. Where we're vulnerable — like this search right now — is if they find physical and digital links between us and those who have helped us."

The others silently nodded.

"If they make those connections, they'll have a fixed location from which to launch intensified surveillance. I mean the kind of surveillance that has never been used on us before." He pointed at Gerrit. "I'll get into that later, or Alena will teach you. These people will torture and eliminate anyone getting in their way."

"You mean like they tried with me last week?"

Joe nodded. "And like they did with your partner and Marilynn… and your folks seven years ago. Like they tried with me."

Gerrit felt the old pangs of anger and loss rise to the surface again. "How do they get away with it?"

"The big three—money, power, and influence. With those tools, they believe they are impervious."

"How do you propose to fight them?"

Joe looked at the others before answering. "One battle at a time. First, we identify those who can be identified—like Kane. We focus our attention on that person—just like they do to us—and watch and wait for him to make a mistake."

"So how do we get to Kane?"

"We let him do that for us. Every move he makes, every communication he generates, gives us connections to follow. For example, we suspect Kane is behind the bombing of your house and the deaths of Marilynn, your partner, and Adleman in Vienna. Now, we work with others to prove it."

"Others? Like who?"

Joe leaned back. "Hey, guys, I need to speak to Gerrit alone. About how we compartmentalize everything. You mind?"

Alena rose. "Come on. I'll make something to snack on. Wouldn't want Redneck to waste away to nothing."

Willy grinned. "It's all fat anyway. He can afford to lose a few pounds."

Redneck smirked. "I could go without eating for a year and still have more meat on my bones than you'll ever have on that sorry excuse of a body you carry around. Your legs are smaller than toothpicks, and your arms...what an embarrassment. How do you get any chicks with that pathetic body?"

"I attract them with my intelligence, Hillbilly. Something you'll never have." Their voices trailed off as they walked down the hallway toward the kitchen, bickering nonstop.

"You sure they like each other?" Gerrit asked, listening to the last of their conversation.

"Yeah, but they'll never admit it." Joe chuckled. "They've both changed. I mean, if you knew Redneck and Willy just a few years ago, they would have pulled guns on each other—not sit down and try to work together."

"You call that working together?"

Joe's expression seemed to shift, a look of concern in his eyes. "I needed to talk to you alone, Gerrit. In case something happens to me."

"What are you talking about? I thought you had everything under control."

His uncle shook his head. "Never get complacent. We're at war. People get hurt—even die—in this type of combat. Just like your experiences in Afghanistan and Iraq. Only this is a quieter conflict, but just as deadly. Like you experienced last week. No rules. No prisoners taken—at least for very long."

"Why are you telling me all this, Joe?"

"If they put me out of commission, I need you to take over. I need you to keep this team safe and functioning."

"How am I supposed to do that? I haven't even figured out how we fight this war yet."

"It'll come. Each of us will help you develop the tools you'll need to lead this unit. I know you will do great. A real asset to our side. And when—or if—the time comes for you to lead, you must be prepared."

Voices in the other room rose for a moment. Alena seemed to be trying to calm them down. Always the peacemaker.

"Beck Malloy will be your contact. I want you to follow his direction—whatever he tells you, do it! Promise me."

"Sure, Joe. But I don't even know the guy."

His uncle gave him a folded-up piece of paper. "Memorize this phone number and then destroy the note. Alena is the only other person who knows about Beck right now. Don't give his name out to anyone. If you ever need help—call it. The man on the end of that line can be trusted. With everything. He's a true patriot. If he ever makes direct contact with you," Joe said, clutching his hands, "it will probably mean I'm dead. It will be time for you to take over and lead the fight."

"Let's hope that day never comes."

"Hey, I plan to be around awhile. Just in case, though, remember what I told you. Okay? No questions asked."

Gerrit shrugged. "You know me, Joe. I never work well with others."

"I've watched you over the years, my boy. You're a born leader. Just remember that those working for you need to know they have your trust and respect."

Again, he heard voices rise in the other room. Louder this time. More intense.

"Let's join the others. The boys and I will need to leave soon."

Gerrit followed his uncle down the hall and into the kitchen. Alena had donned an apron that captured actress Geena Davis portraying an assassin with amnesia in the movie *The Long Kiss Goodnight.* The apron depicted a scene where Davis hurls a long-bladed knife across her kitchen, sticking it in wood with pinpoint accuracy, after discovering she is very handy with sharp cutlery. Her boyfriend and daughter stare at her in shock. The apron quotes Davis saying, "Chefs do that."

Alena looked across the kitchen at Gerrit, waving a knife in her hand, and caught him staring at the apron. "What can I say, I love Geena Davis."

In the movie, he remembered that Davis was not what she appeared to be—a schoolteacher and caring mother. She turned out to be a highly trained assassin. Again, he wondered about Alena's past.

He eyed the knife for a moment. She lowered it to the counter, watching him.

Redneck, straddling a chair, looked up at Gerrit. "So, Mr. J squared you away? How to control us and all that?"

Gerrit leaned on the counter. "He told me specifically how to control you, RD."

Redneck squinted. "*Artie*...what kind of name is that.? Sounds like a loser Pea brain might hang around with. You know, someone a little light in the loafers?"

"Not *Artie*...R. D.," Gerrit said, emphasizing each letter. "Since you like to shorten everyone's name, well, I'm throwing one back at you and Mr. W."

The big man seemed to thinking about it, and his expression telegraphed his displeasure. "I don't know. How about you just call me Redneck?"

"*Arrrrtie*," Willy said, slurring the letters together. "I don't know...

Arrrrrtie. I like it. It has a certain flare."

Redneck stood. "And I can tell you where to shove that flare, Stickman."

Excited, Willy raised up until he was even to Redneck's gut. "Stickman. You—"

"Stop it. Both of you." Alena picked up the knife, waving it for emphasis. "You guys help me set the table. Quietly."

The two men approached the dining table like two male lions, warily eyeing each other. Just as things settled down, Gerrit heard Willy whisper, "*Artie*...hand me the silverware, you sweet *thang*." As Redneck roared back, Willy scurried away, grinning from ear to ear. Alena tried to look stern, but she finally turned away to hide a smile.

Gerrit looked around the room and saw Joe standing off in the corner. The man seemed oblivious to all the bantering, his eyes focused somewhere in the distance. The man's expression looked troubled, his forehead creased and wrinkled with worry.

Then Gerrit remembered what Joe had just asked. *"If something happens to me, Beck Malloy will make contact. I want you to follow his direction—whatever he tells you, do it! Promise me."*

It was a promise Gerrit hoped he never had to keep.

Chapter 30

Seagulls angrily screeched above as Gerrit emerged from a Starbucks, handing a caramel frappuccino to Alena. He peered warily at the fog-riddled gray clouds, waiting for one of those circling dive-bombers to strike.

She cupped both hands around the Styrofoam cup and sniffed. "Oh, how I love that smell."

Gerrit took one sip of his plain cup of house blend and scorched his tongue. "Whoa. Better let that cool."

Alena shouldered a backpack, handed him a cell phone, and began walking along the Embarcadero. "Joe asked that I give you a phone since you lost that last one I gave you in the bombing. Use it only to contact one of us. Once you use it—toss it."

He looked at the phone. "That must get expensive. And how do you know each other's cell number if you keep tossing them each time?"

They crossed the broad thoroughfare in front of the Ferry Building, then made their way along the sidewalk before she replied. "We only use them in emergencies; we have other ways to communicate."

"Carrier pigeons?"

Alena grinned. "We might consider it one of these times." A man in a business suit came up from behind, walking briskly. She eyed the stranger for a moment, waiting until the man was out of earshot before continuing.

"We have a common e-mail service we can all access. The account is listed under a…how do you say *boggie name*?"

"You mean bogus name? Fake name? But they can track those messages."

She gave him a patient smile. "We draft an e-mail but never send it. Each of us can access the account, read the draft, then add to it if we need to share information or need clarification. The last person to read everything is responsible for deleting the entire file."

"Ah, so there's no way to intercept those messages. Sweet. I heard of drug dealers and terrorists using that method to communicate. Fashioned after the old dead-letter drop."

"Try to access the account each day. If there is any hint that the account has been compromised, alert everyone and go to the next. We have a number of accounts, all inactive, all unconnected, until we are ready to use them. Each of us knows the order of those accounts."

Alena slowed down, finally stopping. She turned and looked over his shoulder—searching the sidewalk and street beyond. "Get used to this, Gerrit. Always be on the alert, looking for the unusual."

He was already looking beyond her shoulder, visually scanning the area. "As a cop, I come by this naturally."

"You are no longer a police officer, as you pointed out yesterday," she said, slightly above a whisper. "Everyone is the enemy—cops and crooks alike."

"You talking specifics?"

Her eyes, darker that her coffee drink, looked at him for a moment. "Just before your house was bombed, Kane called someone inside the Seattle Police Department."

Gerrit tensed. "Who?"

She shrugged. "We don't know. The number returned to a secretary's desk in the department. Investigations. However, it was a late-night call and that particular employee was home in bed. We checked."

"So, someone waited for Kane's call."

"After everything was blown sky high, Kane received a call from that same phone. The caller never used that line again to make contact.

They probably have a more secure way to communicate. Unfortunately, a number of people from other agencies had access to that area. Federal and local. Someone from any of those agencies could have used that phone."

Gerrit looked down at the sidewalk for a moment. "You know, there is a way—"

"We know. Joe is following up on that. Contacts he has in NSA. People he trusts. We might even be able to get a voice print off the phone if no one on the other side learns of our efforts."

He looked up. "Kane may have people in place to monitor these requests. Like those he has searching Joe's background and my information right now."

She nodded. "We must be very careful. So far, Joe and Willy have kept our backstory and communications protected—as far as we know. This world is getting so complicated." She shifted her backpack. "Okay, Mr. G. Time to go to work."

"Lead the way, *Al*."

In the distance he saw the blue-gray markings of Pier 39, a high-rent tourist attraction he was sure Alena stayed away from. Too many eyes. Instead, she turned toward one of the older buildings connected to a pier that jutted out into the San Francisco bay. The building, close to the Embarcadero, had a tan stucco front and stone cornices protruding from the edges. A half-oval entryway, like the entrance to an immense cave, gave large trucks access to a colossal warehouse beyond. To the left of that, a doorway—flush with building's facade—provided pedestrian access from the sidewalk.

She fished out a set of keys and opened the door. He followed her up a flight of stairs to the second floor, then down a narrow hallway to an office set back in the building. She slipped a key into the lock of an ancient door, opaque glass in the upper half and wooden panels below, with *Golden Gate Book & Document Restoration Company* etched on smoky-colored glass.

He watched as she quickly opened it. "Do you actually do any restoration?"

"Not if I can get out of it." She shoved open the door. "But I could if someone insisted."

A musky odor of old paper and books greeted him as they entered. He walked into a larger open-spaced room with an enclosed office at the far left. They made their way toward this office, and as she opened the door, he saw a view of the bay beyond. "Hey, nice place to hang out. Great view."

Without saying a word, she knelt before a large safe and punched in a code. The safe clicked open. She reached inside and pulled out a small package, handing it to him. "I've been working on these for some time. Just in case you might need them. I hope you like the name David Marshall. You're stuck with it for now."

"David Marshall? I'll have to get used to it." He opened up the package and saw a wallet inside among other things. In the wallet, a California driver's license with that name. He also found a U.S passport and several major credit cards. "So…David Marshall, huh? Are these credit cards any good?"

"You bet. Up to twenty-five thousand dollar limit on each card and a work history I'll have to go over with you." He examined the wallet and pulled out the driver's license, looking at her for a moment. Alena smiled. "You knew already I like the name David. And Marshall, well I am a fan of that John Wayne movie *True Grit*. You are not like that old lawman, but I think you have the same traits."

"You mean I eat too much, and I have a nasty disposition?"

She laughed. "No. That you are willing to take chances, not afraid of risks."

"How would you know?"

"Remember, I have been watching. Like that incident you got involved with down in San Diego this month."

That shootout in La Jolla seemed years ago in a different life. "I've been meaning to ask you. How soon after my parents' deaths did you get involved with all this? With me?"

"When your dad…" She stopped, her eyes widening for a moment as if she forgot and spilled something she never intended. "I mean—"

"What about my dad, Alena? Do you know something about him? About my folks?"

She turned away. "Ask Joe about all that. He'll tell you."

"He can't tell me anything about my dad prior to the bombing. I mean, they were brothers and all, but they were never that close. I never understood the trouble between Joe and Dad, but they went their separate ways after working together at MIT for years. My uncle would visit me every few years when he happened to be in town. And then that scare in Chicago… I guess they never got a chance to work things out. What can you tell me?"

"I am not the one, Gerrit. You must ask Joe."

"I'm asking you." Anger made his request rather curt. He tried to tone it down. "I mean, what's the big secret? After all this time and everything that has happened, certainly all this can be out in the open. Right?"

"Not everything," she said, quietly.

His cell phone vibrated. He withdrew it and saw a text message had been sent. He punched in the connection and scrolled down to the message. It was from his uncle. His jaw tightened as he read it. He handed the phone to Alena. "You better read this."

She grabbed it and read aloud. "Tell Al danger. Alert. Move quick. Compromised. PU at birdcage midnight. " She lowered the phone. "This is *tsuris*…bad trouble."

He stared at her. "What does it mean?"

She glanced up, frowning. "A breach in our security. We're to meet Joe and the others at the airport at midnight tonight. Bring your new identification and leave everything else behind. Old ID, clothes, everything that's not new. I'll lock them up in the safe here until we know we can retrieve them."

"My old ID? What are you talking about?"

"I mean…everything…can be tracked."

"Aren't you a bit paranoid?"

"That's what keeps us alive," she snapped. "I don't have time to explain everything right now. Use your brain, Gerrit. You know what tracking capabilities are out there. Oy veh! All your scientific background should be good for something. Right?" She turned toward him, angry. "I don't have time to hold your hand."

"I never asked you to hold my hand." He drew himself up.

She ripped Gerrit's cell phone apart, tossed the parts on the ground, and stomped on each one. "If I had not been watching your butt, they'd be fishing out parts of you from the lake. Who knows, maybe they would have whacked you before you even got home." She shook with rage.

He had never seen this side of her. She looked like she could take his head off. "Cool down, Alena. I only meant—"

"Save your excuses. Right now, we need to move." She wheeled around and withdrew a small gym bag from a closet. She carried it over to him and opened it. "I'm waiting, Gerrit."

He handed her his old wallet and felt the pocket watch in his pocket. Hesitating, he slowly withdrew it, rubbing his thumb over the smooth finish. Reluctantly he placed it in the gym bag. He had carried that watch every day since his father first gave it to him. Just clutching it would give him a feeling of connection, a link to his past. Now, that link must be severed. Just like everything else in his life.

She took the bag and flung it into the safe. "Anything else? Watch, jewelry, clothing? Anything we did not give you after the explosion."

He thought back and shook his head.

"Okay, let's get moving." She pushed the safe door closed and locked it. "We need to leave this place and never return until we know it is safe."

"Safe from what?"

"From surveillance, tracking devices, you name it. Until we know no one can link us and this place together. Same with my place in the Haight."

"Just like that. Up and leave everything behind?"

Her expression seemed to soften for a moment. "Look, I am sorry for being so uptight, but Mr. J's message is serious. It means something is really, really wrong. And until we know what the danger is, we have to run and leave everything behind. It is hard, but you will get used to this."

"Have you gotten used to it?"

Alena's eyes tightened. "It seems I have been running my whole life. It is just the way things are. Now, let's move."

Chapter 31

Shop till you drop—or die. Gerrit smiled as he watched Alena eyeing Macy's. They climbed out of a cab in San Francisco's Union Square and entered the large department store, searching for clothing they might need on the run—coats, jeans, shirts and blouses, even shoes. He watched her trying on a black, sporty leather jacket.

"So, this is what you do every time Joe says to run? You go shopping?"

Once they put some distance between them and the office, Alena seemed to relax, although he could see she was as vigilant as a lioness catching the scent of danger. Alena glanced around for the millionth time. "This is the upside of our kind of life. You get to do a lot of shopping." She took off the jacket and tucked it under her arm.

"I have to wonder why you leave everything behind. Kane and the others got close enough to put trackers on us? I mean, I know I met him face-to-face overseas, but don't you think you're a bit dramatic?"

Her face flushed. "Dramatic? You're kidding, right?"

"Look, I'd already be dead if they are tracking me. The fact they didn't find me in Idaho after the bombing tells me they did not have RFID and GPS trackers in place. Otherwise, I would be sucking up dirt right now."

"But they could have tracked us in any number of ways—satellite surveillance, location sensors, you name it."

"I know all that, Alena. My point, they haven't come yet. We might be going through all this for nothing."

"I…Joe and the others can't take that chance. And right now, Joe's calling the shots."

"Maybe he is too careful. Look, Alena, we have to look at this practically. There are endless possibilities for them to track us, but we must look at the percentages. Right now, I'd say the odds are slim they have locked in on us. I think they're just fishing. The net they cast is so broad, going back all those years."

"You may be right, but I trust Joe's instincts." She ran her fingers over an alpaca off-the-shoulder sweater displayed on a faceless mannequin in the aisle. "So, smart guy, dazzle me with your science."

"Dazzle you, huh?" He smiled. "Okay, say I was your husband—"

"My husband? Fat chance."

"Just pretend for a moment. I'd want to keep an eye on your spending spree. I might start with slipping a chip on you. A Radio Frequency ID tag. You have an ATM card, right?"

"Had an ATM card. Left it with the rest of our stuff."

He nodded. "Good, because that's one way of getting to us."

"I thought they had limited tracking capabilities."

"Technology's changed. Now, almost every bank, every financial institution, has the capability of tracking you with that card. Small RFID tags have been inserted in those ATM cards, particularly VIP customers so when you enter a bank, a sensor hidden in the doorways alerts when this card is carried into the bank. A signal is transmitted to bank representatives—such as the manager or tellers—that would allow them to greet important customers by first name and allow them to scan a summary of current transactional history and other information generally only known to the customer."

"I thought Wal-Mart and others just used them for product identification and tracking."

He nodded. "RFID use has been expanded. Theoretically, those tags can be tracked anywhere. Using RFID technology, a manufacturer can trace razor blades you purchased right down to your bathroom shelf. In the past, they've been limited by the signals emitting from the tags and scanners powerful enough to track and locate their product."

She moved farther down the aisle. "So if they know I bought this jacket I'm holding, they could track me anywhere I take it—theoretically?"

"Exactly. That's why Joe wants us to dump our old things and buy new. And this is just the start. RFID and other tracking capabilities have flooded the market. It's in everything. Cell phones, clothing, even woven into our money."

"They track money?" She shook her head. "You are an expert in this technology? I must have missed that in your file."

"It was never my area of interest—I focused in nanosystem integration as it pertained to warfare and nanoelectronics. I knew this technology was out there, but I never paid much attention."

"Well, now would be a good time to start learning. Our lives may depend upon how much you grasp." Her words carried a hard edge. "So, tell me about tracking money."

"I'll let Joe go over all that later when we catch up to them. But I want to look at this with a practical and objective eye. Study the data and determine appropriate responses. To simply toss our belongings every time we smell danger…that's just stupid."

"You calling Joe stupid?" Again, anger flared in her eyes.

"No, but I want us to think in terms of logical and *reasonable* consequences. I know the dangers we face. Any mistake we make, any lapse in judgment, will have catastrophic repercussions. I'm talking arrest, imprisonment…even death. There is a lot at stake. And these guys play for keeps. Winners take all. Losers die. I know all this, but we still must be practical."

She looked away for a moment. "Do not preach to me about the dangers and consequences, Gerrit. Joe and I have been living with them for years. And you…what, less than a week?" There was a look in her eyes as if each word she chose carried with it a history, an event, something painful that underscored her meaning. He could only guess what she was thinking, but whatever it was, those memories must have cost dearly.

He lowered his voice. "I just wanted to make sure we're on the same page. Even though I've been *running* for a few days, I do know the dangers—as a cop, a Force Recon Marine, and a scientist. In Recon operations, I've used satellite tracking stations to hone in on the enemy. Once locked upon a target, I was able to backtrack their movements for intelligence purposes, or hover over their current location until that particular satellite was out of range. I know you've used some of this technology in Israel, too. Tell me, how did you handle our meeting at the airport?"

Alena waited until they'd purchased their items and walked outside, heading toward Union Square before picking up the conversation again. "Prior to contact with you, we needed to reloop surveillance cameras off-site to allow us to spot and track the tail on you—the threesome we tagged."

"Okay, but would they also be able to spot you on camera?"

"Once we locked into the targets and had you sighted, we jammed the signals and made it appear they had a major malfunction. Then we were able to move in and incapacitate the two guys and plant a thumbnail sample of explosives on the woman. That allowed us a brief window of time to have our private sit-down at the airport."

"How did you track those three following me?"

She looked around them, studying each vehicle, each pedestrian. "Joe and Willy will have to explain. They handle the technology; I *handle* the contacts—or enemy. Now, I have to worry about someone planting RFID chips on me."

Gerrit smiled.

"What are you grinning at?"

"I was just wondering where your RFID chips might be hidden. Want me to help search?"

She laughed. "I can take care of myself, thank you. Besides, that is where Joe and Willy—and maybe you, one of these days—come in. Tonight, they will search us and our new belongings to make sure we are clean of bugs before we go anywhere."

"What are they going to do? Strip search us?"

Alena looked at him with mischief in her eyes. "They are going to search you in places where you could never search yourself…and they are going to let me watch."

He eyed her suspiciously. "Why are they going to let you watch?"

She smiled without answering.

Gerrit smirked. "Well, since I need on-the-job training, I'll speak to Joe and see if I can work on you. What do you say?"

"Forget it, Gerrit. Only in your dreams."

Chapter **32**

If Kane's people had tracked their movements, this would be the place for an ambush.

Gerrit watched Alena approach the door. He held his breath as she eased open a gray metal door leading into the hangar, the same location they had arrived from Idaho forty-eight hours earlier. He edged closer in case of trouble, feeling helpless without any weapons. She scanned the area and motioned him inside.

Gerrit glanced at his new watch; it was a quarter past midnight. "Running late?"

She seemed nervous, answering him with a shrug.

"Isn't this risky returning to the same place we used upon arrival?"

Alena grimaced. "I know it's risky, but if we are all clean of tracking devices, we should be okay."

"What if they used some other technique to track us—like satellites?"

"Then we just shoot our way out, Gerrit. How do I know?" She seemed surprised at her own outburst. "Sorry. This whole thing has me jumpy."

A portable MRI machine had been wheeled into one corner of the hangar. He pointed. "Is that for us?"

This seemed to break the tension for a moment. She gave him a quick smile, nodded, then walked to the main hangar door, pushing on a button for a second and then releasing it. The door opened up just enough to see outside. She crouched down and peered into the night. He heard a jet taxiing about a hundred yards away, the sound growing stronger. It was heading toward them.

She studied the approaching aircraft. A moment later, her shoulders relaxed. She sprang to the side and pressed the button to allow the door to open all the way. "Here they come. As soon as they're inside, I am going to shut this door. Keep your eyes open on that back door for anything unusual."

He shook his head and headed for the smaller door. Even if there was something suspicious, what was he supposed to do? No gun. No badge. Couldn't even call the cops. Some army here. Not even a Taser gun between them.

He grabbed the handle and opened the door just a crack and looked outside. Blackness punctuated with stabs of yellow light from nearby streetlamps. No one moving around. As dead as a heart monitor in the morgue.

The aircraft taxied into the hangar, the huge doors swinging closed as soon as the aircraft engines died down. Joe was the first one down the stairs. He hurried toward Alena, where they whispered for a few moments, occasionally turning their attention toward him.

Willy came down the stairs and saw Gerrit standing near the door. He waved and came over to chat. "Wuzup, man?" He gave Gerrit a high five. "See y'all still alive and kicking. That's good."

"Tell me what's going on, Willy. Got that message from Joe."

"Oh, Mr. J will fill you in on everything. Just give him a moment to chat with Al." He eyed the MRI machine. "You ready to get fried?" He jutted out his chin toward the machine. "I heard those things can make a guy go sterile. Any truth to that, Mr. G?"

"I thought you were up on all the computer technology and stuff. You think an MRI will cook your privates?" Gerrit could not hide his grin.

Willy frowned. "You got to be careful with all this stuff. You never know what they got inside these machines." He saw Gerrit's grin widen. "What's so funny?"

"Reminds me of one of the old salts I worked with at SPD. He liked to work motors and used those portable radars for traffic enforcement. One day he backed me up on a call, a domestic violence case where a young punk kept getting in my face. He thought he was a tough guy, and I could tell he terrified the girl. But the guy wouldn't say a thing I could use against him. I knew this clown had been pushing her around, but I couldn't get anyone to say anything. There were no visible injuries, and the house was a mess, so I couldn't tell if he'd been shoving her around the place. I would have to leave without taking action unless one of them came through and gave me a statement."

"So what happened? You have to leave?"

"Nah. The old-timer I was telling you about went outside and returned a moment later with his radar gun. He moved in on this young stud—still sprawled out in the chair without a care in the world—and pointed the gun right at his crotch."

Willy gave him an incredulous look. "What was he going to do with that thing? No power source. It was dead in the water."

"You know that, and I know that, but this piece of garbage in the chair didn't know it. He'd put down a few brews, and his breath was so strong I could have lit up the room with a cigarette lighter. The booze must have addled what little brains this clown still possessed. Anyway, he looks up at my partner and stammers, 'Whatcha gonna do with that, officer?' My partner looks over at me and says, 'Ask that moron one more time what he did to the girl. If he tells you a lie, I'm going to hit him with a blast from this radar gun. This radiation ought to put him out of the baby-making business—for good.'"

"What happened? Did he talk?" Willy looked at Gerrit, then over at the MRI machine.

"Man, that guy low-crawled over to me, got down on his knees, covered his crotch, and began spilling his guts. Gave me enough information that I called a female officer to come check the girl for injuries. Sure enough, that piece of garbage had been hitting her in places where he knew we'd never see and couldn't look without the girl's cooperation. Before we arrived, he'd warned her that if she let the cops take a peek, he would kill her and then start in on her folks."

Willy looked back at the MRI. "Getting back to my question..."

Redneck emerged from the plane, heavy steps causing the metal to groan as he lumbered down the stairway. "You guys miss me?" He acted as if it was a family reunion.

Joe came over to where Gerrit and Willy stood, followed by Alena. She gestured toward the MRI machine. "Well, Gerrit, ready to strip down?"

Joe looked at her. "What are you talking about? That machine's headed for a rural hospital tomorrow."

Willy and Alena looked at each other and began laughing. Willy pointed toward Gerrit. "He thinks we're going to strip him naked and run him through the MRI for bugs and chips? I just played along like I was stupid or something." He wiped a tear from his eye and pulled out a handheld scanner from his backpack. "Here you go. Mr. G. Park yourself over here and let ol' Willy check you out."

Joe stared back. He was not laughing. "Look, we picked up traffic that they planned on sending a team to the cabin in Idaho late last night. We passed it on, and Travis and Frank White Eagle caught a couple of them crossing the river early this morning. The others scattered, and the two they caught clammed up. Couldn't make anything stick. Had to let them go."

Gerrit looked from his uncle to Alena. "They're looking for us."

Joe said, "I think they were looking for you, Gerrit. You contact anyone up there since we left Seattle?"

Shaking his head, Gerrit looked at the others. "What about the rest of you?"

They shook their heads. Alena piped up, "We know better than that."

"So who tipped them off?"

Joe scratched his chin. "Maybe no one. Maybe they found out about the connection between Travis and me and came snooping to see what they could dig up."

Gerrit coughed before responding. "What do we do now?"

Silence filled the hangar. Finally Joe stepped forward, placing a hand on Gerrit's shoulder. "It's time we stopped running and took the offensive. It is time we attack."

"Attack?" He stared at his uncle to make sure the man was serious. "What are we going to attack? Better yet, what are we going to use to attack once we have a target? We don't even have a pea shooter between us."

Redneck drew closer, chuckling. "Man, you have no idea what kind of weapons we have. When Mr. J gives the word, we can go to war with weapons you only dreamed about."

"And who's going to fight this war, R. D.? Willy the computer geek? Alena the book binder? Joe the scientist? And you...what kind of fighting have you done outside of a barroom? No offense, guys, but this is hardly a fighting unit."

Redneck looked at the others. "I think this man just disrespected us, Mr. J. Shall we give him a demonstration?"

Joe shrugged. "Just don't hurt him."

Redneck nodded toward Alena. The next thing Gerrit knew, he was lying on his back, with Alena kneeling on his chest, switchblade pointed at his neck. She had swept his legs from under him in one fluid motion, using his weight to her advantage.

She leaned closer and whispered, "And that's how a chef does it."

Chapter 33

After Alena allowed him to rise from the floor, Gerrit saw they were all laughing. All except Joe. "Are the rest of you as slick as she is?"

Redneck seemed to speak for the group. "Until you joined us, Al and I were the muscle, so to speak, and Mr. J and Pea brain the techno geeks. Now that we've got a jarhead with us, we should be unbeatable."

Willy glared at Redneck before speaking. "Hillbilly, the only muscle you got is between those two cauliflowers you call ears. A waste of space, in my book. Let's line up and get this over with. You first, Mr. G."

Armed with the handheld scanner, Willy searched everyone and their belongings for any readings that might have given them away. He identified and neutralized every signal embedded by manufacturers just to make sure. Once he finished, he let them know they were clean. Thirty minutes later, Joe and Redneck had them in the air.

While Redneck took over the controls, Joe left the cockpit and sat near Gerrit, pulling out a satellite laptop from a carry-all case. "I encrypted this baby to use anywhere in the world. Even if they were able to pick up my IP address, it would be bounced from one part of the globe to the other."

Gerrit leaned over. "What are you planning?" He watched the screen come alive, and a familiar site appeared on the monitor. "NSA? How'd you…?"

Joe didn't answer for a moment as he punched in a series of codes. "The bad guys have their people and we have ours." It looked like his uncle opened up a second program. Once on the screen, it appeared Joe had entered a chat room. Only two people logged in. Joe was obviously one of them. Both active users used a series of numbers as identifiers. "I'm requesting resources to be available when we land. And a search of communications traffic between known identifiers used by Kane—cell phones, IP addresses, the works. I need to find out what information Kane has been trying to access. And what information came to him."

His uncle worked quietly for a few minutes, then paused as if waiting for a response. "I've tried to hold back on this because I am concerned that Kane might have piggybacked his communications with a code that would alert him if anyone else tried to track him. But we need to move forward, particularly since we now know a little about what he's up to."

"Which is what? Trying to find us?"

Joe shook his head. "In the grand scheme of things, we're small potatoes to him. Just irritating flies. Something to be swatted out of the way while he works on bigger things."

"Do you know what he's working on?"

"Remember that project Megiddo?"

"The thing Dad stumbled on?"

"Exactly. After they were…after your parents died, I began searching for a connection between what your dad told me and what happened to your folks. After I recreated myself, I began to develop trusted contacts within the government and business, those I felt I could depend on."

"That's hard to determine, isn't it? I mean, almost anybody can be bought or rolled."

Joe leaned back and squinted. "My, that is a very cynical outlook on God's creatures."

Gerrit stared back. "Tell me I'm wrong, Joe. Tell me there are a lot of people out there you can trust. I mean, truly trust. People who can't be bought, compromised, or just simply paid off to rat on their own mother. It's just the way of mankind."

Joe looked at him for a moment, then leaned over the laptop. "Well, unlike you, I feel I can trust those I befriended over the years. Those I learned to trust in one way or another."

His uncle watched a response come over the screen. "Anyway, I cross-referenced everything your dad worked on and compared it to Kane's life—his business interests, government connections, his communications I could unscramble. Everything."

The jet hit an air pocket and fell for a few seconds. Finally, the aircraft leveled out and Gerrit slowly unclenched his armrest. "So, did you find a lead?"

"Not really. I knew he was interested in the scientific fields your father and I studied. But specifically, no, I didn't find anything. There may be only one place we can get our hands on that information."

"You mean..."

Joe nodded. "Harrogate. It wasn't until he took you to that location that I realized its strategic importance. Not just its proximity to NSA's largest tracking installation in the world, part of ECHELON, with access to all the major world power's intelligence data. But Kane's mansion could become a central clearinghouse for whatever the Megiddo Project sought or a launching site to other locations, other host servers. Plugging into NSA's communications network like some neighbor who runs an electrical cord to your house to tap electricity. Except Kane may have become a part of the household, so to speak. Some very well-connected people may have allowed him to tap into their network from his place at Harrogate. People with the same political agenda—globalization at all costs.

"It wasn't until we tracked you to his place in England that I began to put it together. At least I could guess where he was storing his data and information—none of which was going out over the Internet. That's when I realized he directed the operation in face-to-face encounters with people, very seldom risking exposure by using technology to communicate his ideas and orders. At least until this project Megiddo."

"What changed?" Gerrit leaned back, watching as his uncle continued to search online.

Joe finally glanced up. "Say we're facing a threat of a major WWIII kind of war across the globe. First, military leaders will break down the war into chunks of arenas, say Europe, Asia, North America, etcetera. Within each of these arenas, lines must be drawn and battles waged. But even before all this happens, a massive intelligence operation must be up and running to feed critical information to the command staff, to establish a network of assets and sources, and to acquire vital information about the enemy's tactics, capabilities, and strategy."

Gerrit nodded. "I understand. So, Project Megiddo—"

"Exactly, they are going to use Megiddo to build this massive intelligence base in order to launch an offensive."

"How can they possibly hope to coordinate this on a worldwide front?"

"Through technology used under the operation name of Project Megiddo. At least that's my suspicion. Somehow, Kane's people—or other co-opted scientists—have created a kind of network of proxy servers on steroids, using some kind of quantum-computer breakthrough. I think that is what your dad suspected and began to collect information to prove it."

"I thought we were years away from any usable breakthrough in quantum computers."

Joe shook his head. "We're closer than you think. For example, IBM financed a research group at the Watson Research Center in Yorktown Heights, New York, to actively pursue advances made at Yale University and the University of California, Santa Barbara. University researchers believe that standard microelectronics manufacturing technologies can offer quantum computing using superconducting materials like rhenium or niobium. They face many obstacles, but their findings have been very exciting."

"So," Gerrit said, following his uncle's logic, "if Kane's people have made a breakthrough with quantum computers, they can use this capability to develop an intelligence-gathering tool no one else can match."

Joe looked at him with concern. "That's my point. I believe they already have set up a host of proxy servers to handle and filter all the data they glean from the NSA's system. In some ways, they don't even need NSA; it just makes their search parameters quicker and more efficient. By linking these servers, using quantum capabilities, they can virtually gain access to any system in the world, break it down, manipulate that system, and extract whatever they desire for their own use. And they can do this without leaving a trace in the host server."

Gerrit whistled. "Like using stealth bombers without anyone ever realizing they were there."

Joe nodded. "I believe they have reverse proxies—you know, a computer that appears to be an ordinary server to users—to enable encryption protocols like TLS and SSL to be neutralized and allow access to any secure Web site they choose. God only knows how they plan on using this information."

"I have some good ideas how they might use it. They can gather dirt on anyone, turn them, and then use these assets to gain political and military power. We have to expose this."

"We've got to break into Kane's place in Harrogate to get a better picture of what he's up to."

"Are you suggesting we somehow sneak into that place to steal whatever he's working on?" Gerrit looked around the plane. "With this crew? That's crazy, Joe."

Alena glared at him. "Thanks for the vote of confidence, Gerrit."

His uncle smiled and cocked his head. "You've been in combat many times, son. Are you saying a tiny ol' house in England, protected by a handful of security guards, is going to stop you from saving the world?"

"Saving the world? You have no idea what he's working on. For all we know, he could be working on a new pill that will make the world slim, trim, and attractive. Now, that is something people might kill over."

Joe hit the power button and closed up the computer. "Kane would never have blown up your house and killed your friends and family if the stakes weren't high enough. You might be right about one thing—we don't know specifically what we're looking at, which makes breaking in more challenging."

"Not to mention, we'll be outgunned. I saw some of the security in that place. It's state of the art. Hidden shooters with elevated advantage, walls and doors all heavily enforced. I could go on."

Joe raised an eyebrow. "Makes this operation even more challenging to plan. But first, we need to find out more about Project Megiddo."

"And where we can find that out?"

"Where everything gets channeled through one way or the other. Washington, D.C."

"And who is going to give up this information?"

Joe looked at Gerrit carefully. "The one person who has just realized how expendable he is."

Gerrit suddenly knew where Joe was going in this conversation. "Senator John Summers."

Joe nodded. "And you may be the only one who can make him talk."

Another thought hit Gerrit. "Kane will find out I survived that bombing."

"I believe Kane might already know you're alive," Joe said. "Remember when I said you have to trust someone?"

"Trust a politician? You've got to be joking."

Stretching, Joe leaned back and raised his legs, flexing his feet. "Not a politician, Gerrit. A father. That man lost a daughter to Kane's ambitions. He may still believe it was the work of those Russian gangsters, but sooner or later the truth will break free. You can help him see the truth. If you do that, you can unlock what we have been trying for years to uncover."

Gerrit looked out the side window into the darkness beyond. He wondered about the senator and what the man valued most—power or family.

He'd just have to find out.

Chapter 34

Washington, D.C.

New surveillance vehicles and new faces waited for them as the jet taxied into a private hangar. Gerrit saw a blacked-out Chevy Suburban, midnight blue, and a dirt-spattered white Ford van.

Joe emerged from the cockpit, leaving Redneck at the controls. Joe slid onto the seat next to Gerrit. "Willy did his thing on the computer and tracked Senator Summers to a restaurant just outside D.C. That means he is in town."

"How did Willy...? Wait a minute. You tagged a senator?"

Joe grinned. "Tagging a senator is not all that hard. We snatched one of his credit cards, did a slight modification, and slipped it back into his wallet."

Gerrit raised an eyebrow at Joe.

"Getting into a politician's pocket is easy. We did the dirty deed while he was staying at a really nice hotel after his meeting with you at Dulles." Joe's mouth tightened. "Willy also tracked Kane to D.C. He arrived about an hour ago."

"Kane's here? You're able to track him, too?"

"Thanks to your face-to-face with him, we got close enough to pin down his location and plant what we needed to track him."

"You don't think he might suspect?"

Joe shook his head. "The guy figures he is too untouchable for anyone to get close. What concerns me is that Kane's here…now. Maybe he's having second thoughts about the senator."

"You think they might try to take out a senator? That'd be crazy."

"I don't know what they're thinking. I'd guess he and Summers will have a few words. But if we're lucky, we might get close enough to listen in on Kane's conversation."

"He must be traveling with a security detail. How are the four of us supposed to get close enough for that?"

"We generally never work alone on operations like this." Joe nodded toward the parked vehicles outside. "Those guys only know that they're supposed to report to me—no questions asked. I've been fortunate enough to marshal resources almost anywhere, even other countries, through contacts I've made. That's what makes this whole thing work. We may not be able to be as direct as Kane—who allegedly works as a consultant for any number of federal agencies—but we have our own contacts, our own networks based on those with like-minded agendas."

"Protecting the sovereignty of the United States?"

"And other allies of our government. Like Great Britain, Germany, and France. You can't image the pressure on these countries to bend to a world rule. A one-world government mentality."

Gerrit shook his head. "I'm sorry, Uncle Joe, but I just can't buy this conspiracy theory. I've heard all these wing nuts talking about the Council on Foreign Relations, the Trilateral Commission, and the super-secret Bilderberg Group, organizations supposedly trying to create control and dominance over the rest of the world. As far as I'm concerned, they're a bunch of idiots. No one is going to let our country take orders from a world government. I think Kane and his people are a bubble off plumb if that is what they think will happen."

Joe tapped his fingers on the counter next to him. "Gerrit, we don't have time to go into all this right now. I believe you're wrong…gravely wrong. I only mentioned these contacts so you might see where the lines are drawn. I can't force you to believe that there's a war going on within our own government. That's something you'll have to decide for yourself—if we survive. Until then, I'm going to do my best to keep you and the others alive."

"You seriously believe that what happened to Mom and Dad—to all of us—is connected to efforts by these globalists to control the world? People like Kane?"

Joe stopped tapping his fingers and drew closer to Gerrit. "Not only do I believe it, but I believe you will soon see that I am right. Take a look at what's happened so far. What do you think motivated Kane—and others like him—to take these chances? Bombings? Murder? Theft of technology? Simply to make a buck?" His uncle shook his head. "It's much bigger. The stakes are greater. It's about power and supremacy of a certain ideology. World order. World control."

Joe stood, gazing down at Gerrit. "Just keep an open mind. At this moment, we need to talk with Summers and find out what Kane's up to. Let's get moving."

Alena and the others were already off the aircraft, standing near the vehicles. Several men in casual clothing leaned against the vehicles, arms folded, looking at Redneck with some interest.

As they emerged from the hangar, Gerrit turned to his uncle. "I wonder what those guys think of our little group. Especially Redneck."

Joe chuckled. "My Jewish ninja, my California gangster, and my Chicago head-slammer sure do raise eyebrows. Until they need to blend. Then they leave these surveillance guys in the dust."

Gerrit smirked. "Jewish ninja? Alena? You've got to be kidding."

Joe smiled. "Don't get her mad, or you'll find out the hard way."

As they walked toward the vehicles, Gerrit looked at his uncle. "What's the game plan?"

Joe walked over to the surveillance vehicles, beckoning to one of the men standing near the black Suburban. The man handed him a briefcase. "Our group takes point. These guys will back us up if needed. Otherwise, I want them to stay out of our way."

"What do you want me to do?" Gerrit asked, eyeing the strangers.

Joe placed a firm hand on his shoulder. "You are going to be our star tonight. Front and center." He tossed the briefcase onto the hood of the vehicle and opened it. He reached inside and pulled out a .9mm Beretta. "Here. I want you to have this in case things go sideways at the house."

"What do you want me to do? Shoot the senator?"

After closing the briefcase, Joe turned to him. "I want you to stay safe. Use it if you have to. I just want you to walk out of there alive. After everyone gets some rest, we're going to set up on his house so that you are ready to move tomorrow night when Summers arrives home."

Senator John Summers felt stress tighten his muscles neck as he entered his two-story brick mansion in Bethesda, Maryland. Home at last. After the chaos and noise of his boisterous day on the Hill, he reveled in the silence that greeted him like a long-lost friend. He sent his limo driver and security detail home for the night.

Checking that the readout on the alarm control box read "Armed," he made his way to the bar in his den, pouring a stiff Scotch on the rocks to settle his nerves. The press had been hounding him about Marilynn's death as well as the other deaths in Seattle. They wanted to know whether he was concerned about his own safety, and those newshounds scrambled to wring every morsel of juicy news out of his tragedy. Vultures!

He balanced the drink in one hand as he eased into a leather recliner, yanking on the lever to raise the footrest. He kicked off his shoes and stretched his legs out, flexing aching feet. John placed the drink on the end table next to him, leaned back, and closed his eyes.

"Good evening, Senator. We meet again." A voice cut across the darkened room.

He shot up, dropping his drink and nearly falling out of the chair just as a light flicked on across the room. John struggled to his feet.

Gerrit O'Rourke sat on the sofa, legs crossed, as if he owned the place.

"How'd you…? You're alive."

"Still breathing, Senator. No thanks to you and your friends."

"Me? My friends? What in Sam Hill are you talking about?" It felt like he was staring at a ghost. "They told me you died."

"As Mark Twain once said, 'The reports of my death are greatly exaggerated.'"

"I don't give a rip about Mark Twain. How come they thought you were dead? I mean, Kane told me—"

"Kane lied." Gerrit rose off the sofa and moved closer to John.

"He told me those Russians killed you...and Marilynn."

"If they're Russians, then Kane was the one who hired them. Right now, I don't know who pulled the trigger. But I do know Kane was behind it. In fact, up until a moment ago, I thought you might have had a hand in it."

"Me? You think I might have had my own daughter killed? Are you insane?"

Gerrit edged closer. "Then tell me what Kane told you."

John hesitated as the man drew closer still. John took a step back. "He said the deaths appeared to be connected. That the Russian gangsters retaliated after you killed their boss. Said they'd hit the three of you because of the case you all were working on. I thought..." He fell silent, trying to remember exactly what Kane told him. His face flushed with anger. "That lying son of a—"

"Tell me why Kane seemed to know about the deaths. Think about it, Senator. You do the math."

John looked at Gerrit for a moment without speaking. "What have I done?" Slowly, John sank back into the chair, head in hands, his voice a tortured whisper. "What have I done?"

Chapter **35**

Gerrit didn't want to lose momentum. Maybe the senator had a heart after all. It was time to make his move while the man seemed vulnerable.

Gerrit crossed the room and made a drink for both of them from the wet bar. He felt the handheld radio under his coat and heard someone click a static transmission in his earplug. He hoped Joe and the others were picking all this up.

He glanced over at the senator. The man's shoulders sagged, chest heaving as he tried to stifle deep sobs. Drinks in hand, Gerrit drew near and handed one glass to Summers. "Here, drink this. It might help."

As the senator reached for it, Gerrit's jacket opened to reveal the holstered weapon under his left arm.

"You came into my house armed. What are you going to do? Kill me?"

Gerrit drew back and looked down at the senator. "I didn't know what I'd face here. For all I know, you and Kane were working together to cover up everything."

"You must not think very highly of me to believe I'd be complicit in Marilynn's death." The senator glared at him. "I may be a lot of things, but I'm a father first."

"That was not the feeling I got from Marilynn." Gerrit returned to the sofa and sat down. "She never felt she was good enough for you. Always trying to impress you."

Summers clasped the drink in both hands, peering down into the glass. "I may have pushed her hard, but I did it for her own good. She had the potential to do great things. Maybe even run for office."

Gerrit took a drink before replying. "Yeah, that's quite an achievement, Senator. Look what it got you. Working with bottom feeders like Kane."

The senator scowled. "I have this country's best interests at heart. Always have."

"You mean like selling this country out to those who want our sovereignty to take a backseat to a one-world order?" He remembered what Joe had said, and thought it might be a good time to test out his uncle's theory. See if Joe might be right.

The senator seemed to bite. Summers straightened. "We need to work together as a world community to face the challenges ahead. We cannot be the only gunslinger in town. We need other world powers to deal with terrorism, dictators, and those crazy enough to drag us back to extinction. I'm talking about fanatics like North Korea's Kim Jong-il or Iran's Mahmoud Ahmadinejad."

"So tell me, Senator. How do you and people like Kane propose to create this world community? By lessening our country's ability to protect itself? By allowing others in the world to decide what's in our country's best interests? And at what cost? Just look at what it has cost you already."

The senator stared at him without speaking. Gerrit couldn't tell what the man was thinking. "Tell me what Kane has planned for our future. It looks to me like you have already bought into it. Tell me why he had to kill my father and mother. Why they were so dangerous he had to eliminate them." He realized he was almost shouting.

Summers seemed to shrink in his chair. "I don't know anything about what happened to your parents. Kane said…" And then he stopped speaking. Any anger the man had shown earlier seemed to vanish into the night air. He stared at the floor without speaking.

Any further conversation with Summers would be futile. As Gerrit got to his feet, the senator whispered something. "What did you say, Senator?"

"Megiddo." The man's voice grew stronger. "That's all Kane ever mentioned to me. It was a code name for a project he and others were involved with that would give them the upper hand. Allow them to begin to control the bases of power they needed to create this world power. This world community."

"How were they supposed to achieve this?" Gerrit held his breath, waiting for the man to answer. Naming this Project Megiddo in the context of world domination gave him a chill. Were they dealing with a bunch of suicidal maniacs? He could see Kane in that role.

Summers gave him a dazed look. "It was all supposed to make the world a better place. A safer place." The senator gave a bitter laugh. "Save lives. What a joke. Look what it has done so far. Kane takes the life of my only daughter. What does he have planned next? My execution because I didn't handle her right? Oh, jeez, if he finds out I talked to you—I'm history."

Drawing closer, Gerrit asked again, "What's their plan, Senator? What is Project Megiddo?"

Summers shook his head. "I don't know exactly. They've developed—or are about to develop—a self-replicating technology that can embed itself into any communication system, computer program, or spyware. I don't fully understand its capability, except that they are able to intercept, decrypt, and monitor anyone's communication—online and off-line."

"What do you mean off-line?"

"I mean anything you own that involves technology—cell phones, laptops, eReaders, computers—can be used to intercept anyone's communications. They can gain access to anyone's financial accounts, medical records, tax files—anything you might want kept private—and they can expose it to the world."

The senator shakily rose to his feet. "For all I know, they're listening to us right now. If that program's operational."

"Where is this project housed? And who's working on it?"

Summers gestured helplessly. "All I know is Richard has people coming and going from a place outside Albuquerque, New Mexico. Whatever they are working on can be found there. Kane rarely visits, but he's in contact with someone there on a regular basis. I've been in the room with him when these calls come through. You can tell it's a high priority by the way he acts. I think they must be really close to making this happen—if it hasn't happened already."

Gerrit's radio squawked with a transmission. "Gerrit, can you hear me?" It was Willy's voice, very excited.

In response, Gerrit hit the transmission button twice. He didn't want to interrupt the senator.

Willy almost screamed over the line. "We've got three vehicles bearing down on us at a high rate of speed. Richard's in one of them."

Gerrit wheeled around and faced Summers. "We've got a problem. Looks like Kane and some of his people are headed this way. The way they are traveling, they mean business. I would suggest you come with us."

"Us? There are others with you?"

"Exactly, Senator. And they heard everything we've said."

The man's face paled. "You don't know what you've done. You're going to get us killed."

"Not if we get out of here right now."

"And go where?" The senator rose and screamed at him. "Where could I go to hide from that man?"

"Now would be a good time to find out. Are you coming?"

A look of resignation crossed Summers's face. The man slowly sat down.

"Senator, you'd better get out of here."

The man shook his head. "Nowhere to run that he can't find me." He picked up his drink and took a sip before speaking. "Gerrit. One more thing. Once Megiddo kicks in, watch out. You'll be facing the forces of hell. They'll be able to throw everything at you and anyone else standing in their way. They're about to launch it—any day. Time is running out."

Gerrit spun around and sprinted for the door. As he felt the cold night air, he heard the engines of several vehicles several blocks away. He ran to where Joe and the others sat hidden and jumped inside the vehicle just as Redneck pulled from the curb.

Alena leaned next to him. "We thought you'd never get out of there."

Gerrit glanced back and saw a stream of headlights a block away. Redneck had blacked out their own lights, using moonlight and streetlights to navigate their escape. Joe sat next to Redneck. Gerrit learned forward and touched his uncle's arm. "How did they know we were here?"

His uncle cocked his head to one side. "I think since Marilynn's death—maybe even before that—Kane must have been watching the senator very closely. I wouldn't be surprised if he has the house wired for sound."

"So they know Summers spilled the beans?"

Joe looked back and nodded.

Gerrit settled back into his seat. "Then I just left a dead man back at that house."

Joe looked forward. "I think he was always going to die at their hands. Just a matter of time." He grabbed one of the throwaway phones. "Maybe we can create a little trouble for Kane." He quickly dialed, waiting for the call to be answered. "Hello, Dispatch. I want to report an attempted murder. Someone is breaking into Senator John Summers's residence. I think they're trying to kill him."

He hung up, leaned out the window, and hurled the phone into a field of weeds. Picking up an encrypted phone he always carried, Joe dialed another number. "Hey, it's me. Just left Senator Summers's house in Bethesda. I think Kane is about to take him out. You better start rolling. I'm going to forward a recording of a conversation between the senator and Gerrit. Keep it in a safe place. The puzzle's starting to come together."

Gerrit shot him an incredulous look. "Who was that?"

Joe replaced the phone and stared out ahead of them. "One of the good guys. Someday, I'm afraid, you're going to meet him face-to-face."

"Afraid? Of what?"

Gerrit was met with silence, his uncle motionless, staring out into the blackness ahead.

Chapter 36

Senator Summers finished his drink. Carefully, as if his glass were made of eggshells, he set it down on the table next to him, a trembling hand shaking ice cubes like a gambler rolling dice in a cup.

He flinched when the front door slammed open. Intruders pounded inside, boots heavy on hardwood floors, footsteps echoing throughout the house. Richard Kane emerged from the darkness like an evil apparition, a spirit made of flesh and blood.

"John, you betrayed us." Fury underscored every word.

John's voice, unlike his hands, came across strong, as if he was speaking on the floor of the senate. "We're all traitors, Richard. You, me…all of us."

Richard approached with a semi-auto in his right hand. He knelt down at eye level with John, arms crossed, weapon pointed upward. "Oh, Senator. How I wished you had stayed strong. I wanted us to finish together. But now…?" Richard shook his head. "Now, I must travel alone."

"Just make it quick," John said, his voice now a whisper. "Like you did for my daughter."

"In good time, my friend. In good time. My people have to check out your house. Make sure we have some…privacy."

Collette emerged from the shadows, standing just behind the senator. Richard glanced up. "Did you find anything?"

She drew closer and leaned over, huskily whispering into the senator's left ear, loud enough for Richard to hear. "I found this in his bedroom, Richard." She held up a small revolver with a gloved hand as she ran a finger through Summers's hair. "Hardly big enough to hurt anyone."

She glanced up as Richard silently nodded.

Quickly, she reached down and grasped the senator's right hand around the butt of the weapon. Summers began to resist. With her left hand, Collette drove two fingers deep behind the senator's collarbone causing him to scream in pain and loosen his grip on the gun. She yanked up the gun and shoved it toward his temple, forced his fingers into the trigger well, and squeezed. A blast erupted from the barrel.

Summers slumped in the chair. Dead.

Collette looked up at Richard, her face splattered with blood, eyes gleaming. "I believe a vacancy just opened up in the senate, *monsieur*."

Mirthlessly, he laughed. "And I have just the candidate to fill his shoes. Now, let's get out of here."

Emergency lights from patrol cars and yellow-flashing lamps attached to street barricades filled the night with eerie excitement. Yellow crime-scene tape created an inner and outer perimeter as police and FBI vehicles clogged the streets. A few of the lucky ones were able to drive past the outer line and park in front of the senator's residence.

He drove up to the first barrier, stopping to allow a uniformed officer to peer inside. He patiently held up his identification and badge, waiting for the officer to use his flashlight for illumination.

The officer peered inside the car. "Beck Malloy. FBI, huh?"

Beck nodded, trying to shield his eyes from the flashlight's angry glare.

The officer straightened. "Let me just get you to sign in on this crime log."

Beck shook his head. "Call your boss. Have him speak to the agent running this investigation. Give him my name."

The officer shot him a puzzled look, backing away a few feet while talking into a mike clipped to his shirt collar. He gave someone Beck's name and waited for a reply. "Huh, dark wavy hair, brown eyes, about two hundred pounds, in his forties, my guess." The officer shifted back and forth on his feet, waiting for a reply, then cocked his head, apparently listening to someone through his earpiece. The police officer looked back at Beck, eyes wide. "Yes, sir."

Flashing the light back at Beck, the officer approached. "You can go ahead, Agent Malloy. I guess you're not required to sign in. Really weird. It's like they don't want a record of you. Never heard anything like that in all my years."

Beck nodded. "Appreciate that you checked it out, Officer" He pulled away and drove down the street until he came to an FBI vehicle—a converted RV-size bus—being used as a command post.

He piled out of the car and walked to a side door of the command post. He reached up and flung it open. A large man in a blue FBI Windbreaker stood just inside. The man was on the telephone. "I don't care who they are. Keep all media a block away. If I catch any of them inside my crime scene, I will have you transferred to the Dakotas...in the middle of winter. Forever." He slammed the phone down. Other phones jangled as men and women, wearing identical Windbreakers, jostled around inside as they sought a place to work. The irritated agent spotted Beck standing in the doorway. "Beck Malloy? Let's step outside for a moment."

Beck held the door open as the other man pounded down the stairs, landing on the asphalt so hard Beck thought he felt the pavement shake. "Just got word of this, Ray. Came as quick as I could."

"Just got word?" Ray looked at him with skepticism. "My people say you're the one who alerted the bureau about this fiasco. Give me a break, Beck. How did you know about this?" The man pointed a finger toward the house. "You can't believe the kind of storm that's brewing over this. Every Tom, Dick, and Harry from D.C. is on the phone, trying to get information. Help me out here."

Beck looked at the house. "An informant deep undercover gave me a heads-up. I called PD units to check it out. How'd they do it?"

"They?" Ray looked incredulous.

Beck grimaced. *My big mouth.* He knew where this was going. Joe O'Rourke had called it in minutes before Richard and his people hit the place. He did not mention this fact to the police.

Ray continued to harangue him. "There was more than one? How in the name of everything that's holy did you pull that out of the hat? Is this coming from some of your spook contacts? Counterintelligence? Don't tell me we're dealing with terrorists."

The words just spilled out as Beck watched the man come unglued. "Let's just stick with the facts here, Ray. Tell me what you've found out."

Irritated, Ray rubbed his jaw, eyes narrowing. "Okay. Here're the facts. Victim found in his den, sprawled out in a recliner. No one else at home when officers arrived. Front door wide open. A single tap to the right temple from an S&W revolver, five-shot Model 638, registered to the senator. Found one spent .38 caliber casing in chamber and four live rounds."

"Senator's right handed?"

"My guess. Doubt he did it, though, based upon what you just told me. So you going to tell me what you know?"

Beck shook his head. "Can't, Ray. I'm sorry. Right now, this must remain classified. Dispatch gave the bureau a call, right?" He didn't give Ray a chance to answer. "Cops get here. Find the senator dead. So here we are."

Ray nodded, remaining silent, giving off a look that told Beck the man knew something important.

"What else did you find out, Ray? A witness?"

Almost gleefully, the agent pulled out a clear evidence bag from his pocket. Inside, Beck saw a small electronic device.

"Wiretaps?"

"Federal wiretaps. At least they were federal once upon a time. Stolen from a shipment to one of our no-named spook groups—NSA, DOJ, CIA. You name it. Do you know who might have used these?"

"Not FBI?"

Ray's face tensed. "You tell me, Malloy. How'd you know the senator was in trouble before anyone else—unless you're listening to the wiretap?"

Beck ran a hand through his hair. "Look, I told you. An informant called it in. Swear on a stack of Bibles, I did not know the senator's house was bugged. I cannot reveal my source at this time. He is not involved with Summers's death. That's all I can tell you."

"You mean that is all you're *willing* to tell me."

Beck let the barbed comment go unanswered.

Ray glanced toward the house. "Anyway, we found a bunch of these throughout the house. And one more interesting fact."

Beck looked at the agent, waiting.

"There doesn't seem to be forced entry into the house. But the front door was thrown open with such force that the inner doorknob slammed into the wall. Like someone opened the door with a key, then got mad and kicked it open. Fresh damage."

Several agents hurried past the two men on their way to the outer perimeter. One of the men turned toward Ray. "Sir, the SAC's on his way. I think he is going to handle the media from here."

Ray groaned. "Oh, great. This investigation is going into the toilet fast." He turned back to Beck. "You'd better get out of here while you still have the chance. Once the Special Agent in Charge and his entourage get here, watch out. Everyone better hold their butts with both hands."

Beck reached over and shook Ray's hand. "Thanks for the information. Let me know if anything important comes up. You got my number. I can be reached 24/7."

Ray nodded. "Oh, one other thing. It looks like the senator may have had a visitor just before he got whacked. We found two glasses near his body. Running prints on both of the glasses."

"Thanks. Stay in touch." Beck turned and began walking to his car. As he climbed in, Ray was still watching. Beck gave him a thumbs-up as he drove away. As he reached the corner and began to make the turn, three unmarks with lights and sirens swept past. Beck knew one of them carried the SAC.

The investigative nightmare just got worse.

As he watched them pull away in his rearview, he thought of the information Joe O'Rourke passed his way. Beck eyed the taillights as they grew smaller and wondered who he could trust. For all he knew, one of Richard's men could be sitting in those cars that just passed. In fact, even the SAC could be one of Richard's men.

Beck stepped on the gas to put distance between him and the investigation. When did everything begin to change, when there were no longer clear lines between the bad guys and the good guys? When others—because of wealth, power, and position—were no longer bound by the same laws everyone else lived by? Had it always been that way?

A world of two countries, two governments, two classes. On one side, all the law-abiding, hardworking, taxpaying people who loved this country. And on the other, all the Richards of this world, viewing themselves as unaccountable to no one but themselves.

It seemed futile at times as he struggled to make things right, working with the corrupted system to hold people like Richard to the same standard as everyone else. Beck thought of the cost paid by Joe O'Rourke and his people. Always running, always hiding, always waiting for the executioner's ax to drop. And now, Gerrit had been thrust into that same world.

Beck had been watching over Gerrit ever since he came to know Joe. Now, Richard knew Gerrit was alive. That Gerrit was out there with information and skills that might expose Richard and his people. Unfortunately, Gerrit would now become Richard's primary target, with all the forces that man could bring down. The odds seemed staggering.

A helicopter rushed overhead, its rotors beating the air like a giant hummingbird on steroids. The craft headed toward the crime scene. He pulled out onto Capital Beltway, heading toward D.C.

Last summer, he'd visited New York's Metropolitan Museum where he saw the famous painting of Washington and his bedraggled troops crossing the Delaware to attack British troops. Badly outnumbered, badly in need of supplies, Washington and his Continental Army surprised the enemy and scored a resounding victory with all the odds against them. Just like Joe, Gerrit, and the others.

As Beck sped toward the capital, he vowed he'd do everything in his power to even the score. Until they came for him.

Chapter 37

Richard Kane peered out the window as the helicopter made one more sweep over the senator's residence. Red, blue, and white lights still flashed below, and men the size of black ants crawled around the crime scene. A block away, a parade of media vans blocked the residential street below like one huge parking lot.

Twenty minutes later, Kane directed the pilot to set down at a landing site where a limousine waited. After telling the others to wait in the helicopter, he exited the aircraft and strode toward the car.

He climbed into the vehicle, made sure he was alone, then opened up his laptop, waiting until the video-conferencing software kicked in. An Anthony Hopkins look-alike came on the screen, only he spoke with an Eastern European accent, his suit worth almost as much as the helicopter carrying Richard. "Where are we, Richard?"

He straightened. "Senator Summers just passed on and a major investigation is underway."

"Were you able—?"

"Cops too quick. Somebody tipped them off before the cleanup crew did their thing."

"Is there anything left behind that should concern us?"

Richard shook his head. "Some damage to the front door and…the equipment we left behind. Stuart, I'm sure they'll know it was not a suicide when everything is collected."

"Who alerted the authorities?"

Richard tightened his jaw. "They got to the senator. And Summers shared enough information that we have a situation."

"About Megiddo?"

"Not specifically, although he used the name. He gave up Albuquerque and the capabilities we've developed so we can kick off the project."

A heavy sigh came across the computer as Stuart breathed out. "Do we need to activate the protocol?"

"No. No," Richard said, shooting out the words like bullets. "I'll get this under control. Minimize the damage."

"How do you propose to do that?" Stuart steepled fingers, tapping impatiently. "It seems you've made several mistakes already. Who did Summers reveal all this information to?"

Richard hesitated, not wanting to bring up the subject but knowing it must be answered. He shuddered to think of the consequences if Stuart found other sources. "We know for sure Gerrit survived the blast."

"How do we know?"

"Gerrit confronted the senator in his home. Our spike mikes and video cams picked up his voice and image. Summers spilled this information to Gerrit after the man broke inside the senator's house and waited for him to get home. We can only assume he was wired and transmitted everything that Summers revealed."

Another heavy sigh. "So we can assume this recording is in the hands of whom—FBI, Justice, DIA?"

Richard hunched forward. "My guess is Joe O'Rourke is behind this. He has close ties with someone in the FBI, someone who's been helping them elude my search teams."

"Do we know who this person might be?"

"Not yet, but I have my suspicions. We're working on that. If we can identify this FBI agent, we can use him to lead us back to Joe, Gerrit, and the others. This agent and Joe must have some way of communicating that our systems aren't picking up."

Stuart leaned toward the camera. "Get on this, Kane, and sanitize… everything. Fast. We're days away from springing Megiddo on the world. You have that long to make this good. Or else."

The screen went black.

Richard closed the computer, exited the vehicle and climbed back into the helicopter. As the pilot took off, Richard stared out the thick-paned glass. The lights of the city glittered in the distance. Headlights from vehicles below moved quickly along major traffic arterials, pinpoints of light moving together like an army of fireflies in formation.

Uneasy, he began to map out a plan in his mind, a plan that had so many variables, it made him dizzy trying to figure out each one. Gerrit already knew two weaknesses—Harrogate in England and the lab in Albuquerque. And his uncle was teaching him how to stay alive, to live off the grid, out of Richard's reach.

His one ace in the hole was the imbedded informant in Joe's extended group of acquaintances. Unfortunately, the source must never contact Richard directly unless it was an extreme emergency. Joe O'Rourke and his sidekick Willy posed a threat with all their technological prowess. Richard and the source had to use an archaic communication system to stay in touch. In the past, the source would give him a summary of Joe's activities after the fact. Until now, it helped Richard keep ahead of Joe's meddling. Recent events changed everything. He must get to the source quicker, even if it meant burning that person's cover.

He clenched his hands in frustration. He would have to divide his people in two camps—one in England and the other in New Mexico. He would head for the United Kingdom and leave the other crew behind to cover the lab. Between them, they should be able to lock on to Joe's small army, wherever they might be hiding.

All this money and all these resources, and Joe still continued to elude capture. To be a royal pain in the backside. Richard must bring this to an end, to *sanitize* everyone and everything. Otherwise, Stuart and his organization would make sure that he would be the one taken off this planet.

Permanently.

Richard turned and beckoned to a woman seated behind him. He wanted her close enough so he could speak into her ear above the drum of the helicopter without the aid of headsets. He did not want others to hear. "Collette, can you hear me?"

She drew even closer, leaning over the back of his chair.

As he turned, his lips almost touched her left ear, the smell of jasmine filling his nostrils. "I need you to pull together a team and head down to Albuquerque. If I am not mistaken, our boy Gerrit and his new friends will be sniffing around down there trying to find out where our lab's located. Retrieve whatever resources you need. Locate and take them out. Understood?"

"I saw you take that call in the limo. Any trouble from the boss?"

Shaking his head, Richard played down his fears. "Shoot, that ol' boy thinks the sun comes up just to hear him crow. I'll take care of that end. You just find Gerrit, hear?"

Collette gave him a slow smile. "Can I play with him first?"

He smirked. "As long as he ends up dead, you can do whatever you want."

She raised her eyebrows. "Consider it done. Where will you be?"

"Going back home to England. Need to start ramping up our operations and tie up loose ends. Keep me advised."

"Always here to serve, Richard." She smiled, languidly leaning back in her seat.

He turned and eyed her curves with fond memories, then turned to face the pilot ahead, watching him manipulate the controls as they neared the airport. He must get to Harrogate and make sure it hasn't been compromised. He could have kicked himself for taking Gerrit there. Richard had been so sure the man would work with them—given Marilynn's not-so-subtle charms and other incentives—that he never even thought there might be security issues. He'd misjudged the situation, and now the operation might be exposed.

Trying to control his breathing, Richard leaned back and closed his eyes, listening to the sound of the chopper. He trusted Collette's skills and knew firsthand how deadly she could be. All sweet and nice on the outside, but as lethal as the unrestrained Ebola virus.

Find Gerrit. Kill Gerrit. I will do the rest.

He picked up his cell phone and quickly dialed a number. "Okay, here's what I want you to do," he said, as soon as the person on the other end answered. Richard laid out his plan.

Chapter 38

Richmond, Virginia

Gerrit could smell snow in the air, cold air cutting into his nostrils like a razor. Since they'd pulled into a motel, he sensed the weather might worsen.

Joe rented several adjoining rooms at the far end of the parking lot, away from noisy traffic and prying eyes. Gerrit felt a hand on his arm.

"We need to talk." His uncle led him away as the others grabbed their belongings and trudged to their rooms. "Come into my room for a minute."

Gerrit followed the older man up a flight of concrete stairs and into the room. Inside, Joe turned to Gerrit with a frown. "I'm putting you in charge of this trip to Albuquerque. Give you and the others a chance to work together."

"And where are you going?"

"I'm heading to England. Kane's shield of protection cracked just a tad when he took you to Harrogate. A mistake on his part. I want to take advantage."

"How do you plan on doing that?"

"I actually have some friends stationed at the RAF Menwith Hill site. I plan on setting up surveillance capabilities to identify any visitors Kane might invite to his lair and establish traps to capture electronic communications with others in his group. This is the first time we have had an opportunity to systematically identify our enemy."

"Be careful. Are you taking anyone with you?"

Joe shook his head. "Nah. You'll need all hands on deck in Albuquerque. I'll be fine. I'm not going to do a John Wayne on Kane's place. Just try to find out what we're up against."

As Gerrit turned to leave, doubts started to set in. Splitting up seemed risky. And Joe going solo in Harrogate seemed foolhardy. However, Joe had been doing this for some time. Better not question the teacher until Gerrit knew more.

He got to the door when Joe spoke up. "Oh, wait. I forgot to give you a contact. An Albuquerque PD officer. Here's his number. Tell him Joe sent you and that Oakland Raiders rule. He'll get whatever you need. In fact, I'll give him a quick call to get things started before I leave."

"And what's his name?

"Geronimo Sanchez."

Gerrit raised his eyebrows. "You're kidding."

Joe laughed. "Nope. That's his name. Just don't try to shorten his name to *Geri* unless you want to tick him off. He hates it. His old man tagged him with it when Geronimo was young. Only his family gets away with calling him that."

Gerrit made his way to his own room and saw Alena waiting outside. She watched him unlock the door.

"Joe talk to you?"

He nodded and gestured inside. "Wanna to come in?"

"Only if you leave the door open a crack."

He smiled. "Don't trust me?"

She just laughed.

Gerrit grabbed his bag, followed her inside, and set it on the bed. "Joe said he's headed to England—by himself."

"He told me." She waited a moment. "That makes me uncomfortable. We have always worked together as a team."

Gerrit dragged a chair over for her, taking the edge of the bed for himself. "I don't have a good feeling about it either. No one for backup."

"I know, but he insisted. Claims we are going to need everyone to hit that lab in New Mexico. If we find it, that is. For all we know, Summers might have been, how do you say, full of it."

A knock on the door made Gerrit jerk. The door opened as Willy stuck his head inside. "Hey guys, turn on the tube. Our boy Gerrit's on the news."

Alena and Gerrit exchanged looks. He sprang from the bed and switched on the television. A Fox News anchorman came on, peering into the camera while shuffling papers. "This just in from our reporter Kim Banks outside Seattle Police Department headquarters. Kim, what is the latest on the bombing and murder investigations?"

"Well, Howard, Seattle PD gave a hurried briefing to the press with some surprising information just released. As you know, a joint local, state, and federal investigation has been underway into the brutal murders of federal prosecutor Marilynn Summers, Seattle detective Mark Taylor, and the supposed murder of SPD detective Gerrit O'Rourke, whose home was bombed and the remains of a body recovered among the ruins. And in a related story just in, we've learned Senator John Summers, father of Marilynn Summers, was found shot to death in his Bethesda, Maryland, residence."

The anchorman cut in. "You say the *supposed* death of Detective O'Rourke? Is there any doubt?"

Kim smiled. "SPD spokesman Lieutenant Stan Cromwell brings us breaking news to answer that, Howard."

The screen switched to an earlier recording of Cromwell's press conference. The lieutenant looked older, beaten up, his face contorted with exhaustion and concern. "We have just learned from the coroner's office that the body found inside our detective's resident is *not* that of Officer Gerrit O'Rourke. At this point, we do not know the whereabouts or well-being of Detective O'Rourke. All we can tell you is that the body found inside O'Rourke's residence is that of an identified male adult. We will not be releasing the identity until after the next of kin is notified."

Kim, microphone in hand, cut in as the camera zoomed in on her. "There is some speculation that Detective Gerrit maybe somehow be connected to the deaths of his girlfriend, Marilynn Summers, and his partner, Mark Taylor."

"Any details, Kim?"

The newswoman soberly looked into the camera. "Federal investigators learned that more than five hundred thousand dollars was wired into Detective O'Rourke's account from an offshore business. Investigating further, it has been learned that the source of those funds was an import-export business under the control of a Russian organized-crime group."

"But didn't O'Rourke just shoot and kill Russian crime boss Nico Petrosky?"

"Sources close to the investigation believe there might be an internal struggle for power within that group. To create suspicion elsewhere, they may have paid Detective O'Rourke as a hired gun to eliminate competition."

"But wasn't he a part of a larger task force, armed with a search warrant for that residence?"

Kim nodded. "Yes. But it is believed that O'Rourke may have escalated the situation in order to take out Nico Petrosky."

"This is amazing. So, O'Rourke allegedly kills his girlfriend and partner and arranges for his houseboat to be blown up to make it look like he is also a target. Thank you Kim," Howard said, looking solemnly into the camera while a shot of Senator Summers's residence loomed in the background. "In other disturbing news, federal investigators are launching a full-court press into the killing of Senator Summers. Earlier this evening, there were reports that his shooting death may have been self-inflicted. However, we have learned from sources close to the investigation that the senator's death has been ruled a homicide. The FBI is heading up this multiagency investigation, and they remain tight-lipped about the case. No suspects have been identified at this time."

Howard looked down for a moment as if reflecting on his next words, his brow furrowed. "We can only speculate as to the connection between Senator Summers's death and those in the Seattle area. Two members of the Summers family eliminated in less than a week."

Gerrit stood and turned off the television, just as Joe came into the room, Redneck trailing behind. Gerrit looked at the rest of the group in his motel room. "Well, Kane has just put a target on my back. Every law enforcement agency in the country will be looking to get their hands on me. I would imagine a BOLO is already out."

They looked at Joe. Alena spoke first. "Do we call off this trip to Albuquerque and lay low until we can find out what this is all about?"

Joe raised himself up on his toes, as if exercising a cramp. "Nah, we keep pushing ahead. Laying low is just what Kane wants—to force us into hiding while he tries to clean up his mess. In the meantime, he will be doing everything he can to find us and squash that recording between Gerrit and the senator. Kane's running scared."

"While he is doing all that," Gerrit said, "I'll try to stay out of jail."

Redneck bumped his shoulder. "Hey, Mr. G, jail's not that bad. Three straight meals a day and all the sleep you want." He winked at Gerrit. "You might learn to like it."

Gerrit grimaced. "If I land in jail…if any of us land in jail, we'll be dead. Kane wants to terminate us. And he'll do whatever it takes to hunt us down."

Joe smiled. "I finally made a believer out of you."

Gerrit shrugged. "I've just seen how far Kane will go."

An uneasy silence settled on the group. Joe jerked his thumb toward the doorway. "Come on. Let's get some sleep. We've got a big day ahead of us."

Gerrit watched them solemnly wander out of his room, Joe giving Gerrit a nod before shutting the door.

Joe had placed Gerrit in charge of this operation. It felt like he was back in the military, preparing to go behind enemy lines once again. But now he was leading a group of civilians who seemed to have no training for this kind of challenge.

He hoped they'd make it back alive.

Joe watched his team board the jet bound for Albuquerque. As the stairs retracted, he pulled out his cell phone and dialed a preprogrammed number. A moment later Beck Malloy's voice came on the line.

"Beck, they're just leaving for the lab in New Mexico. I am on my way to check out the jackal's den in Harrogate. I'll keep in touch."

"You going solo?" Concern crept into Beck's voice. "At least let me set up a contact to cover your backside overseas."

"I'll be okay. And I have a contact there if I run into trouble. I'm more worried about our boy and the crew heading for New Mexico. The target had to have heard Gerrit's conversation with the senator. I would bet he already put a hit team together to intercept them once they land."

"That's a high probability, Joe. Our agents found wiretaps in the senator's house. What do you want to do about it?"

A jet roared overhead, drowning out any conversation. Joe waited until the aircraft passed and its blast abated. "Contact our guy at SOCOM. Tell him his favorite Marine is heading into trouble. He and his crew need eyes on their backs without raising any flags with the brass. Keep this covert. Can't let the public know the military is involved."

"Communications will be a one-way street with our contact, Joe. Gerrit cannot be given access to military data. His security clearance with Special Operations Command became inactive when he decommissioned."

"Yeah, but his clearance can be reactivated quickly by the bureau if people like yourself push it. Besides, our contact would never let a security clearance get in the way of protecting Gerrit. They go way back."

Beck hesitated. "With Gerrit being a person of interest in connection to the Seattle murders and now the senator's death, I couldn't get that through the bureau even with the president's help. At least not without raising a lot of eyebrows."

"Okay. Then let our friend with Special Ops handle it from his end like all the others."

"Off the grid?"

"Exactly. It's the safest way for all of us to function right now."

"Consider it done."

Joe killed the connection and tossed the phone and making sure its memory had been wiped clean. Time to pack a bag and visit the enemy's lair.

Richard Kane heard the backblast of jet engines as Collette came on the phone line. "You in Albuquerque?"

"Just arrived, Richard. Any updates?"

"I just learned that the team split up. Joe O'Rourke has designated Gerrit to take the rest of the team to your location and find the lab."

"And Joe?"

"He'll be heading to my location in Harrogate. I'll handle him on my end. You just find and kill that team. I don't want them getting anywhere near that lab. Do I make myself clear?"

"Perfectly," Collette said with confidence. "They won't leave the city."

He cut the connection. His informant came through again. And if Collette failed, he had a backup. The informant would kill everyone on the team.

Chapter 39

Albuquerque, New Mexico

Dry winds and high altitude cleared Gerrit's head as the team exited the plane. A burly man hailed him from across the tarmac. *Officer Geronimo Sanchez*. Joe's description of Geronimo was dead on. Alena, Willy, and Redneck hung back near the plane while Gerrit approached the cop.

Gerrit stuck out a hand. Geronimo, leaning against his car, arms folded, seemed to ignore the gesture.

"Thought you guys would never get here. You ready?"

Taken aback, Gerrit nodded and motioned for the others to join.

Geronimo reached into his car and popped open the trunk. "Throw your things in the back and let's get a move on." The man was all business. "I've set up everything, just the way Joe asked."

Willy was the first to arrive. "So, Geronimo, how did you get that name?"

Gerrit hunched his shoulders. "Leave the man alone, Willy. He's trying to help us."

Geronimo whirled around to face Gerrit. "Stop right there, partner." The cop held up a hand. "No names. Understood? What I don't know, I can't be expected to give up. I'm doing a favor for an old friend. No questions asked. Let's just leave it at that."

Gerrit nodded and the others piled into the car.

Geronimo waited until everyone was settled, then punched the accelerator. He wheeled around a terminal and shot away from the airport as if he could not wait to get rid of them. A five-minute ride found them in a large public parking lot. "Here's your new ride." He screeched to a stop alongside a white van with tinted windows.

Willy groaned as they piled out of the car. A magnetized decal slapped on the side of the van read *Phil's Plumbing: Let us flush your problems away—Cheap and Fast.*

"You gotta be kidding," Willy said. "We're going to run around town pretending to be a bunch of plumbers? This is sooo uncool. Fly in on a fancy business jet and drive out in a plumbing rig that promises to flush our problems away. Give me a break. The ad sucks."

"Well, excuse me, pal." Geronimo glowered at Willy before turning to Gerrit. "It was the only undercover I could snag at a moment's notice. Only the hookers working our hotels know about this vehicle. We used it for a sting operation a few weeks back. I suspect your targets are a step above hookers, so this ride should work."

Geronimo leaned out the driver's window. "Give me a call when you're ready to blow town. Park it right here, and leave the keys in the ignition." He handed Gerrit a sealed business envelope. Gerrit grasped it and felt metal objects inside.

"Keys to a safe house and the address are inside." Geronimo started to roll up the window, then stopped. "You've got my number. Give me a jingle if you run into any trouble. Otherwise—we never met."

With that, Geronimo drove away.

Willy reached down and picked up his bag. "And I was just getting ready to unleash my Geronimo jokes. That would have been a waste of time. I don't think that guy's cracked a smile since Custer's last stand."

Gerrit opened the van's driver-side door. "Get over it, Willy. Climb inside and start working your magic."

Still muttering, Willy opened the side door and climbed into the van and began to gag. "Phew. Someone left garbage in here. It smells like ol'

Phil forgot to flush." Holding his nose, he pulled out his laptop and started to work.

The others climbed in, Alena sitting up front on the passenger side, and Redneck following Willy into the belly of the van. Gerrit turned in the driver's seat and pulled aside a blackout curtain so he could see the two men. "Okay, give us an update."

Willy set his computer on his lap and opened up programs. "I had our home-based computer system begin a search before we took off from Maryland last night. Searching all calls and communications linked to Kane that had any connection to the greater Albuquerque area."

Gerrit nodded. "Doesn't he run an encryption on his system to block such searches?"

"J and W Enterprises will not be trifled with, my man."

Alena caught Gerrit's puzzled look. "Joe and Willy Enterprises. Wasn't Willy exceptionally creative when he came up with that name?"

"Almost as creative as Phil's plumbing business." Gerrit grinned. "Actually, Phil may have been a tad more creative."

Willy scowled at Alena, ignoring Gerrit. "The name is simple and to the point, Al. Don't need more than that in my business." He turned the computer so the others could read it. "Kane did make a bunch of calls here to this unlisted number." He moved the cursor over the number.

"So we don't have the location identified?" Gerrit scanned the computer's display.

"Oh ye of little faith." Willy clicked on the number and dragged it to another screen. "The moron with this unlisted phone number uses a computer-based phone system. I backtracked the IP address with my own magic and traced it to a business just south of here."

"Where is this place located?"

An aerial view from a satellite emerged on Willy's screen. "Way ahead of you, Mr. G. Just got this live feed from one of Joe's friends."

Gerrit eyed him. "Who?"

"Mr. J always says, 'don't ask.' How do I know?"

Irritated, Gerrit glared back. "This is serious, Willy. Whoever's feeding this to you knows right where we are. They can track us."

A gleam of amusement shone from Willy's eyes. "You may have been *Captain America* in the Marines, but in our operation you're still a rookie." He glanced at Alena before continuing. "With Mr. J's help, I've accessed a web of servers worldwide. Anyone tries to track one of my incoming signals is gonna have one heck of a headache. They may wind up sniffing around places like Singapore or New Guinea, thinking they will find me there. Don't worry, Mr. G. We is well protected."

"We *are* well protected, Willy," Gerrit said, smiling.

"Yeah suh, Master G. Yeah suh." Willy shot a grin Alena's way.

She just laughed. "You have just been Willyized, Gerrit. Since we met, Willy earned a bachelor's degree in literature after his computer classes, and he is working on a doctorate online. He has a better grasp of language than most of us." She gave him a look that meant Gerrit had been played. "You just heard his *Uncle Tom's Cabin* rendition. If you try to correct him, his language just gets worse."

A broad grin met Gerrit's stare when he turned toward Willy. "Okay, smart guy. Give me the intel on this place."

The smile slipped away as Willy focused on the computer. "We're here." He slid the cursor over so it blinked on top of the Albuquerque airport. He zoomed in until their van emerged on the screen, shifting the angle so the *Phil's Plumbing* logo became vividly clear.

"That's great, Willy," Gerrit said, "but where's our target area?"

"Man, Joe was right. You are very impatient." Willy shrugged and began shifting images with a few command strokes. "Here we are above the lab. I'll just move us in closer." Fingers sped across the keyboard as Willy entered more commands. A large, single-story building emerged, its structure spread across barren land. He narrowed the picture until they could read the company's sign—Millennium Technologies, Inc.

Willy laughed. "I guess this company thinks they are going to be around for a while."

"Actually, I think they are a bit arrogant using that name," Alena said. "Remember, we searching for evidence of Project Megiddo. For the unenlightened, *Megiddo* is the Hebrew word for the site where the forces of good and evil converge during end times. In fact, I could take you to that site today, if anyone's interested." No one responded, so she continued. "After that battle, Christ will set up His kingdom here on earth where He will reign for a millennium. Somehow, I don't think Millennium Technologies will still be around when that happens."

Gerrit pointed at the screen, trying to ignore Alena's lecture. "Willy, can you zoom in on the building's features?"

"Can a cop find a donut shop?" Willy glanced up with a challenging smirk. "Oh, sorry, Detective. Just joking." He shifted his gaze back to the screen. "Here you go."

Gerrit whistled as the image cleared. "This place looks like Fort Knox." A high cyclone fence, crowned with thorny concertina wire, stretched the perimeter of the complex. It looked like a prison. Only one break in the wire where a single roadway led past a guard shack, the road broadening to create a small parking lot. All vehicular traffic could easily be searched coming and going from the only access point.

"There," Gerrit said. "Show me the area between the guard shack and what appears to be the front entryway." He pointed to the front of the complex.

Again, Willy's fingers worked the keyboard. The view shifted to reveal a small parking lot in front of the entryway, with an interior cyclone fence standing between the parking lot and the rest of the complex. It appeared passengers must leave their vehicles and pass through a second sentry gate before reaching the building.

"Man, that is tight security." Redneck leaned over Willy for a better look.

"Do you mind moving back, Hillbilly?" Willy glared up at him. "Your breath smells like a garlic factory."

Redneck moved in closer. "Oh, come on, Mr. Geek. Let me plant one on you."

Willy pushed him back. "I'm serious, *No Neck*. Give me some space."

Gerrit grimaced. "Come on, guys. Let's focus on the target. You two lovebirds can take this up some other time."

Irritated, Willy peered at the scene and entered more code commands. "Okay, I'll scan the perimeter so we can see what we're up against." He drew the image back so they could see the area between the inner fence and the building's exterior.

Gerrit pointed at the upper right of the screen. "Get me a clear view of that pole. They've ringed the building with a series of concrete poles. I need to see what's on them."

Like adjusting binoculars for a closer look, the computer image expanded as a single pole emerged. A floodlight could be seen attached to the very tip of the pole. Just below the light, strapped to the pole, surveillance cameras could be seen on either side.

Gerrit drew closer, smelling a hint of garlic. "Willy's right, R. D. You need to brush." Willy chuckled as Gerrit peered at the surveillance equipment near the lab. "Those cameras are giving them a 360 of the area around that pole. The next pole's cameras must pick up any dead spots the first ones missed."

"Do you want to see what they can see?" Willy smirked at him.

"You can get into their system?"

"Does a bear—"

"Skip the jokes, Willy. Can you get me a look inside?"

"Can a—?" Willy stopped midsentence when he saw Gerrit's expression. "Sure thing, Mr. G."

A few minutes later, Willy handed the laptop to Gerrit. "Here ya go. Search away. See the camera stations listed along the top? Just point and click. If you hover over the site number, a window will appear to show you what you will be looking at and the location of the camera."

"Say I want to go to the plant manager's office."

Willy reached over and moved the mouse to a midpoint. "Looks like they're divided between interior and exterior locations. The interior are placed in geographical order. Here, start at this point."

Gerrit watched as the first web cam popped up on the screen. It was a hallway in which he could rotate the view as needed. He manipulated the controls until the lens rested on a door identified as leading to the office of *Security Management.*

"While I poke around on this screen, I have a job for you and Redneck." Gerrit crawled back to where the two men sat. "Alena, take the driver's seat. Start looking for a car rental agency. There should be one near the airport."

He turned to the guys. "We need to pick up two chase cars to go with this van. Alena can stay here with me, and you two split up after renting the cars and go solo. Willy, you have the handhelds handy? Everybody pick one up and stay in contact."

Alena slid over and started the engine.

Gerrit continued. "Now, while she's looking for a rental place, Willy, you help search this plant for weaknesses we can exploit."

They began scanning the entire structure, searching each office before continuing to the next. Gerrit turned to Willy. "How can you do this? I mean some people have a problem just getting online while they're traveling. Here, you're accessing the plant's interior security."

Willy gave him a sly smile. "I can get inside just about any security system while miles away." He motioned to portable server he stashed in back. "That is J & W Enterprises own special creation. A mobile server that only needs a power source and provides wireless access to any nearby network. Once we're hooked up, I target any place anywhere in the world. Cool, huh?"

"Yeah. But how do you gain access to this plant, for example? Their system must be self-contained. No hard wires to the outside."

"It's the beauty of wireless, baby." Willy seemed to jump around in place with enthusiasm. "Mr. J. and I figured out how to piggyback on any wireless connections, even though they're only transmitted to on-site locations. With our *special* contacts, we can have a satellite listening station zero in on a specific location, amplify the wireless signals, and transmit those signals back to us. We scan them until we lock into their system network, feeding back whatever we want to see. Just like now."

Gerrit smiled. "Amazing. And you can do this from any location in the world?"

"As long as we connect with the satellite as it is rotating above the target. Impossible if the satellite is on the other side of the globe. Then we need to shift to another eye-in-the-sky orbiting in direct range to the target."

"And who are these sources?"

Willy shook his head. "You're gonna have to ask Mr. J for those. He just gives me the coordinates to access when needed. He keeps all the contacts to himself in case one of us gets captured."

"What if Mr....Joe gets snatched?"

"Then we're up a creek without a paddle."

Gerrit turned back to the screen. He thought of Joe on his way to England. He realized the weakness in their network. If something happened to his uncle, he and the others would be left without any contacts. More important, they would not know who to trust. Joe only left him one name. *Beck Malloy.*

Gerrit focused on the target, trying to shake the thought from his mind.

Chapter 40

A white-coated lab rat kept sneaking glimpses of Collette as she moved around the room, a man who could only dream of getting close to a woman like her—under any circumstances. She smiled to herself as she eyed him in the glass of one of the blank screens. *Men are so weak.* She learned early to use their weaknesses to her advantage. It had served her well.

"Now, you're sure there is no way outsiders can invade this room with surveillance equipment. I don't want them to catch me visiting this plant and I need to monitor whether we have any electronic intrusions here."

The lab rat looked at her, his face reddening. Her glare probably made the guy believe she could read his dirty thoughts. "I'm sure this is safe, miss…"

"I need you guys to be able to tell me if anyone—anyone—tries to invade our security system. Let me know immediately."

Lab rat shook his head. "Yes, sir…huh, miss."

Folding her arms, she studied the screens that recorded all movement inside and outside the building. Her cell phone vibrated. She picked it up, listening for a moment. "Good. Have them escort you here with your equipment. We'll set up shop in this room. I'm told there's no monitoring here and you'll be shielded from any external surveillance. I want you to make sure."

Shoving the phone back into her denim trousers, she watched Lab Rat eyeing her reflection. "Like what you see?"

The man hurriedly focused on the live screens in front of him.

A tap on the door prompted her to open it. "Come on in, guys." She turned toward Lab Rat. "Okay, now that you got an eye full, get out of here and let my team take over."

The man's face looked the color of a red tomato as he scurried from the room. Her team filed in and slammed the door shut.

"I think we got beat, guys." Gerrit turned the screen so the others could see. "Can you rewind that last bit of surveillance tape?"

"Sure thing, Mr. G." Willy's nimble fingers danced across the keyboard, sending the figures on the screen moving backward as the tape rewound.

"There, stop it right there. Now, start the tape. When I give the word, freeze it."

Willy nodded as he punched in codes. The computer screen picked up a signal beamed to them by a surveillance camera in the hallway just outside the plant's security office. Several men carrying large bags worked their way down the hall toward the camera. One of the men tapped on the door with his knuckles. The door opened and a woman emerged.

"There. Freeze that."

Willy complied.

"Great. Now, zoom in on her face."

"Okay." Willy zeroed in until her image took up the whole screen.

"That's her! Kane used this woman in Vienna. She's the one who visited my hotel room." He saw Alena give him a hard look. "Hey, I thought you guys were watching." He saw her eyes cloud. "I guess you weren't watching that close. She left a few minutes after knocking on my door."

Redneck drew closer. "Wow. She looks like she could give Al a run for her money. And you let her get away?" He gave Gerrit a wolfish look. "Yeah, right."

Alena scowled, looking at Collette's face. "So, she came to your room and you...what?" She turned her head toward him, waiting for his answer.

"I think Kane used her to set me up." Gerrit pointed at Collette's face, tying to steer the conversation back to their operation. "This confirms they know we're here and that they heard the conversation I had with Summers before they killed him."

Redneck gestured toward Gerrit. "So what? We go in, find out what we need to know, and get out. If they get in the way, I'll take them out. Very simple, jarhead."

Willy jerked. "Hey guys, we've got trouble."

Gerrit looked his way. "Speak to me, Willy."

"They sent out electronic probes, search signals to read whether someone has tried to enter their system through unusual channels."

"You mean like through a satellite feed?"

Willy nodded. "Exactly. They're more sophisticated than I gave them credit for. They might be almost as smart as Joe and I."

"Almost?"

"Yeah, Mr. G. Almost. They can track my signals. They only know that I've somehow invaded their system. I see them searching, but they're coming up empty."

"Can they track it to where we are right now?"

Willy stared at him as if Gerrit had just suggested the pope sanctioned sin. "Not in a million years."

Gerrit looked at the screen. "This still is not good news. They suspect we're coming and they'll take every precaution to prevent us from getting inside."

Alena shifted in her seat. "So what are we going to do?"

Leaning back, Gerrit looked at each person in the van. "We're going to figure a way to get Alena and me inside. Let's pack it up and find a motel."

Alena shot him a look. "I thought we were using the safe house?"

"Change of plans," Gerrit said. "Just want to switch it up in case anyone has tapped into our plans."

Collette walked over to where one of her crew sat in the chair vacated by Lab Rat. She leaned on the man's shoulder. A large laptop, bulkier than the ones most people carry around, sat on the counter in front of him, line tied into the plant's network system.

"They're gone, Collette. They pulled their probes back and cut the signal. They've vanished."

She slapped the counter. "They are still in the area because they have not gotten what they came here to steal."

The man nodded and turned back toward his computer.

Collette fumed. *Just show me your face once, Gerrit. That's all I ask. Just give me one opportunity to kill you.*

She pulled over a rolling chair and settled in. They had to come to her. And she would be waiting.

Chapter 41

Harrogate, England

Morning was only hours away, but he still hadn't been able to sleep. Joe O'Rourke eased back on the soft pillows, his legs sprawled out on a four-poster, queen-size bed. The Harrogate bed-and-breakfast he'd found online lived up to its high customer ratings, and it was only a few blocks from the center of downtown.

The grueling commercial flight had been stalled for four hours in New York, and then his luggage had somehow been shipped to another airline. He'd kept his laptop and electronics in a carry-on or they might have been lost.

The lost luggage would never be reclaimed because he could not risk leaving a correct forwarding address where he might be contacted. Tomorrow morning he'd pick up a few essentials. Now, he just wanted to rid himself of this brain-numbing headache that plagued him since he got off the plane.

He looked at his passport under the name of Frank Malone. Alena created it just before they abandoned the San Francisco office. No one should be able to track him here in England.

Sitting up on the bed, he opened the laptop, quickly accessing his e-mail account, also listed under an alias and an IP address rarely used. It was an electronic dead letter drop he and the others set up to keep in touch. One of many. When the e-mail program opened, he saw a new document sitting in the Draft file unopened. He clicked on it and saw Willy's avatar on the page with no name. *Captain America*. He scanned down to the message.

Located site. Set up to watch. G wants you to know that C from the Vienna hotel is here with her people. Watching and waiting. G and his girlfriend are going to pay C a visit. They just need to figure out what kind of gift to bring to the party. Stay safe.

Joe stared at Willy's note for a moment before deleting. Kane's people beat them to the lab. He thought of that implication. It was not surprising that they had the senator's house wired up since they trusted no one. So Kane knew Gerrit was alive and connected to Joe and the others.

Kane must know the gang traveled to Albuquerque based on Summers' information. Joe leaned back, resting his head on the pillow once again, his temple beating a dull, painful rhythm. He tried to inventory all their operations, all communications, all points of possible invasion by Kane and his electronics. This has become like a *Star Wars* battle where one needs to worry about more than just linear surveillance. More than just the car tailing behind you or the person peering into your house from a parked vehicle.

Today, everything must be brought into question. When they moved in for contact with a subject or conducted surveillance, they must be worried about a spy satellite thousands of miles overhead or a flea-sized chip tracking their every move. And then they had computers to worry about, an industry that he'd spent most of his life trying to protect people from invasive electronic spying.

People have become extremely vulnerable. Since no one could ensure any privacy, the enemy could use almost anything to spy and invade another person's private life. Even a person's deepest thoughts or fears could be scanned and analyzed by skilled interrogators. Advanced interrogation techniques could render anyone vulnerable. What would it take to break him down? How might he be turned?

Joe closed his eyes and thought how easily he'd been frightened as they dangled him in the air, threatening to drop him onto the concrete below. He learned something about himself in that moment. That he could become a coward. He learned that fear could cripple him. Next time—and with Kane there would be a next time—he might be able to stand firm. Overcome his fear. How much could he take?

An involuntary shudder swept through him. He opened his eyes and put his hands on the keyboard. Quickly, he typed a draft of his own.

The Eagle has landed. Operation look-see about to begin.

Richard Kane met his visitor at the door of the Harrogate mansion. Others bustled with activity around them as he greeted his guest. "George, so kind of you to meet me here. Let's go down to my office where we can enjoy some privacy."

George Lawton shook Richard's hand. "MI6 is always here to serve, Richard."

He smiled and ushered the other man to the elevator. They did not speak again until reaching his office below ground. Once seated, Richard leaned on his desk, staring intently at Lawton. "Any leads on your end regarding my target?"

"This guy Joe O'Rourke?" The intelligence officer shook his head. "If the bloke came in country, he did so under our radar I'm afraid. Checked all incoming flights from the greater New York area, using facial recognition, document profiling, and travel habits. Maybe this guy didn't come in after all. You think they deployed an invisible in this case?"

Richard raised his eyebrows. He knew what the Special Branch officer was suggesting. They may have used someone from inside England, an agent that could operate inside the UK without arousing suspicion because of their nationality of origin.

He shrugged. "Doubt it, George. When Gerrit came here for a visit, their crew left signatures to indicate they'd tracked him here. You came across some of that intelligence. Questionable documents, similar travel routes, electronic signals caught near our London safe house as well as our chat here in Harrogate. They were slick enough to cover their tracks, but it was obvious they used foreign nationals to run their operation. If they had an invisible here, my source would have known."

"So, are you picking up any of this right now?"

Richard folded his hands and rested them on the desktop before answering. "As of last night, we began picking up signals. Someone is close and trying to search for any electronic weaknesses we have on-site."

Lawton gave him an uneasy look. "Right now? They got someone watching you?"

Nodding, Richard eased back in his chair. "Based on the level of activity, my guess is there is only one operative. My people tell me they should have a lock on this person before the day is out."

"And once you find this person—what then?"

"Do you really want to know, George?"

The other man's features clouded as silence followed the question.

Richard knew George's unspoken answer. *Kill him!*

Joe studied his screen intensely. He picked up short bursts of electronic signals ever since he came online about an hour ago. One possible explanation was that Kane's people were searching for any intrusive signatures, trying to determine if someone was trying to gain access to their system. His firewall and access to reverse proxy servers leading to other sites protected him from them locking down his position. He must work fast in order to get in and get out without leaving behind any more telltale signatures.

A few minutes later, he backed out and shut down his exploratory program. Senator Summers's revelation to Gerrit about Project Megiddo had given Joe more information that even Willy and Gerrit realized. Kane's self-replicating spyware and lightning quantum calculations might be able to find a way to track Joe's digital trail. In order to break that link, he pulled out and shut down for short periods, scanning his system to detect any weaknesses or viruses. If his system became vulnerable, they'd be able to slip inside and corrupt or monitor his whole operation.

He had to make sure this never happened.

Joe called up another electronics mail drop and pecked out a quick message:

Target at my location may be aware I am in area. They cannot locate…
if I stay vigilant. Concerned about our birds out west. Gal from Vienna
spotted on-site. You have location of lab. Send them help through our
ops contact. Keep them safe. Thanks.

As he hit the Save button, he hoped Beck remembered to check his messages. Joe shed himself of that concern and began to relax, knowing this man always came through. He never knew much about Beck's background for security reasons. But he knew if the man got this message, Gerrit and the others would have their backs covered.

Beck Malloy always came through.

Chapter 42

Albuquerque, New Mexico

A timid knock on the motel room door forced Gerrit to sit up and clear his head. He'd just closed his eyes for a moment. The others were in their own rooms. Maybe one of them came back to give him an update.

He rose and opened the door. A maid gave him a shy smile and handed him a piece of paper. "A man…he give me this for you, *señor*. Okay?"

Gerrit sleepily nodded thanks and accepted the folded paper before closing the door. He unfolded it and read the scrawl inside:

G.

Meet me down the hall in room 34, upper level. Now! Need to bail you out again.

Jack

Semper Fi

Confused, Gerrit read the note once more. This could only be one person. Major Jack Thompson, USMC, his old commanding officer now located at SOCOM. Here? In this motel? He tensed. If the major knew he was in this room, then the guy must know about the others. As he folded up the paper, another rap on the door drew his attention. He opened the door. Alena.

"We heard a knock on the door and some voices. Everything all right?"

He showed her the note. "I think I know who this guy is. And if so, we can trust him…I think. After everything else I've seen, I'm just not so sure anymore."

"Need me to go with you?"

"Nah. But alert the others. If I run into a problem, you guys jam out of here. I wish we were prepared to defend ourselves right now. That was the next thing I was trying to work out with Geronimo."

"How did this guy know we were here?" She seemed to be thinking about that question for a moment. "Maybe Joe sent some backup. He knows Kane's people are here."

Gerrit shoved the note into his pocket. "That's what I'm hoping. Best-case scenario, Joe sent in the cavalry. Worst-case scenario, Kane knows where we are."

"But if that weasel knew where we were holed up, he would just send in his people and take us out."

"Let me see if this is the guy I know. If not…"

Alena gave him a quick hug. "Stay safe." And then she was gone.

He walked outside, closed and locked the door. Quietly, he walked toward the room identified in the note. The door to room thirty-four was recessed, and he couldn't actually see the door until he was right on it. Curtains to the right of the door were closed, the window sealed up. Gerrit tried to glance at a crack between the two panels of curtains. Only darkness. Once he opened the door, anyone inside would have the advantage. It would take his eyes several seconds to adjust to the darkness once he crossed that threshold.

Major Jack Thompson always maintained tactical advantage. Gerrit smiled as he thought of his old commanding officer. Tough as nails, the major earned the respect of everyone under his command by never asking them to do something he wouldn't do himself. Like running twenty-six miles in full battle gear as they sweated through ninety-degree weather. Or taking on a full complement of Taliban killers with a handful of men during a bitter-cold Afghan winter.

Gerrit took a deep breath and knocked on the door. He heard a deep growl inside. "Come on in, Marine."

Smiling, he turned the knob and stepped into darkness.

"Shut the door, Marine. You want to invite Charlie."

Gerrit closed the door. "We're a long way from Vietnam, Major."

A second later, a light came on. Jack Thompson stood across the room, his hardened face breaking into a grin. "Losing your touch, Lieutenant. Never let the enemy get this close to your people."

"Never thought of you as the enemy, Major."

"I'm a colonel now, son. Gotta keep up."

"Congratulations, sir."

"Stow it, Marine. They thought this old leatherneck might ride a desk for the rest of my career and quit causing them problems. In their dreams."

"Still in Special Ops?"

He nodded. "They'll have to drag me kicking and screaming from that post. The day they move me inside is the day I leave the Corp."

"Never thought I'd see you retire." Gerrit crossed over and shook hands. "Good to see you. But a little surprised that you showed up here."

Jack smiled. "Bet you are, boy. Couldn't believe I could get this close to you without setting off an alarm. You need to run a tighter ship."

Gerrit turned his palms upward. "I'm running nothing right now but a look-and-see op. What brings you here, sir?"

"My man Beck Malloy tracked me down after he got a message from Joe. Yeah, I know him, too. Beck said you and the others might be running into some flack?"

Gerrit shook his head. "I keep hearing about this guy, but so far we've never crossed paths."

"Better that way," Jack said. "Need to compartmentalize these kinds of operations, much like the spooks run theirs. *Need to know* and all that."

"So how much do you know about what we're up against?"

"First, sit down and let me tell you a few things."

They pulled up a couple chairs and settled in. Jack gave him a sober look. "I've had my eye on you ever since our first operation together. Your dad came to me and asked that I watch your back. He wouldn't say much, except he was concerned that others might try to get to him through you."

"My dad came to you? He never said anything about it."

"That's the way he wanted it. And after he died…" Jack paused for a moment. "When Tom was killed—after you returned to the States—your uncle paid me a visit with the same request. Later, he put me in contact with Beck."

"Like I said, I've never met the guy."

"Kind of strange bird. Can't really find much about him. Even through my connections through SOCOM. This guy's a ghost."

"He sent you here?"

"Your uncle, through Beck, sent me here. Small world, huh?" Jack stretched out, flexing his back. "So, give me the lowdown on your operation. How can I help?"

Gerrit laid out what they'd found to date about Millennium Technology and the security layout at the plant.

Jack saw Gerrit smiling. "What's so funny?"

"Come down to my room, sir. I wanna introduce you to the rest of the team."

"I hope you're not hooked up with a bunch of hippies and fruitcakes. I've heard stories."

"Oh, I think you'll find them very interesting. Not your run-of-the-mill Marines. But I think they'll do just fine against Charlie."

Jack eyed him suspiciously. "Whatcha got me into, son?"

Gerrit just shook his head. "Come and see, sir. I guarantee this group won't bore you."

Chapter 43

Gerrit watched Jack Thompson and the others eye each other like boxers entering a ring before the first round. Maybe he was wrong. Jack and Redneck seemed to get along like oil and water. The colonel and the giant looked like they wanted to exchange blows. Gerrit had to find a way to pull everyone together.

"Look," Gerrit said, "I know Colonel Thompson from my days with Special Ops. He's a good man, and I'd follow him into combat anywhere. And make no mistake about it, that is exactly what we face here at Millennium Technologies. It was pure luck I spotted Kane's gal Collette. She's a stone killer in my book, and she has all the resources of Kane's people behind her. So whatever help the colonel can bring to the table, I gladly accept. Everyone on board with this?"

Alena and Willy nodded their consent, but Redneck didn't budge. Gerrit saw a gleam in the big guy's eye that meant trouble. "Spit it out, R. D. What's eating you?"

The giant pulled his attention away from Jack and focused on Gerrit. "It's one thing for you to be calling the shots, jarhead. It's quite another for Mr. Stars & Stripes here to join our party. I don't know him from Adam. For all I know, he's been riding a desk his whole career."

Jack bristled. "Look here, you dimwitted monkey. I won't take any lip from some overweight bar brawler. I only work with someone who'll follow orders, not whine when things get tough."

Redneck's fists closed like two sledgehammers.

"Hey, you guys. We're supposed to be on the same side." Gerrit turned to the big man. "Look, Joe trusts this man. I trust him, and I've been through more than one operation to know this guy is tough. He can help us pull this off with minimum casualties."

He turned to Jack. "Sir, Beck Malloy and Joe have depended on this group to carry off some very tough assignments—including saving my life up in Seattle. I trust them...and I'm asking you to do the same."

The fight seemed to slip from both men's eyes. Redneck's hands relaxed, the man looking at the others. "If you guys wanna work with this guy, then I guess I can, too."

Jack's muscles eased. "Okay, Gerrit, tell me how you want to tackle this op. Let's figure how to get you in and out in one piece."

Gerrit motioned for everyone to gather around a table in the motel room. He laid out his plan, eliciting support information Jack might be able to supply.

Gerrit looked at each member of the team. "I've got to be honest. Based on these plans and the tools Jack brings to the table, we have a 50 percent chance of success. Timing and surprise must be on our side. We'll have a small window of opportunity to make this work. Otherwise, our chances of success drop to 10 percent."

Alena looked at him. "Fifty percent is not good odds. Ten percent..." She just shook her head.

"That's why it is so important that we work together on this," Gerrit said. "Understood?"

Everyone nodded. His estimates made everyone seem to finally draw together. Even Jack and Redneck seemed to be getting along by the end of Gerrit's presentation.

At least for the moment.

Darkness had fallen, and the others had returned to their rooms to get some rest. Jack lay sprawled on Gerrit's bed, snoring, after their strategy session, staying close in case they needed to move fast. Gerrit paced his room, trying to make sure he'd thought of all the contingencies they might face.

He heard the tires of a vehicle rolling across the parking lot. He opened the curtain and peered down from the second floor. A marked police vehicle pulled next to their van, and an officer had quietly opened his door and drawn his weapon.

Gerrit pulled back into the darkness of the room. "Jack, wake up," he hissed, never taking his eyes off of the officer below. The cop approached the vehicle, flashing a light inside the van before reaching for his shoulder mike.

He's calling it in. Did Geronimo sell us out?

Jack stood next to him. Gerrit had never heard the man get up and cross the room. "What do you have, Lieutenant."

Gerrit motioned toward the scene below. "We need to get out of here. I think we've been made."

Jack nodded and snatched up his bag. "Get the others. Meet me in the back lot behind the motel. I'll be standing by my ride. A tan unmarked."

Gerrit nodded, opened the front door, and edged along the outside wall, keeping out of sight from the cop below. Several minutes later, he alerted the others and they quickly snatched up their belongings. He led them down the hall, turning right into an intersecting hallway that spilled into a rear parking lot.

He started down the stairs when a second patrol unit pulled into the back lot. It slowly rolled through the lot, flashing it spotlight on each car. The light illuminated Jack, sitting in a desert-colored Buick sedan. The officer must have spotted the colonel because brakes screeched as the squad car came to a stop. Jack emerged from the vehicle.

Gerrit crouched—motioning for the others to pull back into the shelter of the hallway—as he peered around the coroner. As Jack stepped around his car, the officer sprang from the patrol car, hand resting on the butt of his gun.

"Good evening, Officer. Can I help you?" Jack's voice boomed out across the parking lot.

"We got a call about a possible stolen vehicle, a van, parked on the other side of this building. Did you see anyone drive up in a white van? It has *Phil's Plumbing* on the side."

"No kidding? Stolen, you say?" Jack scratched his jaw. "Can't say I've seen anything. I just came out here to get away from the grandkids. Taking them all the way to Disneyland—a trip of pure torture, if you know what I mean. I've just been sitting out here a few minutes, trying to get a bit of peace and quiet. Haven't seen a soul."

The officer studied him for a moment, then walked back to his car. A vehicle pulled in behind the police car. A police unmarked? Gerrit tried to peer past the cop's headlights and focus on the car. He heard a car door open and a man step out. Another car across the lot started up and headlights flicked on. The headlights caught the surprise in the man's face.

Geronimo Sanchez.

Geronimo walked up to the police car and spoke quietly to the cop. The cop nodded. Both men returned to their vehicles and slowly pulled around to the other side of the building.

Jack climbed back into his car. At least the Albuquerque cop never knew Jack was a part of the team. That would buy them a little time.

Gerrit motioned to the others. They hurried down the stairs and jogged to Jack's car and climbed in just as another patrol vehicle came into the lot.

"Get down," Jack hissed, eyeing the patrol unit slowly approaching. The others sank as far down in their seats as they could. Gerrit heard Willy whisper, "You're sitting on my face, Redneck. Move over."

"I can't," the big man muttered. "And if you don't shut up, I will make sure you'll regret it. I had beans for dinner."

Jack leaned back. "Would you two shut up. The cop's coming our way." He stepped outside and pretended to lock the car. He walked back toward the hotel, just as the patrol car edged past.

Gerrit peered over the dash and saw that Jack had positioned himself on the far side of the patrol vehicle, drawing the officer's attention away from their car. The officer leaned out to talk to Jack when it appeared the officer received a radio call. He gunned his engine, driving rapidly to the other parking lot.

Jack sprinted back to the car, turned on the engine, and hurriedly drove from the lot. "Someone called in two suspicious people near our van, trying to break in. A big white guy and a skinny black guy."

"We were nowhere near the van," Redneck said.

Willy muttered something as he pulled himself up. He leaned forward. "You think Geronimo snitched us off?"

Jack shook his head. "The cops didn't even know the van was theirs. If Geronimo wanted to take us out, there were quicker ways to do that without involving the van. That would only lead back to him. The van is too conspicuous."

"Tell me about it," Willy said, making a sniffing noise. "All they'd got to do is follow their nose. That van smells like a toilet."

Jack pulled out on Main Street and accelerated away from the motel. "The call came in anonymously, otherwise more units would have been flying in on this. The first unit checks it out, then calls for backup if they need it. Someone tried to jam us up—and it wasn't Geronimo."

Gerrit withdrew one of the disposable cell phones and dialed a number A familiar voice answered. Gerrit tightened his jaw. "Why did you give us up, Geronimo?"

"No choice. Your face is plastered all over the news, and we just received a department-wide alert you might be in the area. If they learned I helped you, it would be my badge…or worse."

Gerrit slammed the cell shut and hurled it outside. He shifted, his arm draped on the back of the front seat, trying to give more space to Alena wedged between him and Jack.

Alena squeezed his arm. "You okay?"

His eyes met hers for a moment, nodding. "Let's just focus on the operation. We need to put some distance between us and the motel and get ready to take care of business."

The others fell silent as Jack pushed the engine, staying just under the speed limit. It was going to be a long night.

Chapter 44

Harrogate, England

Joe O'Rourke felt like he was in a drama class. Sporting a wig, a mustache, and a floppy hat, he hoped his amateur makeup would throw off any facial-recognition programs aimed his way. The thick nonprescription glasses added yet another distortion to any photos of him they might have on file.

Now, he was in Kane's backyard. Time to step up his counter surveillance measures.

He moved down the clothing aisle, picking out a pair of trousers and a shirt. He clutched a bag of toiletries he'd gathered from another shop a block away. One more stop at a nearby restaurant, and then he'd head back to the bed-and-breakfast to begin his search once again.

He placed the items on the counter, waiting for the clerk to ring it up. As he started to look out the window, Joe caught the man giving him a quick, worried look. Joe looked back at the clerk, a slim and bony man, who quickly averted his eyes and seemed to study the register more than was necessary.

"Anything else, sir?" The clerk ventured a glance before looking away again.

"No, that's all," Joe said, studying him. "Is there something wrong?"

"No. Nothing at all. Sorry."

Joe gathered his purchases and left the store. As he passed through the doorway, he glanced back and caught the clerk staring again. The man abruptly turned and walked to the rear of the shop out of sight.

Something about the man's look made Joe uneasy. He glanced up and down the street but saw nothing that might arouse his suspicion. A young couple, baby in a pouch, passed by him, the father giving him a polite nod. The mother smiled.

Farther down the street, children played on the sidewalk, completely oblivious to anyone watching. He looked the other way and saw an empty street, two cars passing him, heading for the center of town.

His eyes searched for any danger, anything that might warrant a closer look. Nothing. A relaxed, laid-back afternoon. He walked toward the restaurant just around the corner.

Once inside, he tried to relax at a table in the back that allowed him a view of anyone entering the establishment, and—through a picture window—anyone outside who might be following him. Again, only a normal afternoon outside. Still, he couldn't seem to relax. The clerk's eyes raised a flag in Joe's mind. What could have possibly warranted such a look? Maybe he was imagining all this.

After the waiter took his order for fish and chips, Joe pulled out his laptop and found a strong wireless signal. He tapped in his password, which simultaneously opened and decrypted his files. Joe opened up his e-mail account. No messages. He opened up a new e-mail format and typed a quick message to Willy before closing it up.

A half hour later, after finishing his meal, Joe checked one last time for any messages. Seeing none, he closed it up, gathered his packages, and prepared to leave the restaurant.

Nightfall had finally descended. Joe hurried outside and made his way toward the bed-and-breakfast. He might be able to get in a few more hours studying Kane's computer system before calling it a night. If he couldn't find out anything more useful by tomorrow, he would reach out to his contacts here in the United Kingdom and attempt a closer visual search of the complex. He hoped to get good news from those in New Mexico.

A young man held on to an older woman's arm as they approached a quilt store Joe just passed. The woman seemed to walk with difficulty and the man patiently supported her, matching her slower steps.

Joe rushed ahead and held the door open for them. The coupled swept pass, the man giving him an appreciative nod. Joe let the door close and turned toward the sidewalk just as he felt something jam into his neck.

His body began to convulse as an electric shock coursed through him. It was the last thing he remembered.

"We got him, boss." Richard listened to one of his men over the telephone. "Nobody spotted a thing. We were able to get him to the car as if he'd had one too many drinks. What do you want us to do with him?"

Richard thought for a moment before responding. "Put him under and dump him into a large crate. Bring it here like you're transporting equipment. Move it downstairs and we'll put him in our interrogation section."

"You got it, sir."

"Did he have anything with him?"

"A laptop and a few bags of personal items. Clothes, toothbrush, that kind of stuff."

"Bring it all here—particularly the computer."

He hung up and clapped his hands together. Finally, he'd gotten his hands on the man who had eluded him all these years. Everything was coming together.

His source came through at the last moment. Joe and Willy were very cagey, and they'd built a system that could easily trap anyone trying to send a message to Richard. The source used old-school contact points, messenger and courier services that hand-delivered messages to Richard. Time consuming, but much safer. This time, Richard learned O'Rourke was on his way, although the message wasn't delivered until the man was already in country.

Richard had one ace in the hole. The source had been able to tag O'Rourke before his trip. Though the message got here late, Richard's people were able to use the tag identifier to track the target's location. No matter how many disguises the man used, he could not beat the long arm of technology unless he'd scanned himself and knew what to look for.

O'Rourke made one fatal mistake. He trusted his friends.

How brazen to be walking around in Richard's backyard here in Harrogate. Actually, stupid might be a better word. After all, he knew Joe and the others followed Gerrit here. And to just saunter around like Joe owned the place. Well, now the man would pay the price for his arrogance. After all the trouble Joe's band of idiots caused Project Megiddo, Richard looked forward to making this guy suffer.

Now, with Collette and her crew set up in Albuquerque, they might just get lucky and scoop up the whole group.

Joe woke up, slouching in a chair, his hands handcuffed behind him. His body felt like he'd gone twelve rounds with a heavyweight boxer, his head pounded to a painful beat. His mouth felt dry and his brain sluggish.

A single beam of light above him beat down, leaving the far corners of the room in darkness. He sensed someone nearby.

"We finally meet, Joe. After all these years." Richard Kane stepped from the darkness, letting the light catch his silvery mane of hair. The man moved closer. "Ever since my men paid you a visit in Chicago, you've been a hard man to catch—until now."

Joe tried to appear calm, although his heart raced. He knew what this man had done, including the deaths of his own brother and sister-in-law. Hope began to fade as his situation slowly became clear.

He was mad with himself for ignoring the danger signs. "That clerk tip you off?"

"You think I am going to give away my secrets?" Kane curled his lips back in a sneer. "The sheer arrogance. To think you can just waltz in here undetected and do what? Spy on me? Take my organization down?"

"I got this far, didn't I? With all your money and all your connections."

"And look at you now. Deep underground. Tied up in my interrogation room with nowhere to run."

Joe straightened in the chair, trying to convey confidence. "You think I'm alone? That others don't know where I am?"

"You mean like the rest of your team back in Albuquerque? The ones my guys are moving in on right now as we speak?"

Fear made Joe's pulse spike. They knew where Gerrit and the others were hiding? He lowered his head for a moment. No, they couldn't know that because they couldn't track the probes Willy sent out. Joe was sure of that. He'd built the protections into that program himself. "You're just blowing smoke, Kane. My people are too smart to get caught."

"And yet, here I am looking at their leader, Joe O'Rourke, aka Joe Costello, aka Frank Malone. The guy they thought too smart to get caught. In handcuffs. In my cell."

Almost involuntarily, Joe pulled the cuffs. They rattled as he tugged. "You didn't track me down through technology, Richard. You used plain old-fashioned bribery. Somebody snitched on me right here in town."

Kane leaned over, inches away from Joe's face. Looking him in the eye, Kane whispered, "And how do you know I don't have somebody on the inside? Somebody keeping watch on your band of do-gooders right now?"

Joe glared back. The man seemed very confident. Did they have a Judas in their midst?

He tried to rid himself of that thought. He knew the people he worked with. They had eluded Kane and his henchmen for many years. Each of them had been tested by fire and passed unscathed. They could not be traitors.

Then he thought of Gerrit and the contact Beck sent. Jack Thompson had been used in the past, and he always checked out. Joe was the one who sent him to Beck.

Could he be wrong? If so, Joe had put Gerrit and the others in harm's way. Kane and his people would finally be able to wipe out all resistance.

He prayed that Kane might be bluffing, that the team in Albuquerque might be protected. All he could do for the moment was hope for deliverance. He didn't know how long he could hold out.

Joe knew from bitter experience his lack of courage. Chicago had taught him that disappointing lesson a long time ago. He hoped time and resolve might have changed him. He would know the answer very soon.

Chapter 45

Albuquerque, New Mexico

Collette glanced at the text message and smiled.

One down. Just a few more to catch and they would leave this godforsaken city.

Gerrit and the others would be wary when Joe O'Rourke failed to report in. No matter!

Now, she enjoyed this psychological advantage over her enemy. Their leader captured, cut off the head, the body dies. The others might start running once they found out. At the very least, she and Kane had the tools to plant fear in their targets' minds.

She glanced at her watch. Midnight. Her techies advised the probes had ceased hours ago. Maybe they'd given up. Seen that this place was impenetrable. She toyed with creating an impression there was a weakness somewhere, let them think there was way in. Catch them in a trap.

After mulling it over, Collette discarded the idea and decided to continue with her current game plan. Control, tighten security, and be ready to pounce if these fools tried to get inside.

Checking her sidearm, Collette moved from the security office and began to make inspections. Two men appeared at her side and acted as her escort. She turned to one of them. "Let's make one last inspection to make sure everyone's in place. Then we'll pull back until daylight. If they are going to attack, it will be sometime between now and dawn."

She moved through the lab, eyes darting, searching for any weakness. *That's when I would hit. Hit the enemy just before dawn.*

Gerrit peered down at the schematic Willy pulled up on the computer. "You sure this is the place they have their research stored?" He pointed to a large, rectangular room in the very center of the building.

"I'm telling you, Mr. G. This is it." He pointed around the circumference of the targeted room. "Look at this wiring and the security installation they've implemented. Everything points to this spot. All their security is built around this one room."

Gerrit gave a slow nod. "You have the portable drive Joe gave you?"

Willy pulled out a USB drive and gave it to Gerrit. "This kind of memory storage will soon be obsolete, you know."

Gerrit slipped the drive into his pocket. "Remember my background, Willy. Did my doctoral thesis on how much will change in ten years. We are already into that future."

Jack strode into the motel room. "They're ready for us, Gerrit. Time to move out."

Willy rose and thrust out his hand. "Good luck, Mr. G. And take care of Al."

Alena came in just as Willy finished the sentence. "It's more like I'll be taking care of Gerrit. Like always."

Gerrit gathered his things. *The war is just starting, Alena. Don't start bragging now. Still plenty of time to fall flat on your face and die.* He fought the urge to make a retort.

Looking sheepish, Willy grimaced. "I just meant—"

"I know what you meant, Willy." She leaned over and kissed his cheek. "I'll be okay."

He looked over at Gerrit. "I mean it, Mr. G."

"I know. We'll watch each other's backs. See you when it's over."

Willy and the others climbed into the van Jack had supplied. Gerrit closed the door and waited until Jack brought his car alongside.

Alena and he climbed into the backseat as Jack took off, heading for the edge of town. The colonel glanced back. "Can't believe I'm chauffeuring a lieutenant around. Boy, times have changed."

"So has the war, Colonel. Hard to know which side you're on anymore."

"Amen to that. We should make contact with the bird in about five. You all set, Marine?"

"Yep. Locked and loaded."

Jack gave a smug smile. "That's want I want to hear." The colonel eyed Alena in the rearview. "Want to wish you both a lot of luck. They will be waiting for you."

Alena met the colonel's eye. "Don't believe in luck, sir. God will protect us if it is His will. And if it is not His will…that's fine with me."

Jack looked over at him and then back to her for a second before turning his attention ahead. "Whatever toots your horn, lady. Just be careful."

Alena stared out the window.

At times like this, Gerrit just put everything out of his mind except the mission. Never pondered about the what-ifs. Living and dying became just something that happened. Actions he had no control over. Right now, wasting time on concepts was counterproductive to the mission. Alena's statement, however, seemed almost fatalistic—whatever will happen will happen. She appeared to accept whatever God dished out.

Life or death. Good or evil.

He and Alena seemed worlds apart. He could never relinquish control over his own destiny if given a choice. And if control were taken away, he'd just fight to get it back. Alena seemed willing to accept whatever came her way. It bothered him to see how this might translate into survival tactics in combat. He needed her willing to fight to the death if need be. Passive acceptance was not an option.

He would have to watch her carefully.

Up ahead, Gerrit saw muted lights through the darkness. As they pulled closer, he whistled under his breath. "I never saw one of these in

Afghanistan." A sleek, lightweight helicopter, equipped with rockets and vertical propellers, sat poised on the landing pad.

Jack glanced in the rearview mirror again. "A prototype that Defense is testing for combat—particularly for Special Ops. It's fast, leaves a minimal heat signature, and offers unbelievable maneuverability. Between this bird and Willy's computer, we can drop you on the roof in seconds and pull away before their ground sensors even start recording movement. They will not know what hit them when you touch down."

"They'll signal you when Alena and I are clear of the bird?"

"That's right. Then me and Redneck will move in to cover you from the ground while Willy does his thing."

"Just give us body heat locations as quick as you can. Need to know where they're stationed in that building."

"You got it. We'll light them up before you touch ground floor." He caught Gerrit's look in the mirror. "And the tools you need are in the truck. Got enough firepower in there to start your own war."

Gerrit smiled. "That's exactly what we want them to think. Before they have time to react."

Jack nodded. "Just like old times, huh?"

Gerrit shook his head. "Before, I knew who I was shooting at. Now…" He swung the car door open and stepped out as the trunk popped open. Alena came around the other side as he grabbed an assault rifle—an H&K MP5 as requested—and a sidearm, handing them to her. He reached in and gathered the same firepower, then shouldered a backpack that weighed heavily on his back.

Gerrit slammed the trunk closed, then tipped his head at Jack—standing next to the driver's door, hands on the roof—before he and Alena crossed the pavement and climbed into a side door of the helicopter. A moment later, the engines fired and blades began to turn. The sound seemed muted and quiet, nothing like the Black Hawks they used overseas.

His earpiece crackled and Jack's voice came through. "Son, just remember. This cannot be a military operation. No in-country in the ol' U.S. of A. That would start a firestorm up on the Hill. That bird will not use its firepower unless absolutely necessary. Torch and burn anything left behind. We can't leave any evidence."

"Roger that, sir. Over and out."

The pilot lifted off and the craft immediately shot forward with a burst of speed. They seemed to effortlessly slide through the night toward their destination, the rotors quieter than a silenced gun firing at a target.

Collette sat in the chair, resting. Her eyes felt heavy and she felt herself starting to nod off. She raised her arm to check the time. 4:30 a.m. Her back felt stiff and her eyes wanted to close for a spell. She shook her head and rose, fearing if she sat here for another second she might fall asleep.

Looking over at the console, she saw the technician with his head resting on folded arms. "What are you doing?" she yelled, causing the man to jump and fall out of his chair. "This is not the time to fall asleep, you moron. They could hit at any time."

A squelch came across Collette's portable radio, then a man's voice cut in. "Boss, you'd better come to the front lobby. We've got visitors."

She angrily pressed her transmission button. "I don't have time to screen people. You take care of this."

"You may want to check it out. We have a medivac helicopter setting down in the parking lot. They think we have a medical emergency of some kind."

"Have all units converge there. I want that crew taken down at gunpoint. Search the chopper—now!" If this flight crew worked for the enemy, they'd never leave this place alive.

Chapter 46

Gerrit and Alena slid down the ropes and landed on the roof. The aircraft dipped and slipped away into the night. As it quietly disappeared, Gerrit heard another helicopter's blades noisily beating the night air at the front of the complex.

"They took the bait, Mr. G. I ordered up one medivac chopper. They are attacking that flight crew right now at gunpoint. Looks like you got your window of opportunity. Better use it quick."

Gerrit smiled. "I read you loud and clear. Remember, these transmissions might be monitored."

"No way, Mr. G. Joe and I put an encryption on these babies that only God can break."

"Fine. Right now, you're our eyes and ears. Give me a read on any bogies in the area. We're at the target location and need about five minutes."

He turned toward Alena and pointed to a housing vent a few yards away. "There is our way in. I'll have that removed in a jiffy. Just cover me."

She nodded, taking up a position that gave her a full view of the rooftop.

Gerrit pulled out his tools and had the ventilation cover off several minutes later. "Let's go." He lowered himself down the vent. "Just follow my lead. This heads right to the lab."

Alena moved to the edge, watching his descent. "Come on, slowpoke. We haven't all night."

He started to retort, then saw her smile. "Just try to keep up, or I'm leaving you behind." Reaching the ninety-degree angle in the vent, he moved farther into the shaft to give her room. She joined him seconds later.

"Come on," she said. "I'm getting old here."

He turned without saying a word and moved down the aluminum vent until he reached another ninety-degree turn downward. There was a filtered cover across the face of the downward shaft. Using a penlight, he quickly removed the vent cover and set it aside. "This fast enough for you?"

She moved past and lowered herself down the shaft. "Here, let me show you how it is done." In one swift move, she pushed through a second vent cover and dropped to the floor below, rolling to one side. She whispered up, "Don't hurt yourself, old man."

"Nice move. You made enough noise to set off every sensor in this building."

"We will be long gone before they ever reach us. Now do your thing, jarhead."

"You been hanging around Redneck too much. Wait for me. I'll be right back." He moved farther down the shaft and reached into his backpack for a few surprises he planned on leaving behind. A moment later, he returned and dropped down the shaft to join Alena. "Well, time to get to work."

The lab consisted of a large rectangular room, housing ceiling-high computer servers taking up most of the room. Individual workstations with monitors and keyboards connected directly to the servers.

He moved over to a series of computer consoles. "You will be glad I took that detour. Now, let's get down to business." He keyed his mike. "Okay, Willie, can you read me?"

"Loud and clear, Mr. G. Now, here's what you're looking for." Willie began to guide him through the log-in codes hacked earlier back at the motel. "Just follow my instructions and I'll have you out of there faster than—"

"Cut the jokes, Willy. Just give me what I need to get us out of here." Gerrit glanced at his watch. Two minutes and counting. He tried to move as fast as the programs allowed.

Collette nervously watched her security team sprawl out the flight crew at gunpoint. So far, no face she recognized. One flight nurse screamed when they yanked her out of the aircraft.

Where are Gerrit and the others?

"Hey, Boss." Geek Man from the security office.

"Don't bother me right now. We have a situation at the front of the building."

The man's voice sounded nervous. "I think you got bigger problems. I just saw sensors triggered in other parts of the building—including the lab."

"Could the medivac chopper have set those off?"

"No, these are centralized—the lab and the roof above the lab."

She whirled around and started running. "Check the cameras. Tell me what you find out. I'm coming back to your location right now." She dashed through the building and threw open the door leading to the security office.

Geek Man was hunched over the console.

"What do we have on the camera?" she yelled, causing him to jump. "Time to focus, you moron. They could hit at—"

The lights blinked on and off. Suddenly, all the screens filled with snowlike flakes as if someone had cut the line and all visuals went dead. Everything went black for a moment until emergency red lights flickered on. The man scrambled back into his chair, frantically hitting the keyboard, trying to reload the system.

"What happened?" She leaned over him as he worked.

"I don't know. It is as if they jammed—"

The building shook for a moment, a deep blast sounding somewhere off-site. Collette snatched up her portable radio. No response.

"I think they killed your radio system."

Collette rushed to the door. "I'm heading to the lab. If you can raise any security, get them moving in that direction." She drew her sidearm, pointing at the disheveled technician. "Keep working on that. As soon as you have something—call me if you can."

Geek Man, eyes wide with fear, nodded before turning back to the console.

She dashed into the hallway and ran for the building's central point—the lab. The main power source appeared to be wiped out, and emergency generators juiced up only selected sites in the structure. She heard a secondary explosion that came from deep within the building.

A firefight could be heard outside the building as security apparently came under attack. She keyed her mike, calling for anyone to report in. Only an irritating squelch. Still no way to communicate.

Collette felt like screaming out in frustration. Instead, she ran toward the interior lab, knowing the attackers would attempt to reach that destination. Another explosion shook the building. Were they trying to destroy the whole building?

She reached the last passageway leading to the primary lab. Impatiently, she tapped in the code for entry, only to find that power to the keypad had been cut off. No power to the lab. Without electricity, the lab security automatically froze up.

No way in. No way out.

Unless… She looked at the ceiling.

Gripping her weapon, Collette raced toward the only roof access. An interior door led to a stairwell to the roof, and that door was almost a hundred yards away. If she could reach the roof, she might be able to catch them before they entered the lab.

She would be in position to kill them all.

Gerrit glanced over at Alena before the lights flickered out. "They just got a taste of one of my surprises. Jack and Redneck are about to set off the others."

"That knock out their generator?" Alena flicked on a flashlight. "How are you—?"

A second generator fired up not far away. Lights in the lab flickered back on. "There. Just enough juice to power up these computers. And to get us out that lab door."

He pointed to the vent in the roof where they made their entry. "Collette can only reach us through there. In a minute, I will have the information we need downloaded into a file. Cover me as I try to upload Willy's package into their system."

She nodded and raised her assault rifle toward the ceiling, tightly wrapping the sling around her left arm for sight control and planting it on her right shoulder.

Gerrit typed in a series of commands provided earlier by Willy. The first person to poke his head through that vent above would get an unwelcome surprise.

He opened up a web site that Willy provided. Gerrit typed in a code and connected the program files to the site. He clicked a button to activate it, and copies of the computer files and attached data in the lab began to upload to Willy's Web site. While this function clicked away, he removed the USB drive, inserted it into another active computer, and drove the driver's content into the lab's servers with one click.

A gunshot exploded above them. Glancing up, he saw Alena crouching behind a file cabinet, firing three-round bursts toward the ceiling. Someone had followed their path through the venting system. Several shots ricocheted off the wall in front of him.

"Gerrit, make it quick. It's Collette," Alena yelled back between bursts of gunfire. "She has us pinned down."

"Give me a second and I can give you backup."

"Quick. We're sitting geese here."

"Sitting *ducks*," he muttered to himself, working on the console. Willy's program began to feed into the lab's memory banks like cars on the German autobahns, digital highway where information flowed into and out of the lab at full speed. The content flooding into the lab's storage servers was a gift Willy wanted to leave behind. Sixty seconds was all the time he needed. Right now, that seemed like an eternity.

Alena fired another volley into the ceiling.

Ten seconds left.

He glanced at the screen and saw the final seconds tick off. Suddenly the screen switched back to the primary program. He quickly withdrew the portable drive and shoved it in his pocket.

His earpiece activated and Thompson's voice transmitted. "We are moving into place for backup. Get out of there. Now!"

Gerrit clicked his acknowledgment and yelled over to Alena. "Okay, pull back. Time for Phase II." He grabbed a bag Thompson had given him as they moved deeper into the lab, away from the vent in the roof where Collette lay hidden. He reached in the bag and withdrew a satchel and a package of malleable detonation cord. He packed the explosive cord around the door.

"Alena, time to say good-bye to this place."

She scrambled closer as he blew open the lab door. He waited until she dashed past him, then turned and heaved the satchel into the lab. He slammed the door shut and pointed to where the hallway made a ninety-degree turn to the right. "Wait around the corner and give me a second to catch up."

Once they rounded the corner, he pulled out two radio transmitters. "Fire in the hole," he yelled before triggering both. The ensuing blast ripped through the building, almost knocking them off their feet. As the dust settled, he peered around the corner. The explosion had caved in the entire entryway, leaving a pile of rubble. He was sure the secondary explosion inside the lab had destroyed most of the computers and servers.

"Time to get out of here."

Alena and he ran down a long dark hallway. Gerrit yelled into his mike, "Willy, give me a fix on any security in the area."

Willy's excited voice came over the air. "I've got you in sight. Cameras are out, but our heat sensors show a lot of activity. Keep moving in the direction you're headed. Off to your right, about twenty or thirty yards, a group of security personnel are huddled together. Looks like they're confused."

"And what about the locals—cops and firefighters?"

"On the scene. Firefighters are still back in some kind of staging area, but Albuquerque's SWAT is moving in. They should be hitting the place any minute."

"Thanks, Willy. We're moving out and should be at the rendezvous site in about one minute."

"Got it. Be careful."

Gerrit smiled to himself. Bombs going off. Firefights ranging right and left. And Willy wants us to be careful. He tapped Alena's shoulder. "Let's go home." Into the radio, he said, "We're on the move."

"Roger that." There was a moment's delay until Willy came back on the air. "SWAT is at your twelve o'clock. Move to your left about forty yards. Redneck and Mr. Stars and Stripes blew a hole in the outer wall and cut a path through the concertina wire in all the confusion. SWAT can't see it from their location."

Gerrit acknowledged Willy with two clicks on the radio and moved in that direction.

Willy came back on the air. "Update. Stars and Stripes moved back to the pickup site. Redneck will cover your retreat."

"Ten-four." Gerrit said, as he and Alena moved closer to the outer wall, weapons at the ready.

A huge figure loomed from the shadows as they drew near. Redneck emerged, cradling his rifle. "Took your sweet time, jarhead. Let's get outta here." He pointed toward a jagged hole in the wall. "Made it easy for you."

Gerrit patted him on the shoulder and moved toward the door. He was about to step through when he heard a startled gasp from Alena. Whirling around, he saw Redneck holding a semi-auto handgun to her head.

"Easy there, Mr. G. Lower your weapon, slow and easy."

Gerrit froze.

Alena gazed at her captor with an anguished look.

Redneck grabbed a fistful of hair and pressed the gun against her temple. "I'm not going to tell you twice, Gerrit. Drop it."

He started to lower his rifle, never breaking visual contact.

It happened in a flash. One blink and he saw movement in Alena's left hand. A flash of metal as she plunged a knife into Redneck's upper thigh.

Before Redneck could react, Gerrit squeezed off two rounds straight at the giant's head. His head snapped back and he fell, slamming into the floor with a thud.

Dead.

Alena looked at Gerrit as if in shock. Her expression seemed to ask the unspoken question.

Why?

Chapter 47

Harrogate, England

Oh, God. Give me strength.

Another powerful blow snapped his head to the side. Joe tensed, waiting for another strike. And another. One of Kane's goons kept pounding him with blows. Face, stomach, kidneys. His tormentor knew how to hurt someone.

Pain came in waves, each blow taking away his breath, making him cry out. Fear almost paralyzed him as he struggled to free himself from the chair. It was useless.

Kane emerged from the shadows and waved off the attacker. He moved closer, inches from Joe's swollen face. "We are just getting started, O'Rourke. Remember Chicago?"

Just the mention of that city, that attack, made his heart jackhammer. *God help me stay strong!*

Kane looked into his eyes and leered. "This is going to get much worse. You'll wish my boys had dropped you off the roof in the Windy City by the time I am finished. Unless you tell me what I want to know. Do you understand?"

Joe glared back, fighting his fear.

"Have it your way." Kane stepped back and motioned for the attacker to continue. "I'm going to enjoy watching this."

The next blow almost made Joe lose consciousness.

Joe slowly woke up, his arms still cuffed to the chair, eyes puffy, almost closed from the rain of blows. That had just been a warm-up. A pain in his side told him a least one or two ribs might be broken, and two of his fingers felt painfully swollen after Kane tried to force them in a direction they were never designed to bend.

Joe had finally passed out. How long had he been out?

Running his tongue over his teeth, Joe felt at least one tooth had been loosened. Amid all the pain, he enjoyed a moment of joy. He had not caved in.

The door opened and Joe acted as if he was still unconscious.

"Don't insult my intelligence, Joe. You're being watched 24/7." Kane came closer and grabbed Joe's swollen jaw. "Wakey, wakey. We have more fun planned for you."

Joe opened his eyes, realizing his ploy wouldn't work. The pressure Kane put on his face alone was excruciating. He tried to raise himself and face his tormentor.

Kane stepped back. "Uncuff him and put him on the table. It is time Mr. O'Rourke realized that we mean business." The muscle-bound ape that slapped him around earlier waddled from the darkness and unlocked one end of the cuffs holding Joe to the chair.

Once loosened, he was jerked to his feet as the bigger man twisted his arms behind his back and forced marched him across the large room. Another light came on that illuminated what appeared to be a hospital bed. Flinging Joe on the mattress, Muscle Man quickly produced another set of cuffs. He immobilized Joe's arms, securely anchoring the wrist restraints to two metal stanchions anchored to the concrete floor on each side of the bed. He pulled on each restraint.

Escape was futile.

His captor moved back into the shadows and Kane and another man in a white smock moved closer. Kane leaned over the bed, partially blocking the blinding light above, his face and shoulders silhouetted, his body a black outline like a paper target posted on a gun range.

"You are not going anywhere, O'Rourke. Make this easy on yourself. Tell me what I want to know and you just might live. Resist and I will kill you."

Joe looked up at Kane's unseen face and spit.

Kane slammed his fist into Joe's face. "Get him ready," Kane screamed, moving back into the shadows.

The man in the white smock wrapped a rubber hose around Joe's arm to create a tourniquet. He disappeared for a moment, only to return with a hypodermic needle the size of which made Joe shudder.

One thrust into his veins and soon Joe felt a panicky euphoria creep through his limbs. His head started to spin. He was about to lose consciousness again. A moment later, he blissfully blacked out.

Richard watched Joe's body slump as the injection took hold. "You used sodium pentothal, right?"

The medical technician nodded as he put the serum away.

"You idiot, he's nodding off. You must have given him too much."

Worriedly, the technician thumbed Joe's eyelid to see pupil reaction, then felt for a pulse. The man glanced at Richard, concern tightening his face. "I'm sorry, sir. It's hard to get the right dosage under these conditions."

"I don't want to hear excuses. Let me know the moment he can respond to our questions." Angry, Richard made his way back to the office. A red message light flashed on his phone. Punching the code, he waited for the recording to begin.

A man's voice came over the speaker, an explosion and gunshots in the background. "Sir, we are under attack. We—" is all he heard before the recording stopped.

He glanced at the last number dialed. The call came from the lab in Albuquerque. He dialed Collette's number and listened to her cell phone ring until his call rolled over to voice mail. She was not picking up. Or unable to answer his call.

Something went wrong.

Frustrated, he tried to think of someone on-site who might be able to give him an update. He did not want to leave a phone trail to the lab, and if he called his contacts in Albuquerque, he'd be leaving a trail to those contacts with a timeline corresponding to whatever was happening at the lab.

He dialed a Seattle number. As soon as his contact answered, Richard demanded an update from New Mexico. "You have any contacts there you can trust? I need a quick assessment as to what's happening."

"Call you back in a few, sir."

Richard hung up and thought about Joe O'Rourke and the interrogation. He dialed the medical technician standing by. "Move him back to the holding cell. Something has come up that needs my attention. We'll have to continue this later." He slammed the phone down, waiting for a call back.

Ten minutes later, the phone rang. He snatched it up. "Speak to me."

"Sir, looks like all hell broke loose out there. They got police and fire responding. Reports of a bombing and a firefight going on. The cops are holding everyone back until they can assess the danger."

"They have to get in there right now. Before anyone can escape."

"I know sir, but the cops are playing it real cautious. Things are really volatile. They may be even calling the feds—ATF, FBI, and the rest of the federal alphabet-soup agencies."

Richard shook his head. "No. No. We can't have everyone poking their noses into that lab. We have to contain. Now!"

"It may be too late, sir. It sounds like a war just started."

Richard ended the call and quickly dialed another contact in Justice. He needed to start containment immediately. Before too much information got out. And he needed to kill whoever did this before they could talk.

They needed to be silenced.

Chapter 48

Albuquerque, New Mexico

Alena seemed transfixed as she stared at Redneck's body. Gerrit grabbed her arm, tugging her toward the gaping hole in the wall. "We have to move."

Willy came over the air, his voice frantic. "Mr. G, what's going on down there? I show Redneck down. Not moving."

"He's dead," Gerrit said, tersely. "Guide us out."

"You got movement to your right. SWAT must be reacting to your shots."

"Tell Jack to keep the engine running. This is going to be a close one."

Alena started to move and he released his grip on her. "Follow me," he said, crouching as low as he could to limit the target his body made. Off to his right, he saw a light flash, a police officer in full gear moving along the wall. Apparently they had not spotted the mangled hole in the fence. They must be zeroing in on the blast radius around the outer wall of the lab.

He sprang forward, hearing Alena's quieter tread behind him. They made it through the outer fence when there was a yell behind them. Turning, Gerrit saw a flash of gunfire. One of the SWAT officers was firing. "Alena! Run! Run!"

Gerrit wheeled around and fired, aiming just behind the officer's head. The officer flattened out, then began to rise to fire again.

At that moment he heard the whirl of blades as Jack Thompson's voice screamed into Gerrit's ear. "Run for it, boy. Give that flyboy some room to work."

As Gerrit dashed across the open area behind the fence, he heard the sweet sound of 20mm cannon fire chewing up dirt as the helicopter opened up. Belching across the wire, each round raised dust as the perimeter turned into something akin to hamburger meat. Enough firepower to keep SWAT from chasing them any farther. The pilot made one pass, almost went vertical, then fell back for another run.

Just before Gerrit crossed a rise, he looked back one more time and saw the helicopter crew make a third pass. Those officers trapped on the ground knew better than to cross no-man's land as the helicopter pinned them down.

He dashed down a sloping hill to a waiting car below. Alena reached the car first, diving into the backseat and leaving the door hanging open. Gerrit was a few steps behind. He flung himself inside, yelling, "Go! Go! Go!"

Jack Thompson stepped on the gas and the car hurled forward. Gerrit slammed the door shut, looking back to see the helicopter streaking across the sky into the darkness.

A mile away, Jack slowed down.

Gerrit keyed his radio. "Willy, give us an update. You tracking us?"

"Yeah, Mr. G." Willy's voice sounded subdued. "What happened back there with Redneck?"

Alena's voice came over the air. Gerrit glanced over and saw tears in her eyes. "Willy, let's keep this off the air. Redneck's gone. There is nothing we can do now."

Silence filled the car, oppressive, gloomy.

Another mile slipped by before Jack spoke. "What did happen back there, Marine? We need to know if we've got a security breach."

Gerrit caught Jack looking back at him for a moment, then the colonel glanced away. "It's as bad as it gets, sir. Kane planted Redneck to spy on us. Everything we know, Kane must know by now."

"How could Kane have gotten to him?" Alena looked over at him, her eyes pleading.

Gerrit took her hand. "I think he was one of them the whole time. Working for Kane way back when Joe met him in Chicago. My guess, Redneck didn't have a direct link to Kane, to protect himself from Joe and Willy. Didn't know what kind of protections Joe might have raised to catch messages. They must have done the old spy world thing—maybe a dead-letter trip through an e-mail account, or maybe they did really old school—written only, left at a physical drop site."

Jack piped up. "The good thing is he couldn't get information to Kane on a regular basis. For example, on this op he couldn't let Kane know what our plan was because he never was out of our sight. I mean, they didn't even know for sure we came to Albuquerque until it was too late."

A chill swept through Gerrit. "But he did know one thing he could have passed on to Kane."

Alena gripped his hand. "Oh no!"

Gerrit nodded. "Kane must know Joe is in Harrogate. We need to get word to him right now." He hit his radio transmission button. "Willy, we need to get in touch with Joe. Warn him that Kane might know he's over there."

"I've been trying to raise him. Joe's not answering…" Worry seemed to weigh down every word Willy spoke. "I think they got to him, Mr. G."

They reached where Willy sat with the rental van. He climbed into the car and they sped away, leaving the van and everything else behind. About ten miles out of town, Jack stopped and switched places with Gerrit. "You drive while I make a few calls."

Gerrit listened to Jack phoning his contacts, glanced up in the rear-view to check on Alena and Willy sitting in the backseat. Alena seemed to be fighting back tears. Willy sat expressionless, staring out the window. Neither had spoken since they got into the car.

Jack finished his calls.

Gerrit looked over at him. "We should be good until sunup. By then, I imagine Kane will have his people slip enough information to the local law enforcement that they will be broadcasting a BOLO on our vehicle—and us."

Jack shook his head. "That's why I just made those calls. Let my people know they need to squash any BOLOs if they can. I directed them to put out a bogus alert for known terrorist that just hit the lab. These terrorists are believed to be en route to Mexico. And we all know how well Mexico cooperates with the U.S. on border issues."

Gerrit leaned forward. "Colonel, we need to regroup and head for Harrogate. While there still might be time."

Jack nodded. "Contacted Beck Malloy, Gerrit. He'll be expecting your call about now."

"Why is that?"

"Because I told him to expect it." Jack glanced back at him. "Take my cell phone. It's heavily encrypted, and Beck will recognize the code name that appears on the readout."

Gerrit dialed the number Joe gave him, using his left arm to steer the car. On the second ring, a man's voice answered. "Jack, is that you?"

Gerrit cleared his throat. "This is Gerrit O'Rourke. Beck Malloy?"

"In person. Man, I was hoping we'd never have to talk. What's going on down there? I got all kinds of terrorist alerts going off. Our office is scrambling to try to get on top of this."

"We got in and did our business. But we have a couple of problems." Gerrit saw Willy and Alena look at each other for a moment, sadness in their eyes.

"Like what?"

"One of our guys, Hank Schneider, turned out to be a traitor. Worked for Kane the whole time. He tried to take Alena prisoner. I shot him."

A moment lapsed before Beck spoke again. "And the second problem?"

"I think they've got Joe. He's MIA."

"Oh, man." Beck seemed to be searching for something to say.

"I'm sending you a link to a secure Web site Willy and Joe maintain. Pull the data from that system and have your people start to work through it. It's what Joe was searching for. Project Megiddo. Remember?"

"Yeah, I remember."

"We've uploaded everything from Millennium Technologies. Handle with care, Beck. If it gets out in the open, this will set off all kinds of alarms."

"Gotcha. Let me start pulling some strings on my end. Be ready to move. Now, put Jack on the line. I'll tell him where we can pick you guys up."

Gerrit handed the phone to Jack. "He needs to talk to you, Colonel."

Jack cradled the phone against his left ear, listening. "Got it, Beck. I'll get them connected from my end." He closed up the phone and tossed it on the console. "I'm going to hook you guys up with a pilot and a small plane just across the border in Arizona. The pilot will get you to a major airport, where Beck will have a contact meet you. They will get you across the pond. In England, another contact will get you to within a grenade's reach of Kane's place. Once there, you guys will be on your own. Beck and I have to steer clear of any overseas operations without clear sanction from our bosses. Don't want to ruffle any feathers over at State or the CIA. I'd ask to tag along, but under the circumstances, I don't see me getting the green light." He let that sink in before continuing. "Understood?"

Gerrit nodded. "Got it, Colonel. And who's this contact in England?"

"You'll recognize him when he makes contact. Remember, Kane must be expecting you to show up there. Be careful. And let's hope you can bring Joe back safe and sound."

Gerrit stared out the window. Easy to say from the safety of this car on U.S. soil. Over there, they would truly be on their own. And they were going up against a formidable enemy, one with connections in all the right places. An enemy with unlimited resources.

They had to move fast. If Joe was still alive—and that was big *if*—there was little time left.

Kane was an impatient man.

Chapter 49

Harrogate, England

Staff members seemed to sense something was critically wrong. Their boss sat secluded in his office for hours, rarely emerging. And when he did, Richard yelled and snarled to those around him. After he exhausted himself, he would slam his door shut and remain inside after barking out clear orders not to be disturbed.

Richard had every right to be upset. Collette called four hours ago to let him know what happened at the lab. Security breached. Gerrit and his troublemakers made it inside and toyed with the system before blowing a hole in the door and eluding SWAT with the help of a helicopter gunship.

If Gerrit escaped with the plans to Project Megiddo, Richard would personally shoot everyone in the lab who let those intruders escape. Including Collette. She seemed aware of the depth of his anger and tried to keep her report short and to the point. She was on her way to England.

He knew her flight would be filled with trepidation and fear. *Let her suffer!*

Joe O'Rourke's interrogation did not go well. There had been an overdose of medication and the target had slipped into unconsciousness—again. So far, he remained unresponsive. The medical adviser told him the guy might croak if they pushed too hard. Only time would tell. Richard had been amazed at how the man held up. This was not the same man his people dangled in the air in Chicago.

Again. Major frustration.

He needed to know what Joe could tell him about Gerrit and the others. About who in government aided them in their fight against Richard's people. Unfortunately, Joe kept this information from Hank Schneider.

His phone continued to ring but he ignored it. Just more bad news.

A timid knock on the door caused him to curse once again. "I told you I wanted to be left alone. Get outta here!"

Again the knock. Was this person insane?

He sprang up and hurled open the door. A twenty-something woman with frightened eyes and pale skin stood before him, her hands shaking.

"Sir, you have a call holding. I really think you might want to take it."

The look in her eyes made Richard withhold his fury. The call must be important enough for this young thing to ignore his orders. Her eyes drifted toward the desk and the blinking call-holding light. "He's waiting."

Richard stormed over to the desk and yanked the receiver up to his ear. "Kane here, who is this?"

"Richard. I think you know who this is."

Stuart. Just the sound of the man's voice made Richard cringe. *Uh-oh.* Word was getting out. "What can I help you with, sir?"

"I hear disturbing reports about acts of terror down in our lab in Albuquerque. Are these reports true?"

Richard clutched the phone. "We had an attack, but the intruders have been repulsed. There is extensive property damage. I am waiting for a situation report right now."

"And our...project. Has it been compromised?"

"I assure you we have not been compromised. They tried to get to our computer system, but our people and Albuquerque's SWAT unit got there first. They had to pull back."

"And our guest. Has he cooperated with you?"

"Not yet. He needs a period of rest before we continue."

"This performance is less than I would expect, Richard. Maybe we picked the wrong man after all."

Stuart's haughty tone—as if each word he spoke came down from on high—grated on Richard's ears. He would like nothing better that to screw a .9mm barrel into this guy's ear and force him to eat those words. Instead, he spoke with deference. His life depended upon it.

"Give me a couple days to contain this. Once I get our guest to open up, then I can move on to those causing us these problems."

"You have twenty-four hours. Then we bring in someone else who *will* get the job done."

"Yes, sir," Richard said, gritting his teeth.

"We are committed to the timetable for this operation. Time is ticking."

And you're ticking me off. "I'll get on it right away, sir. You can depend upon it."

Stuart coughed before speaking. "I used to think I could depend upon you. But after everything that has happened this last month, I have my doubts. *We* have our doubts."

"I'll keep in touch. You will know something in the next twelve hours."

The line cut off.

Richard knew his time was short.

Chapter 50

Albuquerque, New Mexico

As Beck Malloy drove up, he saw floodlights set up as dusk settled over the flat dessert terrain.

A small army of federal investigators descended on the torn-up remains of Millennium Technologies. FBI, ICE, Homeland Security, ATF, and a host of other agencies—including Albuquerque PD—milled around the staging area.

The entire compound had been cordoned off. Armed law enforcement—local and state officers, some with dogs—walked the perimeter, guarding against any spectators, rubberneckers, or media slipping inside. It was as if a small army had descended upon this quiet industrial park after someone declared war.

Beck flashed his credentials to an officer guarding access to an ever-expanding parking lot. He parked his car, striding over to where the command center had been set up in an eighteen-wheeler trailer. Occasionally, a helicopter passed overhead, floodlights flashing back and forth as the flight crew searched for intruders from their vantage point above.

His target, a heavyset agent with a protruding gut wearing a blue FBI Windbreaker. "Special Agent Stephen Riker. We spoke on the phone." Beck extended his hand.

The other man squinted at him suspiciously for a moment. "Beck? Beck Malloy?" He shook Beck's hand.

"The one and only."

"Long way from D.C., my man. What brings you out to my neck of the woods?"

"Terrorism, for starters. What kind of lab is this?"

Riker stiffened. "Don't yank my chain, Malloy. I checked you out after your call. I saw your security clearance. You tell *me* what's going on here."

Beck was getting tired of always playing cat and mouse with these guys. They were just hard-working agents trying to do their job. This was the down side of working intelligence. "That's what I'm here to find out, Riker. What have you learned so far?"

Not buying it, Riker looked at him in disbelief. "Okay. You want to play it that way. Fine! I was told to cooperate, but that doesn't mean I enjoy getting jerked around. Not in a case I'm supposed to investigate." The agent gave Beck the detail on the lab he'd already learned directly from Jack Thompson and Gerrit O'Rourke.

"Anybody get hurt?" Beck already knew the answer, but he wanted Riker to believe this was all new information.

Riker studied Beck closer. "After the intruders fled the scene, the chopper pulled away and SWAT found one man dead just inside the building. He must have been a third intruder, but it looked like one of his own killed him. Stabbed in the leg and double-tap to the head. Close range."

"Body been identified?"

"Not yet. Running prints and facial photos through the system. Nothing has shown up yet, which is unusual. The dead guy looks like he may have done time, run up against cops somewhere. But the system isn't giving us any leads."

"Let me see the guy's mug," Beck said. Riker handed him a printout of a digital photo they took at the scene before the coroner arrived. Beck studied the face for a moment. "Not anyone I recognize. White supremacy, maybe?"

Riker shrugged. "Who knows. This kind of operation is more sophisticated than those Nazi wannabe types we normally run into. This was state-of-the-art equipment they used to get into this place. Big money." Riker was still upset.

"Look, I don't know much about this. All I can tell you is this might be connected to Senator Summers's killing and the murders up in Seattle. We're trying to put the pieces together."

"You mean that Seattle cop that went missing?"

Beck played along. "Like I said, we don't really have anything solid at this time." He glanced toward the open door. "Computer forensics going over the lab?"

"They were going over everything with a fine-tooth comb. Taking everything they can...until the call came."

"What call?"

Riker's eyes narrowed. "Somewhere high up the food chain. Orders came down to focus only on the intrusion and murders. Stay away from the lab. National security and all that."

"Is Bobby Chan on the forensic team here on-site?"

"Uh-huh. He's packing up as we speak. You might be able to catch him in the parking lot."

"Thanks." Beck headed for the door. He found Bobby just about to climb into the driver's seat. "Hold up a minute, my man."

"Beck Malloy. I thought you'd show up."

"Whatcha mean?" Beck said.

Chan leaned against the car, arms folded. "I've been here all day, and then we get this order to shut down. Before I can get out of the parking lot you show up. Is this your doing?" He glanced toward the lab, bathed in darkness. "You shut us down?"

"No way. In fact, I was hoping you could tell me what you learned."

Puzzled, Chan unfolded his arms and stroked his jaw. "So if you didn't shut us down, where did the order come from?"

"I don't know, but I'd sure like to find out. I know you, Bobby. You don't walk away because some boss tells you to. Did you get anything?"

A cagey smile emerged on Chan's face. He reached into his pocket and pulled out a USB drive. "I made a backup file to what I downloaded into my own laptop. Just in case some congressional watchdogs come snooping around wanting to know why we didn't follow protocol and seize everything I have. Been down this road before. Politics always seem to come between us and getting the job done."

"Can I take that with me, Bobby?"

A moment of indecision shone in Chan's eyes. Reluctantly, he handed Beck the computer drive. "Guard it carefully. I don't know what's all on there, but the little I saw blew my mind."

Grasping the drive, Beck glanced around to see if anyone might be watching. Riker was standing near the trailer, watching them. Shielding his movement from Riker, Beck hid the drive in a jacket pocket. "What did you see, Bobby?"

The computer specialist shook his head. "I saw plans to invade every electronic device known to man and decrypt anything we have ever tried to protect. I'm talking about code breakers on NSA and CIA encrypted fields, corporate security systems. The works. I have never seen anything like it."

Beck watched Riker disappear into the command trailer. "That's why I am here. To find out just how bad this company has exposed our national secrets. If this got out, it would make the WikiLeaks fiasco child's play. Anyone who controls this technology might easily control the U.S. Maybe even the world."

Chan whistled. "Maybe it's a good thing we were ordered out of the lab."

Somberly, Beck placed a hand on Chan's shoulder. "Just be careful. That information you just downloaded could get you killed. Watch yourself."

"You too, Beck. If the wrong person finds out why you are here, they're going to slap a bull's-eye on your backside and invite anyone to collect a bounty on your head."

Beck thanked the agent and moved away. It was only a matter of time before they started to put the pieces together. Only a matter of time until they learned who he was protecting.

One of them might already be in harm's way. He prayed Joe O'Rourke would survive.

Chapter 51

Phoenix Sky Harbor International Airport, Arizona

Gerrit spotted a sleek-nosed business jet ahead as their motorized cart drew near. He and the others made their way toward the plane, no one talking. Everyone seemed to be moving like zombies, still numbed by the fact that one of their own turned out to be a Judas and their leader turned up missing. Exhaustion and betrayal seemed to zap their strength.

Hours earlier, Jack Thompson arranged to get them on a smaller, luxury craft—a twin-engine 1980 Beechcraft King Air 200. A pilot patiently waited for them on a gravel strip just off Interstate 40 west of Albuquerque. They loaded up, then took off for Phoenix—no questions asked by the pilot. For all he knew, they could have been a bunch of drug runners just in from Mexico. The pilot most likely dealt with the colonel in the past and knew better than to inquire about Thompson's travel partners.

They settled in as the jet began a circuitous trip across the county, bound for the United Kingdom. Jack would be dropped off at a major airport in Virginia before they headed out over the Atlantic. The group remained quiet and subdued, Alena and Willy finally succumbing to fatigue. Gerrit could not seem to fall asleep. Every time he closed his eyes, he saw Redneck's angry face.

Jack, sprawled in the seat across the narrow aisle, leaned toward him. "Hey, you still awake?"

Gerrit opened his eyes. "Can't sleep, sir." Behind him, Willy began to snore and Alena seemed restless as she slumbered. "Redneck still bugs me. How did he slip through?"

"Been chewing that over myself. Kane must have recruited him as a plant years ago. I'm just surprised it took this long for that traitor to show his true colors."

Gerrit nodded. "We have to rethink everything. He knows all our safe houses, all our secrets. He knows where Joe and Willy do business in Virginia."

"That's my first stop after you guys drop me off. Check out their place and clean it out of anything of importance."

"We need to get set up with new identities, new lives, after…"

Jack seemed to read his mind. "Just focus on the mission. Joe will either survive or not. You know the odds."

Gerrit shook his head. They were probably going to rescue a dead man. Richard would already have a trap set. "It seems almost pointless. But we have to know. We have to get in there and make sure."

The colonel looked over at him. "Got a plan in mind?"

Gerrit closed his eyes again. "Got one that keeps coming to mind, Colonel. But I don't like the odds."

"The contact there will give you all the support he can. And I'll start working on the electronic coverage you need. You should have an eye in the sky and a few drone flyovers if you need it. But the ground troops—that's going to be hard to come by. Unless your contact can pull a rabbit out of the hat."

He felt the back of his chair move. Alena pulled herself up, leaning over the seat. "Colonel, Joe has to be alive. He just has to be."

Gerrit turned and saw her face flushed with anger. "We'll do our best."

"We'll do better than that," she said. "We are going to bring him home."

Jack raised himself. "I'm going to check in with the pilot. I'll be back later."

When he left, Alena slid into the seat next to Gerrit . "How are we going to do this, Gerrit? Get inside Kane's place?"

He looked at her. "I got an idea, but I need to talk to our contact before we go any further. Need to know what kind of resources we're working with on the ground."

She rubbed her eyes, a weary expression on her face. "I feel if Redneck betrayed us, that anyone…" She stopped and shook her head.

"We have to stick together. Those of us who are left. And we have to trust each other. No matter what."

She glared at him. "Trust is a hard thing to come by where I am from. Has to be earned. I thought we could trust Redneck, but he turned on us. Makes me wonder about the rest of us."

"Makes you wonder about me?" He searched her eyes, looking for whatever she was trying to hide.

"No. I've seen what Kane took from you. Of all of us, you've lost the most."

"And what have you lost, Alena?"

She turned away, looking out the window at the sun slowly rising in the east. "It is not what I have lost. It is what I have gained."

"I don't understand."

She slowly faced him. "Joe found me. Trusted me when no one else would. He took me in and gave me hope for a better life. He gave me… family. And now, someone in my family has betrayed us."

He reached across the aisle, clasping her hand. "Tell me how he saved you. From what?"

Her eyes hardened, and she moved farther away. "Ask Joe…when we find him."

Gerrit settled back, trying to get some rest, but his mind just wouldn't relax. Different scenarios played out in his head as he tried to figure the best approach to Kane's mansion. Unless they had reinforcements, he did not like the odds.

As he created and studied each scenario, one phrase kept coming to mind.

Suicide mission.

Richard Kane had already put the order out. He knew they were coming. It was just a matter of time. Quickly, he called in those he trusted and laid out the welcoming party he had in mind. If everything worked out, in less than twenty-four hours Gerrit and the others would be his prisoners—or they would be dead.

Either way, I win.

Richard slammed his desk drawer closed and locked it after the meeting, anxiously waiting to hear the final damage reports from Albuquerque. He wanted a firsthand account from Collette before deciding what action he would take. Whatever he decided, he knew she would not be pleased.

Failure was not an option—for her or him. Trouble always flowed downhill when plans went awry. He did not expect leniency from those in power above him, and he certainly was not inclined to give it to his subordinates when they failed.

Albuquerque was a colossal failure. It jeopardized everything they'd been striving to achieve with Project Megiddo and other efforts. This project was just one of many parts to a complicated machine, like one battle in a major war with many fronts. Project Megiddo needed to function so other parts of the machine could move forward.

He only hoped that Gerrit did not get to tamper with what the New Mexico lab had stored. There was only one other facility that retained these developments. They always tried to duplicate their research, so if one facet of the program became exposed, other parts would still function.

If Gerrit's band of troublemakers found out about the other site, Stuart and the others would finish Richard off for good. There was only one weak link. One person whom Gerrit might begin to suspect. Hopefully, he would not put it together until it was too late. After that last phone call with Stuart, Richard knew he was on borrowed time. He must make the most of it.

At least Richard had the brains of the outfit. O'Rourke was in his custody. He rose and strode toward the door.

Time to set a trap.

Chapter 52

Atlantic Ocean, 100 miles from the Irish Coast

Willy Williams sat up and opened his laptop. The aircraft jostled him awake a few minutes earlier and he could not get back to sleep. He saw Alena dozing off again, and Gerrit sat by himself, scratching out ideas on a notepad.

Almost idly, he began to replay a record of all transmissions he'd recorded when they hit the Albuquerque lab. He studied all outgoing traffic from a server located at the lab. One IP address kept popping up every hour at the same time. He isolated the address and ran a history on this site. A pattern soon emerged that must be an automatic transmission generating from the Millennium Technologies lab to the unknown IP address, as if it was a backup system. But the backup site was not linked to any known off-site storage site—either commercially or privately run.

He copied the IP address, then pasted it into a search program he and Joe used as a locator. They used this program when they came across web sites that tried to hide their location of service, sending queries like Willy's colliding into dead ends all over the planet. It would take time for Willy's system to connect to where he and Joe kept these master programs. He would receive an e-mail when the site had traced and identified this unknown IP address. Until then, he would study other data collected from the Albuquerque operation.

He tried not to think about Redneck. Shock over his friend's betrayal still left Willy numb. They always butted heads, but he thought he and Redneck shared a common bond, a common understanding. His mind began dwelling on other concerns, the main one being Joe O'Rourke. Was his friend dead or alive? He shook that thought from his mind, choosing to focus on whether Mr. G's rescue plan might work.

Dark thoughts kept pounding away. Were they too late? Would this be one big trap they were walking into, a trap none of them might walk away from? How much did Kane know about them? Were more traitors in their midst?

He studied Alena and Gerrit for a moment. Could they also be plants? Nah. He knew for sure Al was cool. She had risked everything for them on more than one occasion. She'd left everything behind to join them. She was not a traitor.

Gerrit leaned over his writing pad. Willy studied the man, thinking back over what they knew about him. Once, he'd asked the others whether it was wise to reveal their operation to this man. Someone they barely knew. How ironic that Willy raised this concern with a traitor already in their midst.

Alena and Joe forcibly argued that Gerrit could be trusted. Look at what he suffered and the service he'd already given to his country. No. Mr. G was not a traitor. In fact, he just might be the leader their group needed to survive. Funny, Hillbilly had nothing to say about whether to trust Mr. G. This was about the first time Hillbilly had nothing to mouth off about.

Willy turned back to his computer and typed more commands. There was as wealth of information he could mine from their raid on Millennium Technologies. He was about to open another program when an incoming e-mail alert popped up on his screen. He opened the e-mail. It was from Beck Malloy.

Downloaded this from lab. Tell me what it means?

He clicked on the attachment to the message and waited for it to open.

"Hey, Mr. G. You may want to see this. Just came in from Beck."

Willy returned his attention to the screen. Out of his peripheral vision, he saw Gerrit slide into the seat next to him.

"What do you have?"

"Man, whatever we've got here, this file is huge. Even as a zip file, this thing is taking forever to open."

Gerrit studied Willy for a moment. Something was troubling him. Gerrit suspected it might be related to Redneck. Better to leave well enough alone.

He leaned closer. "Mind if I take a look?"

Willy turned the laptop so Gerrit had a heads-on view. "This has to be what Senator Summers was trying to tell you that night. It spells out how they intend to use Project Megiddo."

He nodded, studying the research paper captured on the screen. He scrolled through the verbiage, getting to the heart of what he thought the project might be about. He spotted an eyes-only synopsis from the Megiddo Oversight Committee. The members of the committee were identified by code. "Look at this. This might be what we're searching for." He began reading out loud:

"'MISSION STATEMENT: Project Megiddo's first phase of this multiphase project is critical to the overall success of the entire operation. Upon implementation, Project Megiddo will be used to aggressively monitor any resistance to our ultimate goal of global unification. Political, economical, and military associates and opponents must be clearly identified and segregated by name, company, and organization. Those enlightened and motivated to work toward global unifications will be singled out for support and assistance to achieve success within their respective spheres of influence. Opponents will be aggressively targeted for isolation, quarantine, and elimination.'"

Alena leaned over the back of his chair. "Oy vey! This lays out exactly what we thought Kane and the others were working toward."

"This is why they killed my father. He was…to put it in their words, 'targeted for elimination.' Mom was just collateral damage." Gerrit gripped the laptop.

She squeezed his shoulder.

He scrolled down the document until he came to the operational plan of the project. "They have already begun to implement Project Megiddo, targeting those they need to put out of business. What they don't spell out is how they plan to achieve these goals."

Alena removed her hand. "Willy, can you find out? This attack on those who oppose globalization?"

Willy leaned over to see the screen from a different angle. "Not from this information. All this data has to be forwarded to centralized storage facilities. I mean, it just can't be allowed to float out there in cyberspace. We need to track where this project dumps its data—that might have been Millennium Technologies—and where the results from Megiddo's invasive technology feeds back to storage and monitoring stations. These may or may not be the same physical location."

Gerrit nodded. "Let's say that the Albuquerque facility became in-operable due to our surprise visit yesterday. Where would they start up? In Harrogate?"

Willy scratched his jaw. "Maybe, but I would think they'd have second-ary locations not known to us. I mean, why did they bring you to Kane's operation in Harrogate if they weren't sure you'd become a team player? That was taking a big risk."

"Maybe Kane was sure he could control me, persuade me to become a part of his operation. He made a huge error, letting us know about his base of operation. Look where it is located. In the same general areas as NSA's global electronic monitoring stations at Menwith Hill. They could tap into their fiber-optics system from Harrogate and wouldn't need to build their own duplicating facilities. They have the one in England tied to the other allied stations like Ascension Island in the South Atlantic, Pine Gap in Australia, other suspected listening facilities in Canada and Japan, as well as many listening posts in the U.S. That is just to access communications over fiber-optics lines. Not to mention all the classified satellite surveillance capabilities of which we may or may not know about."

Willy glanced up. "So you know about some of these places? From your time in the military?"

"Partly. And some of it comes from my research at MIT before my last military duty overseas. Because of my work, they gave me a high security clearance to be able to access some of these intelligence sources. Kane knew this. I guess that was one of the reasons he tried to recruit me. To get access to what I already knew. And to have my clearance reinstated so I could continue to feed him information."

Alena sat quietly listening to the two men talk. She finally broke into the conversation. "What is our game plan?"

Gerrit continued to scroll through Project Megiddo, looking for anything that might lead them to their next target. "Right now, nothing has changed. We need to get inside Harrogate, get Joe out of there, and tear that place apart to find out more about Kane's plans. To find out more about who he's working for."

Willy leaned back in his chair. "And what if Kane is just the tip of the iceberg? What if this is greater than his organization, however big that might be?"

Gerrit eyed him for a moment. "You can count on there being many more Richards running loose out there, layered organizations upon organizations. But I believe above all of them are a select few, an elite, those we may never discover. They've covered themselves with protection, allowing people like Kane to take all the risks."

"But if we can just find one of those strings, and follow it back to those shotcallers."

"Shotcallers?"

Willy grimaced. "That goes back to my days in the gangs. It was always hard for the popos to take down the shotcallers. Too many homeboys and soldiers willing to lie down to protect them."

Gerrit smiled. "Popos? Homeboys? These are the terms you learned in college?"

"Yeah. The school of hard knocks. Not something you pick up in places like MIT, Mr. G."

"Willy, you bring a practical approach to this operation. I appreciate it."

Willy studied Gerrit for a moment, as if trying to determine whether he might be joking. "Thanks, Mr. G…I think."

Alena tussled Willy's hair. "You always made my day interesting. From the second we first met."

"Likewise, Al."

Gerrit watched the two of them for a bit before turning back to the computer. "Okay, enough of this, everyone. We need to figure out how to save Joe and get our hands on Kane."

His words dampened their brief moment of camaraderie. They would touch ground in less than an hour. It was time to pull things together.

He just hoped that whoever met them on the ground would be able to get him the resources needed to pull this operation off. Otherwise, they might be spending the next few years in a British prison or buried in a nearby graveyard.

Chapter 53

London, England

The pilot taxied to a part of Heathrow Airport reserved for private international flights. Gerrit knew they were all carrying solidly built documents that would support their aliases through Security and Customs.

Still, he was on edge when these documents and their faces became subjected to vigorous facial-recognition programs and document searches. Joe had assured him that between his security measures, his contacts inside certain federal agencies, and Alena's expertise, these documents would hold up under intense scrutiny. However, Joe had been captured by Kane, somehow alerted to Joe's illegal entry into this country after Redneck sent a warning. There had to have been a breakdown, and right now they were going in blind. There was no time to back out and try another approach.

Joe's life depended upon them. No second chances when time was a matter of life and death.

The pilot cleared the cabin and made his way toward them. "There is someone from security coming on board. Says he needs to speak to one of you."

Gerrit looked at the pilot. "Do you know who he wanted to speak to?"

The pilot jutted his chin toward Gerrit. "He mentioned your name."

So the pilot knew who he was? Jack had not mentioned that he gave out Gerrit's real identify. "Did you get this guy's name?"

The pilot shook his head and returned to the cockpit. Willy looked at him. "Shall I let him in?"

Gerrit shrugged. "What choice do we have?"

A moment later, Willy popped open the exterior door and pushed outward and a power-operated ramp edged to the opening. Heavy footsteps came up the ramp and a familiar face popped through the hatch.

James Stafford, MI6 agent from Vienna.

"Gerrit, rumors of your death have been greatly exaggerated." Stafford stepped into the cabin, grinning at the expression on Gerrit's face. "Back from the colonies, Doctor?" To the others, he said, "James Stafford, of her Majesty's secret service. At your beck and call."

Gerrit felt peculiar. The last time he met Stafford, the British agent had not been cordial. "I thought you worked for—"

"Lawton?" Stafford laughed. "He just thinks I work for him. Like I said last time, Gerrit, I work for a lot of people. At least I let them think that. Been working with Beck Malloy and Joe O'Rourke for years whenever they come over to my side of the pond. Come, let me help you get through security."

Gerrit and his team grabbed their belongings and followed the muscular man off the plane. They walked across fog-drenched pavement and approached a dreary gray building with a red brick facade. Stafford punched in a security code and opened a heavy metal door, rusted hinges squeaking.

Stafford gestured them inside. "I've arranged the VIP tour for our guests in the most exquisite part of the terminal."

They shuffled across an almost empty warehouse, their footsteps echoing through the building. Passing through another ancient door, they emerged on the far side along a roadway where a single vehicle sat parked, running. Under most circumstances, airport security would be all over this vehicle.

Stafford pointed toward it. "Here's our ride. I've got you set up for the night in a house we maintain on the outskirts of the city. Tomorrow, we'll get whatever you need before your visit up north."

Gerrit raised an eyebrow. "You know about that?"

Stafford gave him an offended look. "You think I don't know what you Americans are up to on my own island? Ever since that trouble we had with you colonists, we've always made it our business to keep tabs on you rebels."

Gerrit smiled. "And I thought you didn't like me."

"I don't, Doc. We just happen to be on the same side in this fight." The British agent grinned before opening the driver's door. "Climb on in, everyone. On our way to the safe house, you can fill me in on what I need to know."

A gray, blustery sky greeted them the next morning. Gerrit was one of the first to rise, quietly opening the front door, stepping out on the front porch. A cold biting wind forced him back inside. He closed the door and made his way to the kitchen.

Stafford was there, making tea and coffee. "What's your pleasure, Gerrit?"

"Coffee, please."

The British agent handed him a cup and saucer. "I made some calls last night after our planning session. I got us a lift—a helicopter—to Harrogate in about two hours. I know time is of the essence."

"Can you tell me anything about what we're going up against?"

Stafford stirred his cup of tea. "I know George Lawton made several trips to Kane's headquarters in Harrogate. Been keeping tabs on the two of them. Even followed my boss up there one time to see what he was up to."

"Lawton doesn't know about you helping us?"

"Man, if he did, Kane would have his hooks into you faster than you could sneeze. Malloy wanted this handled discreetly. That's what I'm doing. On a need-to-know basis. Now, regarding what you might encounter, there's a security net set up around the place. Infrared cameras, laser trip wires, and a security team—"

"Any idea of their strength? How many at the compound?"

The agent took a sip of tea. "Not sure how many. And..." Stafford grimaced "I am not sure how many bodies I can give you for this detail.

The chaps I'd normally pick have been called out for duty elsewhere. In the last twenty-four hours."

Gerrit raised his eyebrows. "Last twenty-four hours?"

"I know. What a coincidence."

"Any chance Lawton is trying to screw up this operation. Kane put out the word?"

Stafford shrugged and set his cup and saucer down. "Thought we covered our tracks pretty well, but this…" The agent stood. They heard someone walking around upstairs. Alena and Willy must be awake.

"How many people can you give me, Stafford?"

Stafford grimaced. "You're looking at him. Me, a chopper and cars to get us in range, and any weapons we need."

"I'll take what I can get." Gerrit tried to hide his disappointment as he recalled firsthand the fortress they would have to hit. His team and Stafford seemed woefully outgunned. There was no more time to think this out.

They had to go in now.

Chapter 54

Harrogate, England

Gerrit flattened himself in the grass. "Willy, you copy?"

"Loud and clear, Mr. G."

Willy had remained in one of the vehicles they left behind a quarter-mile back. Stafford arranged for two vehicles to be waiting on the edge of Harrogate, farthest from Kane's compound, when they arrived in the chopper. In back of one of the vehicles lay weapons, dark camouflage clothing, and an encrypted radio network so each member could keep in touch. Now came the hard part.

Patience.

They waited for darkness to fall before moving toward Kane's compound. A moonless light overhead kept visibility to a minimum, but Stafford's gift—night-vision scopes—allowed the group to move effortlessly toward the compound.

"Give me an update from your eye in the sky." The chopper they rode up in was providing double duty—quick transportation from London and a thermal-imaging camera that could pick out warm bodies to target. The aircraft hovered high above, its muffled engines just under the fog bank, noise almost indistinguishable.

A moment later, Willy's voice came over the radio. "I count four bodies, two on the ground floor and two on the roof."

"No other targets?"

"Nope. Just four. Nothing else registering."

Gerrit keyed his mike. "Stafford, you think there are others down below?"

"Possibly, but if I were calling the shots, mate, I'd put all my resources topside. Down below, they're trapped. Only one way in and out. Right?"

Gerrit tightened his jaw. "Yeah. That's all I saw. So where are all the others?"

"Maybe we got lucky?"

"Don't believe in luck—neither does my partner." He glanced at Alena and was rewarded a smile. "They have to know we're coming. Look for others beyond our perimeter, Willy. This could be a trap."

He turned to Alena. "You ready?"

She nodded.

"We have maybe a minute or two to scale that wall before they come checking on us."

"Let's just get this over with." She seemed nervous.

"Okay." He keyed his mike. "Stafford, you ready?"

"Game on! Once I start a diversion on my side, you'd better make like a track star. I won't be able to hold them off for long."

Willy cut in. "Once he starts the fireworks, Gerrit, I can't give you an accurate thermal reading until they cease. There will be heat signatures popping all over the place."

"Roger that. Here we go, guys. On the count of three. One! Two! Three!" Gerrit saw the first flare rise in the sky a moment later, and a weapon started firing on the far side of the Kane mansion where Stafford lay hidden. "Alena. Go! Go! Go!"

Together, they sprinted toward the building. Ten yards from the outer wall, Gerrit aimed a grappling-hook gun at the roofline. He fired it, watching the hook hurl through the air, an attached rope trailing behind. Once the hook landed, he pulled the rope taut. Suddenly, the rope tension slacked as the hook lunged toward him, narrowly missing his head.

Cursing under his breath, he repeated the action, reloading the rope and replacing the suppressed-air canister. Just as he fired the gun once again, Stafford let loose with another volley, concealing the noise of the grappling hook landing on the roof.

Holding his breath, Gerrit gently pulled the rope toward him until the hook caught hold of the stone ledge. He tugged lightly on the rope and felt it tighten. He could only guess how well the hook gripped the roofline.

"Okay," he whispered, shouldering his assault rifle. "When I start up, pull it taut."

She nodded, watching him hang from the rope and begin his ascent.

They were closing in on two minutes. He had to move faster. The targets—he hoped—took Stafford's bait and shifted their attention to the other side. Alena would remain on the ground. Once Gerrit attacked the targets on the roof, she'd hurl a flash bang through the windows. They planned a simultaneous attack on the two remaining guards below—he from the top and she through the first-floor windows.

So far, so good. They hadn't yet encountered any hostile fire.

Stafford continued his mock gunfight, remotely firing several weapons, making it appear as if more than one shooter was firing from his position. He tossed in a few hand grenades for good measure.

Gerrit heard weapons firing from the roof. They must be trying to locate and eliminate Stafford's weapons.

As Gerrit neared the roof's edge, suddenly Stafford's cover fire ceased. Something was wrong. The bad guys on the roof fired several sporadic volleys, but even they ceased firing. As he neared the roofline, he heard footsteps coming in his direction. A small ledge, about the size to allow a foothold, ran parallel to the roofline and just a few feet below.

Gerrit caught the toe of his boot on the ledge and pulled himself closer to the cold stone facade. The footsteps came closer, a couple yards to his left. With one hand clinging to the rope and standing by one toehold, he grabbed his holstered semi-automatic pistol with his right hand and pointed it toward the roofline.

He miscalculated. If the suspect peered over the edge, Gerrit couldn't get a clean shot. The roofline extended out for several feet from the wall, leaving him under the overhang and at a disadvantage. The gunman could lean over, see Alena below and fire as Gerrit watched helplessly. If the gunman saw the rope, he could lean over and fire blindly—with a great chance of hitting him—or just cut the rope and let Gerrit fall. Either way, Gerrit would not be able to return effective fire.

He froze as the footsteps drew near.

Holding his breath, he strained to listen as the man stopped at the ledge. In the dark, the man might not be able to the see the grappling hook, but if he got any closer, he might stumble over it.

Gripping the weapon, he felt himself slipping on the rope. The exertion of the climb and the gunman only a few feet away made him sweat like a basketball player after a full-court press under a hot sun. Cold night air on his face did little to cool him down. Perspiration on his rope hand caused him to lose more of his grip. He clamped his hand on the rope tighter, trying to stave off a fall.

The gunman's head leaned over the side. The man's broad face, with close-cropped dark hair, seemed close enough for Gerrit to reach. He raised the pistol and pointed it at the man.

Suddenly, gunfire erupted on the far side of the building. *Stafford.* The gunman above him disappeared. Gerrit assumed he was moving back into position to cover his partner. Gerrit reholstered and swung out from the wall, quickly climbing up to the ledge and pulling himself up to peer above the flat roofline.

Both gunmen were on the far side of the roof, firing wildly in Stafford's direction.

Gerrit swung up his right leg and caught it on the edge, pulling himself up and over. He quickly unslung his rifle and brought it up to the ready. He walked toward them keeping the targets in his line of fire.

One of the men glanced back and Gerrit hit him with a short burst. The second gunman heard Gerrit's gunfire and swung his rifle around.

"Freeze," Gerrit said. "Freeze or you're dead."

The gunman let his weapon fall and slowly raised his hands in the air.

Gerrit keyed his mike. "One down and one in custody."

Alena's whisper came over the radio. "Let me know when you want me to make entry."

"Give me a second—" He saw the gunman suddenly make a move. Weapons. Gerrit's trigger finger reacted immediately. The gunman's body fell backward and then over the side of the building.

"Gerrit, what's happening up there?" Alena whispered into the radio.

He started to respond. "I shot—"

Gunfire erupted below. Coming from inside the building. They were shooting at Alena. He swore to himself, lunging for the stairway that led downstairs. He flung the door open and darted inside, rifle at the ready. He needed to get downstairs and neutralize the threat against Alena. He didn't hear her firing back.

"Gerrit, I'm moving in for support." Stafford's transmission broke Gerrit's concentration for a moment. He dared not respond from his position for fear of giving his location away. He keyed the mike twice and continued down the steps.

Nothing from Alena. No transmission. No returning fire. As he edged downward, Panic began to set in. In all the combat he'd been through, never had he felt this before. It almost made him freeze up.

A noise below him forced him to snap back and start moving. One of the gunmen must be moving just below him.

Still no sound from Alena, he moved forward, fearing the worst.

Chapter 55

Seattle, Washington

A brisk ocean breeze made Richard pull his coat tighter as he stood on the deck of the cabin cruiser. The boat churned through the water toward the peninsula west of Port Angeles. The vessel rose and fell beneath him, his feet balanced as the deck pitched with each wave. The last vestiges of the Seattle shoreline disappeared a while back as they plowed ahead for the Strait of Juan De Fuca.

He moved back inside the cabin, feeling warm air circulating. Rubbing his hands together, Richard peered into the sun, almost hidden by the Olympic Mountains beyond. There were quicker routes to the lab atop Angeles Point, but he wanted to protect their destination at any cost.

Gerrit and his people somehow stumbled on the Albuquerque site. This time, Richard intended to keep this lab here in Washington a secret—at least until they launched Project Megiddo. After that, it would no longer matter.

He eyed his cell phone, waiting for confirmation from his people in Harrogate. Grimacing, he hoped the contingent of security he left behind would be enough to wipe out Gerrit and the others.

As soon as Collette finished in England, she had orders to hightail it to the lab here. He wanted all hands on deck in case something went awry and they needed to protect this lab. If all went as planned in England, Gerrit and his crew would not be in any shape to cause him any more problems. It was Collette's final chance to prove herself after the debacle in New Mexico.

That left only Joe O'Rourke. Once confirmation came in that the others were dead, Richard intended to give the order to kill that obstinate scientist after dragging out every last ounce of intelligence the man held inside. It infuriated him to no end that he had failed to make O'Rourke cave in. They threw everything they had at the man and came up empty. Here, they would take their time. Joe would not be able to resist forever.

He must ferret out Joe's federal contacts. They must be hunted down and terminated.

Richard stared across the Strait of Juan de Fuca. Just a short hop across the strait, and he could be on foreign soil if unwanted visitors showed up here. British Columbia would be a good jumping-off place to return to some of his European haunts; countries where his large cache of money greased the palms of those who could offer protection from meddling law enforcement.

Money makes the world go around. And once this project was under-way, money would give him and Stuart's people all the juice they needed to reach their goals.

For a moment, he closed his eyes and thought about the exhilarating use of power that would finally be in his grasp. Power to force armies to stand down, dictators to bend a knee to Richard's will. No more political bickering between countries. A one-world government with enough power to bring peace to every square inch of this planet. No more wars, unless they decided to start one. No more poverty. No more wealthy class taking their undue share—except for those like himself wielding absolute power.

No more pettiness. Richard's people would be able to fairly distrib-ute the earth's resources to benefit all of mankind, not just a few wealthy countries like the United States. It would be a bitter pill for those so-called patriots to swallow, but they would be offered a choice—just like everyone else—either accept this new world order or face extinction.

Disease. Hunger. War. Crime. All the plagues of mankind finally conquered by a unified and centralized power base. Some within this organization even mentioned that a Utopia might be possible, a nirvana in which mankind could live in peace, harmony and accord. There would be no more struggles to survive. Man's technology and research could feed, cloth, house, and protect the world. No more wars. To take advantage of others. He was not one of those dreamers. Nirvana could never be reached as long as human nature imposed itself, but they might come close.

For the last fifty years, he'd been working toward this goal. Finding others with the same interest, those with enough clout to make this happen. Politicians, business leaders, military—all the cogs of society that could be used to wield together one powerful force to create this new world. People not held back by provincialism and self-interested ideology.

His cell phone vibrated. Glancing down, he saw a text message from Collette. He activated the message.

Targets entered the trap. They are about to die.

Richard turned the phone off, smiling to himself. Now he could focus on more important matters.

Every time Beck came to the Pentagon, he felt in awe at the size of this place. Today was no exception. He finally reached the office he sought and tapped on the door. "Mind if I come in?"

Jack Thompson looked up from his desk. "I'm beginning to think you're a ghost. How did you get past security? And how did you know I wouldn't be down at SOCOM in Florida?"

Beck grabbed a chair and pulled it closer to Thompson's desk. "It's all about who you know."

Thompson chuckled. "Well, I know for a fact you do business with a ton of people. I keep running into them all over this globe. What can I do you for?"

"Tracking down Richard Kane."

The colonel nodded. "I'd like to know where that scumbag is right now. I'd be tempted to send in a drone to take him out."

Beck's eyes narrowed. "You may get your chance. I've got a hit on a boat off the Washington State coast. Somewhere in the waters between the U.S. and Canada—Strait of Juan de Fuca."

"How did you manage that?"

"Remember that radio-frequency tracking program DARPA farmed out to private industry?"

"Enhancement of RFID chip batteries? Yeah, but that stuff is only good for close surveillance. Not good for long-range operations."

"Old news, Colonel. An Israeli company came up with a battery-powered RFID chip that can send out a unique identification number read by our satellites. I had one of these chips planted on Kane when he was running around Vienna trying to recruit Gerrit."

"You were watching him over there? How did an FBI agent stateside get clearance to monitor an operation overseas?"

"I'd rather not say, sir."

Thompson smirked. "I'll bet you don't."

Beck leaned forward. "I put a trace on him ever since. He left England just before Gerrit and his crew arrived. I've tracked him to this boat, and we should be able to get a fix on his exact location once he hits land."

"Does Gerrit know Kane is gone?"

Beck shook his head. "I can't seem to raise him on the cell phone. He may have turned it off before hitting Kane's location."

"Well, let him know as soon as possible. Since Kane is not in Harrogate, I wonder who he left in charge."

Beck shrugged. "Even more important…where is Joe O'Rourke?"

Chapter 56

Harrogate, England

Alena whispered over his radio, "Gerrit. Incoming!"

He felt relief for a moment. She was still alive. And she just warned him she'd chucked the flash-bang. Quickly, he closed his eyes and covered his ears. He felt and heard the blast, even with his ears covered.

The gunmen below him must be temporarily stunned. He scrambled down the stairs just as one man rose from the ground. Gerrit fired two quick bursts before the gunman could swing his weapon around. The man slumped to the ground and remained motionless.

He heard movement to his left and swung around to face the next target. A second too late. The second gunman leaped from around the corner and aimed his rifle before Gerrit could zero in on him.

A burst of automatic fire opened up to his right. The muzzle flash gave him a glimpse of Alena coming through broken windows.

The second gunman fired wildly in the air as he fell back.

Four men down.

Alena crept toward him, rifle at the ready. "You okay?"

"Yeah. I was worried. Heard all that outgoing firepower and didn't hear you firing back."

"I knew they were firing wildly. Held my fire until I could get the flash-bang set up to cover you from the roof."

"Thanks for having my back. I was a second too slow for that last guy."

"Yeah. Saved by a woman. You will never live that down."

He smiled. "I could get used to this...partner.

Alena returned his smile for a moment. Then she frowned. "Do you think we have any more to deal with here?"

"Don't know. Our thermal imaging showed these four. We need to take the elevator to the lower floor to check on any others and see if..."

They both knew he was thinking of Joe. She whispered, "They could be waiting down there. That elevator might be a kill zone they set up knowing we'd come for him."

"I know. But we don't have a choice. It's where they might have Joe."

They moved toward the elevator. Alena said, "How are we going to access the code?"

Gerrit held up a card. "Searched one of the dead guys on the roof. Same card I saw Kane use the last time I was here." He slid the card through the reader, and the elevator door slid open. He entered and used the butt of his rifle to shatter the light bulbs in the ceiling. Darkness enveloped them as the elevator door closed.

They descended to the lower level. Gerrit tapped her on the shoulder. "I'll go first. Let's crisscross. I'll move to the right, you to the left. Okay?"

"Yeah."

The elevator shuddered to a stop. "Ready?"

"Hit it."

He gripped his rifle, hit the Open button. He shot through the half-opened door, the tip of his weapon following the direction he scanned as he pressed himself against the wall. Alena moved to his left.

Only silence and darkness beyond. All lights have been extinguished on this floor.

"Stay put," he whispered. "I'll find a light switch."

He worked his way along the wall until he came to a panel of switches. "Got 'em. Get ready." He began to switch one after another. The entire lower floor burst with light. It took a few second for his eyes to become accustomed to the brightness. He scanned the room.

Not a soul in sight.

He crept forward, clearing one cubicle after another. Each desk was cleaned off. Not a scrap of paper left behind. Together, they moved in unison through the room, clearing each spot before going forward.

Still no one.

They came to a doorway. He swung it open and saw it led to a darkened hallway, with more doors leading off from the hallway. He groped on the wall and found another panel of light switches. Turning these on, he saw an empty hallway.

Each room they examined stood empty.

At the end of the hallway, one more door sat barring their way. Peering through the door's window, he saw a much larger room beyond, bigger than all the others. In the center of that room was a metal table equipped with metal rings where victims could be tied down.

Gerrit's gut tightened. He knew how they used this room—to torture and interrogate prisoners. A chill swept through him as another thought came to mind.

Where is my uncle?

If Kane brought Joe here, this is where they must have tried to make him talk. The place was empty and spotless.

"No one here." Gerrit glanced at Alena. "Except for the four upstairs, this place is a ghost town."

Alena looked around her. "And where is Joe? This is where I thought Kane would take him."

"Maybe he was here at one time. But Kane must have moved him. So, where do we start looking?"

"Let's get back upstairs and check in with the others." They rode the elevator and just stepped out when Stafford approached them. "What did you find?"

Gerrit shrugged. "Nothing. Everyone's gone."

Willy's voice came over the radio. Excited. Urgent. "Mr. G. Can you copy?"

Gerrit keyed his mike. "Go ahead, Willy."

"Got another bogey you guys overlooked."

Gerrit looked at Stafford and Alena. "Where?"

"About a hundred yards west of your location. And she's armed."

Collette.

"Can she copy our transmissions?"

"Of course she can't." Willy sounded hurt. "After I got these radios from Stafford, I encrypted our system myself."

Stafford frowned. "They were encrypted, Willy."

"Sorry, Spy Man. I had to make sure."

Gerrit cut in. "Well, we'll—"

"Get out of there now. Now!" Willy screamed into the radio.

Gerrit sprinted to the door, yelling at the others. "Follow me."

He cleared the front door, sprinting toward the nearest tree line, Alena and Stafford a few feet behind. A split second later, he and the others were hurled across the grass like limp dolls as an explosion rocked the mansion.

Gerrit felt himself land on the ground. The only sound he heard after the blast was an incessant ringing in his ears. Alena and Stafford lay nearby. Both were moving.

Alive.

He looked back at the building and saw rubble piled up where the house once stood. Fires broke out among the debris. They had to get farther away in case of secondary explosions. Gas. Explosives. Who knows?

He helped Alena to her feet and they sprinted toward the trees about a hundred yards away.

"We're okay, Willy. Copy?"

"Oh, thank God."

Gerrit keyed the mike again. "Give me a fix on this fifth person. Maybe a spotter?"

"Mr. G, I think she is the one who triggered the explosion. And she has a sniper rifle aimed at your position. Take cover!"

Chapter **57**

Gerrit and the others zigzagged a path beyond the first row of trees. Collette must not have a clear shot and didn't want to give her position way. That bought them a few minutes.

All three caught their breath before Gerrit spoke. "Okay, you guys stay here. I'm going to break off and work my way around her with Willy's help."

Alena placed her hand on his shoulder. "No, Gerrit. This woman is mine. You guys provide a distraction."

"No, Alena, I can't—"

"Because I'm a woman?"

"No, I—"

"There is a lot you do not know about me, Gerrit. This is something I am good at. Trust me." Without waiting, she melted into the darkness.

He glanced at Stafford. The agent just shrugged. "I think she knows what she's doing, O'Rourke. Let's try to take the heat off her."

Gerrit activated his mike. "Willy, feed us any information on the target. Al's going to take point. My partner and I will be the bait. You'll be Alena's eyes and ears until this is over."

"Gotcha, Mr. G."

Gerrit turned to the agent. "Well, let's keep Collette busy."

Alena moved from tree to tree through the shadows. "Willy, guide me in," she whispered into the mike. She heard several clicks. After activating her night-vision glasses, she worked her way in a wide circle around where she believed Collette lay hiding.

"Alena, you copy?" Gerrit's voice seemed like a scream compared to the quietness surrounding her.

She responded with two clicks.

"Be careful."

She smiled to herself, suspecting that Gerrit did not think she could take care of herself. In a way, that was sweet. If only he knew half the operations she'd been in, he would not have to worry as much. But her past she tried to keep locked away. Only Joe knew most of her history. And that was one person too many.

Stealthily, she wove through groves of trees that surrounded Kane's complex, targeting a hill that lay beyond Collette's position. Alena could crest that hill and work down the slope, giving her the high ground and—hopefully—the element of surprise.

It seemed forever before she reached it, clogged with low-lying brush and winter-bare trees. Some were evergreen, but not enough for good cover. She was thankful that whatever noise she made up to this point would not be carried down the hill to Collette's hiding place. At least until she slipped over the crest and began her descent. At that point, she hoped Gerrit and Stafford would kick up some noise.

Just as she reached the apex, she heard Collette fire two quick shots.

Hugging the ground, Alena waited to see where the shots had been aimed. The rifle's blast would not necessarily divulge direction. Only that it had been fired.

"Stafford," Gerrit's voice carried over the radio. "Move to your left, and I'll try to flank her. Don't give her a clean shot."

"Watch your own hide, O'Rourke. I can take care of myself." Stafford sound annoyed.

They were giving her the time she needed to make a move.

She started downward while scanning below for any sign of the target. Moonlight made the hillside light like day through the night-vision glasses. Movement caught her eye. There, behind a rock, facing away. Alena edged forward, using tree trunks as cover wherever possible in case Collette spun around.

Several more shots fired. Those came from Gerrit's position. For a second, she was angry that he fired in her direction, and then she heard one of the rounds zip overhead. He was firing high for distraction.

Stafford fired several shots.

As the sound of rifle fire echoed up the slope, she used the noise as cover to dash down the hill, closer to Collette's position. She jumped behind a tree trunk and waited to see if the woman had heard her. Nothing but silence. She peered around the trunk. The woman lay prone about ten yards away. She could kill Collette from here, but taking her prisoner was a higher priority. The woman knew where Joe might be.

Alena reached down and keyed her radio twice, hoping Gerrit would understand. She held her breath and waited.

Gerrit peppered the air with more shots. He got the message.

She took a deep breath and sprang from the tree, dashing the short distance between her and Collette. With only three more yards to go, Collette rose up and spun around to face her. Alena's momentum carried her the remaining distance as the woman raised her rifle. She slammed into Collette with enough force to carry them both down the hill, knocking the woman's rifle away.

As she leaped from the ground, Alena heard the blade of a knife unsheathed. Her night-vision glasses had been knocked out of place when she collided with Collette. Momentarily blind. She tore off her glasses and reached for her holstered gun before Collette could use the knife. The holster was empty. The weapon must have been jarred loose in the collision.

As her eyes adjusted to the darkness, Alena saw a flash of metal as Collette lunged and slashed her way toward Alena. Moonlight glittered off the blade.

Rookie move.

Alena sidestepped the last downward slash and caught Collette's wrist in midair. Alena torqued the arm to her left and pulled, using her attacker's downward movement as leverage.

Collette screamed as Alena wrenched the arm, practically pulling it out its socket. Collette dropped the weapon.

Whirling, Alena used her forward motion to smash the base of Collette's neck as the woman crumbled to the ground. Unconscious.

Gerrit looked down at Collette, bound and lying on the ground. The woman glared up at them. He looked at Alena and shook his head. "Note to self: Don't get Alena angry. She can hurt me."

Alena tried to smile. "She won't talk—at least for now. We need to find Joe some other way."

Stafford shouldered his rifle as Willy walked up. "Let me get her back to the office and see what we can get out of her."

"Alena is right," Gerrit said, watching Willy search the prisoner's pockets and remove a cell phone. "We have to move now."

"Look at this, Mr. G." Willy had flipped the phone open, scrolling through the menu. "She received text messages from a number I recognize. The boss man himself."

Gerrit felt his pulse quicken. "Maybe we can get Kane to tell us something. Quick, send back a text...*mission accomplished*."

Typing the message, Willy hit the Send button. "Message on its way."

"Okay, let's get out of here before locals come to investigate."

Stafford broke in. "I've got you covered here, O'Rourke. My people will take over as soon as I get them on-site. I'll handle her." He nodded toward Collette. "Maybe I can get something out of her. It would be better if you all were gone when my people get here. Less to explain."

Gerrit nodded.

"Man, that was fast." Willy stared at the phone. "Just got a return text. It reads, *'Congrats. Now, get here as fast as you can.'*"

"Doesn't say where that is?"

"Nope. That's all Kane sent."

Gerrit reached down and turned on his own cell phone. "Hey, I got messages on my own phone." All from one source. "I'll check them on our way. Let's meet by the car."

"Roger that," Willy said.

Gerrit raised the phone to his ear and heard Beck's voice. After listening to all the messages, he joined the others waiting by the car. "Pack your bags. There's one person I trust who might be able to help us. Start driving and I'll try to get a message to him. We're going back to where this all started."

Chapter 58

Vancouver, British Columbia

"We seem to be living out of this plane." Gerrit peered out of the window as the aircraft descended toward the international airport far below. To the north, the Pacific mountains reached for the sky, with Mount Garibaldi rising like a monarch reigning over his mountainous kingdom.

Jack arranged for them to land north of Seattle on the Canadian side of the border and set up a personal escort through security. Sea-Tac would have been the closest airport, but Jack felt Kane's people would be monitoring all arrivals into western Washington. Anyone trying to track their travel would find it difficult to zero in on them once they touched ground in Canada.

A family-size van with tinted windows sat near the terminal when they left the aircraft, and they crossed into the United States with minimal difficulty. Their falsified government-issued documents got them through Customs without a hitch. Once across the border, Gerrit used his credit card—issued under an alias to rent another van to get them near Seattle, leaving the Canadian rental behind.

Alena, sitting in the passenger seat, watched in the rearview mirror. "If someone picked up our trail, I'm not seeing it."

In the driver's seat, Gerrit found himself looking back as often as he looked forward. "Neither did I. Unless someone painted us with markers. Then they could be anywhere."

"Hey, give me some credit," Willy said. He'd been silently sitting in the back until Gerrit hinted at a screw up. "I went over all our gear and personal items on the plane. We're squeaky clean."

"Maybe you missed something." He glanced at Willy in the rearview mirror.

Willy scowled. "I didn't miss anything, Mr. G."

"We're betting our lives on you." Gerrit watched Willy flinch and Alena gave Gerrit a scowl. He got the message. "Look, I'm sorry. I guess I'm worried about Joe. Just forget I said anything."

A slow smile emerged as Willy nodded. "You bet, Mr. G. And if you give me any more grief, I'll just have Al kick your butt."

Gerrit smiled and looked over at Alena.

She did not return his smile. "Gerrit, I'm not sure about this person you called. Can you trust him?"

He met her stare for a moment before turning his attention back to the road. "With my life." He gripped the steering wheel. "He'll have our backs."

As they continued down I-5 heading toward Seattle, he thought about the last month and how everything in his life had been turned upside down. Redneck had been the latest surprise. Since that betrayal, they all seemed to be on edge. He needed to chill out and focus on what needed to be done. He hoped there were no further surprises as they moved ahead. They just needed to find Joe and get him back alive. Everything else dimmed in comparison.

Elliot Bay Marina lay straight ahead. The salt air seemed to cleanse his lungs as Gerrit stepped from the van into the parking lot. He stretched his legs as a familiar figure worked his way through parked cars, waving to get Gerrit's attention.

"There he is. Stan Cromwell. My old boss." Gerrit waited until the police lieutenant drew close, thrusting out his hand.

"Man, talk about rising from the grave." Cromwell vigorously shook his hand and pounded Gerrit on the back. "I can't tell you how good it is to see your ugly face again."

"Likewise, Lieutenant."

"I'm so glad you survived." Cromwell glanced at the other two standing a few feet away. "And who are they?"

"Let's just say they're friends and leave it at that." Gerrit said. "The less you know, the better it will be for you and your retirement."

"My ex is taking my retirement, so I don't have a whole lot to lose." The lieutenant tried to treat his last statement as a joke, but Gerrit could see the words only covered up deep emotional wounds. Cromwell was like a man set adrift without an anchor. "Anything I can do to help, just let me know. I got everything you asked for set up on my end. You want to see her?"

"Yeah. That'd be great." Gerrit motioned for the others to follow as he and lieutenant made their way toward the marina. "Another friend of mine will be sending over some supplies by courier. I'll need to keep an eye on the parking lot. They should be here within the hour."

Cromwell nodded. "When do you want to shove off?"

"In a few hours or as soon as it gets dark."

Looking back, the lieutenant said, "Are you sure? Those waters—particularly as you head out toward open sea—can get pretty tricky at night."

"Darkness works for us. Less likely to see us coming. We can look like another leisure craft as far as they're concerned. Until we get in close. Buy us some time."

"Whatever you say. Here she is," Cromwell said. "A 53-foot Navigator Pilothouse, with a 370 horsepower Volvo engine, 600 gallons of fuel, and a draft of 4 feet, 5 inches. You can practically drive this baby to their front door before they see you coming."

Gerrit studied the boat's contours, pleased that Cromwell came up with this so quickly. "Who is it registered to in case the Coast Guard or crooks run it?"

The lieutenant smiled. "To your deceased friend Nico. Listed under one of his holding companies. We seized it after you—"

"After I died?" Gerrit smiled. "Doesn't a drug seizure take longer before it can be turned over to local PD?"

"I just cut through some red tape. What the bean counters don't know, won't hurt 'em. Just don't run this boat onto the rocks, or I will have a major problem."

"I'll do my best to get this back to you in one piece."

"And no bullet holes. Right?"

"Can't make any promises."

"Don't get yourself dead again, son. This old heart just can't take any more losses."

Gerrit placed a hand on the lieutenant's shoulder. "Sir, I intend to survive. I might ask the same about you. Aren't too many good guys left."

Cromwell walked away with saying another word.

As promised, about an hour later another van entered the parking lot, compliments of Jack Thompson. Gerrit and the others struggled to get the wooden crate on board after the van left. Concealed in a large fish locker, they found enough weapons, explosives, and gear to wage a small war—which is what Gerrit suspected they might face as they continued to hunt for Richard Kane and Joe O'Rourke.

Richard followed a shale-strewn path leading from his compound—built on the crest of a cliff overlooking the Strait of Juan De Fuca—to the shoreline below. In a rare occurrence, the day's fog had lifted in the late afternoon to allow him to see all the way to the Canadian shoreline. A ship bound for open water slowly navigated through the strait about half distance between shorelines.

A Brandt's Cormorant with dark plumage dived into the water a few hundred yards offshore. A pair of seagulls, perched on top of a large boulder, squawked at each other as if they'd been married for years. Richard made his way along the rocky shorelines, taking in the sounds and smells of the sea. The cool air cleared his mind, and he took a moment to relax.

In spite of some setbacks, things were now starting to come together. He just gave Stuart an update on the incident in Harrogate after Collette texted him that the mission had been successful. In spite of having to move his headquarters to another continent, Richard felt a glow of satisfaction that Gerrit and his crew were no longer a threat. Finally, something positive to share with that overbearing man who held Richard's future in those gnarly hands of his.

Stuart was getting old. Maybe it was time for younger blood to step up and take over the reins of power. Those—like himself—who were more in tune with the times. Old warriors like Stuart seemed to be losing their touch, losing their ability to handle all the complexities of this movement. Globalization and world control were not for those who could no longer fight the fight, whose minds were living in the past, minds still resisting change.

Project Megiddo had been Richard's baby, his idea. It had taken everything he had and all the contacts he could muster to get Stuart and the others on board. If Project Megiddo succeeded—*when* Project Megiddo succeeded—Richard would be in line to be elevated to that highest sanctum of power. He would be one of the gods.

He could almost taste the triumph. It was only a matter of time. He glanced at his watch. It was only hours away. At 10 p.m. Pacific Standard Time, Project Megiddo's first assault would be launched. Two banking systems, nine nations known or suspected of possessing nuclear weapons, and one nation with massive intelligence capabilities—the United States—would all fall victim to cyber penetration.

Once Project Megiddo's system infiltrated those systems, Richard and his group would be able to control all those instrumental in each of these critical areas. Weaknesses and vulnerabilities of each of these powerful individuals had been identified. Richard's people, already briefed, stood poised to act upon his command. Financial, military, and intelligence capabilities would be at his fingertips. Their system would soon be able to trigger a financial collapse anywhere in the world, launch nuclear missiles upon command, and tap into any intelligence asset anywhere in the world.

A month ago, they tested the system on one individual who thought himself well insulated inside the White House. Megiddo's technology worked its way into the target's computer systems, meanwhile reaching out to an incalculable number of databases, drawing information specific to the man's life. Using quantum computer technology—thought to be years away from reality—Megiddo's calculations and multisystem access worked at speeds most scientist thought impossible. Every secret, every hidden sin this idiot thought covered up became known to them in a flash, including photos, videotapes, and captured voice messages that clearly made the target vulnerable—and in one instance, eligible for a long term in prison.

Two hours after launch, Richard had sat down with the target for dinner and revealed all he knew about him. The man seemed to melt before Richard's eyes as his misdeeds were revealed: illicit sexual encounters covered up thirty years ago, a business deal gained by twisting political arms using White House clout, and the revelation of an offshore account the man socked away for a rainy day, proceeds from ill-gotten gains. By dinner's end, Richard had an invaluable source inside the White House, a man with direct access to the president.

He laughed, thinking about another staff member in the office of the Director of National Intelligence, who had the audacity to scoff at the notion anyone might be able to penetrate U.S. safeguards protecting nuclear launch codes. As they sat over lunch in a private conference room inside Langley, Richard listened as this moron listed all the safeguards in place. He just nodded in agreement, all the while thinking about Megiddo's pending capabilities. Just for kicks, he had the staffer run through the Megiddo system. Now, he had another convert, a man who had become the CIA director's confidential advisor.

A vibration in his upper pocket alerted him to another incoming text. He glanced at the words and ground his teeth as the message became clear. This was impossible. Anger welled up inside.

Collette must have been captured—or killed. Gerrit and the others were coming his way.

Chapter 59

Strait of Juan De Fuca

Gerrit sat in the captain's chair, steering away from the protected waters of Puget Sound and worked toward the open waters of the Juan De Fuca Strait. To the west, a yellow globe began to set in the sky, although they still had a few hours of daylight left. Just enough to get them past Port Angeles before darkness descended.

They were making good time. He wanted to use these few moments at the wheel to go over their next plan of attack.

Beck Malloy was out of position to help, but the FBI agent made some calls and marshaled reinforcements coming in by chopper once Gerrit gave the word. He was sure Beck failed to mention that they would be following the orders of a person wanted for questioning in several murders. Kane's compound, perched on a cliff, had finally been identified and construction plans for the site emailed to Willy's computer. Aerial shots of the site had also been downloaded.

"Mr. G, here's the layout as I see it." Willy sat at a small table next to Gerrit . "Because of its isolation, I think Kane went a little light on security. The only access to the property is one roadway. There is a large helipad near the main house, and the rest of the property looks like trees, rocks, and heavy forest—stuff like that."

"Where is our best access?"

"From the water—but not directly. Here, take a look." Willy angled the laptop to allow Gerrit a view.

After studying the screen for a few moments, Gerrit pointed to an aerial snapshot of the entire area. "Just east of the cliff, there's a small inlet where we can anchor and cruise our way to shore in the Zodiac. Once on land, it looks like a steep climb to the ridge—tough but doable. Then if we just follow that ridgeline, we'll emerge east of where the lab's located. Once we scout the landing site, Beck's people can land and secure the target. Remember, we need the element of surprise. They may be expecting us. My goal is for us to stay in the shadows and call in reinforcements to take on Kane's security."

Willy nodded. "From there, we can spread out and take the—"

"Not you, Willy. Alena and I will handle any armed security. I need you to focus on the technology we need to gain an upper hand. Heat sensors, aerial reconnaissance, any intel you can grab from Kane's computer system. Until we get Beck's people on the ground, it will be just the three of us against a small army. Bad odds. I want you to feed us whatever surveillance footage you get from the satellite in real time. The colonel is getting you clearance. They have designated airtime specifically for this operation. For you."

"For little ol' me?" Willy said, a look of anger on his face. "Ah, shucks, Massa, you sho' been good—"

"Stuff it, Willy." Alena's sharp tone cut through the cabin. "This is no time for your stupid jokes." She emerged from the galley below, shooting an angry look at both men. She seemed to avert her eyes from the drawing lying on the table.

"How come you and Mr. G. get to do all the kung fu stuff, and I get stuck playin' with a computer?"

Alena frowned. "Frankly, you have no martial arts skills, Willy. Bang'n in the woods back home doesn't cut it. We need your technological expertise. And we need it now."

"It's bang'n in the hood—not *woods*." Willy clenched his jaw. "Can't you at least give me a gun?"

Alena's face softened. "Okay. One handgun…but don't shoot any-one. Deal?"

Willy shrugged and looked back at his computer. "Guess it will have to do until I earn my black belt. Then…watch out!"

Alena's jaw clenched. Even Willy's humor didn't loosen her up. Something seemed to be troubling her. Gerrit turned toward the computer. "Alena, you want to take a look before—"

"Why do I have to take a look? I'll be following you the whole time. You are the one with uncanny recall, Einstein." She whirled toward Willy. "And you, just do what Gerrit says. It is time to get serious. No more jokes, you hear?"

Willy took one look at her and hung his head. "I just thought I'd help you guys hit the place. Not hold back again and watch you have all the fun."

"I need your eyes and ears, Willy." Gerrit jumped into the conversa-tion, trying to calm the others down. "It's critical. Okay?" Gerrit watched Alena looking outside. "You okay?"

She wheeled around and joined Willy at the table. "No, I am not okay." She took a deep breath. "We still do not know where Joe is being kept. And Kane must know by now that we are still alive and kicking."

Gerrit shrugged. "Maybe we got lucky. It might take days for them to dig through all that debris before they find out our bodies are missing."

"What if he tried to reach Collette directly?"

"Stafford's going to take care of Collette and the others. Put her and the bodies on ice until he hears from us."

She gave him a hard look. "Do not underestimate Kane. He has eyes and ears everywhere. Look at…Redneck." A look of sadness washed over her features.

"Everyone here has been tested, Alena. We've all come under fire. Only Redneck failed the test. The rest of us are all good."

Her face stiffened. "Let us just get this over with soon. We need to find Joe and get Kane under wraps—once and for all."

A yelp from Willy drew their attention back to him. "I'm up and run-ning. We have just enough light to get a fix on the place."

The feed zeroed in on the coordinates of Kane's compound. "Print that overview out, will you?"

Willy nodded at Gerrit, sending the image wirelessly to his portable printer. "Here it comes. I'll make several copies."

As soon as a copy became available, Gerrit asked Alena to take the wheel while he studied the layout. "Seems simple. See the main house? Everything must be in that area." He pointed to what appeared to be a large, multistory building. Just like the site plans showed, only one roadway connected to the building and several small structures on the compound. The road led down the mountainside, finally connecting with other roads east of Port Angeles.

Willy was looking over his shoulder. "Mr. G, see that?" He pointed to structures near the main building. "Looks like satellite dishes for sending and receiving. They must be moving massive amounts of data through those towers. I'd sure like to get a closer look."

"You'll get your chance," Gerrit said. "They're going to be watching that roadway for anyone posing a threat to them. Based upon our operation in Albuquerque, they also expect trouble from the air. But a boat—this is where I think they're most vulnerable. We can hoof in from this inlet to the east," he pointed to spot on the map near the water's edge, "and make our way up to the compound. I'd bet they don't even have any ground sensors in place. Just roving security because of the huge area to cover and a perimeter fence."

With one hand on the wheel, Alena leaned over and studied the map for a few moments. "How are the three of us going to slip past security? We don't know how many bodies they have on the ground."

"If everything goes as planned, we'll manage." Gerrit began to lay out their approach. Everything hinged on Beck's contact on the outside. Before they left the marina, Gerrit called that number and gave the contact their radio-frequency numbers. The contact promised they'd be standing by with reinforcements when the time came.

"A twenty-minute response once they get my call." If they didn't get the call, Gerrit and the others would be in a world of hurt. No reason to share this fact with his team. He would make the call—no matter what happened.

"Right now, we have the element of surprise." He pointed the bow toward the shoreline, hugging the coastline as closely as possible.

Richard slammed his fist on the desk. He just received an updated message that Gerrit and the others were closer than he thought.

This time, he must put them down hard. End their stupid antics once and for all. Anytime now, reinforcements Richard called in would be arriving on a secluded airfield about twenty miles away. He wanted to handle this whole matter quietly, but now Gerrit somehow commandeered reinforcements and escalated the situation.

Quiet extermination was no longer an option. This would be a major firefight, and he intended to win.

This could not come at a worse time. In a few hours, Stuart and the others expected Project Megiddo to be in full swing. Every target on Richard's list was going to be hit, a full blast from Megiddo's invasive launch. Data and decryption programs would be flooding their computers from around the world.

Imagine such awesome power. The president of the United States, for example, would be at Richard's beck and call. Absolute power in every country, in every situation—all at his fingertips. Richard and his people were so close to victory, adrenaline rushed through his body.

Now this! Gerrit and his pathetic group of losers.

Search-and-destroy teams had been deployed along the coastline just as dusk set. Any vessel approaching their safety perimeter would be boarded and dealt with extreme prejudice.

Shoot to kill! That was his order. No more traps. No more prisoners. He needed them dead.

Now.

Chapter 60

"Gerrit, you gotta read this. Beck just sent it in." Willy's voice raised an octave. "We've got major problems."

Leaving Alena at the wheel, Gerrit scrambled over to where Willy sat in the forward cabin. "What now?"

"Here." Willy pointed at his computer screen. "Beck knew that darkness would set in before we got set up. The satellites wouldn't do us any good in the dark, at least the close-in images we needed."

"Okay. Tell me what I'm looking at."

Willy clicked on the image. "This is a video feed Beck's people got just a few minutes ago. They sent a drone to sweep the area with a thermal-imaging scan."

Gerrit leaned closer and Willy clicked the feed. Kane's darkened compound suddenly had small specks of heat spreading outward like tiny ants. "More security?"

Willy nodded. "Tons of 'em. It's like they suddenly crawled out of the ground and started spreading all over the property. Look at this!" He pointed along the shoreline.

Heat signatures showed a number of four-man teams sweeping the water's edge, east and west. At least two teams approached the site where he'd selected to hit land. "They know we're coming."

"You think?" Willy scoffed. "They're coming right for us. And we haven't even gotten close yet."

"So, how did they get tipped off? They have some kind of trace on us? Some kind of surveillance you missed?"

Willy shrugged, looking defeated. "Beats the living daylights out of me."

"Not what I wanted to hear, Willy. Right now, our eyes and ears just went blind and deaf." He took a deep breath. No use hammering Willy over what already happened. "I've got another idea. I hope you guys are ready to use a little muscle. You're going to need it."

It was a waste of a good boat, but he had no other choice. Gerrit ordered them to gather their equipment and store it in the Zodiac they had tethered alongside. Once they passed Kane's complex, Gerrit killed the engine and let the craft drift in the current. After the other two climbed in the rubber boat, he untied the rope and leaped into it, letting the cabin cruiser drift away in the darkness.

Alena and Gerrit grabbed the paddles and guided the craft to shore. They struggled to fight their way toward the shoreline against a strong undercurrent. It took almost thirty minutes. Once on land, they faced their next biggest obstacle—sheer cliffs rising straight up for more than a hundred feet.

"Listen up," Gerrit whispered. "I've got to make my way up the cliff first. Once I reach the summit, I'll anchor the rope and lower it down to you. Alena, make sure Willy has his carabineer properly connected and show him how to break his fall using the rope."

"My fall?" Willy hissed. "I'm not planning on falling, man."

Gerrit moved closer. "I just want you to know how to use the rope—in case you slip—to stop your descent. I'm going to send down a second rope around your chest, to give you added support as you climb." *I'm going to be pulling you up that cliff, Willy, So just shut up.*

Alena leaned close and whispered. "You be careful, Gerrit. You have to free climb that rock with no ropes and a full backpack." She glanced upward. "You are the one I'm worried about."

Her breath, close to him, felt warm on his skin in the cool night air. He drew back, almost as a reflex. "Just be ready to move when I get Willy topside. We'll be sitting in an exposed area, no cover all the way to the first building that I can see."

She nodded and moved away, helping Willy slip into his climbing harness.

Gerrit slung the coiled rope and his H&K assault rifle over his shoulder and began his ascent. Although steep, basalt rock formations offered good handholds and jutting edges provided a solid foundation for toe holes as he climbed. But the climb was slow, as he made sure the rock beneath him would hold before he ventured farther. The crashing water beneath him started to diminish as he gained height. Midway, his arms started to shake from the weight of his backpack and ropes, and he rested for a few minutes before continuing. He hugged the rock and looked up. It seemed like he would be climbing forever.

He started upward again, trying to ignore the muscles in his arms and neck tightening with strain and exhaustion. He had to push on. Everything depended on him reaching the top. Resting again, he gazed out over the water. A full moon climbed into the dark sky, a finger of silver light cutting a path across the water toward his direction. The sight might be enjoyable if his body didn't hurt so much.

He pushed on until he finally reached the top. Grasping the edge of the cliff, he raised himself until Kane's complex loomed in sight. Only a few yards away, several boulders lay together, offering limited cover. Beyond the rocks he saw the main structure to his right, and to his left, a heliport that could accommodate several choppers at a time.

No one seemed to be walking the grounds.

He pulled himself up and rolled onto his back after slipping out of the backpack. Catching his breath, he quickly wrapped the end of one rope securely around the largest boulder and dropped the line below.

He knew the kind of weight Willy would bring up the face of the cliff. Stuffed inside a backpack to leave his hands free to climb, Willy carried a 9mm Beretta that he sweet-talked Alena into giving him, his laptop, and a small digital reader. He peered over and saw Alena grasp the other end of the rope. He waited until she had Willy positioned, then he dropped the second rope, tying one end around his waist. Even from this distance, Willy looked scared.

Great, I can see the headlines now: Ex-Cop Killed by Falling Ex-Gangster.

Alena tied the second rope around Willy's chest and under his arms. Gerrit pulled the rope until it was taut, signaling down to Willy to begin his climb. Hand over hand, Willy moved up the face of the rock, using his arms to climb and his feet to brace against the cliff. Gerrit braced himself, set his feet firmly, and began to pull on the second rope to give Willy additional support.

Again, he felt the fire in his arms and strain to his lower back as Willy's dead weight pulled against him. He continually pulled the rope upward. In this position, he couldn't see behind him. Couldn't see if any security patrols came his way.

After what seemed like hours but could only be a few more minutes, Willy reached the top of the cliff. Gerrit pulled even harder, helping the younger man clamber over the edge. Gasping, Willy lay on his back, trying to catch his breath. "Man, I feel like Laurence Fishburne in *The Matrix*."

"Shh," Gerrit warned, glancing around. He untied the rope and started to lower it down to Alena when he saw she was already halfway up. He watched her agilely ascend with what seemed like effortless grace.

A few minutes later, her head emerged and he started toward her to help lift her over the edge. She swung a leg over the top and rolled onto solid ground before he could reach her. He quickly pulled the rope up, stashing both ropes at the base of one of the boulders.

They were ready for the next phase.

Willy lowered his backpack and pulled out the handheld readers before slipping the pack back on. As Willy flicked on the reader, Gerrit whispered, "Okay, when we move out, only use hand signals. We need to make it inside that building without being spotted."

They nodded, and Willy turned the face of the reader toward him.

Gerrit eyed the screen. "Okay, where's the enemy?"

Willy motioned to what looked like a ring of red dots in a semi-circle on the screen, only two positioned near the cliff where they stood. The red dots lay between them and the building.

Alena edged closer to Willy. "They're not going to see our thermal signatures?"

Willy smiled. "Trust me, thanks to Beck and Thompson, we have our own drone overhead to give us cover. Watch what happens when we move out. Oh, don't bother using your night-vision equipment. Just turn it off now."

"Turn it off?" Gerrit shut his system down.

"Yeah, Beck just sent me a message that Thompson made the impossible a reality. And I'd do it real quick. The drone's almost here."

Gerrit shrugged and pointed to where the closest security guards stood. "As soon as Alena and I put those two guys out of commission, we'll move toward the building about two hundred yards away. Willy, stay right behind us. If you spot anyone coming on your reader, tap Alena on the shoulder. When it's clear to move, tap again and point in the direction you want us to move. Okay?"

Gerrit heard the engine of a plane overhead. It sounded like the drone was at tree level.

Willy reached up and grabbed his shoulder. "Wait, Mr. G. One, two...bam."

A man screamed about one hundred yards away. "Man, I can't see anything. What was that—?"

"Shut up, stupid. Our targets are somewhere out there," another voice hissed through the night air. The voice came from the same location where the first man's voice rang out.

"But I can't get a reading. Where is everyone?"

"Will you shut up? You're going to get us killed." The man finally quieted down.

Gerrit felt Willy tap him on the shoulder, motioning toward his night vision glasses. "I can turn them on?"

Willy nodded. "Those two are blind as bats. Their night vision gear is fried."

He slowly rose, flicked on his night vision and signaled the others to follow.

Richard screamed across the room at a man frantically switching from one camera site to another. "Tell me what's going on out there, you idiot. I pay you big money to take care of problems like this. And you can't tell me what's happening?"

The man, huge enough to scare a pro-bowl offensive line, cowered over the console. He was afraid to face Richard. His big paws danced across the keys, trying to access their wireless surveillance monitors.

Flashes of brilliant light had blinded the cameras, and from what he heard over the air, ground-support units were walking around in a daze. The blinding flashes came across intermittently, followed by long periods of blindness as the lens of thermal-imaging readers and night-vision scopes filled with images of snow.

"Someone's got a drone working directly overhead. Each flyover, our guys get hit with electronic pulses that make their Night Optical Devices go blind. Some of their equipment has been permanently put out of commission."

"I can see that, you moron. What I need from you is how to take this drone out."

The huge man shrugged helplessly. "We don't have any surface-to-air capabilities. We never imagined that—"

"Correction. *You* never imagined. And yet, I pay you to anticipate these contingencies. Well, now we must react." Richard paced back and forth, thinking. He thrust a finger at the hapless giant. "Pull everyone back. Ring the perimeter with security units. Gerrit and his people are trying to get inside the compound."

The man turned back to his console.

"I'm not finished with you." Richard peered down at the man seated before him. The man was twice his size, but at this point he seemed to shrink next to his boss. "Start checking for incoming aircraft. I imagine they'll chopper in reinforcements to back up Gerrit. I want to make sure when they land, our welcoming surprise is ready for them. My demolition team set up claymores ready to go off on my command."

Richard leaned over and pointed to a small case on the console. He opened it and carefully pointed to a series of switches inside. "Any aircraft sets down on the pad, I want you to trigger these switches. Just make sure that no one walks away from those aircraft when they land. Think you can handle that?"

The Hulk nodded, starting to disseminate Richard's orders to all security units on the ground. Perspiration ran down his armpits as he watched Richard storm across the room and take an elevator belowground. Relieved, he breathed in easier, his giant forearms laying across the console for support.

Chapter 61

Denver, Colorado

Beck dashed toward the waiting jet as frigid winds cut through his thin suit jacket. He bounded up the stairs and into the belly of the craft. The moment he was inside and the stairs raised, it began taxiing toward the runway.

A crewmember closed and locked the hatch before Beck could grab a seat. Colonel Jack Thompson emerged from the cockpit and made his way to Beck. "Got my pilot initiating takeoff. We need to talk right now."

Beck leaned forward. "What's the latest?"

"Sent that drone in at your request and pulled together a small unit to hit the place as backup. But we can't go in blind. What are we up against?"

Beck leaned back and ran his fingers through his hair. "I wish I knew, Colonel. We have the satellites photos and the images the drone sent back. The trouble is this battle will be over by the time you and I get anywhere near Kane's compound."

Thompson nodded. "We got to trust Gerrit to give us the green light to hit that place. Only one landing pad, and if I were Kane, I'd put that out of commission."

"Any other possible landing sites or clearings the chopper might be able to use?"

The colonel shook his head. "All high forest around that compound, except the road leading in to the place. The best approach is that landing pad. Otherwise, our people are gonna have to repel down with their gear, and if any of the bad guys have them in their sights, it'll be like shooting fish in a barrel."

"Then we just have to wait to hear from Gerrit. And hope he and his people can last long enough for our people to get there."

"Any word on Joe O'Rourke?"

Beck grimaced. "Kane has him squirreled away someplace or the man is dead. We haven't been able to pick up any chatter one way or the other."

"So we know Kane's at the compound."

"Yeah. We picked up his signal at that location. Unless he got wise to our tracking device."

Thompson faced Beck. "Okay, I'll radio ahead to have our people launch the second they hear from Gerrit. But unless he can give us an update, I can't in good conscience send our people in. Just too risky."

The colonel hunched forward. "What's the problem?"

Beck studied Thompson before answering. *The old man must be reading my thoughts.* "Can't figure how Kane knew Gerrit and the others were coming."

"What do you mean?"

"It was like they were expecting Gerrit's arrival. I took a look at the heat signatures the drone shot back. Just as Gerrit and his team left the marina in Seattle, I saw new replacements emerging at Kane's location. They must have brought in more security teams and began fanning out, some heading right toward where Gerrit planned to hit the beach. Fortunately, the drone alerted us to the patrols and Gerrit switched plans. But somehow they knew, Colonel. Who tipped them off?"

"You don't think Willy or Alena tipped Kane off? They've been with Joe for years."

Beck frowned. "Yeah. Just like Redneck."

"Maybe Kane had been able to track them with his newfangled technology."

"Maybe." Instinctively, Beck knew Kane was getting help from someone close to Gerrit. "If they painted Gerrit or his team with trackers, they would have gotten specific coordinates when the three hit land. Our thermal readers indicated that the security force didn't know specifically where they were...just the general area. As if they'd been told where to look."

Thompson tapped his fingers on the edge of his seat. "Gerrit is a straight shooter. He'd never roll. What do we know about the other two?"

"Willy came from the streets. First Alena recruited him, and then Joe took him under his wings."

"And the woman?"

Beck squinted at the window. "Joe connected with her when he started running."

"How did they meet?"

"Just said he trusted her with his life." Beck didn't look at Thompson. Joe shared a few details of Alena's life with him a while back, information that might put her in a bad light right now. All he knew is that Joe trusted her. That was good enough for Beck.

"Yeah, and now Joe's missing. Presumed dead."

The two men fell silent as the jet banked after takeoff, heading for Seattle. They were powerless for the next few hours. It was all in the hands of Gerrit and his team. And one of them might be a traitor.

Gerrit felt Willy's tap again. "Those guys are heading our direction, Mr. G." He held up the reader. Two red dots were coming their way.

"I thought they couldn't read our heat signatures."

"They can't," Willy said, his voice barely above a whisper. "They can't see us. The drone knocked out their system. They're working blind."

Gerrit motioned to Alena, pointing to the approaching men. She nodded back. He peered over the rock and heard them stumbling his way. One of the men continued to complain about his eyes. The other man told him to shut up and they could see just fine.

Looking over his shoulder, Gerrit realized they were trapped for the moment. They could not go forward, and the cliff was to their back. He had hoped they could have slipped through security without detection. Now, they were going to have to take action.

His stomach tightened as he withdrew a serrated Marine combat knife and Alena pulled out her own weapon. Willy held the reader low, and Gerrit followed the path of the approaching gunmen. The security patrol was closing in, about twenty yards away. Gerrit took one more look at the thermal images, then prepared to move in that direction to cut them off. The two men had begun to draw apart, one moving to Gerrit's right and the other coming straight toward him.

He could hear the boots stumble over rocks as the two men approached. Ten yards. Five yards. Gerrit crouched behind the boulder, knife in hand. Alena, also crouching, glanced his way. He pointed to himself, and then jabbed his finger toward the man to his left. He pointed at her, and then pointed to the man on his right.

She nodded. Alena understood.

The boots drew near. "What are we doing over here, you idiot? They said to keep an eye on the perimeter."

"Hey, they told us to check the area. That's what we're doing."

"Okay, we checked. Now, let's move down there beyond the landing pad and check that area between the cliffs and the perimeter fence."

They moved off to Gerrit's left. Soon the guards were far enough away for him to relax. He sheathed the knife and slowly stood. "Okay, any other threats?"

Willy shook his head.

"Then it's time to move out and take care of business." Something began to trouble Gerrit. They'd met minimal resistance. "Wait. Willy, let me see that reader. How are they deployed?"

They all crouched down behind the boulder and Gerrit studied the heat signatures on the screen. None were near the building or the heliport. They were strung out along what seemed to be the perimeter, and he saw other heat signatures inside the building. But no one was stationed where he would have placed people. Near the buildings or satellite towers. No one guarding the landing site. All strategic targets.

He turned to the others. "Stay here. I need to check something out." Alena started to say something, but Gerrit interrupted her. "Need you to cover Willy. If something happens, just call that number I gave you and tell them to come on in. We need to get Willy inside that building at any cost. Stay in contact over the radio. If any patrols come my way, give me a yell. Okay?"

"Hey, Mr. G. I scanned radio frequencies when those two clowns walked by. Came up with the frequency they're using tonight. I fed it into our radios, and we can intercept their calls. It will default back to your communication channel unless they're speaking. Then we can listen in unless you want to override them and communicate with us.

"Sweet, Willy. Thanks. Okay, stay put till I get back."

They nodded.

Gripping his rifle, Gerrit headed toward the landing site. He had to make sure about one thing before they made a move toward the building.

Chapter 62

An open meadow lay between Gerrit and a slab of black asphalt where their backup needed to land. Nowhere to hide. Nowhere to run. If Kane's men caught sight of him here, it was all over.

He sank to the ground and crawled the remaining distance to break up his silhouette. As if to help, dark clouds drifted in front of the moon, cutting visibility to a minimum.

As he drew closer to the landing pad, Gerrit suddenly heard raised voices on the radio.

"Abandon cruiser just beached about a click away." A caller's transmissions ended with coordinates that only made sense to Kane's security team.

They found our boat. Search teams would start looking along the shoreline while security tightens. Time was running out.

Gerrit continued to snake his way forward while mentally trying to put himself in Kane's shoes. *What would I do if I suspected an assault?* Keep security close to the base of operations and make sure the landing site was covered. So far, nothing like that had been set up. It could only mean one thing.

The heliport was a trap.

He drew near the landing pad and inched forward, feeling just above the ground. There. His hand brushed a taut wire stretched parallel to the ground.

Trip wire.

Carefully, he felt along the wire until he reached what he feared. A trigger for a claymore mine. He felt with his fingertips until he located the safety. He flicked it off to prevent an electrical charge from reaching the blasting cap. He crept along the trip wire until he reached the claymore mine, gingerly removing the blasting cap and primer from the detonation well.

Salty beads of sweat stung his eyes as he finished disarming it. First claymore defused. One down. How many more to go?

There must be others.

He studied the position of the claymore and its potential killing radius across the helipad. Picturing where he would place other claymores, he worked along the edge of the asphalt until he came to another wire. Carefully, he disarmed this mine before searching for the next.

Almost an hour later, he defused four claymores set in a crisscross pattern. Whoever laid these mines also expanded the kill zone to include the cleared brush to the left and right where a chopper might set down. They had planned to kill anyone emerging from the craft, including the flight crew still inside. Once the claymores crippled the chopper, they probably planned to use a tractor to yank the disabled craft from the site to make way for their own inbound helicopters.

He activated his mike. "Alena. Use that phone number I gave you and tell our people to start coming. Make sure you use my name. They have two birds. One will soften the perimeter up while the second will come in behind to drop reinforcements. Make sure they have the latest coordinates of each patrol team out there. They must either wipe them out or force them to seek cover until our guys are on the ground."

"Understood."

"And Alena…"

Another transmission click let him know she heard him.

"Relay that four claymores have been deactivated. Make sure they know we're going to hit the main building the second they reach our location. They have to keep the others off our backs as soon as they touch ground. Got it?"

Two clicks gave him the answer.

"Good. When you get that message off, both of you move up to my position. And stay low."

He covered the face of his watch and turned on the light: 10 p.m. Five minutes later, he saw Alena and Willy moving toward him. He waited until they drew near. "Okay, let's start toward the building. I want to be able to move the moment our backup gets here."

He started out and the others followed in single file.

They crawled about ten feet when floodlights came on. The harsh light bathed the open field like a football stadium on game night. They lay there naked to the world.

Someone must have spotted them.

He sprang from the ground. "Alena. Willy. Run for it. Now!"

The elevator door opened and Richard Kane strode toward the security console. "Give me an update."

The Hulk glanced up, blinking twice. "Someone just triggered the laser beams to the landing site."

"I gave strict orders for our people to stay away from there. We have it set up for any incoming visitors."

Nodding, the Hulk seemed to shrink in his chair. "I know, sir. I believe we've got combatants inside our security compound. Look!" He pointed to the color monitor directly overhead.

Richard glanced up and saw three figures darting across the open field. "Zoom in. I want to see their faces."

Feverishly, the Hulk pounded on the keys until the camera swooped in. For just a second, Richard saw the side view of Gerrit as he flashed by. Then the images disappeared.

Richard whirled around. "They got to the building. Lock us down. Now!"

An alarm sounded, harsh beeps pulsating through the building. Richard scurried toward the elevator. "I will be down on the lower level. Keep me posted."

Gerrit pressed his back against the side of the building. Alena and Willy crouched next to him. They tried to catch their breath, listening for any sounds coming their way.

Nothing.

"Cover me." Gerrit pushed off the wall. He peeled away and zigzagged a path to the front steps. Large flagstone steps led to the front door. Seeing a camera above the door, he used the butt of his rifle to smash the lens, although they must have already spotted him.

He lowered his backpack and pulled out a det cord and packed it around the door, letting out the line to the detonator. Gerrit grabbed his pack and retraced his steps down the stone entryway until he stood next to Alena and Willy, dragging the line with him. They stood, shielded from the recessed door.

"Cover your ears," he hissed, a moment before setting off the blast. As smoke settled, Gerrit leaned out to see the damage. The blast punched a hole in the entryway, the door flung inward to allow easy access, one hinge still stubbornly holding it up.

"Willy, let Alena and me do a quick sweep, then you follow."

"Copy, Mr. G. The cavalry's ten minutes away."

"Tell them we need them now! We just hit the building and Kane's security must be moving our way."

Ten minutes seemed ten hours right now. Patrol units would be converging here within minutes. They did not have that long to survive.

Chapter 63

30,000 Feet above Boise, Idaho

Beck looked up just as Jack came into the cabin area. "Bad news?"

Thompson's normally unreadable face wrinkled with concern. The colonel flung himself into the seat across from Beck. "Just got a message from our guys. Choppers took off about five minutes ago and the unit commander just got another message from Willy."

Beck said nothing, waiting for Thompson to continue.

"They've been spotted. Gerrit cleared the landing site of claymores, but they set off an alarm system as they were moving toward the lab. Says they need help now. Not sure they can hold out."

"Anyway backup can get there quicker?"

Thompson shook his head. "They're already slamming pedal to the metal. They can't go any faster."

Beck leaned on the arm of his chair, chin resting on a tightly clenched fist. "They can't hold Kane off for that long."

Thompson nodded. "Willy hasn't been able to break into Kane's system yet."

"Can Willy tell what might be happening once he breaks in?"

"The only good news so far. He reports that he should be able to verify that what we started in Albuquerque is piggybacking on Kane's transmissions. The Trojan horse we sent in should be going to work on Project Megiddo right now."

"So what Gerrit and Alena are doing at the moment may be all for nothing."

Glumly, Thompson leaned back in his chair. "Everything they do now may be just a big smoke screen, one last attempt to save Joe. We still don't know where Kane's main servers are stored. My people—once they get there—have orders to blow the place."

"No updates on Joe?"

"Nothing. Don't even know if he's there, let alone whether he's alive."

"I say again—is this sacrifice they're making for nothing?" Beck seemed to express how both men felt.

The colonel nodded. "Not exactly. Primary mission has been accomplished. They breached Project Megiddo in New Mexico. Gerrit knew what the cost might be going in. We still had to send them in. Even if Joe wasn't there. We had to make it look good."

"Well, it looks like they're did a bang-up job. Kane's sending everything he has to take them out. We've got him fooled."

Both men looked out the passenger window. Below, dots of light lay across the high desert as they flew over Idaho's capital city. Beck stared out into the blackness, feeling helpless as he thought of what Gerrit, Willy, and Alena faced. Sometimes he wished he were God. But that would be stupid. Beck had enough problems dealing with the troubles of this investigation, let alone carrying the burdens of the world.

In his own investigation, he learned to respect what Gerrit's father had tried to achieve. First, Thomas O'Rourke tried to shoulder the whole load after learning how his research would be used by Kane and his people. The father tried to protect his son by trying to bring him back to MIT where he could be protected.

Instead, Gerrit went off to war, unaware of what his own father was struggling with back home, angry that he couldn't make his father understand. Unknown to Gerrit, his father knew quite well what was at stake. Like some international thriller, Thomas O'Rourke struggled against a growing technological invasion that threatened the entire international community.

Ironically, it was the father's death that brought his son home. And then Gerrit struggled to find out why his father died, not knowing his ignorance was the only thing keeping him alive.

Beck hoped Gerrit lived long enough to learn what his father had sacrificed.

This thought took him to a night many years ago when Joe told him he'd recruited Alena to be a part of the team. At first, Beck told Joe he was crazy. They knew what she had done in her past and he thought the risk too great. Joe fought him every step of the way, even though he knew what the woman had brought on Joe's own family.

"People change. Redemption is always possible if a person is willing to confess his or her sins and make amends." That was all Joe would say.

It looked like Joe might have been right about her. Maybe. And Beck hoped Gerrit would still be able to work with Alena once he knew the entire story about his father and that night many years ago.

Gerrit would handle it one of two ways. He'd learn to work with her and put the past behind him.

Or he'd kill her.

This whole conflict might be moot if Gerrit and Alena didn't survive tonight. Help was still minutes away.

He prayed they lasted that long.

Gerrit pulled the pin and rolled a flash-bang into the darkened lobby. Lights inside the building had gone dark the moment he blew the door. They must be waiting inside.

He wanted to even their chances of survival. He counted off the seconds before the explosion. As soon as it went off, he peeled around the doorway and entered the lobby to the left. Alena swept past him toward the right. Once again, he and Alena had to pass through the kill zone.

Red emergency lights flashed on. He quickly scanned the lobby. No movement.

"Gerrit, follow me! Tell Willy to stay right behind us." Alena's sharp command caught him unaware for a moment. She brushed past him and, using her M4 rifle, blew the lock off a door leading from the lobby. "Forget the elevator. It's no use."

Gerrit scanned the lobby once more. Empty. Where was everyone? This place had to have a small army working inside.

She kicked the door open and rolled another flash-bang down a bank of stairs. They turned away from the blast, standing on either side of the doorway, until it triggered below. After the explosion, Alena dashed down the stairs with speed Gerrit thought bordered on recklessness. He quickly tried to catch up, knowing that there had to be more security below.

A pulsating red glow illuminated the stairs in the same way the lobby had been lit up. Somewhere, a lockdown system had kicked in, triggering emergency lights and automatically locking all passageways through the building.

She moved through the building like someone who'd been here before. How did she know the door above led to these stairs? There were no markings in the lobby.

A chill began to work its way through his chest. Unless...? What were the chances Richard Kane had two traitors in their midst? Gerrit had watched her in action, and he found it hard to believe she worked for the other side. She had been genuinely shocked to find Redneck had been a plant. The look on her face was as if Redneck had betrayed her—personally—not just the group she worked with.

He forced these thoughts from his mind. Needed to concentrate on finding Joe and getting out of this building alive. Later, when they had time, he'd confront her.

Gerrit motioned for Willy to rejoin them. "Move ahead of me, but stay behind Alena. I'll cover our six, make sure no one climbs down our back."

Nodding, Willy moved ahead, trying to stay up with Alena.

The stairway snaked back and forth, carrying them deeper below-ground. He'd lost track of how many flights of stairs they traversed. Four or five? The last landing led to a concrete slab, bordered by a wall of cement. A single metal door stood at the foot of the stairs. Off to the left, a keypad.

He moved closer to Alena. "The only way we can get through that door is to blow it with the det cord I have left." He heard a backup generator pounding away nearby, and the keypad lit up.

Alena looked at him earnestly. "Gerrit, do you trust me?"

The thought that troubled him earlier came back in a flash. He paused for a moment, thinking hard about his answer. "Yeah. I do."

"I'll tell you everything later. Right now, just trust me to do the right thing." She strode over to the keypad and punched in a series of letters and numbers. The lock clicked and she opened the door, then held it open. "Stay close." She peeled through the doorway to the right, and Gerrit moved to the left, leaving Willy behind.

At first, the place seemed empty.

They stared at each other and then scanned the room once more. A cluster of consoles and monitors, grouped together at one end of an expansive room, stood next to a forest of tall computer servers. Each workstation was linked to a series of cables that rose to the ceiling, strung together like strands of spaghetti until they reached the servers. The cables came to a glass wall, through which they passed into what appeared to be a climate-controlled and dust-free environment.

Kane's nerve center.

The workstations looked like a duplication of NASA's control center, everyone's desk facing the mammoth screens like so many pagans worshiping their god. On these screens, streams of data code and file directories were broadcast. In the far corner, a half-dozen men and women cowered, their white lab coats broadcasting that they were technicians—not soldiers.

Willy came in behind them and whistled. "Oh my! What do we have here?"

Gerrit moved toward the huddled technicians, ordering them to lie on the ground. He found a box of plastic ties and used these to bind up the technicians. Within minutes, he had the group bound hand and foot.

Willy was already at one of the consoles, his laptop tied to a USB port. "I can get a signal down here. They must have a wireless system set up to reach upstairs. I am going to start sending out data from their system to ours." Willy glanced at one of the screens. "Uh-oh."

"What?" Gerrit moved closer. "It looks like they've accessed NSA, Langley…and the Pentagon."

He and Willy watched a stream of data flow across the screen, files created in directories clearly marked. He saw the names of countries, with subdirectories identified by public and private entities.

Willy quickly zoomed on to the main directory listed as *United States*, and an array of subdirectories formed into two categories, public and private. After clicking on Public, Willy scanned down the list until he reached *Intelligence Agencies*. Clicking on the one for NSA, files began to pop up by division, listing organizational structure and personnel.

Willy chose one file identified as NSA's Central Security Services (CSS) and clicked on the personnel file. A page opened, listing the names of executives in that branch. Some names were in red and others in black. As more data streamed in, some of the names switched from black to red as they viewed the list.

Gerrit pointed. "Click on that one listed as Director, NSA/Chief CSS in red."

Willy complied, and the screen flashed color as hundreds of source documents started to open. Gerrit stared at the screen and recognized the director's face, a brigadier general from the Unites States Air Force.

"Oh, man." Willy clicked on a file where video and voice files seemed to have been merged. "Look at this, Gerrit."

The time stamp on what appeared to be surveillance footage indicted this information has been downloaded earlier in the day. They watched the brigadier general sitting at his desk inside NSA. He was on a telephone, and they could hear the conversation as it was instantly converted to text. Words appeared at the bottom of the screen as they were spoken, like watching a foreign film with subtitles.

Willy looked at Gerrit. "I would imagine that phone has been encrypted by NSA. This means Project Megiddo is able to break through NSA's firewall, gain access to their in-house camera system while simultaneously intercepting and recording this guy's telephone conversation. We're talking top-secret, NSA-protected stuff that anyone in Kane's organization can access at any time."

Gerrit stared at the screen Willy zoomed in on, then glanced at the group huddled in the corner. Several of the bound technicians kept glancing at one man, an older gentleman who just stared at the ground. The man seemed to be listening closely to what Willy said to Gerrit.

Striding over the group, Gerrit pulled out a knife and sliced the plastic cuff binding the man's legs. "You, get up and follow me. Now!"

The man with gray hair and thick-rimmed glasses stood, his hands still bound in front, looking belligerently at Gerrit. He had the look of someone in charge.

Gerrit grabbed the man's arm and dragged him over to where Willy worked on the computer. "Tell my friend what you have just done here."

Barely hiding his look of contempt, the man glared back, saying nothing.

Gerrit drew near and whispered into the man's ear. The man's face paled and he turned toward Willy. "What do you want to know?"

"You just launched Project Megiddo?"

The man looked surprised. "I…we started about an hour ago."

"Where is the data stored?"

"Here. On our servers."

"Anywhere else?"

The man shook his head, but Gerrit distrusted the look in his eyes. "With the right passwords, others can remotely access the information, but it is all stored here. I swear."

Gerrit knew the man was lying, but they didn't have time to push him further. He edged closer, threatening. "Where's Kane?"

The man's eyes shifted to another door at the far end of the room. "There." He pointed with his chin.

Gerrit dragged the man back to where the others were sitting. "Stay here and you won't be hurt. Move, and you die. Understood?"

The man nodded and sank to the floor.

Hurrying back to Willy, Gerrit said, "Keep getting this data pulled from the system, or as much as you can retrieve. Once help gets here, we're going to level this place to the ground."

Willy nodded.

"And Willy, if you hear any movement through the door, dive for cover and call me. I don't want to lose you. Hear me?"

"You got it, Mr. G." Willy moved closer, whispering, "What did you tell that guy to get him to talk to us?"

"It's a secret, Willy. You better hope I never have to use it on you. Now get to work."

Again, Willy nodded, his focus now the computer screen. "You got it, Mr. G. 'Cause I certainly don't wanna tick you off." He shot Gerrit a smile. Willy did not seem intimidated.

An instant later, they heard rifle fire in the building. It came from the ground floor above them, echoing down the stairwell. They had only minutes to finish the job.

"Alena. You ready?"

She backed away from the bound prisoners. "Willy, keep an eye on them."

Gerrit dashed to her side and pointed toward the locked door at the end of the room. "Can you work your magic again?"

Without answering, she ran to the door, waited for him to get into position, and then punched in the code. The sequence seemed to work again because the door clicked open. He reached in his backpack and pulled out a dark-green flash-bang. "If it's dark again, we'll crisscross, hit the deck, and count to three. Then I open up with this." He showed her the stun grenade.

She nodded and reached down for the handle, pausing to see if he was ready, then flung it open.

Completely dark inside. Gerrit rushed in, followed by Alena.

They dived for the floor as a flash of gunfire opened up. He heard Alena crawl to the right as he edged to the left in the ensuing blackness. As the gunman opened again, Gerrit registered the layout in front of him—a large room, office and doors at the far end, farthest away from the door they just came through.

Something else registered in his brain. Yellow light from the gunfire illuminated a man standing next to the gunman, a man with a mane of long silver hair.

Richard Kane.

Gerrit counted to three and hurled the flash-bang deep toward Kane.

Chapter 64

Flashes of gunfire across the room forced Richard to drop. He scrambled through the doorway behind him, locking it from the inside just as explosions shook the door. *Gerrit and Alena made it here*. He needed to call for reinforcements.

His bodyguard banged on the door, trying to get inside. The man failed him, allowing those intruders to get this far. So now, the man could deal with his mistakes. Richard dialed the in-house phone to reach his security office on the top floor.

The Hulk's voice came on the line.

"How did they get down here belowground? I need reinforcements here this second."

"Sir, per your order, the others are manning the perimeter, awaiting your order."

"You idiot! The intruders are inside the lab and blowing things up as we speak. What are you doing up there? Waiting for me to die? Get my people in here right now!"

"Yes sir, I'll put the order out this second."

Richard smashed the receiver into the concrete wall, before rushing farther down the hallway to another secured doorway. He activated the code pad to unlock it, then grabbed the door and flung it open.

There was one last thing he could do that might make Alena and Gerrit stand down. One last chance to make them back up until his people got here.

A message alert flashed on Willy's laptop just as more shots fired above. He reached over and clicked on the message. It was from Beck:

Help has arrived. Keep your head down. All hell's about to break loose.

Gerrit rose, flicked on a light switch he'd seen near the front door. Lights flickered across the room and he dove for the floor once again. Alena lay a few yards away. Catching her attention, he used hand signals, motioning that he'd move to the left and along the outer wall. He signaled her to move to the right and take up a position until he flushed the gunman.

She nodded, moving in the direction he pointed.

Turning his attention toward the gunman, Gerrit snaked his away along the floor until he reached the far wall to his left. This room seemed to be devoted to storage. Boxes of office supplies stored on metal shelves the full length of the room. A wide path cut down the center of the room—where he had seen Kane and the gunman at the far end—and two narrower aisles along each wall. Only three paths to the gunman. He heard a door slam and assumed Kane had left. Leaving one man—armed.

Gerrit inched forward down the center aisle, moving slower as he drew near the gunman's position. Every few aisles, he would dart to the left, using cardboard cartons of supplies, stacked high on the shelves, as cover. He estimated Kane's man was crouching about ten yards away. Or dead. The gunman hadn't appeared in the open since Gerrit heard banging on the door.

Left his bodyguard behind. Kane—the hero.

Gerrit found a large box of computer paper. Above it, he had a clean shot in front of the doorway through which Kane exited. The gunman must be to the right or left of that door. Gerrit reached up and grabbed a coffee mug someone left on the shelf.

Quietly raising himself, he positioned his rifle on a box for support, aiming it about where he thought the gunman might be hiding. Once he had the muzzle pointed down range, he hurled the coffee cup through the air.

He tightened his grip on the weapon, sighting down the barrel. The cup shattered against the far wall.

The gunman lunged into the open and fired down the center aisle past Gerrit. The man fired fully automatic, shooting blindly.

It was all Gerrit needed. He squeezed one round off, and the target lurched backward. Richard Kane just lost one more gunman.

Rising, Gerrit motioned to Alena toward the far door. He knelt by the fallen guard and felt his pulse. Dead. He nodded at Alena.

She dashed toward the remaining door and hurriedly entered the password.

The lock snapped open like the others. He flung the door open toward Alena, who held it open with her foot. He held up three fingers—one at a time. When the third finger rose, he rushed in as they crisscrossed through the doorway. No gunfire. He froze, searching for movement ahead.

Gerrit peered through a reddish gloom, tinted light giving off an eerie feeling as if they stepped aboard a submarine. More storage area. Several rows of shelves blocked his view. A central aisle cut between these shelves like the room they just left. Beyond, he saw what appeared to be an open area, although this part of the room lay mostly in darkness.

He started to take a step when a single light bulb at the far end of the room flicked on. Cascading cold white light illuminated a man slouched in a chair, wrists bound, his mouth covered by gray duct tape.

Joe O'Rourke.

Cautiously, Gerrit started to work his way toward his uncle when Kane's voice cut through the darkness.

"Take one more step, Gerrit, and I will put a bullet in Joe's head."

Gerrit halted. He'd lost track of Alena ever since he saw his uncle strapped to the chair. She seemed to have slipped into the shadows as well.

"What do you want, Kane?" Gerrit peered through the gloom trying to figure out where Kane might be hiding.

"I want you, Gerrit. You and your lovely girlfriend."

Gerrit tried to follow the sound of the man's voice. There was a gap between a row of storage boxes and the next shelving above them. In this space, he thought he might see a figure, standing just to the left of his uncle. He would not be able to get a clear shot.

"Yeah, right. I come up there and you shoot us dead. Not a good proposition for any of us—except you."

The shadow shifted closer to his uncle. Out of the corner of his eye, he thought he saw more movement. It must be Alena, getting closer to the target.

"Believe me, Gerrit. I don't want you dead. You have too much to offer for me to waste a bullet on you."

"And if I come out in the open. What're you going to do?"

"I want you and your girlfriend to put down your weapons. Sit down and talk about this. We parted ways last time without talking this out."

Gerrit heard gunfire above him. Several explosions shook the building. "Sounds like your guys are in a world of hurt. Maybe you ought to just give up." He edged closer, using the shelving to block his silhouette. Two rows away from getting a clear shot at Kane. "What do you say? Give up and we'll let you live."

"Don't come any closer. You think I am an idiot. I got my gun trained on your uncle's chest. There is no way I can miss from here."

Peering around the edge of a gray metallic shelf, he saw Joe's battered face. Gerrit gritted his teeth when he saw what they had done to his uncle. Joe looked back, then shifted his gaze to Gerrit's right. Following Joe's look, Gerrit saw that Alena had sneaked to the first row, one shelf of boxes separating her and Kane.

He swung back toward his uncle, searching the shadows for Kane. The man must have drawn back out of the light altogether, standing just out of sight, watching for them to approach.

There. He saw movement in the shadows. Kane must be getting restless.

Gerrit caught Alena's attention, pointing to where he last spotted Kane. She nodded raised her rifle to eye level.

Kane must be drawn out into the light.

"I'm coming out, Richard. I wanna check on my uncle." Gerrit started to step from behind the shelving.

"You come any closer and he dies." Kane's voice seemed strained, nervous.

"Let me just check on him. You'll have both of us covered—"

Four rapid shots rang out and he saw his uncle twitch. Joe's eyes widened. Blood oozed from a chest wound. Two of the shots came from Alena's direction.

"Kane's down," she said.

"Joe's hit." Gerrit dashed to where he last saw Kane. The man was lying on his back, gun lying next to him. Gerrit scooped up the weapon and stuck it in his waistband, then patted Kane down for other weapons.

Clean.

He moved toward his uncle. "Cover me, Alena. I think Kane's unarmed, but keep an eye on him."

Easing the tape from Joe's mouth, Gerrit looked at his uncle's wound. It appeared to be one shot—a grazing chest wound—sliced the skin enough to cause blood to seep onto his clothing. Kane's second shot must have missed. Relieved, Gerrit pulled out his knife and sliced the tape binding Joe's wrists.

Seeing the older man could function, Gerrit turned and strode over to where Kane lay. The man had been hit twice, once in the chest and once in the gut. Kane was dying, painfully.

Gerrit felt Alena draw near. Kane looked up at them, gaze shifting from one to the other, finally focusing on Alena. The man's eyes, even in death, seemed filled with anger.

"So this is how you repay me, Alena. After all I did for you." Anger from his eyes carried over into his words, weak but harsh in his last remaining breath.

"I owe you nothing, Richard. You brought this on yourself."

Gerrit looked from one to the other, puzzled. "You knew him?" He searched her face for an answer. "You worked with him?"

"Not anymore," she said, walking over to Joe.

Kane turned his gaze toward Gerrit. "Ask her about your father. She has blood on her own hands." The man struggled to raise himself one last time. He wheezed, "Gerrit, your parents…only following orders. Only following orders, boy." The man's last words seemed to take all the strength he had left. Kane closed his eyes and stopped moving.

Gerrit knelt and felt the man's carotid artery. No pulse. He looked over at Alena. What was Kane trying to tell him? Others ordered his parents' killed? More questions left unanswered. More paths to follow. Never ending! He hung his head.

One thing was for certain, Richard Kane was no longer a threat.

Chapter 65

Gerrit heard a blast at their level. One of the doorways breached.

Willy.

"Alena, sounds like they blasted their way to where we left Willy. Keep Joe covered. I'll check to see who's coming our way."

He dashed through the front until he came to the door separating him from where they left Willy. Reaching the doorway, his back pressed against the cinderblock wall to the left of the door, he reached down and quietly turned the knob with one hand. He slowly pulled on the door, opening it just a crack to allow him to see into the next room.

A man yelled across the room. "Gerrit. Hold your fire and stand down. Beck and Jack sent us to save your butt."

Relief swept through him as he opened the door wider. "Show yourselves."

A man in camouflaged gear rose from behind one of the consoles and walked toward him. "The place is secure. All hostile fire has been dealt with. What's your status."

"Main target dead. One friendly in need of medical help. Half dozen of Kane's technicians are cuffed and cornered in this room." He pointed with his chin.

"Don't shoot!" Willy shouted, rising from behind a computer console, hands held high.

"And that," Gerrit said, "is our computer genius. Whatever you do, don't shoot him."

Gerrit propped the door open. He returned to where Joe still sat in the chair. His uncle seemed weak, badly shaken.

"How you feeling, Joe?" Gerrit's chest tightened as concern broke through his resolve. How much pain and injury did Kane inflicted on his uncle? Anger gripped him like a steel vise.

Joe grimaced, his face even whiter under the harsh glare of a fluorescent bulb. "I'm breathing, Gerrit. That's a whole lot better than what I thought might happen."

Patting his uncle's shoulder, Gerrit looked at Alena, standing next to them. "You've got some explaining to do."

She gave him a hard look, then shouldered her rifle, abruptly turning away without saying anything.

He started to follow, but Joe tugged on his sleeve. "Gerrit, wait. Hear me out. I heard what that creep said."

"Is it true?" Gerrit asked, trying to mask his anger, staring down at his uncle. Only his hands shook. "Is my father's blood on her hands?"

Footsteps could be heard drawing near. Several men approached with a stretcher. "These guys are going to check you out and then move you to the chopper."

Grasping Gerrit's wrist, Joe clung to him for a moment. "You have to hear the whole story, son. We all make mistakes. Alena has changed. Just give me a chance to explain."

A medic appeared and began a cursory check of Joe's medical condition.

"We'll talk later. Just let these guys take care of you and I'll see you topside."

Joe tried to push them away. "I'm just fine. I don't need to—"

"Do me a favor, Joe. Let them check you out and get you upstairs. You've been through a lot." Gerrit backed away, allowing the men to cluster around Joe as they began to care for him. Seeing that his uncle's needs were taken care of, he turned and retraced his steps through the building.

OFF THE GRID | 339

A few minutes later, he reached the front doorway and walked outside. Willy joined him. "Jack and Beck arrived at Sea-Tac and will chopper over as quick as they can. They asked for you to stay put."

Alena stood on the helipad, staring out beyond the cliffs to the sea below. She seemed alone in the midst of all the activity. As he looked at her, Gerrit could not shake Kane's last words. A few minutes later, she walked toward the cliff's edge, never looking his way.

He heard men grunting behind him and turned to see two men carrying Joe on a stretcher. As they passed, Joe yelled out, "Put me down for a moment. I need to talk to my nephew."

The man in the lead looked at Gerrit for direction. "Just give us a minute. Then he's all yours."

Joe tried to sit up as they laid the stretcher on the ground. Gerrit squatted and held him down. "Just relax. Let these guys do all the work."

His uncle gave him an exasperated look but lay back, looking up. "We don't have time to go into all the details, Gerrit, but you need to know that you can trust Alena. That everyone—including me—makes mistakes. She has more than made up for her past sins."

"And the death of my father and mother," he said, raising his voice. "Has she made up for that?"

Joe tried to raise himself again. "That's what I am trying to tell you. Kane recruited her many years ago. She didn't know what he and the others were all about. She thought they represented the U.S. at the time."

"So he used her to kill my folks? Your brother?"

"Hear me out. At first, she thought your father was a threat. That Kane—through his government contacts—had been sanctioned to neutralize that threat."

"Neutralize the threat? Give me a break. Dad was never—"

"I know that. And later, so did Alena."

"What do you mean *later*? After my parents were killed?"

Joe shook his head vigorously. "That's what I'm trying to get through your thick head. She came over to our side before your parents died. But by then, it was too late."

Gerrit said nothing, waiting for his uncle to continue. One of the choppers lifted off and began heading toward Seattle.

Alena had moved closer to the cliffs, standing on the ridge looking down. Joe saw her standing in the distance and pointed toward her. "She was sent in by Kane to get close to Thomas. To find out where your father might be vulnerable so a second team could come in and take him out if need be."

"So she spied on them? Betrayed Mom and Dad?"

"Would you put a cork in it for a minute and let me finish?" Frustration tightened his uncle's features. "She got to know Thomas and your mom. They even invited her over for dinner. That's where she first saw your photo and heard stories about you."

Gerrit clenched his jaw, remembering the peace his parents' home always seemed to bring when he visited. When he and dad weren't arguing.

"She came to learn that your dad was not a threat to anyone, and that what Kane and the others were doing was actually a threat to our country. She warned your father about the danger, and he contacted me. Right after that, Kane's men took me to that high-rise and had me do a midair dance."

"So how did my father get lured into the garage? Why didn't he have a security detail on him?"

"There was security. But he slipped away from the detail to be with your mother. He wanted to have a private dinner alone with his wife. It was a stupid mistake and it cost them their lives."

Another thought came to Gerrit as he listened. "Does Alena know who triggered the bomb. Who actually killed my parents?"

Joe shook his head. "She was feeding information to Kane until she came to know and care for your folks. She cut off all communication with Kane and began her own preparations to live off the grid. Once she heard of the bombing, she hunted me down and helped me disappear. That's when I contacted Travis, and he put me in contact with Beck Malloy."

Gerrit's shoulders sagged. His search for the actual killer would still continue. Sure, Kane called the shots, but Gerrit wanted to get his hands on the person who literally built and detonated the bomb. He wanted to find that person and put a bullet in his worthless brain. With Kane dead, he might never find out the truth. Or who, higher up, might have been involved.

He motioned to the medical team. "Can you guys get my uncle on the chopper? Need to have him checked out at a hospital." Joe started to protest, but Gerrit waved him off. "I'll come to visit you as soon as Beck and the colonel get here. Just relax and let these people take care of you."

Resigned, Joe leaned back. "Talk to Alena, Gerrit. Let her tell you her side of the story."

Before answering, Gerrit glanced toward the cliffs and saw her still standing on the edge, peering into the night. "I promise. Now, just let these guys take care of you."

Joe seemed satisfied. "Okay guys, let's get this over with." They scooped him up and made their way to the second chopper.

Chapter 66

Washington, D.C.

Stuart leaned back in his banker's chair, the red leather creaking under his weight. He glanced at the clock; it was now three hours after midnight. Still no word from Kane. Other reports came in about a firefight at the lab in Washington. Outcome unknown.

He fingered the phone for a moment before dialing his contact in Seattle. The phone rang three times before he heard someone pick up on the other end.

A man's voice, tense and alert, answered. "Yeah?"

"This is Stuart." He waited for a moment to let the name sink in. "Kane's associate."

"Yes, sir. What can I do for you?"

"Do you have any word on how our friend is doing?"

"Kane?"

"Exactly."

"I've been monitoring radio transmissions and sent a text message a while ago. Got nothing. Now I'm copying that federal authorities have been alerted. FBI. ICE. Secret Service, and CIA. I think our friend and his people may have…fallen."

Stuart thought for a moment before speaking. "I need you to sit tight. Take no chances. I may have you pick up where Kane failed. Are you up for the job?"

Stuart could almost hear the greed in the man's voice. "You bet, sir. I will have to close things down here first. I assume you want me to relocate to your area."

"Yes. As soon as possible. We need to start assessing the damage and moving forward on our other projects."

"Give me a week."

"Two days." Stuart hung up.

He sat back in his chair, waiting; he knew another call would be coming in at any moment. He grimaced as his phone vibrated on the desk. He picked it up and saw *The White House* identified on its face.

Stuart listened to the caller speak, then cleared his throat. "Project Megiddo has been launched, but the main facility has been compromised."

The caller rattled on as Stuart patiently waited for the man to stop speaking. "No. We need to regroup and push on. This is just a temporary setback. We are taking all necessary steps to sanitize the situation."

Again, the caller launched into a tirade Stuart knew he had to endure. "Yes, sir. I promise you, there will be no blowback. I have already taken steps to make sure this never happens again. Even if they try to live off the grid."

He quietly hung up and stared out into the night.

The war has just begun.

Gerrit watched the second helicopter lift off, carrying his uncle to the nearest hospital in Seattle that handled medivacs. Beck and Jack should be here soon.

As darkness swallowed up the helicopter, his gaze caught a figure standing on the edge of the cliff.

Alena.

He took a deep breath and walked toward her. She stood with her back to him. He drew near. "Hey, they just airlifted Joe out of here kicking and complaining. I think he'll be all right."

She didn't say anything, nor did she move.

"I think we put a real dent in Kane's operation—or whoever's pulling his chain."

"There will always be someone else trying to kill us." Alena's words seemed laced with bitterness and tiredness.

"Then we just keep on fighting. We can't give up."

She finally turned toward him, grief and regret filling her eyes. "I'm so sorry, Gerrit."

He shrugged. "Joe gave me a quick rundown on what happened. That you tried to save my dad."

She ran a hand through her hair, sadness seeming to be pressing down on her. "I tried to think back on all the information I gave Kane about your dad. Before I came to know your folks. It haunts me that that information might have been used to kill them."

"How did you get mixed up with Kane?"

Alena faced the water again. "It is a long story, Gerrit. And not a very pretty one."

"I need to know, Alena. I need to know if we're going to continue to work together."

She looked back, inquisitive. "You would still work with me? After…"

He let her words wing their way into the night, thinking about what her question implied. "All I know is that you tried to save my father. That you turned away from Kane once you learned the truth about him. I need to know about Kane and his group. To help me put everything in perspective."

Alena looked at him for a moment, then turned to gaze at the water once again. "Kane found me in Russia. I was much younger, and my boyfriend—if you want to call him that—used me in his gang activities. Used me to get information. To help the gang set up scores. And he taught me how to fight. How to use weapons and to create false identifications. How to exist in a society in which violence and power were the only commodities others respected."

"How did Kane find you?"

She turned toward Gerrit. "His group—whoever he was working for—would use my boyfriend's connections to get information and access to Russian organized-crime leaders. My *boyfriend* used me in these operations, and I caught Kane's eye about the same time my boyfriend was killed."

"I think he had plans for me way back then. Got me out of the gangs by arranging a visa for me and my folks to move to Israel. Once there, I was recruited into the Israeli army at Kane's direction. Spent a few years learning how to fight, and then an opportunity came up to work intelligence. Again, I think Richard pulled the ropes."

"Pulled the strings." Gerrit gave a half smile. He saw the strain on her face as she dredged up the past.

"One day, he asked if I would like to join a unique unit of people working for him. He said they were trying to create a global community between nations, to help bring peace and stability on an international scale. After my parents were killed by terrorists, it was not hard to persuade me to work for peace. Kane got my Israeli handlers to approve my transfer to his outfit.

"He started working on me the first moment we met, luring me away with promises of a new life, a chance to live in the United States."

"That's how you got connected to my father?"

She nodded, her shoulders sagging. "Later, after I'd been with Richard for a few years and participated in some of his clandestine operations, he assigned me to make contact with your father through Thomas's work and to assess whether he might be a threat to our overall operation. We hit it off right away. Before I knew it, Thomas had me coming over to his house, having dinner with him and your mom."

Her words seemed to choke her. It took a moment before she brought herself under control. Finally, she took a deep breath and continued. "It was the first real home I had ever been in since my folks died. That's where I first saw you...your pictures all around the house. They were so proud of you, Gerrit. Off serving your country."

He thought of the last conversation he had with dad, fighting over the fact he was returning to combat. His father didn't seem proud at the time.

She turned, her eyes glistening as light from the helipad shone on them. He thought she might have been crying, but he could not be sure.

"Your mom even mentioned that you and I should meet when you returned home."

He shook his head, not knowing what to say.

"She was worried about you. That you never took time to enjoy life. To date. Any of that normal stuff."

"She seemed to share a lot about me. Little did she know—"

"—she was talking to the woman who betrayed them."

"But Joe said you changed. That you told them about the threat."

Alena nodded. "At first your dad was shocked. And your mom... well, let's say her idea about us getting together just flew out the chimney."

"Window, out the window," he said, trying to smile. "And yet, here we are." His joke didn't seem to lighten the moment.

"Then your dad seemed to pull things together. For some reason, he became concerned about the threat against your uncle. He tried to warn Joe, but something happened."

"Yeah, Kane's men tried to force him to walk on air. A life-changing event that made him back away from Dad."

"Until after the bombing. Then Joe had a change of heart. We started running from that day until now."

"You probably saved his life, Alena. Joe has faith in you."

"Actually, Joe saved me. Did you know your uncle is a Christian? A believer?"

Gerrit must have looked shocked.

"It is true. He is the one who got me going to church. I was carrying a lot of guilt after your folks. He helped me straighten out my head."

"From what I could tell, Joe believed in you from the time you first met, Alena. I could tell by the way he urged me to give you a chance."

"And you?" Her eyes searched his. "What do you think of me now?"

He cleared his throat. "I think we've all made mistakes. I include myself in that group." He briefly thought of his father's face that day, clouded with frustration. "I walked away from my own father when he needed me most. He may have died because I was not there to protect him."

"He was trying to protect you, Gerrit."

"I never got a chance to clear things up. And now, it's too late."

He heard the whirling thump of rotor blades. Another chopper headed in their direction. "That must be Beck and Thompson. Maybe they have some news." He welcomed this intrusion. He didn't want to dwell on memories he was powerless to change. Nor did he want to talk about a future that might have been.

It was like the last time he saw his folks before returning to the battle-field. Putting his personal affairs in order and placing everything on hold until—or if—he ever returned from war. One never knew whether he would survive the next conflict.

Again, after his houseboat was bombed and his friends were killed, he found himself in the same mindset. Putting his affairs in order. Placing his feelings on the shelf. As far as he could determine, he would never be able to enjoy a normal life again.

It was not his destiny to settle down, have a family, and live as if life offered more tomorrows. He had become a warrior, first in defense of his country and now for his country's survival. He would be fighting a war the rest of the nation—the world—might never hear about. A war fought in the shadows, in the night, in those dark places that are only known by those like him—living and dying in that gray shroud of a secret war.

Take this skirmish tonight. People died, dreams became crushed, and tomorrow—no one would even know they'd been here. A news blackout would drop an impenetrable curtain over this whole affair. The only ones who might wonder would be medical staff watching the wounded and dying carried into their emergency rooms.

He and Alena watched in silence as the helicopter drew nearer, as if the past no longer existed, his folks and their dreams left behind. They both needed to live in the present and prepare for the struggle ahead. Circumstances dictated their lives now. They needed to get used to it.

Gerrit turned to Alena. "Just one more question."

She nodded.

"How did you know the lab code here? You knew right where to go and which codes to press."

"This was our base of operations when I was turned loose on your folks. Back then, this was just a training and housing facility. It wasn't until I saw Willy's site plans that I knew where we were headed. Once I got here, I took a chance that Kane left the same codes in place. I was right."

"Why didn't you tell me?"

"Because I knew that everything would have to come out. We just did not have the time to stand around and dredge up my past."

He nodded, turning as the helicopter approached. "Someone knew we were coming and alerted Kane. I know it wasn't you. So that leaves us with a big problem."

"I've been wondering the same thing, Gerrit. Who turned us in?"

Chapter 67

Gerrit and Alena waited for the chopper to set down before approaching the aircraft. As soon as it came to rest, Beck Malloy and Jack Thompson emerged. They crouched down until they cleared the rotors and then dashed to where he and Alena stood waiting.

The colonel was the first to reach them. "Good work, Marine. You too, Alena. You cut the head off this operation before it could cause further damage."

Gerrit watched Willy running across the clearing in their direction. "I don't know how much damage we did, Colonel. Project Megiddo is still in place."

Willy, out of breath, reached them at about the same time Beck walked up. "I heard what you said about Megiddo, Mr. G." His nickname for Gerrit made Jack scowl, but the colonel seemed to keep his thoughts to himself. "I ran a data systems check just before you guys started WWIII."

Beck interjected. "Did it take, Willy? Tell me you got inside."

Nodding, Willy turned to Gerrit. "Remember how I had you upload their files in Albuquerque?"

Gerrit nodded.

"Well, as you know, I left a surprise present for them, thanks to you, Mr. G."

Gerrit smiled. "I meant to ask you about that, Willy, but everything was happening so fast. What kind of mischief did you get me involved in?"

"Since you guys were already going into their system, I thought I'd kill two birds with one stone. Joe and I created a certain kind of computer program that buries itself inside their system."

Gerrit was incredulous. "You infected their programs?"

"I didn't infect anything. I just *expanded* their program without their knowing it. See, I thought that whoever ran that lab would want to back up their system somewhere other than the site you guys hit. Just in case something like that did happen."

Willy seemed to be waiting for compliments from the others. None were forthcoming, so he continued. "Wherever they transfer their programs or search other sites—in this case, here in the state of Washington—they unknowingly carry my program. I'm calling it the Daemon Files."

Gerrit scoffed. "You didn't come up with that term, Willy. A daemon program is a computer term that's been around for ages."

"I didn't say I came up with the term." Willy looked miffed. "I'm just using it to describe this program Joe and I developed." Willy's excitement grew the more he talked. "As I was saying my little daemon program has a twist. It will sit out in the weeds, so to speak, staying dormant and unde-tected among the program's codes until conditions change in the Megiddo computer processes or we want daemon to come out to play. Then my computer friend kicks in, automatically sending us information on how the Megiddo program is being used or giving it messages we want them to have — unknowingly."

"You mean like a spy telling us what the enemy's up to?"

"You got it, Mr. G. And the beauty of this daemon is that I can trigger a change or a redirection in their program whenever I choose. It gives me remote access and control."

"Give me an example."

"Better yet, I'll just show you. Let's step into the lab's lobby—what's left of it after you two got through—and let me get set up."

Willy led them through the doorway, pausing for a moment until he saw a reception desk a few yards away. He plopped his laptop on the counter and powered up. "I am going to access their program and monitor any traffic they may have initiated since you hit this place."

Gerrit glanced at the screen. "The lab in Albuquerque is down. Kane and Collette are dead. Who do you think might be communicating right now? And with whom?"

Willy glanced up. "I'm sure they have more labs than the ones we know about. And we know Kane was just one of the cogs in a bigger wheel."

"That makes sense." Gerrit nodded, thinking of the events over the last few days. "So what do you hope to show us now?"

"One of the cool things about this Megiddo program is that it monitors not only its identified enemies, but its own people. For example, I can access Megiddo and check on who Kane came in contact with—by computer and cell phone—before you showed up here. Check out these links."

Gerrit and the others gathered around, trying to decipher what the program spit back. "What is this here, Willy?" He pointed to a date and time-stamped entry just before Kane knew they were near the lab.

Willy clicked on the link and expanded the field so they could read the code. "Someone in the D.C. area contacted Kane through their encrypted program. Unfortunately for them, Megiddo knows how to unscramble this. Here is the cell phone tower the phone used to bounce its signal our way."

Beck placed a hand on Gerrit's shoulder. "If we can get that cell phone number, maybe we can track down who used it."

"Look at this." Willy leaned over the computer and clicked on another link. "Hours before you guys hit this place, Kane called this number somewhere in the Seattle area." He minimized that screen, opening up another showing the unidentified Seattle number and calls sent and received from that phone. "And then just a while ago, that same Seattle number received a call from the person in D.C. who had been in contact with Kane."

"Get the cell numbers and tower locations as quick as you can, Willy. I will have my people run this down. We should be able to know who is using both those phones." For the first time since they landed, Beck sounded excited.

Willy started to shut down the program, but Gerrit stopped him. "Do one more thing for me. Take that Seattle number and check its call history. Can you retrieve data going back a few years?"

"Sure, Mr. G. If it was stored, I can retrieve it. What are you looking for?"

Gerrit swallowed, his mouth suddenly dry. He recognized the phone number in Seattle. "Check around the time my folks were killed. Then check that same phone used around the time my houseboat blew up and Mark Taylor and Marilynn were killed."

Willy bent over the laptop, his fingers flying over the keys. "Like I said, this Megiddo program is sweet, but my daemon program is all aces. I've narrowed the scope by date and time. Here, on one screen I'll summarize these calls around the time your folks..." Willy stopped, looking up at Gerrit. "Sorry, Mr. G."

"No problem, Willy. Just isolate both time periods and let me take a look at what you come up with."

Willy finished setting up the screens and stepped away, allowing Gerrit access to the keyboard. "Here you go."

Beck moved back as Alena moved closer, her body brushing against his. "Can I see, Gerrit?"

He glanced up and saw her face, taut and determined. "Sure, come in closer if you like."

She leaned over his shoulder. "Thanks. I need to know almost as much as you."

Gerrit nodded, turning his attention back to the screen. He scrolled down until he came to a series of numbers dialed during the time his parents were killed. His face heated as anger built deep inside. He minimized that screen and began to study the calls around the time his home was destroyed.

He tightened his jaw, clenching his hand into a fist. "Beck, I need a lift back to Seattle. And send word to Joe I know who killed my folks. Now, I'm going to get some answers."

Beck hesitated. "Gerrit, let me do my job. I can bring this suspect in the right way. Who is it?"

"Forget it, Malloy." Gerrit glared at him. "Your people won't get anywhere near this person. Too protected, and he'll wind up dead before you ever find out what he has to say. Let me do it my way."

Alena grasped his arm. "Let me come with you."

He shook his head, taking her hand in his. "Not this time. I need to do this alone, face-to-face. Otherwise, I'll never get the truth."

She sighed. "Be careful." Leaning over, she kissed him on the cheek. Her kiss seemed to soften the anger he felt building inside, at least for a moment.

He glanced at Beck. "I promise you I will do everything in my power to bring this person in. Trust me."

Beck frowned as he studied Gerrit. "Okay, but we'll be nearby as backup. Just in case."

"Bring a coroner if things go sideways." Gerrit looked back at the computer screen one last time. "If he so much as twitches the wrong way, I'm putting him down—for good."

Beck grimaced. "That doesn't exactly inspire trust."

Gerrit shrugged. "It won't be up to me, Malloy. It'll be his call." *Just give me an excuse.* His gaze met the agent's, and he knew Malloy could read his mind.

Beck walked away without saying a word.

Chapter 68

Seattle, Washington

All the tiredness in his body seemed to slip away after Stuart's call. His mind whirled with possibilities as he trudged up a moss-covered walkway leading to his house. The modest, single-story residence was all his ex-wife left after the divorce, after he refinanced and bought out her share. She would get half his pension upon retirement and already squandered all their savings as well as receiving full custody of the children.

His last child-support payment would end next summer when the youngest turned eighteen. However, alimony to his ex would continue until the day he died or she found a new husband who might be able to afford her expensive tastes.

That was all right. The call from Stuart tonight meant his future was about to drastically change. No more bargain-basement suits. No more cars older than his dad. No more meals at budget diners, or cold TV dinners in front of the television. He was about to take a sweet ride into the big time.

Travel. Money. Prestige.

All this from one single phone call telling him he would become Kane's replacement. Kane made one fatal mistake tonight. And even if he had escaped that lab, Stuart was sure to end Kane's life.

Such mistakes were not tolerated by Stuart and his people. A sobering thought he would take into account in his new life. In fact, he had taken care of some of the bodies after Stuart exacted punishment.

Dawn was only a few hours away. He'd slip inside, get a few hours' sleep, and then start planning for his new future. The first thing would be to dump this house. He unlocked and opened the door, then stepped inside and threw his coat on the rack near the doorway. He flicked on the light and turned to walk into the living room.

"Lieutenant Stan Cromwell. Your career ends tonight."

Stan whirled around and started to reach for his weapon.

Gerrit O'Rourke leveled his .40 S&W at Stan's chest. "Go ahead. Make a move. I always wanted to waste the man who killed my parents."

He froze and held out his hands. "Gerrit, my boy. Always too smart for your own good."

Gerrit rose from the chair. "And you're a dirty cop. Sold your badge for a few pieces of silver."

Stan caught the fury in Gerrit's eyes. All the excitement and hope he felt—after talking with Stuart about the future—just blew up in his face. Gerrit wouldn't let him leave this house alive.

The moment Cromwell came through the door, Gerrit knew it would be a battle to keep his promise to Beck. All he wanted to do right now was put a bullet into this man's skull. To end this killer's existence.

His trigger finger tightened as temptation grew stronger. His mind replayed those crime-scene videos of what was left of his mom and dad. Every scene, every frame, seared into Gerrit's soul, imprinted onto his memory forever. It would only take a slight squeeze to end Cromwell's life.

A blinding wave of anger swept over him. A tsunami urging him to squeeze that trigger. His finger began to tighten. Then, like a storm moving toward the horizon, his anger dissipated, leaving almost a feeling of peace in its wake. The faces of Joe and Alena passed before his eyes. For the first time, he realized he was no longer alone. That life offered more than revenge. Life—with all its aches and pains, disappointments and injustices—also offered a glimmer of hope. Killing this man, right now, might erase any chance Gerrit had of moving forward. Of freeing himself from the past. He relaxed his finger.

"Take your gun out, butt first. Left hand, two fingers, and slowly lower it to the floor."

Cromwell studied him, probably debating whether to make a move. Slowly, the lieutenant reached over to his right side, unfastened the weapon, and followed Gerrit's orders.

Cromwell straightened, hands raised in the air.

"Now. Your backup. Slowly, drop it on the floor."

The man raised his pant leg, revealing the holstered weapon strapped to his right leg. The lieutenant carefully withdrew the weapon and placed it near the other weapon.

"Now, take a seat. We need to talk." Gerrit motioned with his gun toward the chair opposite him.

Settling in, Cromwell stared back. "What now, Gerrit? You gonna shoot me?"

"I'd like nothing better than to end your miserable life. But I've made a promise. And I intend to keep it."

Cromwell smirked. "Better be careful what you promise, boy."

"You promised to uphold the law. To protect and serve. But you turned out to be a man without honor, Cromwell."

The lieutenant shrugged. "Spare me the platitudes. Look what it got you. Running and hiding for the rest of your life. If you just listened to Kane, you could have had it all. And now?"

"Now you're going on trial for murder that carries the death penalty."

An incredulous look crossed Cromwell's face. "You think all this will get to trial? People with too much to lose will stop you in your tracks. You and me are dead men walking. And they'll go about their business as if none of this happened."

"Did you trigger the bomb or have someone else do the dirty work?"

Cromwell frowned at him for a moment. "You mean your folks?" He shook his head, his lips pressed together tight. "Man, that was a tough call. I'm sorry, O'Rourke. Nothing personal. I didn't even know them—or you—at the time."

"Doesn't matter whether you knew them or not. You blew them up. For what? Money? Power? To change the world? What kind of excuse did you come up with?"

Cromwell looked at the ground, then raised his head, staring directly at Gerrit. "It was simply business. I got hooked up with some very powerful people. Big enough that they can make your life either really good or really bad. I learned very quickly that you never turn these folks down. Not if you want to keep breathing."

"And Mark and Marilynn? Are they your handiwork, too?"

"No. Kane farmed that out to others. You were the only one I was responsible to take out."

"And my parents. So all these years, you were checking up on me, making sure I never got close to the truth."

Cromwell shook his head, laughing. "I told Kane you'd be trouble. I knew you would never give up. I told him I should just put you in the ground, but he wanted to wait, to see if you might be recruited. He didn't want to raise any more flags after the death of your folks and the disappearance of your uncle. One more death in the family—particularly a military hero and cop to boot—would be too much for the feds to ignore."

"What crossed your mind when you triggered that bomb? When you thought you'd killed me?"

Cromwell just shrugged. Then a steely look crept into his eyes. "Like I said, it was just business, Gerrit. Nothing personal. You just got in the way."

Gerrit rose from the chair. "So how did you think this would end up?"

Smirking, the lieutenant cocked his head to one side. "I'm just a soldier, Gerrit. Just like you. I don't give a flying leap where this all leads. It was just a good move on my part—until now." He eyed the gun pointed at his chest. "So, you are going to turn me in?"

"Since I promised not to shoot you—" Gerrit's cell phone vibrated. He reached into his jacket pocket and pulled it out. Willy sent a text message. Gerrit tapped the screen until the message emerged.

GET OUT NOW! BOMB!

Gerrit hesitated for a moment, then raced across the room and scooped up Cromwell's weapons. "We have to get out of here right now."

The lieutenant folded his arms across his chest. "I'm not going anywhere until you tell me what's going on."

"No time. Move now!"

Cromwell shook his head. "I run out there and someone shoots me. No thanks."

Gerrit dashed toward the door. "Suit yourself. There's a bomb about to make matchsticks out of your house. I'm history." He flung the door open and raced down the walkway.

He reached the sidewalk a moment before the ground shook. A blast hit him like a giant fist, flinging him into the street with one blow. The concussion from the blast swept past. His ears felt like he'd just dived hundreds of yards underwater as the pressure threatened to snatch his hearing forever.

He almost blacked out. Dazed, he felt hands lifting him from the ground. Looking up, he saw Alena, her arms under him as she tried to raise him up. The ringing in his ears kept out all other noise. He knew she was talking to him, but he couldn't hear.

Alena looked around frantically. Her lips moved as if she might be yelling or screaming. It finally registered.

I am deaf.

Chapter 69

The first thing Gerrit saw when he awoke again in the hospital was Alena's soft brown eyes. It seemed like only minutes since he'd closed his own eyes after doctors got through poking and prodding, writing out terms like *perforated eardrum* and *back to normal in months*. Sound began to return, slowly and steadily. Once he knew his hearing would return, he laid back drifted off to sleep.

Now, afternoon light filtered through a stand of fir trees outside the hospital window. Alena's concerned look softened and a smile brightened her face. "You've got to stop this, Gerrit. What is it with you and bombs?"

A shadow fell across them. Jack Thompson leaned over. "Yeah, boy. You really scrambled your brains this time. At least what brains you had left." Beyond the colonel, Willy and Beck Malloy hovered.

Gerrit looked from one face to the other. "What happened? All I remember is Cromwell's house blowing up."

Beck edged closer to the bed. "We sent a forensic team in there, along with ATF. The house was rigged to blow before you or Cromwell ever got there. Someone used a cell phone to trigger it. I guess they thought you and Cromwell would be caught inside when it blew."

"You think they were targeting me, too?"

The FBI agent shrugged. "Who knows? They definitely wanted to take out Cromwell. Guess they thought he had become too much of a liability.

When you came along, they probably thought you'd be a bonus. One less thing to worry about later."

Gerrit looked over at Willy, still clutching his laptop. "How did you know they were going to blow it up?"

Willy cocked his head to one side. "Your lieutenant was a security freak. Had a surveillance-camera system set up around the place. Once you went into Cromwell's house to wait for him, I got bored and hacked into his system just for the heck of it. It was set up on a wireless system, easy as pie to break. Played back the security tapes for the last twenty-four hours and watched them rig the place with explosives. Cromwell failed to check them himself."

"You saved my life, Willy." Gerrit held out his hand in gratitude. "Think you can work some magic on those keys and tell us who is behind this?"

Willy took his hand and shook it vigorously. "Mr. B has already had me working on it."

"Mr. B?"

"You know, Beck Malloy."

"Ah." Gerrit nodded. "And what did you and Mr. B find out?"

Beck came between him and Willy. "Just rest now, Gerrit. We need to move you and the others out of here soon. There's a small lull in this war right now, while the other side regroups. We'll need to start gearing up for a major operation. I'll fill you in later. Once you're on your feet, I have a lot of work for you and Joe and the others. I'm afraid you are going to need to continue to live off the grid, at least until we have a handle on this entire organization."

"Speaking of Joe, where is he?"

"Over here, son." The group parted so Gerrit could see his uncle seated across the room.

"What are you doing way over there, Joe?"

Joe wiped his eyes. "Just thanking the man upstairs that He sent you back to me—again." He slowly raised himself and limped over to Gerrit's bedside. "I'm okay. Kane and his people worked me over pretty good, so it's going to take a while for me to recoup. I should be able to give you all kinds of grief by the time they release you from this place."

"Enough of this chitchat. I'm starving." Jack's voice rang out. "Let the boy get some R&R. If the rest of you can stomach cafeteria food, I'm buying." Before Thompson left, he lingered a moment, letting the others file out ahead of him. He returned to Gerrit's bedside. "Here, I think you should have this." The colonel held his hand open.

Inside, Gerrit saw the pocket watch his father had left him.

"Alena said you might want this," Thompson said. "I sent a team to San Francisco to clean out everything in her shop after it was clear that part of the operation had been blown. I asked them to send this back to me."

Gritting his teeth, Gerrit palmed the watch, feeling its smooth contours. "Thanks, sir. This watch helps me to hold on to the past when all else seems to have been destroyed. You can't..." He couldn't finish.

"I know, son." Thompson moved toward the door. "Take care of yourself."

Gerrit watched the small group wander into the hall, leaving him alone. He started to close his eyes but opened them when he heard someone enter the room.

Alena.

He smiled as she came near. "Missed me, huh?"

"Like a bad heartache."

"You mean headache, right?" he said, pointing to his forehead.

"No, I mean heartache," she said, patting her chest.

Gerrit smiled, "Come here." He reached up and drew her closer. Gently and firmly, he kissed her. He closed his eyes and felt her relax in his arms.

Smiling, she pulled back, cupping his face in her hands. "Don't ever scare me like that again."

Gerrit clasped her hands in his. "Did you know married guys who give their wives kisses every morning live five years longer than those jerks who never kiss 'em?"

Alena raised an eyebrow. "Is this some kind of weird proposal?"

Gerrit grinned. "Just a fact to tuck away for future consideration."

She cocked her head to one side. "Really? Shall we practice?" She leaned over to kiss him.

He pulled back once again. "Did you know—?"

"Shut up and kiss me, Einstein."